Editing: Caroline Palmier—Love & Edits

Cover Design: Brey Shirley—Simply Brey Creative

Book Design: Cathryn Carter—Format by CC

Copyright © 2023 by Ashley Dranguet

All rights reserved.

No part of this book may be reproduced in any form or by any electronic or mechanical means, including information storage and retrieval systems, without written permission from the author, except for the use of brief quotations in a book review.

This novel is entirely a work of fiction. The names, characters, and incidents portrayed in it are the work of the author's imagination. Any resemblance to actual persons, living or dead, events or localities is entirely coincidental.

worth the hurt

ashley dranguet

BOOK ONE OF THE
WORTH IT
SERIES

Content Warning

Worth the Hurt is a contemporary romance novel that contains content that may be triggering to some readers including but not limited to the mention of:

Eating disorders
Anxiety
Violence (not between the main characters)
Death in the family
Abandonment
Other mature subjects

This book also contains strong language and sexual themes.

To all the girls who never felt comfortable in your own skin. Never deemed yourself worthy of love. And never knew how to accept it, but tried like hell anyway. This one's for you.

worth the hurt
playlist

Self Love - Avery Anna

Once - David J

The One - Pierre Alexander

Skin (Acoustic) - Jessica Baio

Before He Could - Halle Kearns

Lose It All - Sam Tompkins

Love Makes You Blind - Kaylee Rose

Almost Always - Rosie Darling

Future Ex - Abigail Barlow

Getting Into - Ashley Cooke

I Guess I'm In Love - Clinton Kane

You're Still The One - Jonah Baker

This Is How You Fall In Love - Jeremy Zucker + Chelsea Cutler

Hard To Love - Lee Brice

Like No One Does (Acoustic) - Jake Scott

Never Been In Love - Haley Mae Campbell

Intrusive Thoughts - Natalie Jane

Gonna Love You - Parmalee

Missing Piece - Bella Lambert

In A Perfect World - Dean Lewis & Julia Michaels

Chapter 1
Macy

Spoiler Alert: It Won't Give You Scoli

Friday, October 12 - 2:30pm.

I sit here with my legs crossed on her brown leather couch. My fingers drum the arm as I scan her office. It's large and spacious. There are three bay windows behind the blinds that are raised, and I can see the entire city of downtown Chicago from up here. The nameplate on her desk reads, Dr. Taylor Reynolds, PsyD, but her certificates all read, Taylor Savell. I wonder which is her maiden name. Did she go through school then get married, or was she married prior and is now divorced? These are the questions my mind contemplates while avoiding her questions. She's sitting across from me, properly positioned, like she's scared relaxing will somehow give her scoliosis. Her legs are crossed as well, and a clipboard rests in her lap. I refuse to make eye contact with her because I know she'll make me talk, and I hate talking about it. She begins writing, but I haven't said a word since I got here, so I don't know what she could possibly be writing about. If I had to guess, she's probably just trying to pass the time, most likely waiting for me to quit wasting hers. She may not have directly said that, but I know she's probably thinking it.

"Macy." I hear her say. I'm still quiet, but I finally meet her gaze. "Can you at least tell me what you're looking to get out of therapy? This is our third session, and all I know about you is that you have an absent mother and a younger sister named Lauren."

I sigh, knowing good and well that this is the most expensive silence I've ever paid out of pocket for. Dr. Reynolds is the best psychologist in the entire state of Illinois, and I wanted the best. I *needed* the best if I was going to get past the fuckery that is my life. I came here ready to spill all my secrets. I wanted her to know everything—from beginning to end—in hopes that she could fix me. But sitting across from a total stranger and telling them how messed up you are, is much harder to admit than I anticipated.

I let out a long drawn out breath and adjust my posture. Here goes nothing.

"I used to read," I say. "Actually, I used to *love* to read." The expression on her face leads me to believe she didn't expect me to finally open up today. Hell, I didn't expect it myself, but the words start pouring out like vomit. She looks pleased to see me finally breakthrough whatever was holding my words captive.

"I would read roughly two or three books a week, getting lost in someone else's made up story. It was my favorite thing to do." I continue. "But I haven't picked up a book in over ten years."

I can't believe it's been that long since I gave up the only hobby that helped me escape my reality. Reading made me feel as though I could have any life I wanted, and I wanted any other life but the one I had.

"Why do you think that is?" she asks.

I think long and hard before answering. It's not a complex

explanation. I know exactly why I don't have the courage to read anymore. In my head, it makes a world of sense, but for some reason, it sounds pathetic when spoken, childish even.

"Reading made me fat." I know it's naïve of me to think, *that's* why I was overweight, when in reality, I just didn't have a lot of opportunities to be thin.

My mother was a single mom raising two kids. Well, not so much raising us, but rather supplying a roof over our head. My dad left when I was two, just after Lauren was born. I don't remember anything about him, so I find it hard to grieve a person I never knew. That was twenty-three years ago, and I still haven't heard from the man since. I know he got married, though—when I was around the age of ten and started his new family shortly after. I only know that because my grandparents insist on keeping me in the loop, even when I have zero desire to get to know him. I know they mean well, but if they really wanted to help me, they wouldn't have allowed him to walk out on his family the way he did all those years ago. And just so we're clear, this isn't me grieving. It's me being bitter—resentful even—for him being the reason we had to live the way we did.

Imagine growing up, bouncing from city to city, state to state, school to school, your entire life. Being the new girl almost never had any perks. In fact, I don't think it had any at all. Once we finally did settle for longer than six months, *if* we did, there would be another random sitter Lauren and I had to endure. My mom worked three jobs just to keep us afloat, so she was hardly ever home. I felt the need to step up, learn how to cook, and do laundry. Because most days, we ate dry ramen noodles and wore stained clothes to school. You can imagine the shit I received for that. I grew up quicker than anticipated, but I somehow felt responsible for making sure Lauren never had to. Most of my days after school were spent watching Food Network so we could eat something other than crunchy soup, and I began reading books—in search of a life where I could be a normal kid. The next two years consisted of the same routine. I'd get us both ready for school in the morning and get us both off the bus in the afternoon. I'd cook us dinner, we'd do our homework, bathe, and get in bed. Only I wouldn't go to sleep. I'd stay up for as long as I could, reading page after page. By this time, I was twelve. I noticed I was gaining weight because my clothes were becoming snug, but we didn't have much money, so I knew that new clothes weren't in the cards for me. I'd go to school and get bullied about my weight, sending me home crying every single day. A daughter should be able to run home and vent to her mom about her troubles, feel her mother's concern, while lying in her lap. But I never had that because my mother was never there.

I speak every one of these words to Dr. Reynolds, but she still seems puzzled over my statement about reading being the cause of my demise.

So, I continue.

"I was twelve when I developed my first eating disorder. I succumbed to the idea that if I ate less, I'd at least fit into the only two pairs of jeans I owned. So that's what I did. I started skipping one meal at first. For weeks, I'd only cook dinner for Lauren. She would question me, wondering why suddenly, I wasn't hungry, but I'd just tell her I was still full from lunch. It was a lie, though. My stomach was screaming from the inside, practically begging me to eat something, *anything*. I didn't give in. Pounds began to shed, and I could finally wear my uniform comfortably. But I was nowhere near the size I wanted to be, so I started skipping more meals."

I grow silent. This part of my childhood is particularly hard to talk about because even at twenty-five, I still struggle with my ED. It doesn't control me the way that it used to, and I've learned healthy boundaries when it comes to food. But the insecure girl I once was, is still trapped somewhere deep inside me. I clear my throat, ready to finally relive my past.

"The less I ate, the better I looked, but the worse I felt. I knew I couldn't survive on the handfuls of cheese cubes or the single slice of bologna I would consume once a day, so after eight months, I developed my second ED, bulimia." I feel a turning in my stomach as the words leave my mouth.

It's painful, thinking about what I endured for the sixteen months after that. Eating just to stick my finger down my throat shortly after. And the worst part about all of it, my mother didn't know a single thing was different about me, until the night of May 11. I'll never forget that day.

Just as I begin to open up about the only date on the calendar I wish never existed, the timer goes off. Dr. Reynold's silences the alarm and begins writing again. I'm curious to know what she's writing. She probably thinks I'm a psychopath, but then again, she did go to school to deal with people like me.

She stops and puts her pen down. "I'm proud of you, Macy. It takes a lot of courage to do what you just did, and I hope you'll continue to be brave. Same time next week?"

I nod and rise to my feet. She guides me to the door, and I shake her hand before exiting.

Chapter 2
Macy

Two Legs & Female Anatomy

I ride the elevator to the ground floor and make my way out of the building. I shield my eyes from the sun as I make my way to the busy street to catch a cab. I flag one down, and slide across the backseat as I pull out my cell phone. I have a text message from Paxton.

> PAXTON
> I scored two tickets to the Bears vs. Eagles game tomorrow, 7 pm. Wanna join?
>
> Football and beer? You don't have to ask me twice.
>
> PAXTON
> Perfect. I'll pick you up at five, and we can pregame at Cheap Shots.
>
> Can't wait. See you then.

The lines of my mouth begin to curve into a smile, and I catch myself becoming hopeful for a split second. I didn't want to sound too eager, but I like Paxton. He's charming, witty, and extremely easy on the eyes. But he's also very smart and driven which makes him even more attractive. He's tall, roughly 6'3 if I had to guess. His slender build makes him look much taller, but in the best possible way. And when I say slender, I don't mean skinny. I just mean that he's proportionately filled out from top to bottom, *especially* in a suit. He has the most perfectly chiseled jaw I've ever seen that's covered with neatly groomed facial hair. His eyes are a mix between blue and green, with a touch of golden yellow in the center. It's so easy to get lost in those eyes. And although I enjoy drinking in his appearance, it's his mind I find myself craving. Something about intelligence in a man lights me up inside and down *there*.

I've had my fair share of relationships over the years, and I do mean a *fair share*, but none ever sparked my interest as much as this man does. His voice is rigid but becomes smooth as velvet when he speaks law to me. And just to clarify—no, we aren't dating. We're not even in the vicinity of dating. Sure, I enjoy his lectures on civil and constitutional laws, or the random non-dates we go on when we're off duty, but I told myself I wasn't going to do this anymore. And by this, I mean, get in a non-committed relationship with anyone, *particularly* not the guy competing with me for the only job I've ever wanted.

Being a criminal lawyer in one of the highest rated crime cities in the world is almost as appealing as being a celebrity, if not better. We're not talking about just *any* criminal lawyer either. We're talking about being a criminal lawyer at *Sterling Heights, LLC*. The most prestigious law firm in the state. They've been involved in some of the largest, most popular cases being aired by the media; this current case being no exception.

When I applied for law school three years ago, I never imagined I'd climb to the top as fast as I did. I will admit, though, I have a bit of an obsession with setting goals and checking them off my list, but I never thought *interning at Sterling Heights, LLC* would come so quickly. Did I mention it's a *paid* internship? I applied on a whim whenever the news of this case first hit the media. I mean, who wouldn't want to sit in on a case where a young girl is being charged with the murder of her twin sister? It's every law student's *dream* to land a case this big. Luckily for me, I've busted my ass to stay at the top of my class before this case ever unfolded, making me a lead candidate. The latter side? They opened *two* intern positions, and Paxton just so happens to be the male version of me when it comes to the books. Not only are we competing to see who scores higher on the bar, but we're also competing for the junior partner spot at the firm.

    I promised myself from the beginning that I wouldn't let myself fall this time. I haven't and I won't. I refuse to let anything—or anyone—get in the way of this opportunity. Not even Paxton Meyers.

My internal alarm clock wakes me up at 6am, so I get up, throw on my favorite Fabletics set and a pair of sneakers. I pull my hair into a ponytail on top of my head before brushing my teeth and head to the kitchen. It's still dark outside because daylight savings has just begun, which means I should probably wait until the sun is up to go for a run. With as many kidnappings and homicides as we've had lately, I'd hate to end up a victim rather than the lawyer. I make myself a rice cake with peanut butter, down a bottle of water and fool around on Instagram before finally heading out the door.

    I live in the nicer part of Chicago, thankfully, but I still carry my pepper spray with me on my runs. I've sat in on enough cases to know that men don't care how old you are or what you look like. They're willing to snatch up anyone with two legs and female anatomy. It's quite frightening. My apple watch alerts me of the rise in heartrate, probably due to the increase in thoughts that I could be picked up and thrown into someone's van at any given moment.

I begin to run faster, trying to drown out my fears with the sounds of my labored breathing. I finally reach my apartment and check my progress on the exercise app. 4.2 miles. *Not bad Macy, not bad.* I have high school track to thank for that.

After entering my apartment, I head to my bathroom for a shower. I decide to shave, *all* of me, in case I have one too many beers and find myself begging Paxton for a one-night stand. I've never had one before, but somehow this man makes me consider it.

This is not a date. Definitely not a date. I somehow try to convince myself of that, which shouldn't be hard, because we have a lot of "not dates."

I spend the next few hours going over notes from the case. I'm trying to dive as deep as I can, hoping to make a better impression than him. My competitive nature really comes out when he's around, and he surely knows how to poke the bear. I smile again, thinking of him once more.

No. Stop. Focus.

Paxton's name appears on my lock screen. I slide open my phone and click on my text icon.

> **PAXTON**
> Justin Fields, Teven Jenkins, or Mike Pennel?

> Fuck Teven Jenkins, Marry Justin Fields, Kill Mike Pennel.

> **PAXTON**
> 🦢LMAO. Not what I was asking, but it made for a good laugh.

> Glad I could be of assistance. What were you asking me, exactly?

> **PAXTON**
> Which jersey?

> Fields, no question.

> **PAXTON**
> Good deal. See you in twenty.

I didn't realize how late it had gotten and now have to rush to get ready. Luckily, I curled my hair before my studies, so at least that's out of the way. I slip on a pair of holey jeans and my oversized Fields jersey.

I'm not from here originally, but I quickly became a fan of the Bears when I moved here for law school. I spent a lot of time watching the games during study breaks and have even been to a few at Soldier Field. They'll never replace my love for my home team, and Justin Fields will never be Drew Brees, but he's growing on me.

I hear honking downstairs in the parking lot. I look out the window to see Paxton's 1967 Shelby Mustang in the spot next to mine. I admire his taste in cars. Most young bachelors would go for something a lot more sporty, so I love that he appreciates the classics. I touch up my lipstick one last time and rush down the stairs. As I open the door and hop in the passenger seat, I can see him studying me from the corner of my eye but try to remain aloof.

"So, we're matching now?" I hear him ask.

I look down at my jersey, completely forgetting I told him to wear that one.

I shrug. "I guess we are."

"You may want to watch it. People might start thinking we're a couple. Only couples do this cute shit." He laughs.

I crack a smile at the thought of people potentially labeling us as a couple. I can't let him know that, though.

"No shot," I say calm and collected. "And besides, you're *totally* not my type." I'm lying. He's actually the very depiction of my type. I'm almost positive if you look up Macy Callahan's type in the dictionary, Paxton Meyers' picture would be right there next to my name.

I'm not sure if I offend him, or hurt his ego, but he scoffs and continues to drive. We make it to Cheap Shots with an hour to spare before the game starts.

Paxton motions towards the left side of the bar, pulling out my chair like a gentleman.

"I think *you* may want to watch it. Acting all chivalrously may give people the wrong idea about us." I tease.

His eyebrow reaches an arch as his lips grow flat. "I don't think we have anything to worry about. I'm not your type, *remember?*"

Ouch.

I guess I did strike a nerve with that indecent comment of mine. If only he knew how wrong he was. If only he knew that I use sarcasm and comical insults as a defense mechanism. Then he'd see how much I really wanted him. But I can't let myself go there. Not this time. Not with him.

Chapter 3
Paxton

Absolutely Not

I don't like the idea of dating. It can be awkward, and it takes up a lot of time. Time that I could be using to study to get ahead in this case I'm working on. But I'm spent, and quite frankly, feeling a little burnt out. I needed to let loose and have a little fun; and what's more fun than beer and football? Not much. I don't know that I'd classify this as a date, though. We're just two friends, unwinding after a long week on trial.

As much as I don't care for female companionship anywhere other than the bedroom, I will admit that I enjoy Macy's company. She's fun and easy going, and matches my sense of humor, so being around her is like hanging out with one of the guys. Only she's much nicer to look at.

I've seen her quite a bit over the last few years. Almost daily. We attend the same law school and will be graduating together come May. If I said she didn't catch my eye from time to time, I'd be lying. She has long, thick, auburn hair that brings out the specs of hazel in her light brown eyes. She has freckles across her pierced nose and rosy cheeks—as if God strategically placed each freckle to make a man weak in the knees every time they look in her direction. And those lips. Perfectly symmetrical, that lifts into the most breath-taking smile. From a distance, she looks poised, untainted, almost virgin-like. But up close and personal, underneath the mirage in the distance, I can tell she's damaged. Even if I wasn't good at reading people, her sleeve of tattoos plaster that message on display like a billboard. It makes me want to know more about her, but like I said, I don't like the idea of dating. Which is why I've always kept my distance from her... until now.

University of Chicago Law School produces some of the top lawyers in the state, so people come from all over to study here. Most graduate and head back to wherever they came from, which is what I imagined she would be doing. What I didn't imagine though, was that she would be interning at the same firm as me, possibly causing me the biggest career loss of the century.

That's right; she's my *competition*. Sterling Heights, LLC is the largest and most successful firm in Chicago, specializing in criminal law. There were two intern spots that opened up for a huge case, available to two students from U of C. And yep—you guessed it—we each landed one.

My family consists mostly of doctors, so you can imagine their disappointment when I chose a different career path. But ever since I can remember, I've wanted to be a lawyer. Defending someone innocent until proven guilty has always appealed to me. Getting to know the defendant and how their mind works, diving deep into their brain to gain knowledge about why they do the things they do; it's all just so fascinating.

Which brings me to how I ended up here, assisting in the biggest murder trial the state of Illinois has seen in over seventeen years, with Macy Callahan as my number one rival. And I only say it like that because there's only one opening for junior partner, and we both want it.

The State vs Sterling case will either make or break my career before it even starts. And yes, you heard that right, State vs *Sterling*, as in the owner of the firm's *daughter*. Twenty-six-year-old Jade Sterling, accused of murdering her twin sister, Josie. She's pleading not guilty and is throwing the blame on her sister's fiancé, Wyatt Lancaster, who also happens to be in custody.

Here I go again, thinking about work instead of enjoying what little time I have off. I snap back to reality, only to find Cole Kmet fumbling the ball for the second time.

"ARE YOU KIDDING ME?!" I hear Macy yell as she throws her hands up in the air. "C'mon man! Do better!"

We're down by thirteen, and usually I would be in a funk about it, but having her here lessens the blow a little.

I let out a subtle laugh.

It's a breath of fresh air hanging out with a girl who knows and loves football just as much as I do. Actually, it's quite *sexy*. She takes a sip of her Blue Moon, and I catch myself paying close attention to her neck as she swallows. I can feel my face get hot and my dick twitch in my jeans but find immediate relief when I hear the crowd cheering.

"TOUCHDOWN!!"

She jumps up from her seat and quickly turns around to shoot me an excited glare—her smile matching mine—then takes her seat once more. I sit there for a minute, admiring her as she continues to watch the game. That Justin Fields jersey hanging off her shoulder makes me feel like I have the best seat in the house. I could care less about the score at this point. She's the only thing I can focus on. The Bears may be losing, but *I* surely am winning.

"Paxton. Paxtooon," I hear, bringing me out of my daze. My eyes meet hers as she's waving her hand across my face to get my attention. I feel a bit embarrassed about losing myself to thoughts of her so frequently tonight. *Get your shit together, Paxton. You can't lose focus now.*

"Sorry, what?"

"Want me to grab us another beer?" She stands up, and I admire her figure unknowingly.

"Hello??" She snaps her fingers. "Earth to Paxton."

"Sure, Mich—"

"Michelob, no foam. I know, pretty boy. We've gone on how many non-dates in the past four months?" she interrupts me. I can see the smirk on her face before she turns and walks away. I think she enjoys torturing me with her words. It's cute, the way she shields herself with sarcasm. I like it. It makes her more mysterious—not like all those other girls who have no problem spilling their baggage on the first date.

But this isn't a date. In fact, she just made that perfectly clear. That all our time spent together is exactly the opposite of a date. She legit just referred to them as *non-dates*. I don't know why that bothers me so much, to hear her so effortlessly admit that what we're doing couldn't possibly be a date. I should be *happy* that she sees our relations this way. After all, *I don't like dating.* I repeat that in my head, over and over. If that's the truth, then why am I trying so hard to convince myself of it?

Macy makes her way back, one beer in each hand. "Michelob for you, another Blue Moon for me. Oh, and here."

She hands me a shot. I put it up to my nose, taken back by the smell of peppermint. *Goldschlager.* I shudder.

"Well, go on," she persists.

I get a whiff of it once again and shake my head.

"Absolutely not."

"Don't be such a baby. Take the damn shot." She raises her plastic cup to mine, and even though I know I'll regret this tomorrow, I clink her cup and down the shot. Immediately, I gag. She takes it like a champ. No emotion whatsoever. What kind of trauma causes a person to be able to shoot two ounces of liquid fire without so much as a flinch?

As much as I like mysteries, I find myself wanting to pry

into her life. I want to know who Macy Callahan is, what her hobbies are—besides criminal law and purposely insulting me. I want to know what fuels her fire to her success. But most of all, I want to know what the hell she went through to make her build walls so damn high.

Chapter 4
Macy

Puking Gold Flakes

My eyelids feel like they're cemented shut with the force of a two-ton cinderblock. I lay here, trying to pry my eyes open, with my head pounding. I somehow manage to open them enough to notice my surroundings do not contain the contents of my apartment. *Where the hell am I?* I roll onto my right side, only to come face-to-face with a sleeping Paxton. A small gasp leaves my mouth and I slap my hand over it as quickly as I can before sliding out of bed.

There's a sharp pain in my head and a hollow feeling in my stomach as I walk down the hallway in search of the kitchen. I try to recall last night, but I can't remember a damn thing after the game; I don't even remember leaving. The last memory I have is taking shots every time Kmet fumbled the ball, which happened to be a lot.

Did we get that drunk? Did I actually beg him for a one-night stand? Did he say yes? What the hell happened?

I feel the nausea rise from my stomach and into my chest.

I need water. I open the fridge and grab a bottle, twisting the cap off and tossing it onto the counter. I drink the entire bottle in less than two minutes, then grab another before making a cup of coffee.

I press my back up against the counter, resting on my elbows while I wait for the Keurig to do its thing. The smell of the caramel-roasted pecan blend engulfs me, and I close my eyes as I take in the scent. A sudden clearing of the throat startles me and my eyes snap open.

Paxton is standing at the far end of the kitchen, in nothing but a pair of gray sweatpants. My throat becomes dry, and the hollowness in my stomach is replaced by a familiar twinge. It's not fair for someone to look this good. Especially when I'm trying to remain focused on the goal at hand. *Junior partner*, I remind myself.

I can see him scanning me up and down, and I've come to the realization that I don't have any pants on. Luckily, my oversized jersey hits just above the knees, not revealing much. The silence is awkward, so I adjust my posture and initiate conversation to erase the elephant in the room.

"Sorry, did I wake you?"

"You didn't. I'm an early riser," he replies with a tussle of his hair.

Jesus, he's beautiful. Why must he be so damn beautiful?

I try to keep myself from smiling at the sight of his hand running through his hair, so I turn around to put fixings in my coffee. "Do you want me to make you a cup?"

"That would be great, thanks. Just—"

"Just cream, no sugar. Got it," I interrupt before he can finish.

I somehow always finish his sentences. Have I really paid that much attention to everything he likes? Surely not. I've never done that in my past relationships. I'm lucky if I remember their middle name, much less their go-to orders. *This is not a relationship*, I remind myself. I stand there for a moment, stirring Paxton's almond creamer into his cup when I realize just how little I know about him. I've become accustomed to his drink orders, and his food choices, and can sometimes even predict what he's going to wear depending on our plans that day. But other than surface-level conversation, I know nothing about his personal life. And why should I? I've never shared anything remotely personal about myself with him, but part of me is interested in getting to know the man underneath the suit. Not Paxton, the law student. I want to know the real Paxton—the shirtless guy standing behind me making me reconsider all my life choices when it comes to men.

I can feel him inch closer to me, and the hair on the back of my neck stands straight up at the heat of his breath on me. I gain my composure and then turn around with an unbothered expression on my face.

I hand him his cup of coffee and slip out from between him and the counter. I take a seat at the island, sitting on one of the bar stools. I notice he doesn't have a dining table, so I guess this is where he eats. He takes a few steps and glides himself onto the counter opposite of the island until he's directly across from me, holding my stare.

Remaining aloof is becoming harder and harder when he's looking at me like that. His eyes burn through me, like he's staring straight into my soul, uncovering all my trauma from my past. It makes me nervous, thinking of him knowing my secrets and what a screwed-up person they've turned me into to. I break eye contact and sip my coffee.

"So, I hate to ask, but um... what am I doing here?"

He looks at me like it's some sort of surprise that I don't remember last night. We drank—a lot—and too much alcohol tends to really taint a person's memory.

"You don't remember?" he asks in a sharp tone.

"If I remembered, Paxton, do you think I'd really be asking you?" And there it is. My unnecessary sarcastic remark. I really should work on that, but for now I'd like to know the remainder of the events after the game.

He took a few gulps of his coffee before answering, then a chuckle leaves his mouth. "It's no question we were both hammered. I told you those shots were a bad idea, but you insisted we drink every time the ball hit the ground. By the time the game was over, I'd guess we had roughly nine shots. I lost count at nine, anyway." He has a grin plastered across his face, and I'm not even sure I want to know the rest.

I look down into my cup, trying to muster up the courage to ask this next question. Normally, I have no reservations. I don't care what guys think of my mouth, but for whatever reason, I tried to be more ladylike around Paxton.

"Please tell me I didn't beg you for a one-night stand." I thump my forehead with the palm of my hand after I say those words out loud.

He laughs and laughs hard. Why does he find this funny? Has he not thought about it before? I'm kind of offended that this whole ordeal could be one-sided.

What ordeal, Macy? There's no ordeal. JUNIOR PARTNER.

He notices the unamused look on my face and continues. "As tempting as that would have been, no, you did not. We did not. In fact, I held your hair most of the night as you puked gold flakes into my toilet."

Wonderful. Delightful. How fucking cute is that? Paxton Meyers, holding my hair as I violently empty the ignorance of my choices from my stomach into the place where he takes a shit. What a fantastic picture that is.

"Well, that's embarrassing. I totally would have rather given you the best night of your life and then snuck out before you woke."

His brows furrow, almost like I hurt his feelings. Why am I

such a bitch? Oh well, can't take it back now. "That's rather insulting," he speaks, with a stoic tone in his voice.

Why does he say it like that? I can't imagine that he would ever want to date me, much less sleep with me. He made it very clear when we first started non-dating that we were just friends, and that he doesn't do relationships. Which was perfect for me because I wasn't looking for anything. The only reason this even became a thing is because we spent so much time together during the case and not having nearly enough fun outside of it.

"How so?" I'm genuinely curious to know how that statement insulted him.

"You just made me sound like a piece of ass. One that you could just sleep with and toss to the side." I can't tell if he's serious or just acting serious to play the part.

I roll my eyes. "Isn't that the definition of a one-night stand? No strings attached. Just sex at night and absence in the morning."

He purses his lips, unable to argue with the explanation I just gave. "Fair enough. But you can't get rid of me after one night. We see each other too much. So I hate to burst your bubble, sweetheart, but those cards are off the table."

Part of me thinks he shot down the idea because he needs to remain focused on the goal at hand, too. But the other part of me thinks he couldn't possibly fathom being with me just one time and never again. I know that sounds narcissistic, and I promise it's not. I'm the least confident person I know. It's all an act—a facade—to get me to that next goal. But I'm a good judge of character, and I think he *might* like me. And the thought of us losing whatever this is that we're doing might scare him enough to keep him out of my pants.

I step off the bar stool and walk my cup over to the sink.

"You're right. No sex. Ever. Not even if *you* beg *me*." I turn around and head back towards his room to find my jeans, making sure to walk in a way that'll make him wish I never said that.

Don't ask me how we've made it four months without even a single kiss, but we have. No physical contact, just the enjoyment of each other's company. And while there have been many times that I have completely undressed him with my eyes, I know it's best to keep that distance between us. And somehow, I know he knows it too.

Chapter 5
Paxton

No Sex. Ever.

"You're right. No sex. Ever. Not even if *you* beg *me*," she says before turning around and making a beeline for my room.

Damn. Her smart mouth *really* turns me on. I watch her walk down the hallway in that jersey, focusing on her legs. I realize she's walking slightly on her tiptoes. Does she always do that? I've never noticed it before, but all I can think about is running after her and slamming her onto my bed. I can't do that, though. It would be a distraction, and I can't have anything distract me right now. But man, I want to. I *really* want to.

How God created someone so elegantly beautiful, yet so erotic, I'll never understand. As he was knitting her together, he probably pondered how he could make me work harder in life than I already have. Yep, I'm convinced that's it. Because up until this point, I've been good at making sure work and school come first. Then she shows up, and I find myself wanting to give her all my free time. I've even caught myself staring at her during class, my mind wandering with scenarios of the two of us. That's one sure way to forfeit the junior partner position, and I wasn't about to let myself do that.

She exits my room, fully dressed, purse draped over her shoulder. "You ready to get rid of me yet?"

I'm a tad bit disappointed that she's so eager to leave, but I have a lot of reading to do for the case if I'm going to secure my spot. I purse my lips, trying not to look like a sad puppy being left by its owner. I decide to give her a taste of her sarcasm to hide my desperation for her to stay.

"I was ready to get rid of you once you graced my shitter with the remains of your poor choice in alcohol. My bathroom is going to smell like peppermint for days."

"That would be an upgrade to whatever smelling potpourri you've got in there now. It smells like my dead grandma's house."

I can't win with this girl. Her wit is too quick. I pick my battles, choosing to end this one on a good note.

Instead, I roll my eyes. "I'll grab the keys and meet you downstairs."

She heads out the door, and I race to throw on a shirt and some shoes. I descend from the stairs of my second-floor apartment only to stop short at the sight of her posted up against my car.

I look up to the sky for a brief second. "This is torture, you know that right?" I say as though God doesn't already know that. I mean *He* put her here, on Earth, and in my life.

I walk slowly to my car, taking her all in as I hit the unlock button on my key fob. I do my best to be a gentleman, but she's already opening the door herself, so I don't fight it. I know she'll just make another remark that'll leave me feeling miniscule.

The ride to her place is quiet. The silence almost deafening. I'm not sure what to say after the playful banter we exchanged, so I feel it's best to keep to myself. Judging by her lack of conversation, I'd say she feels the same. We pull up to her apartment complex, and she unbuckles her seatbelt, stalling for a quick moment before reaching for the doorhandle.

I grab her arm, and her head whips around to meet my gaze.

"I'm sorry if I offended you earlier. It was just a joke."

A smile peaks on her lips. "I'm not easily offended, Paxton. I'm just sorry you didn't get to see me naked."

She exits the car without another word, leaving me speechless once again. I close my eyes Dand release the breath I wasn't aware I was holding. *I'm doomed.*

Chapter 6
Paxton

I'll Take Nightmares Any Day

Monday, October 15 - 4:00 pm

"Good afternoon, Paxton. It's good to see you," Dr. Reynold's says as I step into her office.

"You too, Taylor." It slips off my tongue. "I mean, Dr. Reynolds."

She grins. "Taylor is fine. Take a seat."

She motions to the brown leather couch I used to spend so much time sitting on. It's weird being back here, yet everything still looks the same as it did during my last session. The familiarity causes a wave of chills to inhabit my skin. It's been three years since I first sat in this spot, opening up to a complete stranger about my failed engagement and how I believed my ex tried to kill me.

My phone vibrates, and a text from Macy lights up my screen.

> **MACY**
> You seemed distracted today. Everything okay? We can grab your favorite Chinese takeout and talk about it. Ya know... if you're into that sort of thing.

> Mondays aren't good for me. Raincheck?

> **MACY**
> Sure. I'll see you tomorrow in class.

I silence my phone and turn my attention back to Dr. Reynolds.

She looks at me, and I feel as though she already knows the reason I'm here. I wouldn't be surprised if she did, honestly. It's not like the news is a secret. I swallow, unable to speak any words. I'm relieved when she breaks the silence first.

"It really is good to see you," she reiterates. "How have you been?"

I want to tell her I've been miserable. That I can't sleep. That I have nightmares of that night. That they sometimes wake me up out of dead sleep in a cold sweat. And that the Trazodone the doctor prescribed me only worsens the nightmares. But I don't. I don't say any of that because I feel crazy. The only normalcy I feel is when I'm with Macy. But I can't tell her that either because I can't go there with her. Not if I want my career to take off.

She notices the hesitation in my stiffened demeanor.

"I've been... better." I manage to get out.

"Better than the last time we spoke, or better overall than your current state?"

I contemplate lying, but what good would that do me? Her time is expensive, and although I'm not really strapped for cash, I'm sure I could find other things to spend $95 an hour on. Like a massage, which I so desperately need.

"The stress of this case is really weighing on me. It's a lot. The workload is far more than any other case I've been part of. And not to mention, Mr. Sterling has me staying after hours at least three times a week. I'm just really exhausted."

"Do you ever think about stepping down? Giving yourself a break? You're a hard worker, Paxton, but sometimes I think you might work *too* hard." She emphasizes the *too*.

She's not wrong.

"Have I thought about it? Plenty of times. But this opportunity is just too good to pass up. *Junior partner*, straight of out law school? Do you know how many people would kill for that? I can't just quit."

I really do think about it often, though. Not because I don't love law—because I do—but because this case in particular has only caused me stress. I would never fully give up the career, but I have contemplated walking away from this firm. I just worry that if I do, my name will be tainted and dragged through the mud in the entire state of Illinois, and I can't let that happen. Reputation is everything when it comes to clients, *especially* high-end ones.

I try to convince myself, knowing those aren't the only reasons I've managed to stay this long. I know deep down that a sarcastic firecracker of a woman has kept me coming back, day after day. In all honesty, sometimes I feel like the competition isn't really for me, but more for her. I feel like I owe it to her to secure the position, just so she doesn't have to work for a man like Jack Sterling. I somehow feel the need to protect her from him, but I'd never admit that. Instead, I'll just work harder than ever, killing myself in the process. But if it allows her to be free from the grasp of that man, I'd do it a million times over.

"Okay, well how are your meds working for you?" She redirects the conversation. "Have you been taking them regularly?"

"More or less." I stall. "Mostly less." I start picking at a loose string on my slacks, knowing she was most likely about to scold me.

"Any particular reason why?"

I shrug. "They don't really do anything for me other than enhance my nightmares." I immediately regret letting those words slip out. I've been so careful up until this point, and now I'll have to relive the thoughts that haunt me.

"Nightmares?" she repeats. "They're back again?"

I nod. The last time I had them, I ended up spending a week in the hospital for severe panic attacks. They drugged me every single day, forcing me to lose consciousness. The medication only reminds me of my inability to function as a human being. I'd take nightmares over that feeling, any day.

I notice Dr. Reynolds peeking at her watch, only for the timer to go off shortly after. I'm slightly relieved that I don't have to rehash the one night that scared the living hell out of me, but I also know if I don't come to terms with it, it'll haunt me forever.

"Next Monday, 4:00 pm," she says.

"I'll be here."

Chapter 7
Macy

Am I Going to Have to Run You Over?

I can hear sirens in the distance, followed by a plethora of lights that have no business being that bright. Humidity fills the air as a light mist hits my face. All I can see is the night sky through blurred vision. I don't know what's going on, but I can faintly hear my mother screaming my name. Before I can locate her, the two double doors slam shut, and an oxygen mask is placed over my nose and mouth. I inhale and exhale, trying to fill my lungs to max capacity. Next thing I know, the doors fly open and a parade of people in scrubs await my arrival. I can feel what I now realize to be a gurney beneath me, scrape across the ground, making a squeaking noise. It sounds like nails on a chalkboard, and I try to focus on anything else. I somewhat remember being rushed into the E.R. and am surrounded by a team of nurses. I can hear everyone speaking at once, and the voices began to blend together. I can't make out any of the words. Breathing becomes harder. I can feel my chest tightening and my head spinning. Then everything falls silent. Until it doesn't.

Beeeeeeeeeeeeeeeeeeeeeeeeeeeeeeeeeeeeeeep. "Code blue!" someone yells.

And then I wake up.

I'm lying in a pool of sweat, the back of my tank top soaking wet. The nightmares continue. It ends the same way every time—with me flatlining. Even though I'm alive now, for the first year after my incident, it felt like I was dead. It felt like the ending to my dream became my reality, and I sometimes wish it had happened that way. Maybe then, I wouldn't be damaged goods. Maybe then, I would have a sense of normalcy. I'd be a twenty-five-year-old adult who has her shit together. Instead, I'm broken, with no idea how to do this thing called life.

It's been eleven years since that day, and it only grows worse with the passing years. Maybe it's because I have yet to seek help until now. Maybe it's because every year on May 11, my mother finally decides to show concern and check up on me, never letting me forget. I know I should be grateful, but I don't need a reminder every year how my obsession with my eating disorder almost ended my life.

I look at the clock, it's 4:11 am. What the hell is up with me and the number eleven? There's no going back to sleep now, so I begrudgingly throw the covers off me and head to my bathroom. I peel off my sweat-soaked top and let it fall to the floor, along with the rest of my clothes. Steam seeps over the glass shower door, and I step in, making my way under the showerhead. Scalding beads of water fall onto my skin, and I finally feel like I can breathe again. I close my eyes, soaking in the warmth that contrasts with my cold flesh. Thoughts of Paxton standing in his sweatpants inhabit my brain. I smile, unable to wash away the feeling that I can potentially see a future with this man. I quickly snap back to reality once I remember who I am and how I could never drag him into my mess.

Why do I do this to myself? Why do I push away every guy I've ever shown interest in? I'll tell you why; because I'm selfish. Because no one ever gave a shit about me before I became this way, I stopped giving a shit about other people. I solely focused on what was going to carry me to the light at the end of my tunnel, never caring about who I hurt in the process. That cycle continued for the past eight years—until I met Paxton. And even though I'd like to think I could change for him, I have a feeling it might be too late.

My heart breaks at the thought of never knowing what real love feels like. I've never allowed myself to fall that hard, but I really think I could with him. I force myself to push back the thoughts. Today is a big day. It's the day we take the first part of our mock exam, so I need to focus. I finish my shower and walk into my closet, grabbing the nearest pair of workout clothes I can find. After getting dressed, I make myself some breakfast and do some studying before my run.

I'm disappointed that I'm only able to get two miles in, but that's all I had time for. I rush into my apartment, run some dry shampoo through my hair, and throw on a dark gray pencil skirt and a pale pink button up. I opt for light makeup since I'll be sitting at a desk most of the time. I grab a bottle of water out of the fridge and my keys off the hook by the door before I head out. I get to my car and hop in when I notice a text on my lock screen.

PAXTON
Good luck today; not that you need it, but I wanted to say it anyway.

Thanks, you too. Although, to beat my score, you are going to need it.

PAXTON
I forgot how pleasant you are in the mornings.

No wonder I'm in therapy. I seriously need help. I try not to think about the regret I feel for possibly ruining Paxton's day, but I'm showered with guilt. *Why couldn't you just stop at 'you too'?* Because I'm an idiot, that's why. Some days, I don't even know why he bothers to entertain this *situationship* we have going on. I would've dropped me a long time ago. I feel a pang in my chest, realizing how upset I'd genuinely be if he ever ended things. Which I know will happen eventually, since graduation is only a few months away, but I'm not ready for that just yet.

I pull up to school and head to the auditorium, taking my seat three rows in front of Paxton. I try to slyly peek at him without him noticing, but that would require him not already staring at me. I give him a shy smile and turn back to the front of the room.

"Everyone please login to your computer and pull up your mock exam," Professor Prelow voices. "The password is GRAD, in all caps."

We all do as instructed and begin our six-hour-long test. I am the fourth to finish, which is a surprisingly pleasing number, considering there are over one hundred people in our class.

By now, it's a little past two, and I patiently wait for Paxton to exit the building so I can rub my score in his face. With a minimum of 133 to pass, and 165 being the highest possible score, I'd say a 159 is a pretty good score for the MBE portion.

Finally, he enters my view and I stride with pride towards him. He doesn't have a single emotion present on his face, and now I'm wondering if he didn't do so well. But because of the person that I am, I ask anyway.

"Well? How did you do?" I ask eagerly.

"161, you?"

That's damn near a perfect score. The gloat leaves my

body, leaving my face pale and my soul crushed. *He beat me?* I know I should be happy for him, but all it means is that I'm not reaching my goal. I've been distracted by the man standing in front of me, possibly costing me Summa Cum Laude and the junior partner position. I've spent the last four months playing pretend girlfriend instead of focusing on being the best. Four months too long, and now that must end.

"Uh… 159," I say, almost embarrassed.

"Holy shit, that's amazing, Macy. Not many females score that high on their first try."

A feel a flush in my cheeks. He's so sincere in his compliment, not at all returning my vindictive attitude from earlier today.

I grace him with a shrug. "Well, I'm not most females."

"No, you certainly are not," he mutters under his breath.

"What was that?"

He lowers his head, watching his feet and sticking both hands in his pockets as we continue to walk across the courtyard to the parking lot. "Nothing. Do you wanna go to Cheap Shots to celebrate?"

I think long and hard, wanting so desperately to say yes, but the war inside my head leads me to say otherwise. "Paxton, it's a Tuesday. And we have the writing portion tomorrow. I think it's best if we don't."

"How about Friday then?"

Everything inside of me wants to take him up on his offer. But I know if I do, cutting him off would be even harder than it already is. I can't get back these last four months, but I can certainly prevent indulging in any more wasted time. *Is that really what I think of my time with him? A waste?* I certainly don't believe the tricks my mind is playing on me, but time with Paxton means less time to study. And I need to study.

"I'm busy Friday, sorry," I lie.

I can see the disappointment on his face, but he doesn't push the issue any further. We reach our cars, and he opens my door for me. I slide in and put the key in the ignition, cranking my Audi. But Paxton doesn't move. He stands between me and the door, and I suddenly feel all hot inside. If he stands here any longer, I just might give into temptation. I need him to leave. I need to get out of here. So, I do the only thing I can think of.

"Are you just going to stand there or am I going to have to run you over?"

He bends over and sticks his head inside my car, coming inches from my face. Normally I'd entertain the stare-down, but this time, I keep my gaze ahead. There is no way I can look him in the face right now.

Inching closer, he whispers in my ear, "Friday night. 7 pm. Be ready."

I can hear my heartbeat in my ears, and I wonder if he can hear it too. He shuts my door and walks away towards his car. *This man isn't going to make it easy.*

Chapter 8
Macy

Safe Haven

Friday, October 17 - 2:30 pm

"Macy."

I nod. "Dr. Reynolds."

She begins writing then peeks her eyes up from her clipboard. "You can call me Taylor, if you'd like."

Although I'm certain she's barely older than me—thirty at most—I don't feel comfortable doing that. "I'll stick with Dr. Reynolds, if you don't mind. Calling you by your first name makes me feel more like I'm talking to a friend, rather than receiving the professional help I'm seeking."

"I never thought of it that way. Dr. Reynolds it is. I suppose I did earn that title. What a waste it would be not to hear it." She chuckles.

I like her. She has a calmness about her that makes me feel comfortable and not judged like the last therapist I tried talking to. Dr. Sanchez was an older woman, in her late fifties, if I had to guess. She reminded me of a less pleasant version of Professor McGonagall. She was very punctual—not that there is anything wrong with punctuality—but she wouldn't start a second early or end a minute late. Her clothes were always neatly pressed, making me feel severely underdressed most days, and she never cracked a smile. Not even once. Safe to say, I barely lasted three sessions before taking my money elsewhere. Which is how I ended up here.

"So, Macy. Where did we leave off last week?"

As much as she writes during our sessions, I can almost guarantee she remembers, but I think she wants me to *want* to talk about it on my own. I appreciate that she doesn't push me, but I think I'm finally ready to open up to someone other than my mother—who constantly scolded me for "having a problem."

I tense up at the thought of my mother's reaction once I was finally home. Even after almost losing her own daughter, she still found a way to place blame on me. Yes, it was my fault, but a little compassion would have been nice. I remember her lecturing me about how stupid I was for doing such a thing, and how I could've died and left Lauren alone. As much as I hate to admit it, she did have a point there. It was a selfish thing for me to do, leaving my little sister in the hands of our mother or even worse, another random babysitter. I was the only safe haven in Lauren's life, and I should've considered that.

"M-May 11." My voice cracks. I'm shifting in my seat, feeling uncomfortable as the date rolls off my tongue. I know Dr. Reynolds can see my struggle by the unsettling look on her face.

"If it's too hard, Macy, we can come back to it."

"No. I'm ready. It's just a miserable day that I try to suppress," I admit. "But I know I have to face my demons head on, or else the nightmares will continue."

"Nightmares are common after trauma, but I see you're smart enough to know how to break the cycle. I'm impressed."

I crack a smile. No one has ever thought I'm smart *or* impressive, so I silently accept the compliment and try to figure out how to begin explaining this tragic day.

"I just turned fourteen earlier that year. My eating disorder had been in full swing for almost a year and a half, but this particular week, it was at its worst. I hadn't eaten in days. I was scary thin and so pale that I was almost translucent. I could feel myself growing weaker by the day, but I couldn't bring myself to eat anything. The hunger pains were excruciating, but still, I didn't give in." A long-drawn-out breath exits my mouth. "My mother was set to arrive home that evening after being gone for the week, so it was just me and Lauren until then, as per usual. All morning long, I had been vomiting—unintentionally. There was nothing left to expel, other than the contents of the lining of my stomach, which continued on and off for hours. Eventually, it let up. I remember standing in the kitchen, making Lauren dinner, when everything went hazy and the room went black."

I can feel my hands trembling at the thought of Lauren watching me collapse. She was only twelve, and although she's no stranger to trauma, I'm sure that scared the living hell out of her. Guilt fills my stomach. How could I have been so selfish to allow her to witness something so disturbing?

"I don't remember anything after that. Doctors said I was severely dehydrated and suffered a concussion from hitting my head on the stove, and then the tile" My eyes divert to the floor, and I start picking at my already chewed nailbeds. "In my nightmares, I vaguely remember the drive to the hospital in the ambulance. The neon lit emergency room sign over my head as they rushed me into the trauma bay. The slurred speech of everyone around me. And then... I die. Every time."

It's so quiet I can hear the pressure of Dr. Reynold's pen on the paper as she's writing. What *is* she writing? I'm sure she has other clients just as messed up as me, if not worse. But somehow, I feel the most in need of repair.

I don't know what I expect her to say, but it definitely isn't the next words that she speaks.

"Were you trying to kill yourself?" she asks so nonchalantly.

My mouth falls a little, taken aback by her question. "I'm sorry?"

"You don't have to answer if you don't feel comfortable, but you mentioned that in your nightmares, you die at the end. So, my question still stands. Were you trying to kill yourself?"

Could I be honest without being sent away in a straight jacket? I don't know if I ever *intended* for things to get as bad as they did, and I know my life wasn't picture perfect, but I also don't think I wanted to die. *Did I?* Thinking back, maybe I was a little depressed. Maybe the stress of being my sister's keeper at such a young age did take its toll on me. But did I really want to end my life?

"I don't know," I say, feeling unsure. "I didn't intentionally do what I did to end up almost dying, if that's what you're asking. It wasn't an act of premeditated suicide. I could've found better, *faster* ways to do that. I simply needed to feel better in my own skin. Then, it became an addiction that spiraled out of control. Did I sometimes wish I had a different life? Absolutely, all the time. But I wouldn't purposely leave my sister to fend for herself. So, I guess that answers your question."

"It does. I only asked because maybe your nightmares are a result of your subconscious thoughts. Do you ever try to convince yourself that things would've been easier on you had your life ended as such?"

She's really digging deep today, forcing me to do the same. It's like she's in my brain, and all her questions are causing my insecurities to resurface. She really *is* the best psychologist in the state.

I fidget some more before finally telling her the hard truth. "Yes."

That was it. That's all I could admit. And then, my session ended.

Chapter 9
Macy

Thank You, Grandfather Clock

Today was a hard day. I felt fourteen all over again, and nothing made me feel worse than that. I stand in my bedroom, staring at myself in my full-length mirror that is leaning up against the wall. I begin to pick apart the body I've worked so hard for over the last ten years. I am in good shape. I am healthy. Yet I somehow find the ugliest things to say to myself. *Your hips are too big. Your stomach isn't flat enough. Don't get me started on those stretchmarks on your thighs.*

The knock on my front door silences the voice in my head, and I run to my living room. Who the heck is here at this time of night? It's 7:00 pm. I reluctantly swing the door open, and find Paxton standing in my doorway. He's dressed in jeans and a relaxed tee but holding a black garment bag in his right hand. A cunning smile cuts across his face, then falls once he examines me in my pajama shorts and tank top.

"What are you doing here?" I ask with an uncanny tone in my voice.

"It's 7:00," he answers, as if I'm supposed to know what that means.

"Thank you, grandfather clock. I'm well aware of what time it is."

"Always with the sarcasm." He rolls his eyes. "Our non-date? Also, you should probably be more cautious when opening the door; I could've been a serial killer."

Shit. I totally forgot about our non-date. I had been so distracted today after my session that it didn't even occur to me that today was Friday. This week has been so stressful that all my days have blurred together.

Paxton is still standing outside of my apartment, waiting for me to invite him in, but I have one last smart-ass remark to make before allowing him inside.

"Oh. You were serious?" I drum my fingers along the door frame, still blocking him from entering.

He stares at me blankly, then grazes his eyes over my body once more. "By the looks of it, I'm going to assume you forgot." He ducks underneath my arm that's stretched across the frame and enters my place without warning. "Lucky for you, I have options."

"Of course, you do," I reply unpleasantly. I watch as he pulls a small stack of notecards from his bag. I notice he has slacks and a button up in there as well, along with his shiny brown loafers. *Are we going somewhere fancy? What is he up to?*

He separates the notecards into two stacks of three, all turned over so I can't see what is written on the other side. "Here." He gestures. "Pick one."

I'm hesitant at first, but I really could use a night to unwind. I stand there, my left arm taking hold of my opposite elbow, my right hand resting on my chin as I debate which to choose. I pick the right one and turn the card around. *Cute and casual,* it reads. "What do the other ones say?"

"That would ruin the fun. Go change. You look like you're

ready for bed." He tries his best to use my tactics against me, but I know better.

"I *was*. Then you stormed in and ruined the night I had planned."

"Let me guess. Murder documentaries and ice cream?"

Damn. Am I that predictable? Or does Paxton actually pay attention to me as much as I pay attention to him? Either way, I'm quite impressed, but have to play it cool. I stand there with my arms folded, not listening to his demand. "Maybe."

"Go get dressed. You're wasting precious time."

As much as I don't want to obey his command, I do as I'm told—with attitude of course. I opt for a pair of jeans and a knitted cream-colored sweater that hangs off my left shoulder, revealing the dandelion tattoo just beneath my collarbone. I pull my hair into a low messy bun, pulling strands of my bangs out to frame my face. Since my contacts are on backorder, I also decide it's best to throw on my glasses so I can enjoy tonight's festivities, whatever they may be. I stroll down the hallway and head back to the living room to find Paxton making himself at home on my couch.

He catches a glimpse of me and swallows hard, obviously unable to form words. I kind of like it when he looks at me like that. Makes me feel confident, *sexy* even. I try to hide the look of satisfaction on my face. "Well, are you just gonna sit there all night or are we going to do something fun?"

"I was just about to compliment you." His mouth snaps shut. "I changed my mind."

I rarely ever feel remorseful for my choice of words, but this time, it's in full force. I really know how to screw shit up. "Sorry," I manage to whisper. "Carry on."

He looks a little surprised that I apologized. I normally don't do that either, but I guess he takes it as a peace offering. "You look… nice. I love the business attire, but casual really suits you."

"Thanks." I can feel a dusty shade of pink tint my cheeks. It takes a lot to make me blush, but Paxton has no trouble whatsoever causing me to feel like a lovestruck teenager. It's quite cute how open he is with his compliments. Judging by his inability to date, I would've never pegged him as the romantic type.

"Next card." He holds out his arm, both cards facing him, the blank sides facing me.

I pick the left this time. *Drunken laser tag.* I let out a laugh, then look up at him. "This should be interesting."

He smiles, and I just know he was hoping I'd pick this card. It does sound like fun.

We take the stairs to the first floor and make our way to his car. Per usual, he opens my door for me, and I climb in as he shuts the door behind me. I'm not sure where we're getting drinks, but the familiar sign of Cheap Shots comes into view once we turn onto Plaza St. The bouncer welcomes us as we walk inside, and Owen, the bartender, greets us with a wave. Instead of sitting at the bar tonight, Paxton grabs us a corner booth. It's one of those small ones, only one person per side, and I start to think he's trying to avoid sitting next to me.

We sit across from each other and pick up our menus. I already know what I want, but I pretend to look over the menu anyway. Our waitress appears and introduces herself. "Hey guys, my name is Drew, and I'll be your server tonight. Can I get you both started with something to drink?"

"I'll take a Michelob, bottle please. She'll have a Blue Moon, extra oranges."

She nods and writes down our drink order on her notepad. "I.D. please."

We both hand her our licenses, and she quickly checks over them before handing them back. "Anything else?"

"Oh, wait. Yes. And an order of your famous cheese fries. They're her favorite."

"Yes sir. I'll go put those in and grab your drinks," she says as she walks in the opposite direction.

I can't believe he just did that. I can't *believe* he knew my order, without me saying a word. I pinch myself under the table to make sure I'm not dreaming. I wince, pinching myself a little too hard. Yep, definitely awake. *I think it's time I ask for his hand in marriage,* I joke to myself. He adjusts his posture, accidentally kicking my leg, breaking my focus.

"First you don't allow me to speak for myself and now you're assaulting me? What kind of non-date is this?"

He seems puzzled, maybe even almost offended that I wasn't appreciative of his generous actions. "I... I'm sorry. I didn't mean to overstep." He dips his head below the menu he's holding. Now I feel bad. I lower the menu in front of him to reveal his face.

"Paxton, it was a joke. I might be slightly impressed that you knew exactly what I wanted." I don't want to give him any time to boast, but I do think I may have insulted him just a little, so I figured I should play nice.

"I expect nothing less from you," he shoots back with a grin. My stomach does a flip. What the hell am I going to do with him?

We spend the next hour pouring back the troubles of our week. But only enough to feel slightly intoxicated. There is no way I'm going to have a repeat of last week.

We stumble our way down the street and cross over to the next block until we reach Battle Royale. It's packed with underaged kids, as it should be, but we decide we can't back out now. The cashier gives us our vests, and we make our way to the control room to grab our laser guns. A deep voice comes over the intercom, explaining the instructions of the game.

I shoot a stern look at Paxton, raising my two fingers to my eyes then gesturing them to him, as if to state I'm taking him down. He can't help but laugh.

The doors open to the playing room, and all fourteen of us step inside. It's dark, only lit with glowing targets posted on the walls. As soon as the doors shut, the voice reappears and shouts "You may begin!"

Everyone takes off in different directions, and I lose Paxton almost immediately. It's so dark that I can't make out who anyone was, but then again, a 6'3 man shouldn't be that hard to locate.

I look down, a laser beam centered on my chest, and before I can run, my vest taps out. I see Paxton pop his head up from behind a half wall, cracking up laughing. That's it. *Game Over.*

I'm running into walls due to my inebriated state. I'm almost positive I take out at least three kids in the process, but I try not to feel bad about it. I need to win, after all. I spend the remainder of our time smoking the shit out of everyone I can get my laser to land on. I notice there's only three minutes left on the clock, and once again, Paxton is nowhere to be found. I sneak around a wall trying to hide when a hand covers my mouth from behind and pulls me into a corner. My back is plastered against the wall, a very unsteady Paxton standing in front of me, his chest touching mine—well, his vest is pushed against mine. I'm almost afraid to look up at him, in fear that I might try to take him right here on this very floor.

He lowers his gaze to meet mine, inching his face closer until I can feel his staggered breath on my lips. This is it. This is the moment we cross the line of whatever this is that we're doing. But before we have the chance, the lights flicker on.

Chapter 10
Paxton

Ricky Bobby

I can't remember the last time I had this much fun. This woman surely does bring out the teenage boy in me, and I can't complain one bit. I love how effortless our friendship is. And even though she's hellbent on pushing me away with her words, I don't plan on going anywhere. If anything, it makes me want to get even closer to her. I can't tell if it's the buzz, or my subconscious mind playing tricks on me, but everything is screaming at me to kiss her. *Just kiss her Paxton,* the voice screams louder.

It's dark, and I can barely see anything but silhouettes and laser beams. I stand in a corner, waiting to see the reflection from her glasses. *Ah, there she is,* walking towards me without the slightest clue. She rounds the corner in front of me, and I grab her from behind. She lets out a shriek, but my hand is covering her mouth. I push her up against the wall, her ear at the height of my chest, and I wonder if she can hear how fast my heart is racing. It's been almost four years since I ended my engagement, and I haven't had a girlfriend since. Bedmates? Sure, but nothing that has ever felt like this. My nerves are getting the best of me, but I manage to lower my eyes, focusing on what little I can see of her. My hands rest against the wall on either side of her. I'm so close. *Kiss her, idiot.* Just then, the room grows bright with fluorescent lights, and my forehead falls to hers. I blew it.

―――

Both now completely sober, we walk to the car in silence, not really knowing what to say. My lack of words stems more from my embarrassment than anything. I can't say I know where hers comes from. Was she also embarrassed? Was she upset I got so close? Was she disappointed I didn't make it to her lips? The questions are racing a mile a minute and my ears are burning for answers. I want to approach one but am afraid she will ask me to take her home.

Instead, I pull out the final two cards from my pocket. We stand in front of my car, and I stretch my arm toward her, both cards in hand.

"Last one. Choose wisely," I dare.

She grabs both notecards and starts running from me.

"Hey! That's cheating!" Luckily, I'm a foot taller than her, so it doesn't take many strides to catch up to where she is. She hasn't looked at either card yet, so I snatch them back and hold them up above my head. She tries to tickle me, but she doesn't know I have the composure of steel. Her 5'4 attitude really shows up after that. She gives me a soft punch to the gut, but my position remains intact.

"Ugh, you're no fun," she huffs. I'm not backing down though, and she finally chooses the left card.

BomboBar. Her smile insinuates she's excited about that choice. "I've never been there, but I've heard great things. I'm especially excited to try the s'mores hot chocolate."

"That's my favorite. Come on, let's go."

I drive us across town and pull into the parking lot of *THE* dessert place in the West Loop. We each order a hot chocolate and decide to split a cookies-and-cream bomboloni and a small cup of their homemade hazelnut gelato.

We take our dessert out to my car. She doesn't ask questions, but I know she's confused as to why we didn't just eat inside. I can tell by the expression on her face. I made the decision so that I could spend time with her, just the two of us, without any bystanders. We chat for a bit then finish off the bomboloni and place our hot chocolates in the cupholders after sipping on them. She takes a bite of the gelato, and a low moan leaves her mouth. I shoot her a playful smile. Yet, she doesn't even seem ashamed in the slightest.

"What? Dessert does it for me." She laughs.

"Seems I've found a sweet spot."

"Don't get any ideas," she warns me with a glare.

I chuckle, noticing she has gelato on her lip. Without a second thought, I lean over and place my lips on hers, slightly biting her bottom lip with my teeth as swipe my tongue over the creamy residue. Instantly, my dick grows thick and electricity zaps down my spine. If this is what just one small taste of her does to me, I can't wait to taste the rest of her.

I feel her hand snake behind my neck, pulling me in and kissing me harder. *She wants this too.* My hand makes its way into her hair as the kissing grows deeper. I slip my tongue into her mouth, feeling hers wrapping around mine. *God, I've wanted to do this for so long.* My pulse quickens, and I pull her into my lap, setting the cup of gelato on the passenger seat. I can almost guarantee she can feel me against her jeans, but at this point, I don't even care. She breaks for a quick breath, then comes back slowly, *softly.* The ache for her is becoming too strong to control. We need to get out of here.

I pull away and stare her straight in the eyes, a hungry look on my face. "Your place, or mine?"

She doesn't even blink before whispering, "Mine."

She makes her way back into her seat, and I press on the gas a little too hard, causing her to topple over and hit her head on the door. I try my best not to laugh, but it's inevitable.

"Ow! Watch what you're doing, Ricky Bobby!"

Again, I laugh. "Whoops, sorry!" I peel out of the parking lot, trying to get to her place as fast as I can. "You know what they say, baby; if you ain't first, you're last."

Her eyes narrow in on me, trying to hide her smile. *Are we really going to do this? Do I even have a condom? If I don't—which I probably don't because I wasn't expecting this—does she?* Jesus, Paxton. Get a grip. Quit making things so weird.

I finally pull into to her apartment complex and throw the car in park, almost too eagerly. We climb out and walk up to her floor. My heart is racing, my palms are sweaty, and there's a nervousness filling my stomach. *What am I? Fifteen?* A twenty-six-year-old grown man should not be making a big deal out of this. Yet here I am, acting a fool, as if I've never slept with a girl before.

209.

I've never been so excited to see a number before. I stand behind Macy as she unlocks her door. She enters and just before I make it over the threshold, she turns to me, barricading the door. Her eyes are tired, but her smile is genuine. I'm so confused. I stand there with a perplexed look on my face.

"You didn't really think you were coming in, did you?" Her eyebrow arches.

Now I really feel stupid. Of course, I thought that. Isn't that what the whole fiasco that just happened implied? Did I misread the context? Again, *I'm so confused.* I rock on my heels for a moment, both hands in my pocket, a disheveled expression taking over. I've lost all ability to speak.

"One moment," she says, as she partially closes the door. I

watch her grab my things. She hands them back to me. "Here you go. I had a really good time tonight, Paxton. Let's not ruin it."

She backs away and slowly closes the door.

What just happened?

Chapter 11
Macy

I've Changed My Mind

My back is against the door, and I slide down it until I'm sitting on the floor, elbows resting on my knees with my head in my hands. I can feel tears form at the brim of my eyes. One slowly falls down my cheek as I blink, and I can't help but feel guilty for allowing things to get that far.

I can't go there with him.

Paxton deserves so much better than the broken mess of a person I am. He deserves more than the damaged girl who's incapable of love—or a normal relationship for that matter. I'm twenty-five-years-old and have never had a relationship last longer than six months because that's my limit. Six months and not one day longer. I can't love someone when I don't even feel like I deserve to be loved myself. My father didn't love me, or else he wouldn't have left. My mother sure as hell didn't love me, or else she would've been present. *I don't even love me.* So, how can I expect anyone else to take on that task? I didn't. And I don't.

My phone buzzes. It's Lauren.

> **LAUREN**
> Hey stranger. Just wanted to check on you. I haven't heard from you in a while. I miss you! I'm making plans for Thanksgiving and wanted to see if you mind having company. Specifically, two. There's someone I want you to meet.

Great. Even my little sister can find it in her to move past all the bullshit and live a normal life. Although I held my composure most days when we were kids, I always knew she was stronger than me. She never once complained about the way we lived. She just took it as it was and made sure to console me in the process. I was lucky to have her then; I still am, but it's hard to stay as close as we once were when you live half a country away from each other. I'm in Chicago, and Lauren ended up in California for college and graduated from UCLA last year. I haven't seen her since I moved here—almost three years ago.

> Sorry I've been distant. School has me swamped, but I'm doing just fine. Only eight more months until I cross that finish line! And I'd be happy to host, but you're sleeping with me. No playing house under my roof 😉

> **LAUREN**
> My God, Macy. You're such a mom. Does this mean you still don't have a boyfriend?

> Well, we never actually had a mother, so it's my duty to make sure you don't become one. Until you're ready, of course.

> **LAUREN**
> You didn't answer my question.

> Goodbye Lauren.

> **LAUREN**
> You know I love you, Mace, but you can't keep doing this to yourself. It's not healthy. I don't want you to end up alone.

> I'll see you at Thanksgiving. Love you.

I drop my phone to the ground, still sitting against the door. Her words hit me like a ton of bricks. *I don't want you to end up alone.* For someone who never lets anyone get too close to her, you'd never guess I am a victim of monophobia. The physical act of being alone doesn't scare me, but the fear of ending up alone at the end of it all does. Still, I push any guy away that could possibly care about me. I'm terrified to end up like my so-called "parents." If my dad could just get up and walk away from his wife and two kids, how can I be sure that someone wouldn't wake up one day and decide he didn't want to be with me anymore? And that's where my atelophobia settles in.

Atelophobia (n): the fear of not being good enough or fear of imperfection.

I've chased perfection my whole life, and all it has done is set me up for disappointment. I wasn't good enough to keep my dad around. I was never good enough for my mom, who picked me apart my entire childhood. So, nothing inside of me believes I'll ever be good enough to become someone's wife. And Paxton deserves a wife one day—even if he isn't ready to date right now.

A familiar knock sounds on my door, so I rise to my feet. I open the door and there's Paxton, standing there like he hasn't even left. Before I know it, both hands are cupping my face, his lips on mine. I nearly stumble backward, but he quickly releases his left hand and catches me by the waist, pulling me in even closer. This kiss isn't like the one we shared earlier in the car. This one is pure desperation. Whether it's for sex, or for me, I can't tell, but I know whatever it was, he wants it. And he wants it *bad*.

Before the kissing can escalate, I pull back. "Paxton, what are you doing?"

His breathing is uneven, like he just ran a marathon, but he remains focused on me. He takes a step toward me. A very stern expression is plastered on his face, and I'm unsure of whether I should be worried.

The tension melts when he speaks; he sounds almost hurt. "Why do you do it?"

I'm not sure what he's referring to.

"Why do I do what?" I ask genuinely, not in the mood for sarcasm.

"Push me away. I can handle the sarcasm. I can handle the insults. Because I know they're a defense mechanism that you hide behind. But what I can't handle is you making me feel the way you do and then just shutting the door in my face like none of it matters to you."

I feel sick. I can almost guarantee I look like I've seen a ghost. Because I now know that the desperation in that kiss was for me. *He wanted me. Wants me.* But there's no way I can give him what he wants, though—what he *deserves.*

"Do I not matter to you, Macy? Have these last four months meant *nothing* to you?" His voice is demanding, and I know he isn't leaving without an answer.

"Paxton…"

"No. Answer me. I wanna know."

"It's not that simple." The uneasiness in my voice doesn't sound very convincing.

"Yes, Macy. Yes, it is. I like you. I enjoy being with you. I *thought* you felt the same, but I guess I've been misjudging everything."

I lower my head, staring at the floor until I find the courage to speak. "You don't want me, Paxton. I promise you that."

"I'm standing right here, telling you that I want you. How can I be clearer than this?!" His voice grows louder, which sends a chill down my spine.

"But you said—"

"I don't care what I said four months ago," he interrupts me. "Four months is enough time for someone to change their mind. I changed my mind, Macy. *You* changed my mind. The way that you chew on your pen during class when you're pondering your answer to Professor Prelow's question. Or the fact that you laugh at 98% of my jokes, even though I'm not nearly as funny as you. Your quick wit and unnecessary smart-ass remarks you make, just for the hell of it. The way you stay quiet and keep to yourself but then turn around and have no problem putting me in my place. All those things *changed my mind.*"

My heart is beating out of my chest. No guy has ever fought this hard for me when I tried leaving before. So, why is he?

"Why?" I blurt out. "Why now, Paxton? Why, after not wanting to date anyone for years, do you suddenly want a relationship?"

"Because I didn't want to date anyone. I didn't want to *want* to date anyone. But you're not just *anyone*, Macy. I was doing just fine before you, and I sure as hell didn't expect you to walk into my life and wreck my plans of solitude. But you did, and I can't change that; I don't want to. I just want *you*. Do you not feel any of that for me? Just tell me, and if your answer is no, then I'll leave you be."

Tears sting my eyes. A heaviness courses through me, my entire body feels like lead. Can I really stand here and lie to him, just to push him away? His words feel like a wrecking ball that has just demolished the sky-high walls I've spent forever building. All in one swift motion, they've come crumbling down at the sound of his despair.

So, I do something I know I shouldn't, but can't stop

myself from doing. I tell him the truth. "I want you too, Paxton. But I'm hard to love, impossible even. I'm a handful, maybe even two. I have a bad habit of overthinking things. I don't trust easily, and I tend to push everyone away. The last thing I want to do is hurt you."

Without a second thought, he embraces me in another kiss. This one much more delicate. My eyes flutter shut. My breathing evens out, and every worry I have melts away. He breaks from our kiss and rests his forehead on mine.

"I'll be the judge of that," is all that escapes his mouth before his lips are back on mine.

Chapter 12
Macy

Sixth Month Rule

Saturday, October 18

Eight years ago, today was our sixth-month anniversary.

Blaine was taking me out to dinner, so I showered and stood in the doorway of my closet, trying to decide on an appropriate outfit for that night. He said not overly dressy, but not too casual either. I opted for a high-waisted skirt and a long sleeve bodysuit. I slid the top over my head and pulled it down my torso. It was a bit snug, but I still managed to snap it between my legs. I grabbed the skirt and slipped into it, sliding it up my thighs. Only, I couldn't get it over them. I tried again, pulling at it more aggressively. This time, it ripped. A surge of self-consciousness washed over me, and I was instantly transported back to twelve-year-old me, feeling completely uncomfortable in her clothes.

The first year after my trip to the hospital was the hardest. I took so much pity on myself, never taking responsibility for almost ending my own life. It took a lot of isolation and self-reflection before realizing I wasn't a victim in this situation. I did this to myself, and I was going to take back control of my life. My sophomore year of high school changed everything for me. I put the books away. Instead, I focused on becoming active. I joined the track team and used the weight room every day after my last class. I even met with the school nutritionist to get my relationship with food under control. It wasn't easy and I failed a lot at first, but eventually, my habits became a lifestyle. I started liking the person staring back at me in the mirror. Girls wanted to be my friend, and boys finally began taking interest in me for once.

I stayed away from dating for as long as I could though, because I had absolutely no idea how to feel confident in my own skin when it came to boys. But finally, at seventeen, I had enough courage to say yes to having a boyfriend. Blaine Evans was the very first guy I took a chance on, and he was the very first guy to ever break my heart.

I don't know why I took it so hard. Maybe because I'd never dated before. Maybe because I felt inadequate. Or maybe it was because every girl thinks they're going to marry the first guy to make them feel like they know what love is. But he was a typical teenage boy, and I shouldn't have been surprised in the slightest when it came to an end.

I vividly remember him picking me up for our date, only to comment on the bit of happy weight I had gained over the last few months of us dating. He always had something to say about my appearance, whether good or bad, but never cared about anything deeper. Now that I think about it, he was quite shallow, but at the time, I didn't care. He was a boy, and I hadn't been a girl worth looking at until then. After our date, he parked his car in my driveway, and we made out as normal teens do. Then, he tried to take it a step further, like he always did. And I turned him down, just as I always did. I knew he was a boy with needs, but I just wasn't ready, and apparently, he was tired of waiting. He gave me an ultimatum—sex or it was over. It's not hard to figure out which I chose. I broke my own heart that night, but there it was—the fuel I needed to set myself on fire.

Goal number one: lose twenty-two pounds. And so, I did. I worked my ass off for the next three months to shed that extra weight I had been harboring. Once I knew what I could achieve after heartbreak, I made a deal with myself. I vowed to date for success. I'd date, but I'd never date anyone for longer than six months. Because any longer than that and I'd fall, and *that* wasn't part of the deal.

Chapter 13
Paxton

Very Un-Macy of You

I haven't heard from her since I confessed my love for her two days ago. Well, not love. I don't love her. Do I? No. Not *yet*, anyway. But I do like her, a lot. *A whole lot.* I may like her even more than I liked my ex-fiancée when I proposed to her. Not that I didn't love her, because I did once upon a time, but she grew into a person I eventually fell out of love with. And after the accident, someone I absolutely hated.

There's no proof that the accident was caused by her, but I know deep down it was. The investigation didn't last long because candles cause fires all the time. Only in my situation, I never use candles. I never lit candles. The only reason candles were ever burning in my house was because of her, so I know the fire was no accident.

Maybe it was rage on her part because I left her just a few weeks before our wedding, which wouldn't surprise me in the least. Her temper is one of the reasons I decided to end things in the first place. And maybe that lit a spark in her, and that spark grew into arson. But I couldn't argue that in court because there was just no proof. No trace that she was there that night, other than one flickering candle that eventually sent my house up in flames.

The flashbacks start, and I feel the heat rising in my face, just as it does whenever I frantically jump out of the shower after smelling smoke. Had I not been awake, there's no telling if I'd still be here today. I remember opening the bathroom door, thick black clouds coursing through each room. I couldn't see a damn thing, but somehow, I managed to make my way through to the kitchen and out the back door. It was freezing outside, and I was in just a towel, still wet from the shower, but the chill was far better than the heat put off by my ex's poor attempt to erase me. That night, I appreciated that I designed the build of the house. I knew the layout like the back of my hand, which is probably the only reason I was able to make it out alive.

I remember standing in my driveway, sirens and lights racing into the neighborhood to come to my rescue. I didn't give any of them a second thought. I just stood there with my back to them, facing the one thing I had worked so hard for. I was proud of that house. I not only designed it, but I put months of manual labor into making sure it was something that would last forever. Maybe not for me, but for any owners after me. I wanted it to be something someone loved so much that they wouldn't feel the need to change a thing about it. And then, it was gone. Engulfed in the mistakes I made when choosing to *almost* spend my life with a possible criminal.

My phone vibrates, pulling me back to planet Earth. It's a text from Macy. She's agreed to let me at least *try* to love her, her words not mine. It came with unwanted sarcasm and a shit ton of warning signs that I paid no mind to. Because things in my life have never been as easy as they are now since she came into it. She makes things better for me. She's given me the ability to feel something for someone after four years of solitude. She's given me the ability to be *happy*. And although that happiness may come with a price of whatever she thinks deems her unlovable, I'm willing to take the risk.

After my confession and her agreement, we kissed for a bit, but I didn't push it any further than that. I left, respectfully, leaving the ball in her court. I was hoping she'd stop me from walking out of that door, but she didn't. And I can't say I wasn't a little crushed that she didn't ask me to stay. But I understood her need for space and clarity. I just didn't think she'd need two whole days of it.

> **MACY**
> So, does this new arrangement of ours warrant me a real date?

I grin at the smart remark. Not that I expect anything less, because I absolutely don't, but I find comfort in it now. It seems almost flirty, rather than a tactic to keep me away. I like that. I can handle that.

> Were all of our non-dates that bad?

> **MACY**
> Well, no. I enjoyed them. All of them. But I'd like to be able to label them now. Even though I always kind of pretended we were on real dates anyway.

I feel a swelling in my chest that tumbles into my stomach, almost as if I just got butterflies. Do grown men get those? The last time I was this giddy over a girl, I was in high school, so I really can't remember.

> I can't believe you just admitted that. Very un-Macy of you.

I tease, though I hope it doesn't come across the wrong way.

MACY

> You're right, I take it back. I don't even want to go on a real date with you now.

    I laugh. She is something else, that's for sure. But she's something so unlike any other girl I've ever met, and I'm drawn to it. I can't leave it alone. She invades my thoughts throughout the day. She even seeps into my dreams at night, and in my dreams, I get to have her. *All of her.*

> I'll be there at five. Dress nice. And make sure you yell before answering the door. I could be a kidnapper.

> Better yet, don't. I'd love to kidnap you

sense of pride, like I'm in complete control. Which is what I need to make sure I'm able to detach myself from him when it's time. It's never been a problem before, but I have a feeling Paxton won't make this easy on me.

"That's it, we're staying in," he demands. He kisses me, softly at first, but it quickly grows deeper. The feeling of his tongue on my lips causes me to part them immediately, allowing him to completely intertwine his tongue with mine. My whole body is tense, wanting so badly to lead him to my bedroom, but I'm dressed nicely and want to take full advantage of dating him before I end things in a few months. It takes everything in me to break free from the desire to strip him right here in my living room, but I finally pull away. His expression is full of disappointment, so I try to sound as convincing as I can.

"We look too good to hide ourselves away from the world; let's go on our date."

I know he would rather stay now that I got him riled up, but he still manages to peak a smile. He helps me slide on my coat, then guides me out the door by hand. As soon as we enter the elevator, Paxton pins me up against the wall and kisses me once more. How we went four months without ever kissing, I'll never know, but now I don't want it to stop. His body is so close to mine that I can feel him against me, and once again, I debate undressing him this very instant. He is hard to resist.

The elevator dings, and Paxton removes himself from me just in time for the doors to open. We walk to his car, and he opens the door for me as I slide in. He hops in the driver's seat shortly after, and I can't help but take in all his features. He is so handsome in all the ways my exes weren't. Everything about him only makes me realize that at the end of this, I'm going to be in trouble. Guilt starts setting in, thinking about potentially hurting him. It always felt wrong, no matter who the guy was, but something about Paxton makes it even more painful to imagine. Maybe if I make

Junior Partner before the six months are up, I won't have to do this again. I can finally be happy for longer than half a year. Maybe even forever this time; I can see forever with him.

I try to push those thoughts out of my head. "So, where are we going?"

"It's a surprise." He places his right hand on my left knee, so I cover his hand with mine, giving it a small squeeze. He smiles.

We drive in silence until we pull up to Alinea's. In the two and half years I've lived here, I've never been able to get a reservation here. They book months in advance, and thanks to my dating history, it's never worked out.

Alinea's has been named the Best Restaurant in the World by Elite Traveler, Best Restaurant in North America by The World's 50 Best Restaurants, and the Best Restaurant in the U.S. by Gourmet and Business Insider. *How did Paxton manage this?*

He can tell I'm stunned by my inability to speak. I'm sure the fact that my jaw has dropped is also a dead giveaway.

"You're surprised. Good." He's proud of himself. Hell, I am too.

Paxton leads the way, and I follow him into the two-story restaurant. It's beautiful, breathtaking even. The bottom floor is lined with a dark grain hardwood floor and consists of big, wooden, round tables surrounded by fabric chairs. On each table there are perfectly placed cloth napkins and empty chalice glasses. On the far-right side, there are floor to ceiling glass doors that allow you to see straight into the kitchen. Everything is exceptionally clean, and not one thing is out of place.

Behind the hostess stand, a carpeted staircase spirals up to the second floor. Luckily for us, our table is upstairs. We enter the stairwell, a glass chandelier hanging from the ceiling, hovering over the middle of the steps. Paxton is standing behind me, guiding me up the stairs with his hand on my lower back. We reach the top and the floor is nothing but windows. It's dimly lit, allowing us to see the entire city from this view. It's better than I ever imagined. The hostess seats us at a tall, marble table towards the front of the dining room and places menus in front of each of us.

"Nate will be your server this evening. Thank you for visiting Alinea's and enjoy," she says before sauntering away.

I open the menu, glance over a few of the dishes and immediately close it. "Absolutely not. We're leaving," I say as I place the menu flat onto the table. Paxton looks at me confused, with a small tilt of his head.

"What's wrong?"

"$190 A PERSON??" There is no way I will let him pay that. No fucking way.

He laughs, as if this is a common occurrence for him. "Calm down. It covers everything, from appetizers, to the meal, down to the dessert and a bottle of their best wine."

That is still absurd to me, and after the battle I had with myself earlier today, I know I am *not* worth $190.

"Paxton, please. There's no way I'm allowing you to spend that on me."

"Good thing it's not your choice," he says with furrowed brows. "It's already paid for. Has been for months."

Months? How many months? Did he make these reservations for someone else, or was he planning to take me here as a non-date? Surely not. There is no way he would spend this kind of money on someone who he wasn't committed to, would he?

"I'm sorry, what?"

"I made these reservations when we first started hanging out. After our first few encounters, I've wanted to take you here. I didn't mind that it was a few months out because I was hoping you'd give me an opportunity to prove myself to you," he admits. "I like you, Macy. A hell of a lot more than I ever intended to, but I'm not mad about it."

Fuck. Fuck. Fuck. I can feel my pulse becoming rapid, and my stomach is in knots. He's already falling for me with zero idea that I can't allow myself to reciprocate. *Even though I feel like I already am.*

Chapter 15
Paxton

You're a Pain in My Ass. You Know That?

I'm beginning to think that confessing my feelings for her is just scaring her at this point. I might be coming on too strong, but I'm only being honest about how I feel. Is that such a bad thing? Maybe for her, it is. I don't know what all she's been through, but I'm sure it must've been traumatic for her to still be single. Or maybe I'm just being judgmental. Maybe she's just strong-willed and independent and chooses not to depend on a man for anything. But I wouldn't know because we don't talk about anything deep. She keeps me wondering, and I want to know everything about her, but she's not the easiest person to get information out of. I'm honestly surprised she agreed to actually date me. And now that I'm thinking about it, I never even asked her to be my girlfriend officially. I guess that'll come later, when she's not so wound up about the price of our dinner.

Nate brings us some water and our appetizer, but Macy is just sitting there, not touching her food and looking completely uncomfortable.

I reach over the table and place my hand on hers. Her shoulders fall into a more relaxed state, as if she didn't realize how tense her own posture had been.

"Relax. Enjoy our date, please. For me."

I can tell from her sigh that she feels thankful that I asked, almost like she's relieved that I'm assuring her she's worth this. Of course, she is. I wouldn't have brought just *anyone* here, which is why I've never come before. I can see Macy as my end game. I just hope she can see me as hers.

"What's your middle name?" Maybe I can start with surface level questions and dig deeper as the evening goes on.

She has a puzzled look on her face. "Don't tell me you're going to ask for my social security number before the night is over." The slight grin on her face lets me know the sarcasm is never going away. I'm okay with that, as long as she still allows me in. I shoot her a pleading look, hoping she'll be keen on answering my questions.

"Fine," she agrees, rolling her eyes. "It's Brooke." Macy Brooke Callahan.

I'm not sure why that makes me smile, but it does. Even if it's something as small as divulging her middle name, it's a piece of her that I can now hold onto.

"It suits you. What about your birthday?" I'm trying not to push my luck, but I can't help but want to know every single thing about her, starting with the basics.

"I'll only tell you if you promise not to get me anything. I don't like gifts."

I have never met a more stubborn person in my entire life. How can I promise her that without breaking the promise? I can't just *not* spoil her on her birthday, or any other day for that matter. I'll figure it out, even if it means surprising her the day after her birthday. I wouldn't be breaking my promise then because then *technically*, it wouldn't be her birthday anymore.

"You're a pain in my ass, you know that?" She shrugs, still not answering me. "No gifts, got it."

"January 1st."

"A New Year's baby. That's cute and easy to remember."

"Why are you all of a sudden curious to know things about me?"

"What makes you think I haven't always wanted to?"

"You've never asked before."

No, but I've wanted to.

"Don't take this the wrong way, but you're probably the least easy person to pry information from. I'm fully aware of how distant you keep yourself, and I never want to make you uncomfortable or feel like I'm overstepping by wanting to get to know you in a personal way. Therefore, I've always kept our conversations light. I'd like for that to change, though."

I can see the wheels turning in her head. Remaining in the friend zone long enough finally got me here, so I'm not complaining. But I would like to be closer to her in all the ways she'd let me.

"I guess that's fair," she admits, taking a sip of the red wine Nate just placed on our table. "What about you? What's your middle name and birthday?"

"Andrew and May 11," I reply without hesitation.

But something in her demeanor changes when I say those words. Her face becomes devoid of color, and her eyes shoot down to her lap. Is my middle name a reminder of a past relationship that didn't end well? Does my birthday signify a date that haunts her? Again, I have all these questions and not a single answer to any of them.

"Are you okay?"

She shifts in her seat, avoiding eye contact. Taking another sip of her wine, she answers, "I'm fine." Her response is short and curt, and not at all convincing.

How can something so simple as a name and birthday trigger her? Maybe she's right. Maybe loving her and getting to know her *will* be hard, but not impossible. If she would just let me in, I can help her. Be there for her. Nothing she can say will turn me away from wanting this, but I have a feeling she won't just allow me to walk into her past, present, or even future without putting up a fight.

We're not even halfway through our first real date, and I'm already beginning to feel defeated. I put an end to the questions—for now. Maybe I'll try again later, but now, I just want to enjoy her company without the pressure of swapping trauma stories.

Chapter 16
Macy

From This Moment

Of course, his birthday is May 11. Why wouldn't it be? I can't escape my past, no matter how hard I try. The thought of potentially spending the rest of my life *celebrating* that date makes me feel sick to my stomach.

How can it be that the one person making my world go round, is born on the only day of the year I wish I could erase from my memory? This is just another reminder that I can't drag this on any longer than planned. I can't end up with him —no matter how badly I might want to.

The wine is making me flushed with heat, but I pour another glass, and then another. By the end of dinner, I think I drank the entire bottle by myself. I don't think Paxton minds though because wine makes me flirty. I'm still stable enough not to reveal any important information, but I have him laughing and even catch him blushing after complimenting him all night. It's not something I normally do, but divergence is key. Luckily, he takes flattery way better than I do, so it only feels right to continue, keeping him from breathing down the neck of my past.

That smile of his does something to me. It makes me tense in all the right places, and I want nothing more than to get him back to my place. Tonight might be the night I finally let him have all of me. Besides, it's just sex. It doesn't mean the same thing to me as it does to other girls. I've perfected being able to shut off my emotions when it comes to physical contact, and if I hadn't learned to do that, I'd still be a virgin.

Earlier tonight before getting dressed, I snapped a picture of myself in my towel, from the neck down. And because I'm a tease, I decide to send it to Paxton now.

> Ready to get out of here?

I barely raise my eyes up from my phone, just enough to remain indifferent but still catch a glimpse of his reaction. I can see his right eyebrow form an arch, and a slow breath exits his mouth, his chest falling.

PAXTON
> Let's go. NOW.

He wastes no time. Paxton leaves a cash tip on the table and grabs me by the hand, guiding me back down the stairs. I thought for sure he'd stop to kiss me at some point, but he doesn't. He walks me back to his car and helps me in, following shortly behind me.

I'm not normally the dominant type, but before he clicks his seatbelt, I take hold of his collar and pull him to me, attempting to embrace him in a kiss. But true to my drunken state, we clash foreheads instead. The blunt force mixed with the copious amounts of wine creates an instant headache. Suddenly, I regret drinking so much.

Paxton laughs as I press my hand to my forehead, then he places a kiss over the reddened area. The embarrassment is almost too much, so I turn on the radio to drown out the silent screams in my head. "From This Moment" by Shania Twain is on, and I can't help but sing along. I've never seen Paxton's head turn to me so fast. He has the biggest smile on his face that ultimately falls into a frown whenever I quit.

"I didn't know you could sing."

Have I never sung in front of him before? I guess not. Singing is something I do in my own comfort. It's a vulnerable part of me, so it only makes sense that I've kept it to myself.

"There's a lot you don't know about me, Paxton Meyers."

His expression is almost too much to handle. I know he's coming to the realization that we're practically strangers, which I had already concluded. It's hard not to be when you're constantly in defense mode. Sometimes I wish I had the courage to be honest with people about the things I've gone through, but I just don't want anyone's pity. That's the last thing I need. I'm stronger because of what I've endured, but I'm also damaged in ways that I can't bring myself to share with others, especially guys.

"Well, please continue," he insists.

I'm hesitant, but since he already heard me, there's no sense in hiding it now. I sing three songs for him before we arrive back at my place. It felt nice to show him a part of me that I've never shown to anyone else. Even more than that, he appreciated it, and that just makes me like him even more. He places a kiss on my cheek before running around to grab my door, then we take the stairs to the second floor. Our walk is quiet, even after we enter my place. I kick off my heels and head for the kitchen.

"Do you want anything to drink?" I yell from around the corner. "Water? Coffee? A beer?"

"Water is fine." I hear him say.

I grab us each a bottle of water and make my way back to him. He's sitting on the arm of my couch, the top two buttons of his shirt undone. I try to swallow, but my throat is dry, so I hand him his water and take a few sips of mine. I'm not sure why there's an awkward silence filling the room, but it's making me uncomfortable. This is why I don't share things about myself with people. It makes me susceptible to discomfort, but for some reason, I want to show him more.

    I take his hand and guide him to my bedroom. I push him onto the edge of the bed, sliding my coat off and onto the floor. I can only imagine what's going through his head, but he isn't about to experience what he's thinking.

    In the far-left corner of my room sits a keyboard with a stool placed in front of it. I make my way over to it and sit down, turning it on. I make no prompts. I don't even look back at him. I just start playing. My heart is beating so loudly that I can barely hear the tune being played beneath my fingertips. It's weird, exposing all the raw parts of yourself to someone else. But it's even more weird when that person makes you *want* to, without them even asking. No one in my life, besides my sister, knows I can sing or play piano—but now Paxton knows. And I love that he does.

    I feel a warmth on my skin, and shortly after, fingers trail from my neck down my right shoulder. Goosebumps cover my entire body, but I continue to play through the desire for him to touch me again. His lips press against the crook of my neck, and I can't help but close my eyes. My hands go still for a moment as my head falls back onto him, and before I know it, he turns me around to face him. He embraces me in a kiss that causes me to fall backward onto the piano. All the piano keys mash at once, producing a loud lattice of noise, but the only thing he's focused on is me.

    Paxton lifts me from the chair and lays me down on my bed while still locked on my lips. I run my hands through his hair as he lowers himself on top of me. My need for him is becoming more than I can bear, so I begin to unbutton the rest of his shirt.

    If I could describe his body in one word, it would be *perfec-*

tion. He's completely chiseled. Strong, broad shoulders. Large pecs that lead down to mouthwatering abs. A sexy V that dips below the waistband of his pants. I continue to graze my hands over his shirtless torso when I feel a small area above his waistband. The patch of skin is smooth—delicate even—but my eyes are closed, so I can't see it. If I had to guess, I'd say it's a scar. I roll Paxton over onto his back, taking control. My curiosity gets the best of me, and I break free from our kiss to try and examine it. Sure enough, a burn mark, about six inches long, stretches across his lower abdomen. I can tell he feels insecure, but now I'm intrigued.

I run my fingers across his skin. "What happened?"

He winces, sitting straight up, using his arms as a shield to cover the scar. "It's a long story." He grabs his shirt and begins buttoning it back up. "It's getting late. I should probably go."

A surge of guilt takes over my entire body, and now I'm regretting my decision to inquire about his past. I should know better. I don't like people digging into mine, so he has every right to exclude that part of him as well. I just wish it didn't require him to leave in a hurry. But I get it, and I don't feel right stopping him.

"Okay."

He seems bothered by my failure to intervene in his choice to go, but I know if he stays, I'd pry, and I can tell he isn't ready to talk just yet. So instead, I walk him to the door and watch as he exits into the stairwell.

No amount of therapy is going to pull me out of the quicksand that is Paxton Meyers.

Chapter 19
Paxton

So. Much. Baggage.

I know I should've stayed. I should have told her the truth, but I'm a coward. And I'm a hypocrite. It's selfish of me to want to know her deepest, darkest secrets, yet run away when she takes the slightest bit of interest in mine.

The truth is, though, that I have the same fear as her. What if my past is too much for her? What if my trauma proves that I'm not worthy of being loved by her? The scar that stains my body is just a painful reminder of the most irresponsible decision I've ever made.

I don't hear from her for the rest of the evening. I've fucked this whole thing up, and I know the only way to fix it is to be honest. But I'm not sure I'm ready for that.

There are only three people who know about the life-altering mistake I made that night—my mom, Dr. Reynolds, and Jack Sterling. Unless you include the parents of the fifteen-year-old girl. They don't know it was me though, so I'm not sure that counts. Painful memories flash across my mind, and I do everything I can to not think about it.

I take a handful of melatonin, hoping I'll be able to get some sleep tonight. I'll ask Taylor's advice tomorrow during my appointment, but until then, I'll close my eyes and try to drift off to sleep.

Monday, October 20 - 4:00 pm

I don't bother stalling as I enter her office. I rush to the couch and take a seat, eager to speak.

"I need help," I blurt out.

"Well hello to you too, Paxton." She laughs. Dr. Reynolds takes a seat across from me as she does every week, but this time she doesn't jot down any notes. She sits up tall and focuses on me, as if I'm about to spill news she's never heard before. "Is everything okay?"

"I don't know if I'm asking this as a patient or as a friend, but I'm having trouble in the relationship department."

She seems taken back for a moment. "You're dating again?" A surprised tone in her voice.

"Sort of? I'm trying," I admit, not fully knowing where this is going. "I've been unofficially seeing someone for almost five months. I don't even know that I'd call it 'seeing someone' considering we're just friends. *Were* friends. Our time spent together was just that; something she classified as 'non-dates.' Until the other day, when I practically stormed into her apartment and told her how I felt about her."

"Okay, I think I'm following. But what is the problem, exactly?"

"She's hard to read. Closed off to the world. Impossible to get to know. I've been trying to break down her walls, to learn as much as I can about her. And I started getting somewhere last night, but then…" I trail off. "Then she saw my scar and wanted to know more."

"And you're not ready to share that, I'm guessing?"

"I know I shouldn't be trying to uncover her past when I can't bear to resurface mine, but my desire to get to know her is unbearable at times. I just wish I could learn more of what she's gone through before unloading the worst parts of me onto her."

"Are you afraid she won't accept things, or are you still stuck on the fact that *you* don't accept them?" She pauses. "I'm strictly asking this as your friend and not your therapist. So, it's off the record."

"Both, I guess." The truth catches in my throat. "You know how bad off I was after what happened. If I can't forgive myself, how could I ever expect someone else to? Not to mention, all the crazy shit with my ex. I have so much baggage. I don't know what I was thinking, trying to get involved with someone. There's a reason I've been single for so long."

She adjusts her posture to a more comfortable position, and I know she's about to be really honest with me. "Paxton, you're too hard on yourself. People make mistakes. Accidents happen. You were twenty-one-years-old and on a high from happiness after just proposing. I'm not excusing the lack of attention you paid for just a split second, but you've been doing your best to do right by her for the last five years. It's time to do right by yourself now."

I know she's right, but I don't know that I'll ever fully be able to accept that I ruined an innocent girl's life with one brief moment of distraction. But if I ever want to move on, I have to try. "So, how do I tell her then? I'm terrified of losing her, Taylor."

"I've known you for three years, and I know you're a good person and an even greater friend. I've understood your need for seclusion, but I'm relieved that you've finally found someone that makes you feel scared to be alone. It means you're letting yourself be happy again. If this girl is the one for you, she'll accept you as the person you are and everything that comes with loving you. And in return, she'll receive a man who I know would give her the world and nothing less. Just be honest with her, Paxton."

I nod just as the timer alerts me that our session is officially over with. "Thank you," I say as I stand to my feet.

"I'm not charging you today. Consider it a favor for all the times you peeled me away from the bottle after my divorce last year. Now, go be happy."

She hugs me, and I feel a sense of relief. I don't particularly want to open the wounds to everything that's helped aid in my isolation, but Taylor is right. I can't run from it anymore, and if Macy really is the person I'm going to keep forever, she deserves to know what she's getting herself into.

Chapter 18
Macy

I'm Calling Bullshit

PAXTON
We should talk.

The text lingers on my screen until I'm brave enough to open it. There's a sinking feeling in my stomach, and I'm not sure where this conversation is headed. Is he ready to talk about the scar? Has he decided that we made a mistake and shouldn't be doing this? I wouldn't blame him if he did. I'm a lot to deal with, and I haven't been the most open with him. It's hard to date someone who you know nothing about. At least that's what I'm telling myself to brace myself for whatever it is he has to say to me. I let the message sit unopened for another five minutes before my curiosity takes over, and I respond.

Okay. Tomorrow after class?

> **PAXTON**
> Will Friday work? This week is a busy one for me.

> I have something Friday.

> **PAXTON**
> I don't want to talk about this around people. I'd like for it to just be the two of us.

> Okay. Friday it is, I guess. Come over around six. I'll make dinner.

He hearts my message, and I throw my phone on the couch cushion beside me. I sit there, leaning my head back, staring at the ceiling.

Why the hell are our plans always so anonymous when it comes to describing reasons why we can't see each other? I know good and well why I don't mention my therapy on Fridays, but what the hell is he always doing during the week that he can't ever come over? I try not to let my mind wander, but it's no use. I'm making up scenarios in my head that probably aren't true, but it's hard to convince myself otherwise. Maybe he's seeing someone else and that's what he wants to talk to me about. He wants to tell me that he's found someone less fucked up than me. Someone who is honest and shares her feelings *and* her body — two things I have yet to do.

Until Friday, I'm going to be uneasy. I don't even know how to act around him after Sunday, but I can't focus on his words right now.

Tomorrow is a big day in the court room. Jade is giving her statement after being silent for months. I need to worry about the case, not whether my boyfriend is about to break up with me before we even get started. Can I even call him my boyfriend? He didn't exactly ask me to be his girlfriend. Ugh. Why the hell is dating so damn complicated?

My stomach makes a loud grumbling noise, so I make my

way off the couch and into the kitchen. There's leftover potato soup in the fridge that I dig out and reheat. I sit back on the couch with my bowl of soup in my lap and turn on the news. I don't know why I watch this crap when I get a front row seat to the trial. Most of what they cover doesn't even touch the surface of what's said in there.

"After four months of silence, Jade Sterling will finally be releasing her statement tomorrow." I hear the reporter say.

I'm sure everyone is interested to hear her side of things. I mean, being accused of murdering your twin sister must stir some unimaginable thoughts in your head. She refuses to talk to anyone except her dad, and sometimes Paxton—which is weird to me. But even then, she usually doesn't provide much information. I don't know if she's conjuring up a story good enough to try to prove her innocence, or if she really *is* innocent. Her sister was found dead in her apartment, with multiple stab wounds to the chest and abdomen. Her fiancé was the one who called the police. He claims he found her after coming home from a work trip that evening. Conveniently, no one was there to back up his story, which is why his alibi didn't stand up in court, and he was brought in.

Jade, on the other hand, is a suspect because her hair was at the crime scene. Although it proves she was there, it doesn't prove she has anything to do with the murder, just yet. It was her sister's place. They hung out all the time. Of course, her hair would be around the apartment.

Do I think she's innocent? I don't know. It's hard for me to judge because I didn't really know much about their relationship. Her silence could be a testament of her devastation, or it could be a testament of her guilt. It's hard to say.

Between my thoughts about the case and my anxiety stewing over Paxton's text, my head is beginning to throb. I run myself a hot bath and turn on my classical playlist. I shut my eyes for what feels like only five minutes, but when I open them, it's been forty-five. The water is now chilly, and I realize it's now 10:30 pm. I rinse off and grab a towel, dry myself and wrap it around me. My body feels tense and sore, even though I haven't worked out in three days. Maybe it's the stress of everything. I collapse onto my bed, and within minutes, I'm fast asleep.

Morning comes, and I wake up still in my towel. I head to my closet and pick out clothes for today. Since I'll be in the court room all day, I reach for a pair of black, jogger-style slacks and a long-sleeved black turtleneck. I throw on my black and grey checkered blazer with some nude, closed-toe heels. My hair is down, and my makeup is on the neutral side, bringing out the specs of hazel in my brown eyes. I throw on my glasses and a light brown lipstick, then head to the kitchen. I'm not particularly hungry due to the churning in my stomach, but I know it'll be embarrassing if my GI tract decides to make itself known during the trial, so I decide on a protein shake and banana. I quickly grab my briefcase and keys, then head out the door. I force myself to drink at least half the shake and eat three quarters of the banana on my drive to the courthouse.

When I get there, Paxton is stepping out of his car, so I wait patiently until he heads towards the doors. I figure I can try to avoid him as long as possible until we're forced to talk on Friday. I'm not sure how that'll work exactly, since we're both forced to see each other here and in class, but it's worth a shot. I open Facebook and scroll long enough for him to walk inside. When I lift my head, he's nowhere in sight, so I close the app and head in.

As soon I make my way inside and round the corner, I catch Paxton standing with his back against the wall, arms folded across his chest. He's in an all-black suit, with a gray tie and brown loafers. The same ones he had in the garment bag the night of our last non-date. The expression on his face tells me he wants to say something, but he keeps his mouth closed, so I fake a smile as I walk past him. But before I can get too far, he grabs my wrist and pulls me back. He's positioned so that his right shoulder is supporting him on the wall as he faces me.

"Are you avoiding me?" His tone is clipped, and I try not to give him the satisfaction of being right.

"And why would I be doing that?" My tone is just as sadistic. I don't even know why I'm angry at this point, but everything feels wrong, and it's putting me in a bad mood.

"Maybe because you waited in your car until I was out of sight, then decided to come in once the coast was clear."

Well shit. So much for being inconspicuous. Why the hell was he watching me anyway? And if it was that big of a deal, why didn't he come to my car to say anything? Does he not want people to know we're together? My mind races with questions that I have no answers to but am too afraid to ask.

"I just assumed you didn't want people to know about us, so I thought I was doing you a favor." I scoff. Although that is partially true, I really was trying to avoid him. There's too much going on today for me to be distracted by him.

"I'm calling bullshit, Macy. We've walked into every hearing together since we started this trial, and no one has had two thoughts about it. If you're trying to avoid me, just admit it, and we can be on our way."

I roll my eyes. "I'll see you in there." Then I turn on my heel to head towards the direction of the courtroom. I don't hear footsteps behind me, so I imagine he isn't following me. When I make it through the doors, I sit in the first row behind the counsel table. Not long after, Paxton arrives and drops onto the bench next to me. I continue to look forward, not daring to make eye contact with him. He slides closer to me, making me feel awkwardly uncomfortable. I press my lips into a flat line, trying my hardest not to smile.

I see his smirk out the corner of my eye, and that's when

he places his left hand on my right thigh. The warmth of his hand feels as though it's burning through my pants. This is inappropriate for so many reasons. I reach to knock his hand off me before someone sees, but it's too late. The guards are escorting Jade into the courtroom, and she glances at us both, locking eyes with Paxton. Her eyes are like daggers. Though she never meets my gaze, I can tell that death stare is for me. Does she have a thing for him? Were they friends before all of this? If so, he's never mentioned it.

I smack his hand off my leg and adjust my posture, an unnerving feeling settling in my stomach. I try to pay attention as she takes the stand, but my mind is far from present. So many thoughts consume me, and I don't come back to reality until everyone is standing, making their way into the hall.

What the hell just happened?

I missed her entire statement, all because I was distracted inside my own head. There's no way I can continue with whatever it is that Paxton and I are doing. When he comes over Friday, I need to end things.

Chapter 19
Macy

Twisted Games

Friday, October 24 - 2:30pm

I've been sitting on the couch in silence for roughly ten minutes. The only words Dr. Reynold's and I have exchanged thus far have been our greeting. Other than that, it's been quiet. Our last session didn't end on the most positive of notes, so I'm struggling to find the words I want to say.

Today, I don't want to talk about my past. I want to talk about my present. Mostly, I want to talk about Paxton. My head is swimming with thoughts of him. Thoughts of his hand on my thigh, burning a Paxton sized handprint onto my skin. I think about how that one small touch radiated every single cell in my body, leaving me unable to focus during the case. And no matter how hard I try, I can't stop thinking about him. He's like a drug that I can't quit, and I haven't even had him yet. My heart begins pounding at the thought of what will happen when I *do* get a taste of him for the first time. And this —this is why I can't.

"Is it okay if we talk about something different today?" I say finally, to break the silence.

"It's your session, Macy. We can talk about whatever you'd like. I work for *you* during this hour."

She does have a point, but I'm not sure my love life qualifies as therapy. Or maybe it does because it is pretty fucked up. Either way, I just need to get this out to someone, and it has its perks that she can't share this information with anyone.

"So, there's this guy I'm sort of seeing. If you can even call it that. And I like him—more than I anticipated I would. But I don't know how to be in a serious or committed relationship, and I'm afraid I'm going to screw things up. The way I always do. I don't even know if you're qualified to advise me on this topic, so I'm sorry if it's not something you're used to. I guess I'm just looking for a female's opinion. Someone who isn't going to judge me."

"Why do you think you're going to mess things up?"

"It's just what I do. I never date with the intention of getting serious."

"Is there a reasoning behind that?"

"I've never admitted this to anyone, except my sister, but even that wasn't intentional. She just kind of caught on to my antics as she got older, and by the time she was old enough to realize what I was doing, I couldn't exactly lie to her. But I didn't start dating until I was seventeen. No one had ever shown interest in me until I was skinny enough to be deemed pretty. The first guy I ever dated was a shallow prick, but that was to be expected, I guess. He was a teenage boy who had needs that I couldn't or wouldn't fulfill, so he made me choose between sex with him or a broken heart. We were only together for six months, but I still loved him because he was the first relationship I ever had. Ultimately, I chose to end things, causing my world to come crashing down."

I take a pause, letting my thoughts wander as she writes on her notepad. With a heavy sigh, I continue.

"During the duration of our relationship, I had put on a little weight, so I didn't get much attention after our breakup. Which led me to set a goal for myself. I wanted to lose twenty-two pounds, which was equivalent to the weight I gained over the six months. Though my heart ached, I let that be the factor that drove me to success. By the end of the school year, I had lost all of the weight and was back on the market. And that's when I told myself I'd never let myself go longer than six months in another relationship. Since then, I've only ever dated people to fuel my fire. I set goals for myself—small ones at first, but they grew bigger over time. First weight loss, then valedictorian, then a promotion at work, and acceptance to law school. I let myself fall just enough to inflict pain, then sabotaged each relationship so they'd break up with me before the six months were up. I chose guys that I know are incapable of commitment. Over time, I got good at reading people—or so I thought. Because every guy ends up falling for me, and every single time, I break their heart. Until him."

I'm sure that's a lot for her to digest. She's writing again, and I'm thinking I should've just kept my mouth shut. But once the words started coming out, I couldn't stop them. At this point, she's been writing for a solid three minutes, and I consider heading for the door. I'm embarrassed at the path I've chosen, and the people I've hurt. I don't welcome remorse but saying those words out loud for someone else to hear almost felt cynical. She stops writing, and I release a breath I've been holding for quite a few seconds.

"You said you're a law student?" she asks me this, as if that's all she gathered from the ten-minute long rant I just went on.

Despite my confusion, I answer anyway. "Yes?"

"Sorry. We've just never discussed what you do for a living, or any surface-level details about your life, so it stood out to me. Anyway, based on your history of dating, are you afraid you're going to repeat the same pattern now? With this new guy?"

"I already am. I have one goal left. To become junior partner at the firm I'm interning at. And although I really do like this guy, he's become a huge distraction in the case I'm dealing with. I think about him all the time. I space out during the trial. It's ruining my chances of reaching my final goal. So, when he confessed his feelings for me, I agreed to date him—strictly so that he can hurt me. If that happens, I'll be forced to focus solely on the objective at hand. The only problem is, I think I might *actually* see a future with him. At least I could. If he wasn't in my damn way."

Her wheels are turning, as if this is some sort of twisted game I'm making up. And honestly, I wish it was. Because this is why I'm alone. It's why Lauren worries about me. It's why my monophobia controls my life. I'm a fucking sociopath.

"I'm not a relationship guru, and I don't think you need one to tell you that what you're doing is unhealthy. Not just for you, but for the other person involved. If you're not going to commit to someone with the decency of reciprocation, then it should be obvious not to start a relationship." Her mouth snaps shut, and I can tell she didn't mean for those words to come out in the way they did. But I can respect her honesty. I needed to hear it. That's the whole reason I brought the subject up in the first place. "I'm so sorry, Macy. That was completely unprofessional, and I apologize. I know you weren't asking for—"

"No, it's fine. I deserved that. And even though I didn't directly ask for the advice, I was hoping you'd give it to me anyway." I uncross my legs and smooth out my dress. "I know it's wrong, and I'm scared to hurt Paxton. I don't want to, which is why I'm planning on ending things tonight."

Her pen falls to the clipboard at the sound of his name. Is that just a coincidence? I don't have time to overthink it because the timer goes off and concludes our session for the day.

I'm heading to the store to gather ingredients for dinner tonight. I know Paxton's favorite food is Chinese, and mine is Thai, so I'm meeting in the middle and making Pad Thai. I grab a basket as I walk into Mariano's and begin filling it with everything necessary for tonight's dish. Rice noodles, shrimp, fresh vegetables, peanuts. I even grab a bottle of red wine, hoping it'll give me the courage to lay it all out for him.

When I get back to my apartment, I shower and change into my oversized Def Leppard t-shirt dress, staying barefoot. I put my hair half-up, securing the ponytail low, against the middle of my head, and I slide my glasses back onto my face. It's 5:00 pm when I start dinner, and only fifteen minutes later, when I hear a knock at my door. I leave the vegetables to simmer while I answer it, and not to my surprise, it's Paxton.

"You're early." I'm not trying to be rude, but of course my tone comes across that way.

"And you're sexy as hell," he says as he reaches for my waist and pulls me into him.

I can't deny the jolt of pleasure that runs through my body as he grips me tighter, but I also can't do this right now. He lowers his head until his lips are at the shell of my ear, and I shiver at the mere heat of his breath. Playfully, he nips my earlobe which elicits a small moan of pleasure from me. But before he can go any further, I place my hand on his chest and use it as leverage to push him away.

"Dinner is almost ready. Make yourself comfortable," I say as I disappear into the kitchen.

I love that my kitchen has a view of the living room because I can see Paxton removing his sweatshirt. It gets snagged on his t-shirt, causing the bottom half to rise just above his waistline. Both hip bones are fully exposed, and a silent gasp escapes my mouth. *Why is he so fucking hot?* I try to keep my eyes off him while I finish cooking. It's almost impossible, but I manage. Sort of. Not really. It takes me a little longer than expected, but I finally finish making dinner. I fill two bowls with the noodle mixture and pour each of us a glass of wine and set everything on the table.

I make my way to the living room to find Paxton slouched down onto the couch, watching football.

"You hungry?" I ask, catching his attention.

"Starving." He stands up and follows me to the dining room, taking the seat next to me. "Smells amazing."

A grin spreads across my face. I've never cooked for him before, so I hope he enjoys it. "Thanks."

We eat in silence for a few minutes before I set my fork down. I take a sip of my wine, then set that down too. Paxton looks at me and mimics my motions but doesn't say a word.

"Well, are we going to talk or what?" I take the first leap into this burden of a conversation we're about to have. I'm not ready for whatever it is he has to say, so I take another sip of wine. I'm trying to mask the fact that my hand is shaking, so I place one in my lap and rest my chin in the other. I don't know if he can tell, but my heart feels like it's about to explode. My adrenaline is racing so fast, I wouldn't be surprised if he can see it pulsating in my neck.

He lets out a breath and forces his head into his hands as his elbows rest on my table. I don't like where this is going. Not one bit. The hunger I once had is now replaced with worry and nausea. *I'm* about to break up with *him*, so why am I feeling like this?

I open my mouth to press on, but he cuts me off before I can say a word.

"Look, the other night... I didn't mean to walk out on you. I should've stayed, and I should've talked to you. It's just..." He pauses. It's almost painful to watch him be at a loss for words. He never is. Whatever he's trying to say is weighing really heavy on him, and I feel guilty for allowing him to get to this point.

"Paxton, we don't have to go there. Your personal life is your business, and I had no right to pry." Even though I wanted to know, I didn't feel right making him explain himself.

"That's the point, though. I *want* you to know things. I *want* you to know *me*. But up until the other night, I never realized how hard it is to allow someone else to get to know all of you. All your flaws, your baggage, the quirks that make you who you are. I've selfishly wanted to know all those things about you, but never prepared to give them to you in return. So, I mostly wanted to say I'm sorry, and I'm willing to let you walk down memory lane with me if you'd be willing to do the same."

I think long and hard about everything he just said. This isn't at all where I was expecting this conversation to go. I thought he was coming here to tell me he wanted out, and that someone else was better suited for him than I was. I thought we were breaking up, whether it was him ending us, or me. That's why I invited him here—to call it quits. But the words Dr. Reynolds said to me today rings in my head, and it sends an outpouring of guilt through me. *If you're not going to commit to someone with the decency of reciprocation, then it should be obvious not to start a relationship.* I shouldn't have agreed to this, but now I'm in too deep. And as much as I tried not to, I'm already reciprocating his feelings.

Chapter 20
Paxton

Easy Enough

She's just staring at her bowl of Pad Thai—not eating, not responding. I force down a thick swallow then follow it with a sip of wine. Something tells me she wasn't prepared for this conversation, and I can't blame her, but waiting for a response is damn near killing me. If she says no, I'll understand. Opening up to someone isn't easy. I rarely open up to anyone —besides Taylor—because I don't like to feel vulnerable or misunderstood. It's a scary feeling, being judged by your past. It's why I've decided to keep women at arm's length for so long after my failed engagement. No one deserves to be pulled into the fucking mess that has been my life since I called it quits with my ex. Not to mention, I've always feared what my ex would do had she found out another woman was in my life.

I use my fork to push around the vegetables and swirl the noodles until they're tight around the tines, and then I slip it into my mouth. I don't know how much more deflecting I can do before I'm forced to walk out of here with whatever dignity I have left.

Macy finishes off her wine, so I do the same, and she finally meets my gaze. For a brief moment, she parts her lips, and I'm hopeful she's about to agree. But just as soon as they're opened, they shut again. A heavy breath leaves my mouth, and my chest falls with uneasiness. If she's going to end things, I don't want to be here for it. I can't bear that thought.

With no more fight left in me, I scoot my chair back and stand to my feet, collecting my dishes. Just as I'm about to walk away from the table, her voice catches in her throat, and she finally speaks.

"Paxton." I hear her say softly. "We don't have to do this right now. We don't have to rush it."

My heart pangs a little. The words may not be the end of us, but it does sting a little knowing she doesn't want to get to know me and vice versa. I could love her. I know I could, and I want to someday, but she tries so damn hard to make sure I won't.

My ex was clingy and obsessive and controlling. Macy is anything but that. She's vague and easygoing and independent. It's nothing I'm used to, but it's what attracted me to her in the first place. She's secretive—which is intriguing to me—and smart. Goddamn, is she smart. I never knew conversing law with an intelligent woman could be such a turn-on, but she sure renders me speechless sometimes with her rants. I just want the opportunity to know her, and what makes her, her.

"I want to get to know you, I do," she continues. "But I want to do it at our own pace. I don't want you thinking you need to know every single detail about me right now, and I don't need to know every little thing about you at this very second. I just want us to enjoy getting to know each other. Why don't we start with the basics tonight, and we can move into deeper conversations over time?"

I can respect that answer. After all, if I spilled every part of my past to her tonight, she could very well decide she wants nothing to do with me. At least going at a slower pace will allow her to get to know me now, versus the person I used to be. Not that I was a terrible person. It's just... I've made some questionable decisions in my past, some I'm not proud of, but it's what changed me.

I sit back down across from Macy and set my bowl on the table, fidgeting with my food.

"That's fair."

I take another bite of Pad Thai, and she pours us both another glass of wine. Before I can open my mouth to initiate conversation further, she asks the first question.

"What's your family like? Do you have any siblings?"

Easy enough.

"I come from a pretty large family. My parents are still married, both doctors. My mom works in the E.R.; says she likes the thrill." I chuckle. She's always been the more fun parent of the two. Takes life by the horns and never lets life get too serious. My dad, on the other hand, has always been the stern one. I know he means well by it because we're all successful, but sometimes I wish he was a little more easygoing.

"My dad has his own family practice. I have an older brother, Preston. He's a plastic surgeon. And my younger sister, Payton is in school to be an obstetrician." I pause.

Penelope's name sits on the tip of my tongue. A wave of sorrow runs over me. It hurts to think of her sometimes, wondering what she would be like now. I often think she would've paved her own way if she was still alive. She was the youngest, yet the most independent of us all. She always reached for the stars and beyond, literally. I remember her saying she wanted to be an astronaut when she was older—not a doctor like the rest of them. It was because of her that I made the choice to follow my own dreams of becoming a lawyer. I didn't want the pressure of people putting their health in my hands. It felt too heavy for me. And although my client's lives are still resting on my ability to keep them out of jail, it isn't instant life or death.

It's as if Macy knows I'm not finished speaking. A crease forms between those perfectly plucked brows of hers, and she waits for me to move forward with my family lineage.

"I had... *have* a younger sister. Her name is Penelope, but we called her Penny for short. She's four years younger than me. Would be twenty-two this December." Tears sting my eyes, but I try my best to bite them back. *Fuck, I miss her so much.* "She passed away when she was twelve."

It seems that even the most basic of questions escalated to a dark place I didn't expect to visit tonight. Missing her comes in waves. When I see a commercial she used to love or hear a song she would scream on the drive to school. I feel a hot tear streak down my face and quickly brush it away. Macy's hand lands on mine, giving it a squeeze. I can see the sympathetic look in her hazel gaze, but I can't seem to look away. Even with the open-concept dining and living room, the air still feels heavy.

"I'm sorry, Paxton. I didn't mean to—"

"Don't apologize. I want you to know everything there is to know about me. Family is the easiest thing for me to talk about. We're all very close-knit, and I'd love for you to meet them someday. When you're comfortable, of course." She nods, and although it doesn't convince me she will, I push forward. "What about your family?"

She seems uneasy. Her posture stiffens, and it's as though all her comfort disappeared with the words I've just spoken. I run my hand down her arm, trying to soothe her discomfort. She grabs a strand of her hair, twisting it around her finger as if she's trying to avoid answering. Her silence is remarkable. But finally, she gives way.

"I wish I could hold a flame to your family tree. But truth is, I don't really have a family. Just a sister. Her name is Lauren. We're two years apart. I'm the oldest." She sighs.

"My dad left us when Lauren was born, and my mom was never around. We moved all over the country, fleeing wherever her boyfriend-of-the-month took us. She was selfish in that way. Always picking dead end jobs and failing relationships over her kids. I was forced to become the parent at an early age so that Lauren didn't suffer."

Her head falls in defeat. No wonder she's so damn closed off. She's had to be that way her entire life, never being able to depend on anyone—not even her own mother. It makes so much sense now. The walls she built were never intended to shut people out, but to keep her and her sister safe.

My need to protect her just increased tenfold. I know she's more than capable of handling her own, but she shouldn't have to. I want to be the one she runs to. The person she can rely on. The one she reaches for after a long, shitty day. I want to prove to her that she doesn't have to do life alone if she doesn't want to. I have no doubt she'll put up a fight, but I'm going to try like hell.

I scoot my chair closer to hers, resting one hand on her thigh, and I use the other to brush the strand of fallen hair out of her face. "Where's your sister now?"

She looks up at me, tears sitting at the brim of her eyes. I can tell she's doing everything she can to remain strong.

"She lives in California; moved there after she graduated high school." Macy straightens herself in her chair, collecting her emotions.

It makes me sad to see her so afraid to be vulnerable. I lift her chin, forcing her to meet my gaze, but her eyes quickly avert. She's staring at my lips, and all I can think about is kissing hers, so that's exactly what I do.

Chapter 21
Macy

As You Wish, Baby

He deepens the kiss, and the weight of our conversation slowly floats away. I snake my hand behind his head and into his hair, pulling him closer, if that's even possible. Everything I thought I wanted tonight became obsolete once his lips met mine. This feels right, no matter how much I try to convince myself otherwise. I'm falling for him, and I'm falling for him *hard*.

The next few minutes are a blur. Somewhere between the overwhelming feeling of butterflies in my stomach and the inferno burning between my legs, we end up in my bedroom. He puts me down, and my feet hit the floor, never breaking our kiss.

We're frantic now. We're a mess of bruised lips and grazing teeth. I'm biting his lip, he's sucking on mine, and I can't get his clothes off fast enough. My hands fly between his t-shirt and his bare chest, lifting it above his head. His fingers are grazing my thighs, removing my dress in one swift motion.

And for one brief moment, I freeze. I realize I am now

partially naked, only in my bra and underwear. Thank God it's a matching satin set. But still, I'm exposed, and I feel every bit of it. Thoughts come whirling back into my head. Self doubt creeps in, and every ugly thing I've ever said about my body is at the forefront of mind. Instinctively, I wrap my arms around my stomach to shield myself from the gaze he's now burning me with.

Paxton closes the small distance between us, running his hands up and down my bare arms. He lifts my chin with his fingers and forces me to look him in the eyes, my mind still going rogue.

"Macy." I hear, creating a catapult to my thoughts. "We don't have to do this if you don't want to."

His sincere words have my heart beating out of my chest. Of course, I want to. It's all I can seem to think about. But letting someone see all of you for the first time is scary as fuck. Sex has always been physical for me, but I never cared much for the guys I've been with, so it didn't matter what they thought of me. But Paxton matters, and part of me is afraid he won't like what he sees.

I shake my head. "It's not that," I whisper as I look away.

His fingers find my chin, and he guides my gaze right back to his. "Then what is it, baby? Talk to me."

I tilt my head back as I look to the ceiling, willing these stupid tears that are forming to disappear back to where they came from. I blink numerous times before I finally let out an exasperated breath and meet his eyes once more. I muster up every ounce of courage I can find and finally am honest with him.

"I'm afraid I won't stack up to the countless women before me. I'm not very thin. I have stretch marks. I—"

I don't even finish my sentence before my back is against my mattress, and he's dangling above me while he punishes my lips in a searing kiss. My arms automatically go to his back, pulling him closer.

"Don't you ever say anything like that again," he says once he finally removes his mouth from mine. "Do you hear me?"

I nod, all the air leaving my lungs, causing my inability to form words.

"You're fucking perfect. This mouth is perfect," he whispers against my lips as he kisses me gently. "This neck." Another kiss, this one down the column of my throat. I can feel my skin prickle with heat as his lips linger, his words causing a pooling sensation in my gut.

His mouth travels further down to my chest, pulling my bra down below my breasts. "These fucking tits," he groans against my breast as he slips my right nipple into his mouth, growling and sucking. For a moment, he pops it out. "They're perfect, and they're fucking *mine*." Moving to my left breast, he sucks and swirls while he tweaks the right nipple between his fingers, and I nearly lose the power to breathe. Every single molecule in my body is on fire, desperate for his touch.

I want him. I *need* him. And I'm done holding back for the sake of my own stubbornness.

I pull him up until he's resting on his elbows and our torsos are touching. He's hovering now, and I'm doing all I can to not beg him to take me right here, right now. His breathing is uneven, his chest falling heavily with every exhale. His right hand meets my jawbone as he lingers over it with his thumb. I wonder what he's thinking. Why he stopped. It's clear he wants this as much as I do, right?

"Don't you ever, for one second, doubt how fucking sexy you are, Macy. I could come in my pants right now like a damn teenager just from touching you." He pauses, looking at me, piercing me to my core. "But I want you to be sure this is what you want. Because once we cross this threshold, there's no going back."

I'm lying here in my bra and underwear, and he thinks I don't want this? I'd call him crazy, but I guess he has reason to believe I don't since I'm why we haven't made it this far yet.

I'm no longer making excuses anymore. I'm ready. For him, for his body, and maybe even his heart. All of it. I want him and everything that comes with him.

"I want to," I whisper so faintly I almost can't hear my own words.

That's all it takes.

"Sit up, now," he demands as he pulls me to my knees.

I oblige and Paxton makes a quick work of unhooking my bra. His right hand finds my neck and with a slight pressure and he pushes me back down to the mattress. I swallow hard, anticipating his next move, when he ever so slowly drags his hands down my body until he gets to the satin underwear I'm wearing. He hooks his fingers in the sides and glides them down my thighs until they're discarded onto the floor. His fingertips trail the inside of my legs, starting with my ankles and make their way up to my inner thighs. On instinct, I clench my knees together, feeling so wholly exposed that it's almost embarrassing.

But the heat in Paxton's eyes does something to me. It lights me on fire from the inside out as I wage war against the insecure thoughts in my head. He grabs both of my legs and spreads them apart, and once again I'm on full display. The chill from the fan is nipping at my bare pussy, and I've never felt more vulnerable than I do right now.

Paxton comes closer, lowering his head above my breasts, taking turns sucking my nipples and a breathy moan escapes me. His teasing is torture, and yet I love every second his mouth is on my skin. He dips down lower, placing chaste kisses down my belly, and it clenches under the feel of his lips. His face comes into view as he stares up at me. "I love every inch of this body. Every. Fucking. Inch." His kisses trail lower until he's right above my pubic bone. "And I will worship it every single day until you believe me. Got it?"

His praise has my brain short circuiting, and all I can manage is another nod, which seems to satisfy him because he continues his conquest. He moves lower, kissing across my pussy until he finally swipes his tongue through my lips for the first time. My entire body comes alive with that one motion, and my hips involuntarily buck from the mattress against his face. *Holy fucking shit.*

I can feel his shit eating grin against me, but I don't even care. His spreads me with his fingers as his tongue circles my clit, and when he sucks it into his mouth, I know I'm a goner.

"*Paxton,*" I cry out in pleasure.

My back arches from the bed and he continues circling his tongue lazily as he pushes a finger inside of me. My hands fly to his hair, holding him in place and he enters me with a second finger, causing the pressure in my core to build. He pauses for a moment, lifting his mouth from me, and I nearly whimper at the loss.

"Fuck, Macy," he says with a crack in his voice. "You taste like fucking heaven."

I don't have time to respond before he dives his tongue back into my pussy. His fingers curl, hitting that spot that not even my dildo can reach, and he doesn't stop until he sucks the life right out of me. Literally and figuratively. I think I may be lifeless.

My breathing is ragged as I sink into the mattress, unable to move.

"I need you, please," is all I manage to speak because *fuck*, do I ever need him inside of me.

The rest of his clothes become nonexistent, and he climbs back onto the bed, positioning himself on top of me. His mouth is coated with the remains of me, and something feral inside me unleashes at the sight of me on his lips. I bring him down by the back of his neck and suck his bottom lip between my teeth. I've never kissed anyone after oral—ever. It's always grossed me out, but hell if I don't say that tasting myself on lips doesn't turn me into a starving woman, I'd be lying.

A throaty moan leaves his lips before he kisses me desperately. I can feel his erection pulsing between my legs, and it's taking everything inside of me not to wrap my legs around his waist and pull him into me.

I break our kiss, leaving me breathless. "Get inside me, *now*," I demand.

"Yes, ma'am," he complies, lifting himself off me for a quick second to retrieve a condom from his pants. My tongue swipes across my bottom lip as I watch him roll it onto his hard length. He finds himself between me once more and lines himself up at my entrance. But before entering me, he brushes the hair from my forehead and places a kiss there. It's the smallest gesture, but it has my insides completely turning to mush.

"You're beautiful, Macy. So damn beautiful that my chest aches at the thought of you. At the thought of this moment, which has been a fucking lot. You need to know that you're the best thing—"

My lips land on his before he can finish that sentence. I don't want to hear it. I can't. Because then I'll cave. I'll give him anything and everything he asks for, and that's not part of the deal I made with myself. I just want him to shut up and finish what he started, which is to make me come.

"Just fuck me, *please*," I beg.

"As you wish, baby."

And so he does. He gives me exactly what I ask for. Three times.

By the end of it, we are exhausted and sweaty, and tangled in each other. It isn't until it's over that I realize separating emotions from sex isn't going to be possible with him. If we keep this up, I'll fall in love with him in a matter of weeks. And something about that terrifies me.

Chapter 22
Macy

Why Didn't We Do This Sooner?

I wake up the next morning and slide out of bed while Paxton is still asleep. I slip into the shower, washing the remnants of last night off me. Standing under the hot stream of water, I begin battling with my mind once again. Every time I let myself become invested, it only ends in heartbreak. I don't want that for him or for me. Not this time. I want to be happy with Paxton. So why can't I just let myself do that? I stand there, back against the wall, letting the water trickle over me before finally finishing up.

When I exit the bathroom, Paxton is no longer in my room. He's made the bed, and his clothes are missing. Did he really just sleep with me and leave?

I throw on a pair of joggers and an oversized tee before heading to the living room. A whiff of waffles hits my nose as I open my bedroom door, and I realize he's still here. Standing in my kitchen in his sweatpants, Paxton is making us breakfast. I can feel my mouth watering, but not because of the waffles. *What the hell is up with this man being shirtless in the kitchen?*

He finally notices me, and a grin spreads across his face. "I thought it was only fair since you cooked dinner, that I make breakfast. You hungry?"

My heart swells. *He cooks.* Just one more thing for me to love about him. A loud noise escapes my stomach, signifying that I am, indeed, hungry. I pull out all the fixings and set them on the table. I grab everything from peanut butter and Nutella to fruit and honey. I normally try to stay away from the processed shit, but my obsession with reading labels had to stop. It's not things I eat every day, but I do allow myself to indulge once a week when I'm wanting a treat. I guess today is going to be that day.

I sit at the table, and Paxton brings over two plates, piled high with homemade waffles. Accompanying our breakfast, he pours us a glass of orange juice each—mine over ice, just the way I like it. We're both clearly starving from the aftermath of our night because we eat in silence until we're both doubling over from fullness. I clean up the mess from breakfast, after almost having to assault Paxton to let me do it, while he takes a quick shower. By the time he reenters the living room, I'm laying across the couch watching LSU get smoked by Georgia. He picks my legs up and drapes them across his lap, and just stares at me.

"Is there something you'd like to say?" I tease in a sarcastic tone. Just because we've slept together doesn't mean I'll retract the banter.

"Nope. Just admiring." He gives me a cheesy grin, and I roll my eyes. "Ouch!" His shoulders tense as Jayden Daniels gets tackled to the ground. "That had to hurt."

"Ugh. I miss Joe Burrow." I slide my hands down my face in agony of this game. We're losing 28-3 in the third quarter. I know we still have time to come back, but it's not looking very promising as most of our first-string players are out with injuries. Still, I guess there's a chance we could come back and win. If we're lucky. I cover my eyes with my hands, peeking through my fingers every now and again, when Paxton grabs my feet and starts massaging them. Every tense muscle in body becomes liquified, and it almost makes me sick how perfect this man is.

There's a minute and a half left in the fourth quarter and we're only down by seven now. One touchdown—that's all we need to go into overtime. Daniels throws the ball downfield to Kayshon Boutte, and just as it hits his hands, he's knocked from the left side and fumbles the ball, with Georgia scooping it up and recovering it. That's it. That's all I can watch. I shut the tv off and let out a loud huff, startling Paxton.

He pats my leg. "Now, now. I'd say I'm sorry, but that's what you get when you cheer for the number sixteen team in the NCAA."

First, I smack him in the back of the head, then I catch an attitude with my arms folded across my chest. "It's called *loyalty*. Ever heard of it? You're from here and you cheer on the Buckeyes for crying out loud."

"It's called *talent*. They're number four in the league, and it just so happens to be where your precious Joe Burrow got started. You know, in case you forgot."

He's an asshole, I've decided. "I officially hate you. Just want you to be aware of that."

The smile across his face proves he believes otherwise. He climbs across the couch, lowering his body on top of mine until he's just inches from my face. My breathing becomes labored due to his body weight and the inability to think clearly when he's this close. I can feel his warm breath on my lips. They're close enough that I could kiss him if I wanted, but far enough to make me work for it. Paxton lowers his head, placing a gentle kiss on my neck that electrifies every inch of me. My eyes close in response.

Suddenly, he slips his hand into my shirt, trailing his fingers over my bare skin. My body is screaming in torment, aching for him once again.

He whispers in my ear as his hand circles my breast, "Do you hate me now?"

Yes, for torturing me. All I can manage to do is nod, and it lights a fire in him. He walks his fingers down my stomach and slowly creeps them below the waistband of my joggers. My breath hitches, unable to make a sound as I imagine what's coming next. Continuing down this path, his fingers meet my inner thigh, spreading them apart. He grazes me with his thumb, teasing me with his next move.

"How about now?"

This time, I shake my head, unable to lie. He places the lightest kiss on my lips as his fingers enter me, causing a surge of pleasure to course through me. My back arches and a moan escapes my lips. He takes pride in that, causing him to deepen his hand inside of me. His thumb circles me in agonizing bliss, but before I can peak, I pull his hand from between my legs.

He sits up and pulls me on top of him until I'm straddling him. He has a look of sorrow plastered across his face.

"I'm sorry, Macy. I—"

I shut him up with a kiss. One that is deep and full of desire. I slide my tongue into his mouth, wrapping mine around his, biting his bottom lip in the process. One of his hands is tangled in my hair, the other is pressed firmly against the small of my back. I need to get closer to him. I need him inside of me. So, I lift myself off his lap and drop to my knees.

I look up at him while hooking my hands in his waistband and lowering his sweatpants to his ankles. I slide my joggers off, leaving myself lingering in my tee and lace thong. Paxton's breathing is shallow, his eyes dark.

By the looks of it, he clearly doesn't need any help getting started, but I choose to please him anyway. I never cared to satisfy any of the men who came before Paxton, but something about him makes me want to dominate his sex life. I want him to never want to experience sex with anyone after me. So I make sure he never forgets it.

I dip my head down and lick him from root to tip in one slow, torturous motion.

His head drops to the back of the couch as a guttural moan escapes him. "Fucking hell, Macy."

A smile forms at my lips as I take him into my mouth. I lap the precum from the tip of him and suck him deep into my mouth until he's hitting the back of my throat. His hips involuntarily buck off the couch, causing me to gag. I push him back down and quickly recover, sucking and working him with my free hand.

Filthy noises leave his mouth, and I can already feel the heat burning so hot in my core that I might explode just from giving him head.

"I'm going to come, baby," he pants. I suck harder, faster. "Fuck, fuck, fuck."

And then he spills into my mouth. The hot liquid soaks my tongue and slides down my throat with ease. His eyes are closed as he tries catching his breath.

Pleased with myself, I stand up and straddle him again. He wastes no time. Paxton slides my underwear to the side and lowers me onto him with force. The full length of him fills me, and I drop my head forward into the curve of his neck.

"Jesus Christ, you're fucking soaked," he breathes into my ear. "So fucking wet for me, Mace."

"Yes," I manage to whisper.

"There's nothing I want more than to fuck you slowly. Show you every way I can make you come undone for me. But now isn't one of those times," he says. "Right now, I'm going to fuck you so hard that you're screaming my name, over and over, until you're dripping down my cock. Understood?"

The heat of his words has my clit throbbing, begging to be demolished. I don't want slow. I don't want gentle. I want to be fucked six ways to Sunday and have the inability to walk tomorrow.

"Yes," I whisper again.

A feral noise escapes his throat, and he lifts me then slams me down once more.

"Paxton!" I cry out his name just like he promised I would.

He's buried to the hilt. Any further and he'd be rearranging my organs. But I welcome the fullness. I crave it. His fingertips bite into my hips and we find a steady rhythm while I ride him. I can feel myself seeping onto his lap, but he doesn't seem to care. He grips me tighter slamming me onto him repeatedly, and I grind against him with every motion.

We're both panting, at this point. I'm holding onto his shoulders for dear life, he's creating indentations on my waist, and I swear my orgasm hits me like a freight train when I least expect it. Paxton follows shortly behind me. One last collision of our bodies and he's tossing me onto the couch next to him while his release paints his entire stomach. We're both breathless, unable to move.

And all I can think is, *Holy shit. Why didn't we do this sooner?*

Chapter 23
Macy

Ready to Attack

It's almost Thanksgiving, which means it's been roughly a month since Paxton and I agreed to be more than friends. It also means that Lauren will be here this evening, and I have yet to tell her about us. I don't even know how to introduce him. He still hasn't confirmed whatever it is that we're doing, which puts me a little on edge for them to meet. I've never let my boyfriends meet my family because I knew they weren't long term, plus my family is so screwed up, so I'm exceptionally nervous for him to meet the only person in the world I love.

Although she's my little sister, she's always been protective of me and my heart. And while I don't fear that Paxton won't live up to her standards, I worry that she's going to bring up my past relationships. I know she wouldn't do it out of spite, but more so out of concern, and that isn't a conversation I'm ready to talk about in front of him.

PAXTON

I know it's short notice, but did you want to come over for Thanksgiving? I know my family would love to meet you.

Thank you, but Lauren will be here this week. I told her I'd host her and her boyfriend.

PAXTON

Oh.

Okay. No big deal. Just wanted to ask.

I know I should invite him, and I was planning to, but now I'm having second thoughts. Surely, he understands, right? We haven't been together that long. Unless you count us hanging out as friends, which has been almost six months. Maybe he doesn't understand, though... he *did* just invite me to his parent's house.

Fuck. Why am I being so complicated? It doesn't have to be this way. I just make everything in my life so fucking hard for myself. Ultimately, I decide not to ask him. It's the only sense of control I have left, keeping him at arm's length for now.

It's Sunday, and I know I should be preparing for class tomorrow, but I need to work out and get my mind off things. I throw on some biker shorts and a tank top and head to the gym. There's a spin class starting at 3:00, so I have an hour to spare. I hit the treadmill for half an hour—getting in two and half miles—then I work on abs. My stomach has always been my biggest insecurity, so I'm always focusing on it the most. My set consists of four rounds of fifty crunches, leg raises, mountain climbers and planks. By the time I'm finished, my core is on fire. Sweat is pouring from my scalp and dripping down my face. I'm almost tempted to skip the class but decide against it because my head is still reeling with guilt for not inviting Paxton over for Thanksgiving.

I stand next to the window overlooking the parking lot,

chugging my bottle of water when I feel hands wrap around my waist. I instantly turn around to hit whoever the hell thinks they can touch me like that.

"Get the fuck—" I start to say with my hand raised, until the guy catches my arm mid-smack. The guy just so happens to be Paxton.

"Well, I'm glad to know you can hold your own." He chuckles.

I playfully punch him in the chest as I smile, the pissed off look fading from my face. I take a few steps back and rest my back against the windowsill. My eyes trail him from bottom to top, eventually meeting his face. He's wearing black gym shorts with a plain white tee that hugs every single chiseled muscle from the waist up, and a black hat—which he's wearing backwards. I can't decide which version of Paxton I like the most, but Gym Paxton surely has me feeling all sorts of things I shouldn't be feeling. I drink another sip of water, hoping it'll cure the drought that's in my mouth right now.

"Sorry about that," I say shyly. "But you really should watch yourself. You can't be sneaking up on a girl like that. Especially one ready to attack."

We both laugh in unison. God, that laugh, that smile, those eyes, and the way he looks at me. All of it aids to the pulsing between my legs. We haven't had sex since that day on my couch, and right now, I can think of a million things I'd like him to do to me. I force the thoughts back, for now.

"So, what are you doing, anyway?"

He walks closer to me, and I feel myself growing anxious as he closes the space between us. He grips my waist and looks down at me. My watch buzzes, notifying me that my resting heart rate has spiked to 105. *Yes, I am well aware of what's going on in my chest right now, thank you.*

"Well, I *was* working out. But then this really sexy woman caught my eye and I thought I should come ask her why she hasn't text me back."

I like it when he's needy. It's cute and not at all annoying like all the other guys I've been with. Part of me wonders if it's because I might need him too. Not in a desperate way, but in a way that I need him to *change me.*

I don't really know what to say to him as to why I ignored him. Mostly because I can't tell him I didn't want him to come over in fear that he might uncover some of my past. Sure, we've gotten a lot of surface-level conversation out of the way, but the deep stuff is still buried.

"I... I uh..." I stumble over my words as he nears closer to my face. "I just needed to clear my head is all," I manage to say.

He pulls back just enough to be able to study my face. *No, come back. Please.* I silently beg. Chewing on the inside of my cheek, I realize that probably wasn't the best answer. I don't want him asking questions. Yet, I knew it was coming anyway. He doesn't step away though. He just stands there, still holding onto me, a concerning look on his face.

"Are you having second thoughts?"

Yes. No. I don't know. What the fuck do I say?

"No, of course not. I just haven't seen my sister in almost three years, and I haven't exactly told her about..." I pause. "You... us."

His face falls, along with his hands, taking my heart down with them. I wasn't prepared to have this conversation, and now I feel like I've just ruined his day. My stomach twists, forming a pit. I probably should've eaten something before coming because I feel a wave of nausea hit me.

"Is that why you haven't asked me to spend Thanksgiving with you? Because you didn't want your sister to know about us?" He doesn't seem angry, just genuinely hurt, making the queasiness in my stomach build even faster. *I really should've eaten.* A familiar feeling of dizziness appears in my head, so I grip the windowsill to steady myself. Paxton grabs a hold of me, and I hold onto his biceps in return. "Macy, are you okay?" His voice is stern. I look up at him, and his expression has changed from upset to worried.

I feel bad making him worry, but I can't tell him I haven't been eating much. We've been spending a great deal of time together, and I've neglected eating well and going to the gym. I haven't put on a ton of weight, but enough for me to notice. It's been a little over week since I've relapsed into old habits.

I feel the room starting to spin. Black spots begin to cloud my vision, and suddenly, everything is dark.

Chapter 24
Paxton

Just Wake Up

"Macy!" I yell.

She's slumped over in my arms, and I'm panicking. I lower her down to the ground and pull out my phone to dial 911. I check her pulse, which is beating slowly but at a steady rate. I sit there with her until EMS arrives, running my hands through her hair, trying to wake her up. In a matter of minutes, she went from lively to lifeless. Her skin is cool and clammy, completely opposite of the fire that was ignited between us just moments ago. Before I know it, they're hauling her onto a stretcher and into the ambulance. I try to ride with her, but they won't allow it since I'm not family. What they don't know is that she doesn't have any family. I'm the closest thing she has right now, but I do my best not to dwell on that. I drive as fast as I can to Northwestern Memorial, where I assume they're taking her since it's the closest.

By the time I make it there, she's already been put into a room in the E.R. I rush through the doors to find her.

"Sir! You can't just go in there!" I hear someone yell, but I ignore them and continue until I get to the nurses station.

"Macy Callahan, where is she?"

A familiar face turns around to greet me. Marissa, an old fling of mine. If you'd call casual sex a fling, then that's what she was, but nothing more.

"Hey to you too, Paxton," she says with a sarcastic tone. I hate the way sarcasm rolls off anyone's tongue except Macy's. It pisses me off. I give her a nod, hoping to shut her up so she will tell me where to find Macy.

"Can you please just tell me where she is?" At this point, I'm begging, and I don't even care. I just need to get to her. She points to room six, and I head in there as quickly as possible. She's lying in the bed, still in the same state as when she left me. Her eyes are closed, her breathing still labored but continuous. She's hooked up to an IV with fluids slowly dripping. I sit in the chair next to her, watching each drop empty itself into the tube.

I need her to wake up. This is agonizing. I don't even know what happened. How will I answer questions? I haven't a clue about her medical history. The motion of the sliding door breaks my thoughts, and I look up to find my mother in her white coat with a stethoscope around her neck. I didn't know she was working today.

She seems just as shocked to see me as I am her.

"Paxton? What are you doing here?" She looks at me, then at Macy, then down at her chart. It doesn't take her long to put the pieces together, and this is not at all how I wanted her to meet the girl I plan to bring home for the holidays. "Is this—"

I nod before she even finishes her sentence. She walks over to me and lightly grips my shoulder, as if she's apologizing. I look up to her with pleading eyes, begging for her to tell me, something, *anything*.

"I really shouldn't share her information with you without

her consent." I know it's a violation on her part, but I can't bear the thought of sitting here without answers. I hang my head in my hands, circling my thumbs over my temples. A breath leaves her mouth, as if she's about to go against her better judgement, and I look back up at her. "Her iron is low, as well as her blood sugar." I breathe a sigh of relief. That's easily fixable. "She also has a bit of dehydration," she continues. None of this makes any sense to me, but surely, it's just a coincidence, right? "Do you know if she suffers from any deficiencies or struggles with eating?"

I shake my head. I wish I knew more personal things about Macy, but I don't, so I can't provide my mom with any accurate information. I wouldn't peg her as the type, though. She's always cooking and working out. Her figure is perfect. But then I think back to a month ago when she was trying to shy away from me before sex. How insecure she felt, covering and shielding her body. Maybe she does.

"Okay," she says softly and pats my back.

"Thank you," I say. "I'm sorry you had to meet her this way. I planned to bring her home Thursday, but——" I drop my head down again, feeling slightly embarrassed that my mom will judge her. She hasn't always approved of my choice in women—my ex-fiancé included. But I've also never been serious about anyone since her, which honestly is probably the reason she's never liked the rest.

She gives me a sympathetic look. "It's okay, son," she says calmly. "We'll have a proper introduction when she wakes up."

The breath I was holding releases itself, and I feel somewhat relieved. I return her generous words with a half-smile, and she exits the room.

I scoot closer to Macy, and run my fingers over her hand, eventually raising it and placing a small kiss on the top. Her skin has warmed up, and I take that as a good sign. I just wish she would open her eyes. Her phone buzzes on the counter next to the rest of her things. *Lauren* lights up the screen, and without thinking, I answer it.

"Hey, Lauren." I'm an idiot. I know I shouldn't have answered the phone, especially since Macy didn't tell her about me, but I'm impulsive.

"Uh, who is this and where is my sister?" she snaps. Okay, this was a bad idea.

"Paxton, a *friend* of your sister's. Please don't freak out, but I'm sitting with her in the hospital right now."

"What? What happened?" I hear the panic in her voice, and it reminds me of the feeling that consumed me when she passed out in my arms. "She's supposed to pick me up from the airport in two hours. Is she okay?"

"She will be. The doctor said her iron and blood sugar could use some work, but no signs of further distress…" I pause, waiting for her to answer me, but she's still silent. "As far as picking you up, I can come get you."

"I'm sorry, who are you again?"

"Your sister and I are in the same law class, and we're both interning at the same firm." I'm not lying, but I also don't want to give her any more information without Macy's permission.

"I can catch a cab; it's fine."

"That's an hour drive; I'm coming to get you." I know I'm being demanding, but I refuse to let her sister wander around Chicago.

"Us. Coming to get *us*," she corrects.

I do remember Macy saying something about her bringing her boyfriend. It does ease my mind that I won't have to make small talk for the entire ride.

"Right, the boyfriend. I'll leave shortly. See you in two hours."

"See you," she says before hanging up.

"Who was that?" A weak voice from behind startles me, and my heart jumps out of my chest when I see her eyes open.

I leap over to her, laying the rail down to her bed and sliding in next to her. I wrap around her, and I just hug her for a moment, then place a kiss on top of her head. "Paxton," she says with a rasp. I completely forgot to answer her question.

"It was your sister," I admit. I feel her body tense beneath my arms, and I have a feeling I shouldn't have answered her phone without her consent. "I'm sorry, I know I shouldn't have answered, but I remember you saying she was coming to town, and I didn't know if it was important." In reality, I just wanted to speak to her, let her know I existed, but I can't tell her that.

"Shit. I need to get out of here. I have to go pick her up from the airport." She throws the blanket off, and I cover her back up just as my mom walks into the room. She stands next to the bed and introduces herself. I feel slightly nervous about this encounter, but I can't really do anything about it now.

"Hi Macy," my mom says as she lends out her hand. "I'm Dr. Meyers. It's nice to finally meet you. How are you feeling?"

I'm not sure she comprehends what's going on right now, but she shakes her hand and answers anyway. "I'm okay. Tired... *really* tired, but okay otherwise. How long before I can go home?"

"I'd like to keep you for overnight observations, so as long as everything comes back clear, you may leave tomorrow," my mother responds. "Paxton has told me a lot about you. You're just as beautiful as he led on."

"Mom," I say giving her a knowing look. I didn't exactly get a chance to tell her my mom was her doctor in the few minutes she's been awake.

"Mom?" Macy looks at me. It's all beginning to make sense to her now. I can see it in her expression. I suddenly feel a sinking from my chest to my stomach. This is bad, so bad.

"Paige Meyers," she reintroduces herself. "I'm sorry my son is rude and didn't inform you of my presence." She jokes with a playful smile. Though that doesn't ease the tension in the room.

Macy gives her a small grin, but I can tell she looks uncomfortable. "I apologize we're meeting at your place of work, with me as your patient. What a wonderful impression I've made." That small bit of sarcasm relieves me of the growing angst that was forming within me. *There she is.*

My mom let's out a laugh, and the room finally feels less suffocating. "I'll give you two a minute to talk." She nods then opens the glass door to the room and exits.

"I offered to pick your sister up from the airport, but I need to leave soon if I'm going to make it on time. Are you going to be okay here?"

She looks pissed off, and somehow, I know she's going to protest. "You did *what?*"

Her arms are now folded across her chest, and I instantly regret going behind her back. But how else would her sister get here?

I raise my hands in defense. "I'm just trying to help. I didn't want her to have to get a cab when I could easily just pick her up. *Them* up." I correct myself. "She seemed genuinely surprised to hear me answer the phone, though. You haven't said *anything* to her about me, at all? Not even that we are friends?"

Her eyes divert to her lap, and she begins picking at her nailbeds. The one thing about Macy is that she always answers my questions, even without speaking. I feel a little defeated. I was ready to take her home to meet my family, and she's kept me a secret this entire time. Maybe we aren't on the same page. Maybe she doesn't care about me the way I care about her. It hurts a little, knowing that I might be more invested than she is. Yet somehow, it doesn't make me care about her any less. It just makes me want to try harder.

"You don't get to just answer my phone and make decisions without talking to me first, Paxton. That's an invasion of privacy. They're perfectly fine getting a cab." Her tone is stoic and distant. "Or, if you can convince your mom to let me leave, *I* can pick them up myself."

I now find myself standing, facing her. "You don't even have your car here. It's still at the gym, you know—where you *passed out.*" *You're a fucking idiot.* "I'm sorry, I shouldn't have said that. I just—"

"Just go. Now," she directs with a harshness in her voice.

Nothing inside of me wants to leave her, but if I don't, I'll be late. I try to walk towards her, but she holds her hand up in defense and points to the door behind me.

"I'm sorry," I apologize again before walking out and sliding her door closed.

Chapter 25
Macy

Do Not Make Small Talk

I'm angry. Angry at myself for allowing this to happen again. Angry at Paxton for going behind my back. Angry at myself *again* for making a fool out of myself in front of his *mother*. Angry at him again for not telling me who she was. I'm just angry at all of it. And now, he's going to be in the same car with my sister for an hour. Who knows what information will be revealed about me. Panic starts to set in, and I rush to text Lauren.

> Do not make small talk. Please.

The message delivers with a green bubble instead of a blue one, which means she's still in the air. Hopefully she will read her texts first thing when she gets off the plane. If I don't distract myself, I will have an anxiety attack over this.

I've done so well at keeping my life private from Paxton, and now he has the upper hand. I don't like that. I need control. My heartrate kicks up and sets off the alarm to my EKG monitor. My nurse rushes in. Her badge says, *Marissa*.

"Are you okay?" she asks with little concern.

I realize I'm being delusional. There's absolutely nothing I can do about any of this right now, and I don't need to cause a scene while Paxton's mom is on duty. I've already embarrassed myself enough.

"I'm fine, thanks."

She scans me up and down, and I wonder why she's looking at me like that.

"So, you know Paxton, huh?"

Well, now it makes sense. She's curious about the girl he was just sitting with for God knows how long. I wonder if she's an ex-girlfriend. She's certainly pretty. Petite. Long, dark hair curled to perfection. Eyebrows perfectly manicured. Icy blue eyes and a smile straight off a dental poster. I feel myself growing jealous of her, and I don't even know her tie to him. All I can do is nod.

She must sense my apprehension because she gives me the most malicious smile, as if it seems impossible that we could be together. "Never thought I'd see him outside of the bedroom with a girl." She silences the machine and walks out with her head held high. My stomach coils, and I'm instantly angry all over again. I yank my pulse ox off my finger and begin removing my leads. *I'm getting the hell out of here.*

The machine alarms once again, but this time, Dr. Meyers walks in. She scans the room; I'm assuming she's looking for her son who is no longer here. "Did Paxton leave?" I nod. A breath leaves her, and it almost feels as though she's relieved. She walks towards my bed and takes a seat on the far end. "I'd really like for you to stay overnight, Macy. But ultimately, we can't hold you without your consent. I do think you need to finish your evaluation though, so we can go over treatment options."

She knows. *Of course, she knows. She's a damn doctor.* I can't look at her. I'm ashamed. Horrified. Humiliated. "How did you know?" My voice is quiet, almost a whisper.

"All the signs are there. Fatigue, vertigo, dehydration… scabbing of the throat." Her momentary silence is deafening, and I quickly wonder if she's told Paxton.

"Does he—" Before I can finish, she shakes her head. Though I'm relieved, it still makes me uneasy that she now has something over me. How fucked up am I to think that about his mother? That she would somehow use my eating disorder as blackmail?

"It's not my business to tell, but if you plan to be part of my son's life, I think he deserves to know. He was very worried about you. And between the two of us, I haven't seen him that way about someone in a very long time."

The guilt is rolling in. I know she's right, but how do you just come out and tell someone something so personal? I don't want him to pity me, nor do I want him worrying about me. Although I don't plan on sharing it with him, I nod anyway, hoping she believes me enough to stay quiet.

"Wonderful. Well, we're moving you upstairs to room 301 for the evening. Dr. Stokes will be taking over, and I'll be back in the morning to check on you. You should be cleared to leave around nine if all goes well." She puts a hand on my shoulder, and I meet her gaze. "It's good to see Paxton happy again."

Her words matched with her genuine smile makes my heart twinge as she leaves the room.

Ha. Fuck you, Marissa.

———

True to her words, they move me upstairs. At least this room is bigger, and the bed is more comfortable. There's also a tv, and somehow, I'm lucky to find my favorite show is on. I pull up the guide and notice that there's an entire *One Tree Hill* marathon playing. I'll be busy for hours. It's the episode where Nathan is freaking out on Haley after they had unprotected sex. He's yelling at her for possibly jeopardizing his future career, and then I think back to me and Paxton on my couch. We had used protection the night before, but not that morning. It was a spur of the moment decision, and neither of us were thinking clearly. Even though he pulled out, I know it isn't always effective.

I really need to get on birth control.

The sorrow I feel for Haley instantly becomes my own. I imagine having this conversation with Paxton, wondering if he'd say the same thing as Nathan. But he hasn't mentioned it. Not even once.

I hear a knock on the door, and then three bodies enter my room. Lauren turns to both Paxton and someone who I assume to be her boyfriend, and I watch as the two guys turn and leave through the door they just came in. She walks over to me and climbs into bed with me, snuggling up to me before saying a word. I'm not very affectionate, not even to my own sister, so I lay there awkwardly, as stiff as a board. She just laughs because she knows she's making me completely uncomfortable.

"Good, now that I've made you as uncomfortable as I have been for the last hour, we can talk," she teases. "What the hell is going on with you? And *who in the world* is that fine ass man who picked me up? I mean, I know his name, but he has given me zero context, which I'm assuming is your fault."

"Remind me why I agreed to let you visit again?" I huff as I roll my eyes. I know there's no getting out of the conversation. Lauren is very persistent and lets me get away with nothing.

"Because you missed me. Now spill, so we don't have to keep them eavesdropping outside of the door." She laughs. "I obviously know you've relapsed. Your little birdy at least told me what happened at the gym." The look on my face is insulting. "And before you get mad, I pushed him. You know how persuasive I can be." She grins, and I just want to smack her. "Why do you keep doing this to yourself, Mace?"

I didn't realize how much this had been affecting me—all the secrets. Keeping everything bottled in. No one is here to call me out on my bullshit like Lo does, so it's easier to get away with it. But now that she's here, I'm unravelling. A tear escapes me, and I wipe it away, as if I can hide it from her.

"Stop trying to be so damn strong all the time! Fucking cry! Yell! Scream! Whatever you need to do, just do it. *Please*," she begs. "We're not kids anymore, Macy. You can quit keeping it together all the time. All this shit you're harboring is going to *destroy* you."

Her words cause me to erupt into tears that I've been desperately holding back. It's exhausting, this life I'm living. The battles I'm at war with. My mind. My body. My heart. It's all too much to deal with on my own, yet I've made sure to never burden anyone with my problems. Lauren comforts me, as she always has, and I finally gain my composure long enough to explain about Paxton.

"We were friends, for a while. We were assigned to the same case in the firm we're at, and we hung out for about four months, as friends. No physical contact, not even a kiss."

Her eyes widen, and I'm not sure if she believes me. My expression doesn't falter, and her mouth immediately opens in shock.

"You mean to tell me you've been around *him* for *four* months and never even kissed the dude? Are you out of your mind?" She picks her jaw up off the floor. "I'm impressed. You're crazy, but your self-control is astonishing. I debated leaving Dillon at the airport when I saw Paxton waiting next to his car." I can't contain my laughter after that statement. Mostly because I know how good he looks posted up against that damn Mustang. "It's good to see you smile. Now continue."

"*Anyway*, one night, he finally made his move to kiss me. I led him back up to my apartment and..." She's getting antsy. Like a kid needing to use the bathroom, she's shifting uncontrollably in her seat, hanging on to every last word. "I closed the door on his face, basically."

She jumps to the floor, throwing her hands in the air. "You did *what!?*"

There's a rap on the door, and we both turn our attention to the creaking sound of the rusty hinge. The door is slowly opening, with two heads peeking in.

"You guys okay in here?"

"Fine! Now, out!" The boys jump back and shut the door at her demand. She turns her attention back to me. "You've got to be kidding me."

"I'm not. And then ten minutes later, he was banging on my door, and when I opened it, he barged in, ranting about his feelings for me. Calling me out on my bullshit, just like you do. And that's when I knew I couldn't deny my feelings for him. So, now we're dating. Sort of, I think. I don't know. He hasn't technically asked me to be his girlfriend."

She cocks her eyebrow, and I know exactly what she's thinking. "You've never cared about labels before. Why now? I mean I know why—*look at him*. But imagining you serious about someone is foreign to me." And before I can speak, she starts again. "This is a good thing, though, Macy. *Do not* hurt that boy, or I will be forced to marry *both* of them."

Marry? We've been so busy that I hadn't even noticed the 3-carat cushion cut diamond weighing down her ring finger. I unknowingly take her hand in mine, admiring the way the ring fits perfectly on her bony, white-polished finger. A pang of jealousy hits me. It's not that I'm not happy for my sister, because I am, but I fear this is something I'll never get. It's something I *know* I'll never have if I keep this shit up.

"Well, what do you think?"

"It's beautiful, but I didn't even know you were dating, let alone *engaged*. Why didn't you tell me?" I know it's been a while since we talked, but I thought I would've at least gotten a call.

"I am telling you—that's why I'm here. He proposed before we left, and I didn't think it was something to celebrate over the phone. So, surprise!" Her excitement makes me smile.

My baby sister is getting married, and I'm going to be alone, forever.

The boys enter the room once again, without warning.

"We're bored out there," Paxton shrugs.

Dillon follows closely behind him as they make their way to the foot of the bed. He's handsome. Dillon isn't exceptionally tall, but he's taller than Lauren. Not that it's hard to be. She's only 5'1. He has light brown hair that's tussled on top. His face is slender, which matches the rest of his build. He's dressed in jeans, converse, and a long sleeve striped button-up that hangs open over a white tee. There's also an expensive watch on his right wrist and glasses on his face, completely tying his outfit together. A little edgy, yet sophisticated.

He smiles at me and holds his hand out for me to shake. I hate that I'm meeting my sister's fiancé while in the damn hospital. But luckily, I'm still in my gym clothes from earlier, so I don't look completely awful. Lauren and I both climb out of bed, and I take his hand in mine.

"Dillon Brady. It's nice to officially meet the infamous Macy." His smile and demeanor are charming. I can see why Lauren likes him.

"I'd say the same, but I didn't even know about you until about five minutes ago," I joke, shaking his hand back. Lauren elbows me in the ribs. "What? It's true." I shrug my shoulders with a genuine smile. I guess Lauren and I aren't all that different in the confidentiality department.

Paxton stifles a cough, which I know is him agreeing. I shoot him a glare, aware that he's waiting for a proper introduction. I roll my eyes and drag him to my sister. "I don't know why we're doing this. You guys have already met."

Lauren holds her hand out, as if she didn't just take an hour-long car ride with him. "Hi, I'm Lauren, sister of the broody, misunderstood, red-headed girl standing next to me."

Paxton lets out a chuckle. He reciprocates her handshake. "I'm Paxton, her——" He stands there, staring at me, unsure of how to identify himself to her.

"Boyfriend," I interject. "He's my boyfriend."

Chapter 26
Macy

I've Reached My Crazy Meter

And just when I think Paxton can't get any cuter, the huge smile on his face proves me wrong. The fact that those simple words made him happy makes my stomach flip. He snakes his arm around my waist and pulls me toward him, placing a kiss on the top of my head. PDA has never really been my thing, *especially* in front of my sister, so I give him a fake smile and awkwardly pull away, returning to my position next to Lauren. It's after nine, and I'm exhausted. I just want to go home. Being here is depressing. But I know there's no way they're going to let me go tonight. I'm ready to be alone again and try to forget about today.

"Here's my key. Ya'll go to my apartment and get some rest. I'll see you tomorrow." I remove the key from my keychain and hand it to Lauren. Then, I turn to face Paxton. "Would you mind dropping them off, please?"

"Not at all," he replies. "Do you need me to grab you anything while I'm there?" I contemplate asking him for clothes and my toothbrush for a moment, but then I realize he'd have to come back, and I'm not really up for a conversation tonight. I just want to get in bed and get the night over with.

"I'm okay, thank you though."

His expression reads complete disappointment, and I can understand why—especially after I just called him my boyfriend— but I'm not ready to tell him about everything just yet. And I don't know if I'll ever be ready. It's just another fucked up part of me that makes me feel unworthy of love. I say goodbye to Lauren and Dillon, and they walk into the hallway, leaving Paxton and me alone. It makes me uncomfortable, standing here in a damn hospital room with the guy I just started dating. Not because I feel uncomfortable with him, but the whole situation is awkward. He doesn't even know why I'm here, and I'm sure he's waiting for an explanation—one which I don't plan to give. His fingers trace the tattoos on my left arm, and he looks into my eyes as if he's searching for answers. The silence between us is cut by a loud grumbling of my stomach, and I instantly feel embarrassed.

"Let me bring you dinner at least. You haven't eaten since you've been here," he offers. I'm starving, I won't lie, but I'm not eating anything this late. It'll just make me feel worse.

"I'm fine, really. You should get going. It's getting late, plus they're waiting on you." I really don't feel like arguing about this right now. I just need him to leave. "I'll see you tomorrow." I place a kiss on his cheek and walk him into the hallway. I can tell he's apprehensive about leaving, but I force him out the door anyway.

"I'm going to skip class tomorrow, so I'll be here first thing in the morning to come get you."

"I can catch a cab to the gym to get my car, it's no big deal. I appreciate the offer, but don't miss class for me," I basically beg. I don't need him to come to my rescue, and even more so, I don't want him to. I can see the pity in his eyes. This is exactly the reason why I didn't want to get involved.

"I haven't missed a single day thus far. I'm coming to get you. Now, go get some rest." His tone is demanding, but I don't have the energy to argue with him, so I do as he says. He places a featherlight kiss to my lips before turning around and walking away. I close the door as he heads toward the elevators.

Shortly after, a nurse walks in the room. She introduces herself as Alex and hands me one of those hideous hospital gowns that feels like sandpaper. I don't particularly want to wear it, but my gym clothes smell like sweat, and I desperately need to shower. I guess I'm going commando tonight.

Before I'm allowed to shower, Alex takes my vitals. She checks my blood pressure, pulse and my temperature, all of which are within the normal range. *Thank God.* Hopefully this means I'll be able to leave without any issues.

"I'll be back to hook up your IV once you're finished. Just press your call button."

I nod and head for the small bathroom in the corner of my room. The shower is tiny. It's cattycornered to the right, with the sink to the far left and the toilet right next to it. It's been so long since I've been in a hospital, I forgot how miserable it is. I turn the water on to the hottest setting and begin peeling off my clothes. I release my long hair from my ponytail and shiver as it falls down my back. The water is finally warm, so I step in and close the paper-thin shower curtain. Of course, there's only generic soap and bodywash, but it'll have to do. I wash my hair and scrub down my body with the bodywash that smells like antiseptic. It makes me want to gag.

When I step out of the shower, I dry off and slip into the gown. I throw my hair in the extra towel and head to my bed. It's nearly 10:30, and I'm ready to sleep. I press the call button as Alex instructed, and within minutes, she's entering through the doorway carrying a bag and Tupperware bowl. She places them both on my tray table and refills my saline. As she's connecting the tube back to my IV, I can feel her eyes on me.

What the hell is up with all these nurses eyeing me like they hate me? This one is blonde. Her pin-straight hair meets the top of her shoulders. She looks to be around my age and around the same height as me. Much like Marissa, her eyes are blue, but they're darker. And although her smile isn't perfect, she's a very pretty girl.

"Paxton brought these for you," she says as she gestures to the small bag and bowl containing food. I'm just going to assume everyone here knows Paxton because of his mother and not because they're a part of his past. Even if that isn't the case, I'm going to pretend it is. I've never been the jealous type, but for whatever reason, it bothers me to think about him with someone else after finally giving myself to him.

"Thanks," is all I can manage without questioning her. I figured she would walk away after my short response but clearly, I'm wrong. She stands there, looking at me with some sort of territorial expression in her eyes, and I understand that his presence isn't well known due to his mother's job here. *How many girls has he been with?* Not really wanting to know the answer, but forcing myself to ask anyway, I blurt out, "So, you know Paxton then?"

She shrugs, which annoys me. "As well as anyone can *know* Paxton, I guess. He's not really the dating kind." Her tone is so nonchalant. My blood is reaching boiling temperature. I know exactly what she's insinuating. They've fucked. My skin crawls at the thought of them together, and at this point, I'm ready to walk over there and bash her head into the wall. I've already reached my crazy meter for the day, so I refrain, but the image was nice.

"I see he's found a new type." She smirks as she gestures up and down my body, and I feel the need to cover myself up. I know I'm not everyone's cup of tea, but I'd like to think I'm not so far from someone's type that it seems impossible that Paxton would be with someone who looks like me. Piercings and tattoos are normal these days, so why do her and that bitch Marissa feel the need to judge me so quickly?

Rage flashes through me, but if I want to leave here tomorrow, I very well can't beat the shit out of my nurse. Nothing says I can't be a bitch, though.

"Seems as though he's upgraded. Have a nice night," I spit back. Her face falls, and I can tell I hit a nerve. Good. She doesn't say another word, just walks out and slams my door. *Bitch.*

I open the small black bag sitting on the table. Much to my surprise, or lack of, are a few clothing items. Underwear, socks, a pair of sweatpants, a tee and my U of C sweatshirt. He also packed me a pair of jeans, my toothbrush, and my hairbrush. A smile traces my lips at his thoughtfulness, but then manages to fall at the thought of him going through my things. Something really is fucking wrong with me. I should be appreciative of this kind gesture, not pissed off. Yet somehow, I always manage to find the negative in something nice done for me.

Despite my sour attitude, I decide to shoot Paxton a text to thank him after changing into more comfortable clothes. I don't wait for a response. Instead, I put my phone on *do not disturb* and fall fast asleep, leaving the meal completely untouched.

Chapter 27
Macy

Ambushed in Front of the Canned Corn

Morning comes quickly, and I'm woken to a knock at my door. In walks Dr. Meyers. I check my phone and realize it's already 8am. *Shit.* Paxton will be here within the next hour. Hopefully we can discuss a plan before he arrives. I don't want him involved in this.

I sit up as she enters the room and begin smoothing my hair and wipe under my eyes so I don't look like a total train wreck.

Dr. Meyers greets me with a smile on her face. "Good morning, Macy. How did you sleep?"

It feels weird, still, talking to my boyfriend's mother about my problems, but what choice do I really have? As uncomfortable as I am, the only way to get myself out of this bed and back home is to play along.

"Fine, I guess. I sleep better in my own bed, though," I admit. "Look, I know how this goes, okay. I'm going to get better. I already see a therapist. I'll make an appointment with a nutritionist, too." I already workout, so that's another thing I can cross off the list of I'll-fix-myself.

"If this is regular behavior, I suggest checking yourself into a rehabilitation center to seek the help you need, or else you're just going to continue relapsing."

Her suggestion makes my stomach turn. There is absolutely no way I'm checking myself into any facility. I've beaten this before, and I can do it again. I just need to be stricter on myself. I need to stop letting my time with Paxton detour me from hitting the gym, and I need to stick to eating right. No more leisure.

I let out a breath before responding. "With all due respect, I haven't done this in a very long time. I've had it under control for years, and I know the precautions I need to take. I've almost finished law school, and taking a leave of absence would not be in my best interest. It'll only fuel my anxiety, thus causing me to backtrack even further." All of what I'm saying is the truth. I don't need to hinder my chances of making junior partner, and I absolutely do not need to push back graduating school. "I don't take your consideration lightly, but I overcame this as a teenager, so I'm positive I can do it again as an adult."

She seems apprehensive about pushing any further, so she gives me a nod instead then hands me a few pamphlets. "In case you change your mind."

I accept them with a nod, then shove them into my bag. Dr. Meyers informs me that she signed my discharge papers, and that I am free to go. Once she exits the room, I pull on my jeans and sweatshirt, then brush my teeth and hair. Not long after, I hear the door creak open and a familiar face peeks in: Paxton.

"Uh, hey. You ready to get out of here?"

I stride out of the bathroom and grab my things, tossing the bag over my shoulder.

"More than ready," I respond, walking up to him. He

leans slightly forward, placing a kiss on my lips then leads me out of the room towards the elevator. "Are you going to say goodbye to your mom?"

"No. I'll see her later. Let's go."

We walk to his car, and he takes my bag from me when he opens the passenger door. He tosses the bag into his backseat then grips my hips, pinning me up against the car before I can get in.

"Paxton," I let out in a low whisper. My breathing is uneven and a dull throb sets between my legs as his car meets my back. *What is he doing, and why can't I stop him? Why don't I want to?* Before I can comprehend what's going on, his mouth is against mine, his hands cupping my face. His kiss is deep, not at all subtle. His hands move from my cheeks and down my body, roaming over every little curve. I should've done more. I should've matched his energy, his curious hands, but I don't. I just stand there, taking it, without a single reciprocated touch.

He takes a breath then lowers his forehead to mine. "Don't ever scare me like that again." His words are breathless, and I know he means them down to his very core. My stupid decisions, my losing battle with my eating disorder, my inability to be a decent human being, caused him to worry. And what scares me the most is, this is only the beginning.

―――

The drive is quiet, and I'm silently thanking God for that. I think he knows not to ask questions, but I can see the intent in his posture. His grip on the steering wheel is tight, his shoulders stiff, his jaw ticking with every passing moment. I do my best to ignore it because we finally arrive at the gym so I can retrieve my car. I pull my bag out of his backseat and turn to face him.

"Thank you," I manage to say. I reach for the door

handle, but his arm catches me until I'm facing him once more. I'm almost certain I know what he's about to ask, so I divert my gaze to the windshield.

"Macy," he says as he lets out a sigh. "What happened in there?"

I knew it was coming, I just thought he would've given it more time. I stare at the building in front of us, my stomach turning in knots as I search for an answer to give him. My thoughts are swirling, and I can't come up with one single excuse. Until…

"You heard your mom. My iron was low, and I was dehydrated. I guess I haven't been drinking enough water." *Whew. Good thinking on your feet, Macy.*

His shoulders release the built-up tension, but his face is still set in stone. I can almost guarantee he doesn't believe me, but that's all I've got for him right now. So, I change the subject. "Do you want to come over for Thanksgiving? Dinner is at four, but you're more than welcome to come over whenever, if you want."

I'm not sure if he realizes what I'm doing, but a small smile crosses his face. It looks almost forced, but I don't call him out on it.

"I'd like that. Sneaking away from my parent's house shouldn't be a problem," he says reluctantly. "If you need any help, feel free to ask. I make a mean sweet potato casserole."

"I think Dillon might appreciate your company even more than me," I tease. "It's doubtful that he will want to assist in the kitchen while we catch up."

He gives me a genuine smile this time, followed by a low chuckle, and butterflies fill my entire stomach. I don't think I'll ever get tired of that sound.

"I'll swing by around noon if you're good with that."

I nod, and he places another light kiss to my lips before allowing me to crawl out of his car and head to mine. I slip into the driver's seat and watch in the rearview as he pulls out of the parking lot. I sit there for a moment, replaying the last twenty-four hours in my head, trying to figure out how I allowed this to happen. I'm usually more cautious, more careful—I don't know what happened this time.

I pull onto the highway and head towards my apartment. When I arrive, it's almost ten. I knock on the door, since Lauren has my key, and she opens it shortly after. I step inside, then shut the door behind me.

Before my sister can question me, I walk down the hall and into my room. Lauren trails quickly behind me, entering and throwing herself on my bed. She rolls onto her stomach, feet in the air, chin resting in her hands as I unpack my bag. I can feel her eyes burning a hole in the back of my head, but I don't plan on entertaining her interrogation.

"Where's the boyfriend?"

"Home, I guess. I don't really know." My tone is curt, but I really don't feel like discussing Paxton right now. I need to figure out how to get my life in order. "I don't keep tabs on him."

"Jesus, Mace. What the hell is your problem?"

"Nothing. I'm just not in the mood to talk about everything. I have to go to the grocery store to grab everything for Thursday. Do you want to come?"

"And leave Dillon here?" She cocks her eyebrow in question, acting like he isn't a grown man who can take care of himself while we're gone.

"Forget I asked. Ya'll go and explore."

I walk into my bathroom and slam the door. I pace back and forth, trying to calm myself down. I know the anger is just a side effect of my malnutrition, but I can't seem to get my shit together long enough to not be a bitch to everyone in my path. I run the shower and step in, hoping the scalding water will relax me. Luckily for me, it does just enough. I wash my body, followed by my face, and wrap myself in a towel. When I return to my room, Lauren is no longer lounging on my bed.

Thank God. I throw on a pair of black leggings with a nude sweater and a jean jacket. I grab my brown boots and place a tan beanie on my head before retreating to the living room.

Lauren and Dillon are nowhere in sight, so I go into the kitchen to grab a water bottle from the fridge. She left a note on my dry erase board pinned to the door that reads:

Went out for brunch. Be back later.

Honestly, I'm relieved. I'm happy she's here to visit, but I'm so high-strung right now, it's best if she's not around me. I take a bottle of water and fish through my pantry for a granola bar. Once I have both in hand, I lock up the apartment and walk downstairs to my car. I put my favorite playlist on to drown out my thoughts while I make my way to the store.

Once I arrive at Mariano's, I walk inside and find myself a cart. Taking my time walking down the aisles, I put the ingredients in, one by one, until I notice the familiar figure standing in front of the canned vegetables. Although I really need green beans, I opt to turn around and head in the opposite direction without drawing attention to myself, but it's too late. I hear her voice yell my name.

"Macy!" she calls out behind me, and I'm forced to turn back around.

I plaster the best smile I could onto my face, and I don't think she can tell the difference because she's smiling right back at me.

"Doing some last minute shopping?" Dr. Meyers drops a few cans of green beans as well as yams into her basket.

If I'm going to be standing here talking to her, I might as well do the same. I nod as I grab a few handfuls and place them in my cart as well.

"Yes, ma'am," I say. "Are you off work already?" I don't know why I even asked that, but it just slipped out. Hopefully she doesn't hear my displeasure at our run-in.

"I'm not working today. I just came in this morning to

sign your papers and make sure you were set to leave." She keeps her hands busy, tapping on the handle of the cart, then looks at me with another smile. "I was wondering..." Oh no, I don't like where this is going. Please don't. "Would you like to come to our house for Thanksgiving? I'm sure Paxton would love for you to be there, and everyone is excited to meet you."

And there it is. The question I'm dreading. My heart is hammering against my chest, not wanting to be rude. It's bad enough, our first encounter was in the hospital, but I really am not ready for introductions.

"Oh, that's okay," I say as politely as I can. "I don't want to intrude." I can feel the heat in my cheeks rise, and I can only hope she doesn't think I'm being disrespectful. I'm just not used to meeting parents, or family for that matter. I never let myself go there with any of my other boyfriends, and I don't really want to start now.

"Nonsense. We all want you there, dear. Please, it would mean a lot to us. Paxton doesn't bring girls home, ever. So, for him to want to include you is a big deal—to him, and to us."

Fuck.

Me.

"I really do appreciate the offer, but my sister and her fiancé are visiting from California, and I promised them I'd host this year."

"Ah, I see. They are more than welcome to join us as well. We have plenty of room; lots of food. Game night is always enjoyable, too. It'll be fun." Her eyes light up with endless possibilities, and I can't very well turn her down now.

"That sounds great. We'd be happy to join you." I swallow the thick lump lodged in my throat. Dr. Meyers lets out a tiny schoolgirl squeal and embraces me in a hug. I tense up because I'm not a hugger, but she doesn't seem to care. "Should I abandon my cart then?" I ask with a small, uncomfortable laugh, which again, goes unnoticed by her.

She then nods and responds, "I have everything taken care of."

"Can I at least bring dessert? I'll feel awful showing up empty handed."

Her hand comes flush with my cheek. "Anything your little heart desires," she says. "We do dinner around five, but feel free to come any time. Payton likes to make her special mimosas, so we will be in the kitchen most of the day sipping on cocktails and trying not to butcher the food."

A laugh falls between the two of us, and somehow, I feel a little more comfortable knowing they're not snobby rich people who hire people to cook their meals.

"My kind of party." I wink, and she giggles again. "I will see you Thursday. Thank you again for the invite."

Dr. Meyers goes to finish up her shopping while I return my cart to the front of the store and exit the building. I shoot Lauren a quick text before backing out of the parking lot.

> I may have gotten us into a little problem.

LAUREN
> Do I even wanna know?

> Well, it involves us and the Meyers on Thanksgiving. So, there's that.

LAUREN
> And you managed to do that, how?

> Long story short: Dr. Meyers basically cornered me in the vegetable aisle, forcing me to say yes. I tried to get out of it, but she was persistent, and I caved under pressure.

LAUREN
> Nothing like a good ole ambush in front of the canned corn.

> It was green beans, actually.

LAUREN
> Whatever. So, now what?

> Now we go and be merry, or whatever it is families do on holidays. Hell, if I know.

LAUREN
> Well, this will make for an interesting Thanksgiving. Can't wait!

> I hate you.

LAUREN
> I love you, too, sis.

Chapter 28
Paxton

Thank You, Dr. Phil

Monday, November 21- 4:00 pm

I'm feeling particularly aggravated today. The last thing I feel like doing is sitting in this session, but because I know it'll probably do me more good than bad, I stay.

I never suspected that Macy had any problems in the health department, but again, what do I really know about her? Not much, obviously. When my mom presented the question about her struggling with eating, it didn't sit well with me at all. Macy is always working out, cooking, taking care of herself. From what I've seen, anyway. She has a great body. Slim, yet toned, so I would have never pegged her to be the type to fall into the pressures of an eating disorder. But again, what do I know?

Her abruptness earlier only led me to believe that it was true, but I also know that when Macy doesn't want to talk about something, she isn't going to talk about it. There was no sense in pushing the issue any further, but eventually, we will have this conversation—whether she likes it or not. I want her to be healthy, and I refuse to let her do something so detrimental to her body. Not to mention, I cannot withstand another episode of the near heart attack that she almost gave me. Seeing her go limp, then almost lifeless, brought me to my knees. I felt like I couldn't breathe. My muscles felt like they had ceased to exist as I held her body in my arms. The only reason I managed to call 911 was the pure luck of momentary adrenaline that seemed to rush through me due to panic.

Taylor greets me as she gestures me to sit down in front of her, so I do just that. My head is anywhere but here, and I know she can tell. Across from me, she adjusts her posture so that she's sitting up straight and places her hands in her lap. They rest on the clipboard sitting on top of her perfectly crossed legs. The silence is thick, neither of us breaking it, just holding eye contact like we're in some sort of staring match. Normally, I'd find it awkward if it were anyone else. But Taylor and I have become good friends over the last three years. Though we've never crossed the line with each other, I can't say I didn't think about it before. She has that sexy, intelligent presence about her. Her frame is tiny with a golden tan. Her hair is a rich, dark brown; long and thick, it falls to the middle of her back. And deep brown eyes that crinkle at the ends when she smiles. She is definitely easy on the eyes. Which is why I insist on visiting her during office hours instead of letting her be the voice of reasoning as my friend.

I don't look at her like I once did; not since Macy made her way into my life. Sure, she's beautiful, and she has a way about her that makes me feel comfortable talking to her, but it hasn't been like that for me after spending so much time with the girl who has a serious hold on me. *All* of me. I haven't been this serious about a girl since my ex, and it scares the shit out of me. Macy has the ability to either make me the happiest man in the world or destroy any future chance I have at love. Because if she ever walks away, that's it for me.

"Paxton, are we going to talk, or just duke it out through mindless eye contact?" she asks, breaking my focus. "I mean, whatever you need. But I figured you'd want to take advantage of that high dollar you're paying me." She laughs with a wink.

If we weren't friends, this would be totally inappropriate, but ever since her divorce, we've allowed playful banter to fall between us. I think that's what grants me the ability to relax and be open with her. It eases the tension.

"Sorry, I just have a lot on my mind."

She leans forward and adjusts her position, uncrossing her legs. Now, her forearms are resting on the clipboard and her hands are clasped together, hanging over the thin piece of wood stacked with papers. "Talk to me. What's going on?" There's a kink in her eyebrow as she leans back into her chair, which means she knows exactly what's up. "It's the girl, isn't it?" A knowing grin plasters across her face, and I can't help but roll my eyes. Sometimes I think she knows me *too* well.

"Something of that sort." I let out a breath. "I think she has an eating disorder. She passed out on me at the gym yesterday and had to be rushed to the hospital. My mom was her doctor, and I basically forced information out of her because Macy never lets me get close enough to know anything about her life. So, there I was, sitting in the hospital room of my own girlfriend, not being able to answer even one damn question and looking like a fool to my mother for being clueless." I feel slightly hesitant about telling Macy's business to a stranger behind her back, but I don't really have anyone else I can talk to about this. Normally, I'd talk to my sister, but in this case, I want her to *like* my girlfriend for once, so that's out of the question.

"In her defense, you've only been officially dating for a month or so," she says with a shrug of her shoulders. "Maybe she has deep rooted issues that she doesn't want on display, in fear that you'll high tail it out of here the minute she lets herself get comfortable with you."

Does she really think I would do that? If my past is a testament to anything, it's that I would never judge her based on hers.

Taylor cuts the silence. "On the contrary, maybe she just doesn't see a future with you and doesn't want to get in too deep."

"Wow, that's comforting. Thank you, Dr. Phil." An ache in my chest becomes present at that thought. Maybe she's right. Maybe that's why Macy has kept me at arm's length this whole time. She doesn't see me as someone long-term.

A soft laugh leaves Taylor's lips, but I find this to be anything but funny. "I'm just being honest with you, bud. Do I think she would be crazy to pass up the opportunity to keep you forever? Sure, but that doesn't mean she sees it that way. My biggest advice here would be to just be honest with her. It sounds cliché but tell her what you want. Let her know how you're feeling, and if she doesn't reciprocate that, then at least you didn't spend three years of your life with her just to propose and break off your engagement weeks before your wedding."

"Just coming for my throat today, huh, Tay?"

"All in good fun," she banters back. Taylor stands and rounds the table between us, and with a pat on my shoulder says, "Now, get off your ass. Your time is up."

She nudges me, and I finally manage a genuine smile.

Time to go get my girl.

―――

Without warning, I arrive at Macy's apartment. I figured if I asked to come, she probably would have made an excuse to avoid talking about yesterday. I thought long and hard about Taylor's words on the drive over, and she's right. If I don't lay everything out there now, we could end up wasting our time, and I'm done doing that.

I step out of my car and enter the building, climbing two steps at a time to get to the second floor. Once I reach 209, I knock. My heart is rapidly beating, in fear that she's going to reject me once I tell her how badly I want this— us, her, and every single part of her.

To my surprise, Lauren opens the door. She gives me a sly smile as she motions for me to come inside. I step in and look around. "Where's Macy?"

"She's still napping. Probably trying to sleep off the encounter she had with your mother earlier today." She laughs. I stand there, confused, which I'm assuming she notices. "When's the last time you spoke to her?"

"My mother, or Macy?"

"Either, I suppose." But before I can answer, she continues. "They had a run-in at the grocery store earlier today, and your mom invited us to Thanksgiving at their house on Thursday. Cornered poor Macy right in front of the veggies, allowing her no escape." She laughs even harder, and the thought causes me to let out a deep laugh as well. If my mother is known for anything, it's being persistent. She doesn't take no for an answer.

"I guess I should be thanking her for getting Macy to agree to something she wouldn't when I asked. But now, I'm thinking I should be running for my life before she wakes up," I admit with another chuckle.

"Please stay. I'd love to watch this unfold," Lauren responds. "I'm lacking drama since I moved away from home," she jokes.

"As much as I'd love to be a pawn in your reprise of hardcore teen drama, I think it's best if I head home. I'll see you all on Thursday though, right?"

She nods, and excitement overcomes me as I head back to my car. I guess this conversation can wait just a little bit longer.

Chapter 29
Macy

Tequila Sunrise

I hear a faint rapping at my bedroom door, followed by Lauren yelling at me to wake up. I roll over to check the time. The screen on my phone lights up and reveals that it's only 8:00 am. I groan and bury my head back into my pillow, pulling the covers over me. Lauren pokes her head in my door.

"Get your ass out of bed. We have Thanksgiving to attend," she says as she walks over and yanks the blanket off of me.

I give her a death glare, to which she sarcastically smiles back and heads toward the door.

"It's barely breakfast time," I yell back. I am *not* looking forward to today.

Mostly because I'm being forced against my will to say yes, but a small part of me must admit that I'm excited to see Paxton. I haven't seen him since he dropped me off at my car on Monday, so I might miss him just a little.

"Yeah, but I'm ready for mimosas, and I'm sure Dillon is ready for male companionship."

I can't argue with her there. He has spent a great deal of time dealing with all our gossiping and girly charades. I guess I could grant him the extra hours for some male bonding. I sit up in bed, rolling my eyes.

"Fine," I growl. "Give me an hour."

With an excited nod, she leaves me alone to get ready. I hop in the shower, then enter my room in just a towel, in search of something to wear to Paxton's parent's house. I opt for a chunky, sage green sweater dress with thigh high brown boots. I curl my hair and pin it half up, half down, then add some light makeup. I finish off the look with my thin rimmed glasses and nude lipstick.

By the time I walk out of the room, it's nearly 9:30 am, and Lauren and Dillon are both dressed and ready to go. Setting eyes on my little sister, my stomach sinks. I feel strangely insecure standing next to her; I always have. She's a petite little thing. Standing at only 5'1, she's perfectly proportionated with an hourglass figure. Lauren has always been the smaller of us two, and I let my comparison of us fuel a jealousy I've never revealed. Where she has naturally blonde hair, while mine is tinted red. Her eyes are as blue as the waters of Bora Bora, and I took after my dad with light brown. She has the most flawless skin, yet my face is skimmed with freckles. If you didn't know our parents, you'd never believe we came from the same two people.

I suddenly begin to rethink my outfit choice. Lauren is dressed in a long-sleeve black turtleneck tucked into a brown, suede skirt. Black tights cover her legs, but accentuate them, making them look longer than they actually are. Her black ankle booties make her an inch taller, too. Somehow, my appearance makes me feel skimpy, almost. I don't need that to be his family's first impression of me. I turn on my heels before Lauren catches me.

"Where do you think you're going," she challenges.

"To change."

"Oh no you're not. You look hot."

My cheeks flush. If anyone is going to hype me up, it's my little sister. Our entire lives, she has always made it a point to make sure I feel good in my skin. Most of the time, she succeeds in the moment, but obviously not enough for me to believe it. Otherwise, I wouldn't have felt the need to starve myself or consume food only to have it come up moments later.

I try to protest against her, but she isn't having it.

"We're leaving. Now." Lauren grabs me by the wrist and calls for Dillon as she drags me to the front door.

We decide to catch a cab, in fear that Payton's special mimosas might have us on our asses later. I give the driver the address that Paxton texted me, and we ride fifteen minutes through the city until we hit a long stretch of highway. It's nothing but trees for miles until large houses come into view. They're separated by at least five acres or so, each house bigger than the last. When we finally pull into the long driveway, his parent's house comes into view. It's breathtaking. The pavement runs through an iron fence with a brick column on each side, both mounted with a gas lantern. The driveway makes a complete circle in front of the large, white stucco house. It's warm and inviting, yet modern and sophisticated. I pay the driver before stepping out, Lauren and Dillon following closely behind. Nerves hit me like a ton of bricks, unsure of what to expect today. I do my best to take a deep breath and then ring the doorbell.

The sound of the deadbolt clicks, and the door opens wide. Standing in the doorway is Paxton, with a boyish grin on his face. He's dressed in black slacks with a brown and white checkered button up, which is neatly rolled to his elbows. A watch sits on his left wrist, and I follow the chorded muscles of his forearms up to his biceps. His hair is styled in a messy, yet flattering, way. My insides are tingling at the sight of him, and there's lust between my legs. I need to get inside before I rip all his clothes off this instant.

He signals us inside, giving Lauren a quick hug and Dillon a brief handshake, while taking my hand. Paxton points down the hall, explaining to them that the kitchen is on the left, and tells them we will meet them momentarily.

Before I can protest, he pulls me into a dark room and shuts the door. My back immediately meets the wall as he pushes up against me and grips my waist. The only light present is from a lamp on the opposite side of the room. It doesn't give off much, but it's enough to illuminate Paxton's perfect facial features. His eyes are blazing with hunger, and by the way his tongue meets his lips to wet them, I know what comes next.

"God, I've missed you," he says in a hushed tone.

I didn't want to come today, but now that I'm here, I couldn't be happier.

A smile flashes across my face, and I let out a staggered breath. "I've missed you, too, Paxton."

And then, his lips come crashing down on mine. I thread my fingers through his hair, pulling him into a deeper kiss, parting my lips in anticipation for his tongue. It comes quickly, exploring mine, and I moan into his mouth. He presses up against me, the length of him grazing my hip. My need for him triples in this moment, but there is absolutely no way we are doing anything in his parents' house. I let him kiss me for a few more minutes before breaking away and placing my hands on his chest. He lowers his forehead to mine, both of us trying to catch our breath.

"Come on. Let's go. I have games to kick your ass at," I tease.

He lets out a deep laugh but releases me from the wall and smacks my ass as I turn towards the door. I shoot him a playful glance over my shoulder, then make my stride out of the room in the direction of the kitchen.

Laughter and conversation fill the air as we enter the large, spacious room. The kitchen is just as beautiful as the exterior of the house. Light, natural hardwood floors with white cabinets lining the brick wall behind the industrial sized double oven. There's a large island in the center, painted a dusty gray, topped with a dark marble slab. Waist-high bar stools surround it, which is where Lauren and Payton are sitting, having a drink, and Dillon and Preston are leaning against the counter, both with a beer in their hand.

Dr. Meyers rushes to us as soon as we enter, bracing me in another unwanted hug, but I do my best to return her affection. "There you two are!" She pulls back, studying me from head to toe. "You look beautiful, dear. I'm so glad you made it."

I manage to smile. Paxton slides up behind me, wrapping his arms around me and places a small kiss on my temple. I don't do PDA, especially not in front of parents, so I feel extremely uncomfortable. I don't want to make things awkward though, so I just roll with it. I thread my fingers through his and lean into him.

"Thank you so much. You look wonderful too," I say shyly. "Did Lauren hand over the dessert? Caramel apple dump cake is her favorite. I figured she might try to keep her for herself," I joke.

Dr. Meyers lets out a laugh. "I had to fight her for it, but I eventually I enticed her with a tequila sunrise." She gives me a wink and I giggle. "Payton, I think Macy here needs one," she says as she gestures to me. Payton makes me her famous tropical mimosa and hands it over. I take a sip, basking in the delicious flavors.

"Hi, I'm Macy," I say and lend out my hand for her to

shake. She grabs it and pulls me in for a hug instead. *What is with this family and hugging?* I slowly pull from her embrace. "I've heard a lot about you."

"All good things, I hope." She turns her glare to her brother standing behind me but finishes with a sarcastic smile.

I nod. "Of course."

Paxton's older brother strides towards me and takes my hand in his. He raises it to his lips, placing a kiss on my knuckles, then lowers it. "Please excuse my impolite brother who doesn't know how to properly introduce his family. I'm Preston, the older, more handsome Meyers brother." Jesus Christ. Their gene pool is fucking ridiculous. I don't understand how one family can be so damn gorgeous, yet here we are. Preston is handsome in a whole different way than Paxton. He's a bit more rugged, even though he's a surgeon. I'm not really sure that that has to do with anything, but I feel like surgeons should be daintier since they have such an important line of work. Not him, though. He's very masculine, with broad shoulders and rough hands. He has dark, sandy blonde hair and blue eyes to match his sister and mother's. I didn't think guys came much taller than Paxton, but he's here to prove me wrong on that as well. He has *at least* two inches on him.

"Nice to meet you," I return with a smile. I notice he's not wearing a wedding ring, so I'm going to assume he's still single. I can't imagine dating a doctor is easy work with their long, demanding hours. I turn back towards Dr. Meyers. "Is there anything I can help you with?"

She shoos the men out of the kitchen then puts us girls to work. The drinks are flowing as we put together each side dish.

During our time spent swapping stories, I learn that Paxton was scared of the dark until he was ten. He played football, baseball, and soccer in school, but sucked so bad at basketball that he didn't make it past the first tryouts. He's also weirdly afraid of birds, which makes me chuckle. We manage to finish cooking all the food without burning the house down, and I feel slightly buzzed from all the tequila.

The boys are in the living room watching football, of course, and yelling at the tv when their teams are losing and cheering every time they score. I press my lower back against the counter, taking in my surroundings, and my chest begins to swell. A wave of emotions run through me, and I can feel the tears stinging at the back of my eyes. The realization that Lauren and I never had this type of experience with family growing up has me appreciating these moments even more. We never got to cook in the kitchen with our mom during holidays, or settle around the tv, enjoying spending time together. We didn't laugh until we cried or were embraced in hugs every so often. I didn't know what it was like to have a parent that loved you so much, the way Dr. Meyers loves her kids. It feels nice to be part of something so heart-warming, and I'm not sure I ever want to give this feeling up.

Payton pours each of us another glass, and Dr. Meyers gathers everyone in the dining room as we set the table. The long, mahogany dining table is run with food. We have everything from green bean casserole, to baked macaroni, and everything in between. Paxton's mom insisted on making ham *and* a turkey because he tipped her off that I don't eat ham, which was oddly sweet, but wasn't necessary. We all take our seats. Paxton next to me, Lauren and Dillon across from us; Preston next to Paxton with Payton directly in front of him, and Dr. Meyers at the head of the table. The only person missing is their father, but I don't dare ask if he'll be joining us.

I watch as everyone links hands, so I nod to Lauren to follow suit. His mom leads us in prayer over our dinner, and when the room falls silent, we begin to dig in. As everyone eats, we make small talk, and I've never felt more at home than I do right now. Nothing else seems to matter in this moment, not the partnership, not my past, not even the future. I'm here, having what I assume to be a normal family get-together, with the one guy who I can see myself spending every single holiday with from this point forward. I'm genuinely happy for once; so why am I so damn scared?

Chapter 30
Paxton

Wolverine's New Discovery

This feels so damn good. Having her here, enjoying herself, perfectly fitting in with my family and looking so fucking happy. I watch her intently as she brings her fork up to her mouth and takes a bite of her food. She's smiling and laughing at whatever is being said, while dabbing her lips with the napkin then setting it back in her lap. Everything seems as though it's in slow motion, and I can't help but revel in the feeling that's brewing inside of me.

I'm falling in love with this girl, and I'm falling fast.

My focus shifts as my mom stands up from the table, announcing it's time for game night. It's a tradition we've done every year since I was a kid. I've always loved it, but it's become more fun once alcohol became involved. Preston and I offer to clean up the table, while Dillon assists us, and the girls make their way into the living room to get the games set up. They picked out Monopoly, Cards Against Humanity and Hearing Things.

We start off with a few rounds of Cards Against

Humanity but eventually move to the next game because Preston and Payton almost end up in a WWE match over who is *not* the funniest. It's clearly me, since I had the most cards in hand, but I wasn't going to step foot into that battle.

My mom pairs each of us up during Hearing Things, and Macy gladly accepts her onto our team since my dad isn't here to play with her. It makes my heart feel all sorts of things for this girl, but I need to pace myself or else she'll run for the hills. This game is much more enjoyable. It causes belly laughs that none of us have had probably in years. Tears are spilling down our cheeks while trying to guess our partner's sentences, but painfully butchering them every single time due to our inability to drunkenly read lips.

With her earphones on and the static loud, Macy tries to guess my words, "I hope it's covered by the warranty." What comes out of her mouth has me doubling over in complete, uncontrollable laughter. "There was a new discovery by Wolverine" has taken the cake tonight.

Payton comes into the living room with another round of drinks as we set up the Monopoly board. While Macy and Lauren take a bathroom break, I relax on the floor with my back up against the couch. My mom plops a seat next to me, leaning onto my shoulder. She's giving me *the look*, and I know that could only mean one thing.

"What?" I ask in a knowing tone.

"You know I don't say this lightly, because quite frankly, I've never liked any of your girlfriends, but she's a keeper, Paxton."

I feel a rush of adrenaline through my veins as my mom openly admits to *finally* approving of someone I'm dating. The smile on her face lights me up because I know what she said is true. Although I know my mother loves me, she's always been impossible to please when it's come to my dating life. Not just mine, but Preston and Payton's too. It's why we're all still single this late in life. My brother is thirty, for crying out loud, and he still refuses to bring a girl home. Payton, on the other hand, is only twenty-four, so she still has time to settle down, although she has no interest in relationships right now.

Over the years, our mom has engrained success into our brains. While Preston and I have been very driven in our fields of work, we haven't been shy about entertaining a love life. Payton has always been independent and headstrong, always focusing on college, and now, med school. She says a boyfriend would only deter her from being successful and that she doesn't want to date until she has the letters PhD behind her name. Seeing as though we're her protective big brothers, we've never really minded.

I give my mom a small nudge in agreement. She places a kiss on my cheek then stands to her feet. "I think I'm going to get some much-needed rest," she announces. "Don't let Monopoly get too out of hand." She chuckles. "And girls, if you don't want to go back across town, you're more than welcome to stay the night; you too, Dillon. We have two extra guest rooms, and both bathrooms are stocked with freshly clean towels and amenities." She kisses Payton and Preston goodnight and heads up the stairs.

The six of us play Monopoly and have one last drink before things quickly go downhill. To think my mom insinuated the game getting too out of hand as a joke. Clearly, we had no idea Macy does *not* take board games lightly. She cleared the board and ended up with everyone's property in a matter of four rounds. And let me just say, she is *definitely* a sore winner. She threw money in the air like she was at a strip club and taunted me for being the first to lose all my earnings. Yet somehow, I'm oddly turned on by her behavior.

I excuse us from the common area, setting Macy's drink down and slinging her over my shoulder. She's kicking and yelling for me to put her down, while also still bashing my Monopoly playing skills. We reach the end of the hallway and enter my old bedroom. I sit her on top of my empty dresser, and she immediately spreads her legs for me to stand between.

Still insulting me, I slide one hand around her waist and cup her cheek with the other. My lips meet hers, finally putting an end to her incessant remarks. Her arms quickly wrap around my back, digging her nails into my shirt and raking them all the way down to my ass. My cock starts to pulse, becoming tight against my slacks. Our kissing becomes sloppy and needy, and before I know it, Macy is undoing the buttons on my shirt.

She grabs each side of my button-up and slips it over my shoulders and down my arms. Within seconds, my hands trail up her thighs, sliding slowly under her dress. She doesn't protest, so I pursue it further. As I inch closer, I can feel her need for me. It's just as strong as my need for her. I swiftly drag my finger across her underwear, and they're soaked. I moan into her mouth and she swallows it down, gripping my hair and pulling me in closer. *God, I love when she pulls my hair.*

"I've been waiting to get you alone all night," I say against her lips.

"Please, Paxton," she begs, and I nearly lose it.

"Tell me what you want, baby." I stroke her over her panties, teasing her.

Her breaths are coming out in pants as I slowly circle her center. Her honey eyes meet mine, and she leans in close to my ear. "I want you to fuck me with your fingers, then bury yourself so deep inside me that I'll feel you tomorrow," she whispers.

Jesus fucking Christ. I'm gone. Dead. Goodbye.

Something deep rumbles from my chest, and all my self-control flies out the window. After pulling her panties down her legs and tossing them to the floor, I slip two fingers inside her. Her head falls back in pleasure, and she uses her hands for stability on my shoulders as she bucks her hips forward onto my fingers. My core is roaring, my cock praying for a release. I pump into her a few times before pulling out and setting her onto the ground while she stands in front of me.

"What are you doing?" She pouts, and I take her bottom lip in between my teeth before sucking on it.

"Turn around," I demand. She doesn't ask questions; she just does as she's told. "Good girl."

I dig in the top drawer where I used to stash my condoms and pull one out. She instantly turns to face me and snatches it from my hands. In shock, I apologize, "I'm sorry. We don't have to do this."

Her eyes narrow in on mine, holding me hostage in a stare. That's when she begins moving her hands, and it takes me a minute to realize she's undoing my pants. At this point, I'm throbbing, and I need her to touch me before I explode. Once my pants and boxers are around my ankles, she opens the gold foil packet and removes the condom.

Never breaking eye contact with me, she moves so close I can feel her breath on my lips. "I want to do it." She places the softest kiss on my lips as she rolls the condom onto my thick length, and I completely lose all train of thought. I spin her back around quickly and bend her over the dresser. My cock twitches as I slowly enter her from behind.

"Paxton!" she screams, as her hands grip the wood in front of her. I immediately cover her mouth with my own hand.

"As much as I love hearing my name from those gorgeous lips, I need you to be quiet, Mace."

My hips begin rocking back and forth, and I put my hands on her waist to steady myself.

"God," she moans. "Go faster."

That's it, I'm a lost cause. Her demands are causing me to come undone. I somehow manage to hold it together for the next three minutes. I thrust into her forcefully, causing her to scream my name over and over. *Fuck being quiet.* I'm so close to my release; I can feel it bubbling up my spine, but I can't finish before her, so I reach my right hand around to her front and circle her clit while I continue to pound into her.

"Fuck, you're so tight baby," I manage to say through my ragged breaths. "Are you gonna come for me?"

Macy's head falls forward and her breathing is erratic. "Yes! Yes! Mother fuck—"

Her words fall short. I can feel her about to fall over the edge, and with one more intense thrust, she falls back onto my chest as I spill into the condom.

I hold her tightly for a minute or two, then guide us over to the bed where I let her sit in my lap until she's ready to move.

She turns her head and snakes her hand around my neck, pulling me into a lustful kiss, but then stands up and searches for her underwear. I pull my boxers up then walk over to the bedside trashcan and dispose of the condom. I make my way back to Macy, slipping my arms around her waist from behind once she's fully dressed. Resting my chin on her shoulder, I place a kiss on her cheek. The urge for me to tell her just how she makes me feel is on the tip of my tongue, but I know it's too soon.

So, until then, I'll have to make sure she falls in love with me too.

Chapter 31
Macy

Stay with Me, Please

It's dark, and I'm feeling dizzy. Whether from the alcohol, or the high I'm still riding from what just happened, I don't know, but I need to lie down. I climb onto Paxton's childhood bed and collapse. I'm on my back, staring at the ceiling when I feel the mattress sink. He scoots next to me, draping his left arm over my middle, but I can't seem to shift my focus. I've been thinking about tonight, and how it made me feel. My emotions are in overdrive as I replay everything from the moment I stepped into the home he grew up in.

I try to imagine what he was like as a kid. I wonder if he was tall and lanky. If he had braces or had a naturally perfect smile. Was he always this charming, or did he go through an awkward phase?

A faint burning in my chest begins to sting at the thought of teenage Macy and Paxton ever meeting, knowing he probably wouldn't have looked twice at me. Insecurity washes over me as I remember the insulting stares from the nurses, presuming that I could never be his type. I feel a sob getting caught in the back of my throat but quickly swallow it down.

Paxton's stare isn't subtle at all. Even out the corner of my eye, I can tell he wants to speak, but isn't quite sure what to say. After another few minutes of complete silence, he finally breaks.

"Who knew you were such a master at Monopoly." He chuckles. A small laugh escapes my lips, but my mind is still racing with thoughts.

"The ugliest version of me is the version that comes out when I play board games," I say with amusement. "I don't know who she is; a monster really, but she is not fit for human interaction."

I warrant a deep, husky laugh after that. It's my favorite sound, yet I still can't make myself feel better about everything playing in my head. I let out a huff, and Paxton adjusts himself so that he's resting on his elbow, with his body shifted toward me. His left arm is still laying across my stomach.

"What's going on in that pretty little head of yours?"

"How many girls have you been with?" My hand immediately covers my mouth in response to my drunken outburst. If I was sober, I probably wouldn't have been brave enough to ask that question but drunk me doesn't really care. She's determined to embarrass me. I am so good to her. I put her in cute little outfits, get her ready, feed her alcohol, and what does she do? She ruins me.

"Macy…" he trails off. I can see the shift in his demeanor. Drunk me has made him as uncomfortable as I feel in this moment, and I wish I could take it back, but in retrospect, I'm curious. Not that it matters, because it doesn't; we're adults here. I just need to hear it in hopes it'll calm this unsettling feeling inside of me. "Why are you asking me this?"

I sit straight up and look him directly in the face. Although my vision is a little hazy, I can tell he doesn't want to answer this question. His head is dipped, and his eyes divert past me. "Because Paxton. Because I spent an entire day in the hospital with two girls, both of whom I assume you've fucked, basically telling me I couldn't possibly be your type. It's humiliating, being looked at like there's no way you'd ever be interested in me. Every time I meet someone in your presence, I'm reminded that you don't date. So, excuse me for being curious about who I should avoid in this town."

He shifts his position again, this time removing his arm and laying on his back. His arms rise and settle behind his head as he stares up at the ceiling, still avoiding the question.

"That many, huh?" A sarcastic laugh falls from my mouth, and I begin to slide off the bed. Before I make it to the edge, he grips my wrist and sits up. My head snaps towards him, my eyes blazing with anger. I've decided I don't want to hear the number after all. "Let me go, Paxton."

"No," he says with a passive tone. "You don't get to use this as an excuse to push me away. So, stop trying. What good is going to come from this conversation, Macy? Have I kept myself busy over the last four years in that department? Sure, but it's a part of my past. The past I had before I met you, and it's not fair for you to hold that against me. Nothing I've had with any girl after my ex-fiancée has meant anything to me. Not the way you do. And that might sound shallow on my part, but it's not like they didn't know prior. I made my intentions very clear. But with you, it's different. I've wanted more with you since the very beginning, and I just wish you'd understand that."

Ex-fiancée is all that's ringing in my ears. My stomach is twisting and the words stabbing like a thousand knives.

"You were engaged?" Though I don't mean for it to, the question comes out breathily. "When?"

The color drains from his face, and in that moment, I know he didn't mean to let that slip. I sit here, watching him search for an answer, any answer. Hopefully it's the truth because I can't handle any more surprises. A long exhale leaves him, and I brace myself for what he's about to say.

"When I was twenty-two," he admits. "My high school girlfriend became my fiancée, and I broke off our engagement five weeks before our wedding."

I really don't think I can handle this. Not sober, and definitely not while drunk. I know we have secrets, but I didn't think I'd be so affected by them.

"I should go."

I slide off the bed and head towards his bedroom door, but he stops me once again. Turning me to him, he lifts my chin so I'm meeting his gaze. It's stern, yet full of pleading. That look sends a pooling of sensation into my stomach, and I suddenly have the urge to hold him. Ultimately, I send that thought as far back as I can.

"I don't owe you an explanation, Macy, but I'm willing to give you one if you want it," he says, stifling back his fear.

Part of me wants one, but the other part of me doesn't—in fear that I won't be able to walk away. I don't want him changing my mind, yet here I am, nodding unknowingly. I'm really going to have to sit down with drunk me later and give her a scolding.

He guides me back to the bed and sits next to me, positioning himself to face me. I'm thankful that I'm beginning to sober up so I can comprehend his next words.

"We started dating our junior year in high school, and I proposed to her our junior year of college. Those years leading up to the engagement were great. I was in love with her, but after we got engaged, she became a nightmare. She was constantly keeping tabs on me, controlling when I could hang out with my friends, always searching through my phone in hopes of finding something so she could start a fight. It just became too much, and I was done. I no longer loved her enough to commit the rest of my life to her, so I ended it."

My heart sinks for him. The accidental slip of an ex-fiancée doesn't matter so much to me after hearing the ugly truth. He gave five years of his life to someone who robbed him of a future by being a total narcissist. The longevity of his commitment has my head reeling, while I'm over here cutting off any chance of happiness at six months. That's all I've ever known, yet something deep inside of me wants to give myself more than that with him. But I know I can't, and he doesn't deserve to have the rug pulled from under him again.

"I'm sorry," is all I can say.

"Don't be sorry. Just stay with me, please," he begs.

I feel my chest shatter, and somewhere in the midst of this, the lines have blurred. My rules are fading, and I can feel myself falling in love with the guy sitting in front of me, pleading with me not to leave him.

Chapter 32
Macy

Are There More Secrets?

We sit in silence for a moment until he leans over and places his forehead against mine. His breathing is slow and steady, releasing an exhale.

"Please," he begs again.

The constriction around my heart tightens, and I immediately give into temptation. Nodding my head, he sweeps his lips over mine so faintly that it almost doesn't seem real.

"Thank you. The bathroom is across the hall if you want to shower. I'll go check on Lauren and Dillon." He walks over to his closet and pulls a plain tee off the hanger, as well as a pair of boxers from the top shelf and tosses them to me. "I'll be in the living room if you need anything." He kisses the top of my head and walks out of the bedroom.

I make my way to the bathroom and turn on the shower. With my back against the wall, I sink down to the floor, pulling my knees close to my chest. I rest my forearms over them and drop my head backwards toward the wall. Tears start streaming down my face as the room fills with steam. I don't even know why I'm crying, but they're falling hard with no end in sight. I don't know if it's because I'm inside my head, praying I'll get over these feelings of self-doubt. Or if it's because I'm scared to fall for him in fear that I'll ruin everything with my inability to commit. Or maybe I'm just scared of loving someone who could easily decide to walk away from me, just like he walked away from his ex.

After finally undressing, I step into the shower and under the hot stream of water. I close my eyes as I let it wash away my tear-stained cheeks. Once I'm clean, I wrap myself in a towel and take a long look in the mirror. My eyes are puffy and bloodshot, my hair a knotted mess. I find a brush in the top drawer and rake it through my auburn tinted hair until it's smooth then remove a brand-new toothbrush from its box and brush my teeth.

By the time I make it back to Paxton's room, he's lying in bed wearing just a pair of basketball shorts. They're sitting low on his hips, creating a clear view of his perfectly lined V, and I bite the inside of my cheek to prevent myself from smiling. His hands are resting behind his head with his eyes closed.

I walk quietly to his dresser, placing my clothes on top of it while I replay the moment we had earlier. My pulse quickens, thinking about him behind me, slamming me against the dark wood. I lean forward, imagining it again as heat pools between my legs. My head hangs in front of me as I grip the dresser, my eyes fluttering, my breathing heavy while the replay consumes me.

Paxton's deep voice scares the shit out of me, snapping me out of my trance. My attention turns to him as he's now sitting up, staring at me.

"Jesus, you look so fucking good in my clothes," he pants.

The burning sensation between my legs grows hotter, and I feel myself gravitate towards him. Pulling myself onto his lap, I straddle him and drag my index finger down his perfectly toned chest and stomach. I lean forward, grinding my hips and placing a trail of kisses from his lips, across his jaw, down his neck and across his shoulder.

"Woman," he groans as his head falls back in pleasure. I continue moving my hips in a circular motion to get a rise out of him. I feel his hands slowly make their way from my waist down to my ass when he grabs two handfuls, squeezing me gently. Our lips are on each other's once more, the kiss intensifying.

The effect this man has on my body is undeniable. I speed up my movements, his groping matching my pace, and before I know it, he has me on my back. Paxton settles between my thighs, now doing some torture of his own. His hips roll into me, his cock pressed hard against my center. A small whimper escapes me and a victorious smile spreads across his face. He leans down and places a kiss on the shell of my ear, causing my whole body to set aflame.

"I want to taste your pussy," he whispers, and I nearly fall apart at those words alone. He lifts my shirt until it's sitting under my chin. His tongue flicks down my neck to my chest, before he claims one of my breasts with his mouth. I can't help but let out a moan as he uses his teeth around my sensitive nub while he caresses my other breast with his hand. He switches sides, tending to the left one, just as he did the right. My orgasm is climbing up into my stomach, and I know I won't last much longer.

Though unspoken, I think Paxton can sense my release coming to surface. He peppers kisses down my stomach until he reaches just above where I want him. His fingers dig into my hip bones as he runs his lips across my waistband, slowly pulling his boxers over my ass and down my thighs. I watch him attentively as he crawls back up toward me, his eyes never leaving mine. In one very slow motion, he swipes his tongue over me, and my eye contact is lost as my head hits the pillow.

"Eyes on me, baby," he demands. "I want you to watch me while I eat my favorite meal."

Every single stroke he makes causes a haziness in my head, but I manage to open my eyes. His fingers enter me as he laps over my clit, causing the air from my lungs to seize.

"Oh my God," I scream over and over. My hands find their way to his hair, putting pressure to keep him in that specific spot. He doesn't slow down, but rather speeds up, sucking my clit between his teeth. My orgasm erupts, sending the entire lower half of my body into paralysis.

Pleased with himself, he makes his way back up to my lips, kissing me ever so gently. The lingering feeling left on my lips only enhances the euphoric state I'm in. All I can do is smile.

Paxton retrieves his boxers from the edge of the bed and slides them back up my legs. He kisses my temple and snuggles up next to me, wrapping me in his arms.

"Get some sleep, baby," he says with a sleepy rasp in his voice.

It doesn't take me long to close my eyes and drift off to nothingness.

A continuous buzzing invades my dreams, causing me to wake up. Paxton has now moved to his side of the bed, sprawled out onto his stomach. His back muscles are tight, and I take a moment to drink in his shirtless appearance before peering over to silence the constant vibrating on his nightstand. A familiar name lights up his phone, *Jack Sterling*. It's 9:40 on a Friday morning, and we're still on break for Thanksgiving. What could he possibly be calling him for? I check my phone, but I have no missed calls from him, so why is he personally reaching out to Paxton?

That unsettling feeling becomes present in my stomach once again, the same one that appeared when he spilled about his ex. *Are there more secrets?* Before I can allow myself to dwell on the scenarios I'm creating in my head, I slide out of bed and into my clothes from yesterday.

I shoot Lauren a text, and she responds back, letting me know that she and Dillon are having breakfast with Payton and Preston in the kitchen. After brushing my teeth and taming my hair, I walk in and greet everyone with a half-smile, hopeful that no one heard the events that took place last night.

There's a breakfast spread laid out on the island with charcuterie boards full of pancakes, waffles, bagels, fruit, and jellies. Another board contains all types of eggs, sausage patties and links, as well as strips of bacon. Bottles of different flavored juices are stacked behind the boards, accompanied by empty crystal glasses. It smells heavenly.

Payton gestures to the array of foods. "Help yourself, girly. I'm sure you need it after last night." My cheeks instantly become flushed, and embarrassment consumes me. "I imagine you're feeling just as hungover as the rest of us," she finishes with a low groan.

Oh, thank God. The tension in my body eases, and I grab myself a plate.

"Like death," I lie. I'm tired, but not because of the alcohol, though I won't admit that out loud.

Scanning over the contents, I choose scrambled egg whites, a few pieces of fruit, and two slices of avocado, then I fill a glass with ice and pour in my orange juice. Making healthy choices has been harder lately, especially with all the sugar and carbs tempting me. But in order to get back on track, I have to be smart about my eating. I secure a spot at the island next to Lauren and begin eating my breakfast. A shirtless Paxton rolls into the room, and he makes his way over to me, pressing his lips to the side of my head. The taught muscles of his stomach flex against my back, and my insides turn to putty.

"Dude, my fiancée is in this kitchen," Dillon jokes, causing an eruption of laughter.

Lauren nudges his shoulder and places a kiss on his jaw. "You know I only have eyes for you, babe," she assures him with a wink.

Paxton roams around the island, packing his plate full of food and grabs himself a bottle of water, taking the bar stool next to me. He sneaks me a glance while eating, grinning with that charming smile of his. I return his gesture with a smile, but questions are resurfacing as to why our boss is contacting him. Surely, it's nothing, right?

"What are your plans for the day," he asks, interrupting my thoughts once again. Besides bringing Lauren and Dillon to the airport this evening, the only other thing I have planned is my session with Dr. Reynolds, but he doesn't need to know about that.

I shrug. "Nothing specific. They have to be at the airport by seven, so we'll probably just hang out until then." Only Lauren knows where I'll be for that hour, so I can't invite Paxton over or else he'll have questions about my disappearance. "What about you?"

He continues eating his breakfast, only stopping to answer my question. "Was thinking about going to shoot some hoops with Max and Preston. Dillon, you wanna join?"

Lauren and I direct our attention to Dillon. I can tell he so desperately wants to go, but he waits for Lauren's approval. She rolls her eyes but gives him the permission he was seeking.

"Just don't be late," she scolds with a hint of laughter. He nods and slings his arm over her shoulder, pulling her into his side.

Everyone finishes breakfast, and Lauren and I help Payton clean up the kitchen while the guys chat amongst themselves. It was the least we could do since they picked up last night.

"Is your mom still asleep," I ask Payton.

"Oh, no. She had to work today, so she made breakfast then went in." She's loading the dishwasher and I'm wiping down the countertops while Lauren sweeps the floor. "She did tell me to say goodbye to you both, and that she can't wait to do this again."

I give her my best comforting smile and continue to finish off the counters.

Once everything is taken care of, Paxton walks us out to his car. We all hop in, and he backs out of the driveway, heading towards the highway. The drive seems shorter today than it was yesterday, which I'm chalking up to the nerves that were running through my entire body.

Arriving at my apartment, I open the door and lift my seat forward, letting Lauren and Dillon exit from the back. Paxton steps out of the car and motions for me to go to him. I slowly walk around the front of the car until I'm standing in front of him. He grips my waist then slides his hands around, connecting them at the small of my back. I peer my eyes up at him through my lashes, melting when I see that sexy grin of his.

"I want to see you again. Tonight, preferably." His demanding tone does something unexplainable to me, and just like every other time, I can't refuse.

"Okay," I say quietly. "I'll let you know when I get back from the airport."

He cups either side of my face and kisses me, deep. Before it escalates, I break our connection.

"Make sure he's back by five, and not a minute later," I lecture as I direct my finger to him in a teasing manner.

He chuckles and nods his head. "Yes ma'am."

Chapter 33
Paxton

I've Never Been Good at This

The rec center was only fifteen minutes from Macy's apartment, so Dillon and I didn't get much conversation in. My phone, however, wouldn't stop going off. This is the fourth time Jack Sterling has called me in the short drive to the gym and the seventh time since this morning.

"Do you need to get that," Dillon asks before I silenced it once again. "Whoever it is seems very persistent."

It isn't lost on me that he's implying something heavier, like I'm ignoring it because I don't want him to see the name on my screen. Although he doesn't know Macy all that well, he's playing the protective brother-in-law, which I can't be mad about. She deserves to have someone else in her corner other than Lauren, and well, me. I want nothing more than for her to be surrounded by people who love her, and that's why I wanted her over for Thanksgiving. I wanted to show her what having a real family is like, and I so desperately hope that one day, she will be part of mine forever. The thought makes me smile for a moment but is quickly derailed by yet another call from Jack.

"He can wait," I say coolly. "It's just my boss, and I'm off the clock. Plus, we've got some hoops to shoot. I don't feel like thinking about work." Dillon nods and steps out of the car once I put it in park. "Max and Preston are inside warming up if you want to head in there." I tipped my chin toward the side door that leads straight to the court. "I'll meet you in there in a sec."

Again, he nods, and jogs up the sidewalk and through the glass door. I pull my phone out of my pocket and dial Jack's number, hoping he wouldn't pick up, but sure enough, he answers on the second ring.

"Why the fuck haven't you been answering my calls?"

I am well aware of his temper, but I'm not going to let him get to me. The thing about Jack Sterling is that he always gets his way, and he never plays fair. He's a businessman who's *very* good at his job. Once upon a time, I respected him and his work ethic. I admired the way he could step into a courtroom and command everyone's attention without so much as a single word. The way he protected his clients, winning every case, is what I dreamed of doing. *He* is who I aspired to be as a lawyer. At least, he used to be, until I learned what he was really like behind the scenes. I have spent a lot of time with him outside of the courtroom over the years, but never as his intern, until the past few months. There was a lot to uncover, and man, did I underestimate the depths.

"I've been busy," I say, returning his snide attitude. "It's the day after Thanksgiving. I'm with my family."

"Busy with your family or my other intern?" His tone is very much suggesting what he already knows, but it's not his business. What I do outside of his office has nothing to do with him.

"What do you want, Jack?" My patience is wearing thin at this point. I don't have time to sit here and play games with him. Not today, or any other day for that matter. I don't even know why I've been fighting for this position so hard. I've come to the realization that I don't even want it anymore. Not if it means I have to keep answering to him. But I'm reminded once again that I'm doing it for Macy, so that she doesn't ever have to experience this side of him.

"You need to come into the office tonight. We have shit to discuss." The statement is non-negotiable, I know that much. No matter what plans I have going on, it's him who controls my whereabouts. I am tired of the blackmail, but what other choice do I have? I can't let Jack destroy my life the way my ex almost did.

"Tonight? Really? This can't wait until Monday? You know, during business hours?"

Anger roars to life inside of me. I'm fuming, ready to just say "fuck it" and let him throw me to the wolves. Because honestly, having my secret out in the open might finally set me free. But then again, it would destroy my future as a lawyer, and my career is the only thing I have left.

"Don't get smart with me, boy. You have too much to lose. I *own* you. Don't you forget that. Be at the office at eight."

And with that, he hangs up. I'm livid. I want to punch something, but nothing is within reach other than a brick wall, and I'm not that stupid. I shove my phone into my pocket and run into the gym before I can think about it any further. The only way I can release my anger at this point is to play ball, even if I suck at it.

―――

We play two on two, Max and Preston against Dillon and me. Unfortunately for Dillon, I never did get better at basketball over the years, but that never stopped me from having a good time. He passes me the ball and I go for a three-pointer. The ball leaves my hands, gliding through the air, only for it to hit the rim and bounce off.

I curse under my breath and give him a shrug, "Sorry man, I've never been any good at this."

We both laugh it off. Dillon regains the ball and slams it right into the hoop. He's much better than I am, so I'm thankful he's carrying the team on his shoulders.

When I look at the clock, I see it's already 3:30. My t-shirt is soaked through, and the sweat in my hair matches the sweat on my back. Dillon and I take a break to rehydrate while we sit on the bench.

"So, how long have you and Lauren been together?" Small talk seems like the easiest way to deflect from talking about my poor basketball skills.

"Four years this past August. We met at Freshman orientation at UCLA. I thought she was the most beautiful girl I had ever seen, but she didn't even look my way after that first weekend." He laughs.

I know that feeling all too well. Even if I didn't directly ask for Macy's attention, she was very focused and barely noticed me until we started working together on this case.

"I spent the better part of my freshman and sophomore year doing whatever I could to get her attention," he continues.

"So, what did it for her then?"

"Lauren likes grand gestures. She's not interested in small talk. I followed her around campus like a lovesick puppy, always trying to sneak conversation in when I could, but she was very short with me and never seemed to want to hold anything beyond a few words," he admits.

I don't know why that takes me by surprise, but it does. I guess because Macy and I have never had any issues communicating. Things with us are always light and fun. Although sassy and sarcastic, Macy makes conversing easy, even if she is constantly insulting me and bruising my ego.

"Finally, the start of our junior year, something inside me snapped. I wanted her so bad, dude. I *had* to have her. I don't know that I went about it the right way, but she was sitting at a table with her sorority sisters in the middle of the campus cafeteria, and I stood on their table."

"You didn't." I dare.

"Oh, I did. I confessed my feelings for her to the entire student population there that day. Then I hopped off the table, grabbed her face between my hands and placed the biggest kiss I could manage on her lips before striding straight out of the door without another word."

I lose it. I can't help but laugh as the scene plays out in my head. I give him a playful swat on the arm.

"Talk about a story to tell the grandkids, huh?" I tease. The smile I'm wearing falters for a second, thinking how Macy and I don't really have a meet cute. I'm not a hopeless romantic or anything, but there is nothing significant about the way we met. I didn't do anything spectacular to woo her. And for whatever reason, that makes me feel slightly guilty, like maybe I'm not doing enough for her. Dillon brings me back to with his answer.

"Ha, yeah. She's it for me; she has been since the day I laid eyes on her. I couldn't propose to her soon enough, but also didn't want to freak her out, ya know?"

I nod. In fact, I do know. I know exactly what he means because I, too, feel like that about a certain future-sister-in-law of his. I had my fun over the years after my engagement ended, but Macy is the one for me. I've known it since our very first non-date back in June. I want her for the rest of my life. I am finally ready to admit to myself that I love this girl. I am *in love* with this girl. And it's only a matter of time before I need her to know it too.

―――

We play two more rounds of ball before I need to take Dillon back to Macy's. I stop at our favorite taco joint to grab us all a quick dinner, then we head to the apartment.

Before Dillon opens the door, he turns to me, a wary expression on his face. "Are you serious about her?" He asks as if he's known her all her life and wants me to assure him that I wasn't about to hurt his own sister.

I don't hesitate, not even for a second. "I am," I promise. "I'm more sure about her than anything else in my life. But like you said, it's hard to be honest about stuff like that without scaring her."

I can see the understanding on his face, but I know he believes me. "Must be a Callahan thing," he jokes. "I know I don't have a firm foot to put down, seeing as I just met her, but she's my fiancée's sister, and I'll protect her all the same. Because hurting Macy means hurting Lauren, and that won't sit well with me."

I like Dillon. He's a good guy, and I absolutely understand where he's coming from. I'm glad Macy will have him in her life for the long-haul, and I only hope I will too. He claps me on the shoulder.

"You're a good dude, I know that much, and I trust that you'll treat her how she deserves. But if I'm being honest, it's you I worry about. She's dealt with a lot, and Lauren says it's clouded her perception of love. Just be careful."

That bit of information gains my attention. It's a full circle moment for me, bringing me back to the realization that the girl I want to spend my life with has a dark past. She's still as mysterious to me as she was almost six months ago.

What don't I know about you, Macy Callahan?

Chapter 34
Paxton

Baked Ziti, or Gym Socks?

We all sit around the coffee table in the living room while we eat our tacos—Lauren and Dillon on the couch, Macy and I on the floor across from them. *Thirty Minute Meals with Rachel Ray* is on the TV. She's cooking chicken marsala in this episode, one of my favorites. Sometimes I forget how much I love to cook until I watch someone else do it. Both of my parents are great cooks, and I'm the only one who liked to help in the kitchen when I was growing up, so I learned a lot.

"Hey, Mace. Remember that time you were thirteen and tried recreating her baked ziti, but it ended up tasting like old gym socks?" Lauren snorts. "I think that's the *only* dish you've ever made for us that scarred my taste buds."

I try to picture what Macy was like at thirteen. Probably still just as beautiful as she is now, but less damaged; more youthful and livelier. I wonder if she had a glow to her that somehow faded over time. I try to picture her walking down the hallways in school, guys constantly raking their eyes over her as she passed by. I know I would have. She's gorgeous.

Then I try to imagine her at home, standing in the kitchen, cooking. Did she cook with her mom just like I did, or was she self-taught through Food Network? So many questions I want answers to. Macy interrupts my thoughts when she responds to Lauren, and I intently listen, hoping for a glimmer of information.

"Oh, I remember alright. I think the cheese was bad, but I didn't check it before I cooked." She scrunches her nose up in memory of what I assumed was an awful smell. "I've never used an ingredient without checking the expiration date again."

They both laugh in unison, and it's quite a sight, seeing them both look so happy together. I hate that her sister has to leave because I know Macy misses having her around. As much as I try to keep her company, I can't fill the void of the only family she has.

"I think that's what you were making for dinner the night you—"

"Lauren." Macy cuts her off and her eyes meet her sister's with a sinister glare that the devil himself would be afraid of. "Memory lane is officially closed." She says it with so much conviction that the air suddenly feels thick.

Lauren's gaze flits, as if she's about to reveal some big cinematic secret. Macy folds her arms over her chest, her eyes wandering, thoughts drifting miles away. There she goes, shutting down again, leaving me completely in the dark.

"You should go get your bags. We have to leave shortly." And on that note, she gathers the mess from the table and walks into the kitchen. I remain seated, contemplating my next move, but ultimately decide to follow her. When I go to dispose of my trash, she tries to walk past me, so I hook her elbow with my hand, reeling her back.

"Are you good?" *Really, Paxton? Are you good? Not, are you okay? Not, what's going on? Not, I'm here if you need me, just "are you good?" Smooth.*

Her eyes meet mine, but her face gives away nothing. No hint of emotion whatsoever.

"Fine," she states matter-of-factly, but I'm not buying it.

Lauren struck a nerve with whatever memory she brought up, so I know she's not *fine*. I also have a sister and know the universal word *fine* is a lie in girl language. It means you're feeling like shit but avoiding it.

"I have to go."

She releases her arm from my grip and pulls away, leaving me standing alone in the kitchen with my thoughts. I don't know why I ever thought we'd get past this stage of secrecy. The woman is fucking infuriating. I should just take Dillon's warning and run now; get out before I'm in too deep.

And that's when I laugh at myself. Because who am I kidding? I'm already in the trenches.

It's six by the time we all go our separate ways; Macy is heading to the airport, and I'm heading home to shower and change before my meeting with Satan. I feel particularly anxious about this one-on-one because I don't know what else we could possibly need to cover that we haven't already. He hasn't mentioned a break in the case, so what is this about?

I pull up to his office and walk in without making my presence known. Jack is sitting at his desk, feet resting on the top, legs crossed at his ankles. He has a stack of papers in his hands, notes from the case I'm assuming. His brow is furrowed as if he's in deep thought. There are black rings around his eyes, indicating he probably hasn't slept in days, maybe even weeks. And how could he? One of his daughters is gone, and the other is on trial for her murder. Jack may be a lot of things, but he's always been a good father, that much I know. His world revolved around those girls—it always has—as long as I've known them.

Without prompting, I sink down in the seat in front of his desk. "Well?" I'm not beating around the bush tonight. I don't want to be here in the first place, and I'm furious that I had to cancel my plans to see Macy, not that it seemed like she minded. In fact, I think she was grateful that I couldn't come by because it gave her an out to the conversation she knew we'd have.

"We need to prove Wyatt is guilty or else Jade is going to plead insanity." The words strike me hard in the chest. She doesn't even have any history of mental illness, not that I'm aware of anyway. I know she's crazy, but I didn't think she'd been clinically diagnosed. The first part of that statement? *We need to prove Wyatt is guilty.* If he *is* guilty, it would eventually come to the surface. If he *is* guilty, why the hell is Jade even thinking about pleading insanity? It's not like she's doing it as a favor. Maybe she really *is* guilty, and her conscious is finally hitting her. "I can't lose *both* of my daughters, Paxton."

I sit there with my thoughts for a moment before responding, trying to figure out how to have this conversation without it being a conflict of interest. Although I'm pretty sure it's a little too late for that.

My heart starts racing at the question I'm about to ask, and I'm not even sure I want his answer, but I need to ask anyway. "Do you think she did it?"

I watch as his face falters. He removes his feet from the desk and plants his elbows down instead, hanging his head in his hands. He rubs his temples, the way he always does when he's stressed, and I think I know what he's concluding before he even speaks.

His daughters were complete opposites. Josie was bright and kind. She was very loveable and sincere and could light up a room the second she stepped foot inside. She had that way about her, and I think Jade envied that.

Jade had to work hard to make people like her. She and Josie may have had the same face, but their personalities were like oil and water. Jade could be all the things Josie was, but it always seemed forced. And maybe that's because she was bitter towards her sister, but now that I think about it, maybe she really did have something scary going on inside that head of hers. When I met Jade in high school, I got to really know her. She was jagged at first. Honestly, she was a real bitch, but I later learned it's because she always felt compared to her sister.

Jade opened up to me over time, and I understood why she constantly felt inferior to Josie. I couldn't argue that her sister was easily likeable, but I'm a fixer. For whatever reason, I was attracted to Jade in a way that I wasn't attracted to Josie. I don't know if it was because she felt like a project I could work on, or if it was because she was a challenge.

Jack groans, pulling me from memory lane. "If I say I'm unsure, does that make me a terrible father?"

I can tell that answer hurts him to say. This is the most vulnerable I've ever seen him. The love he had for his girls was unmatched. He'd do anything for them, even if it meant trying to prove a possibly innocent man guilty for the sake of saving his daughter.

"You loved her once. What is your perception?"

I'm not expecting that question. I hadn't really let my mind wander there before because he's right—I did love her once. I loved her for years. Hell, I almost married the damn girl, so my judgment isn't black and white. Even after the fire incident, I still couldn't bet my life on a possible verdict for her.

I let out a sigh as I drop my head. "I don't know, Jack. The girl I got down on one knee for is not the same girl sitting in that holding cell."

His expression confirms I'm right, and he knows that. Jade had gone off the deep end a few times since I'd known her, but she somehow always found her way back to solid ground. This time, I'm not so sure. After I ended our engagement, she lost her mind, and I wasn't there to pull her back to safety like I always did. So, there's no telling what she was capable of.

"I can't let my mind go to the possibility that she's guilty. I have to believe with all my heart that she wouldn't do something so cruel, especially to her own flesh and blood." His eyes brim with tears, and I finally get a glimpse of the man who almost became my father-in-law. The man who protected me on the scariest night of my life. Not the man who blackmailed me into working on this case. "Sylvia and I knew she had problems, but nothing to this extent. We sent her to therapy. She spent time in an institution, but she always seemed to come out better."

I want to comfort him because I know he's mourning the loss of not only one, but two daughters, even if one is still alive. But nothing I can say will make this situation any easier. The truth is, *someone* had taken away his little girl way too soon, and nothing will bring her back. And if Jade really was the reasoning behind that, I don't know if her parents will ever recover.

"I wish I had answers for you. I really do. But I'm just as lost as you are." I shake my head, carefully treading my next words. "Jade was everything to me for a long time. She was difficult to crack, but once I got to know her, she was fun and caring. She didn't care for many things, but the things she did love, she was passionate about. I loved that about her. Had you asked me six years ago if I thought she was capable of something like this, I would've gone to bat for her in a heartbeat. But you know as well as I do, that she and Josie had their ins and outs. They rarely got along." I pause for a moment, then continue. "We're both adults here, Jack. Think logically about the situation, and before you throw blame on Wyatt, who loved your other daughter something serious, make sure you're accusing him for the right reasons."

Those words feel so heavy, like I just came to the conclusion for him. His eyes are now devoid of any emotion. He stares blankly at the wall behind me until he closes his eyes and rests his head on the back of his large, leather chair. I don't know what's going through his mind at this point, but when he lifts his gaze back up to me, all that leaves his mouth is, "You can go now."

So that's what I do. I stand up and walk out without a second thought.

Chapter 35
Macy

My Safe Place

It's midnight, yet I can't sleep. I've been lying in bed, staring at my ceiling for the better part of two hours. Truthfully, I was thankful to be alone tonight, but the loneliness started creeping in about ten minutes ago, and all I want to do is call Paxton. It's a weird feeling, wanting to be alone, yet wanting to be close to someone at the same time. I've gotten used to his presence, but I'm too stubborn to ask for it when I need it most. That's the thing about being independent. You learn not to need people. You learn to depend on yourself—and only yourself—because you don't want to burden anyone else. But pride is a scary thing. It can take you into the deepest depths of darkness in a split second, and I am so damn tired of being prideful. I'll never admit this to her, but I miss Lauren so much, and I didn't want her to leave. This past week has been so good for my soul. It helped me heal, even just for a little while, and I didn't realize how much I needed that until I watched her walk through the terminal to head back to her own life. I felt empty, and I desperately need to be in good company, so I break down and send Paxton a text.

> Are you awake?

Five minutes pass, and my phone finally lights up.

PAXTON
> I am now. Is everything okay?

> Sorry, I didn't mean to wake you. Go back to sleep. I'll be fine.

PAXTON
> I'm coming over. See you in twenty.

I lock my phone and roll over onto my side. There's never been any question that Paxton cares about me, but the way he's willing to drop everything just to come to me makes my chest ache. The more he does for me, the more he proves himself, the harder I fall for him. If I didn't know any better, I'd think that maybe I'm in love with him, and that scares the hell out of me. I shouldn't love him; I can't, but I also can't stop myself. I feel safe when I'm with him—happy even—and I crave him when I'm not with him.

The door to Paxton's car shuts, and I can hear him lock it from outside my window. I hop out of bed and check my reflection in the mirror. I'm wearing an oversized U of C t-shirt and a pair of underwear. I pull my hair out of its bun and the curls fall down my shoulders and around my face. Then I swipe my glasses on my face before heading to the living room.

A soft knock sounds, and I slowly open the door to find Paxton with a sleepy smile on his face. His hair is disheveled, making him look extremely sexy, and he has day old stubble surrounding his jawline. The black crew neck he's wearing clings to every muscle on his torso, and he's got on those damn gray sweatpants. *Fuck.* Heat flashes through me just looking at him. The way my body reacts to the sight of him is just sad, but I don't mind it one bit.

"Shit," he says in almost a whisper. His tongue swipes his bottom lip as his eyes roam my body. A flutter erupts in my stomach and a smile stretches across my face. He takes it upon himself to close the space between us and shuts the door behind him. His hands meet my waist and his forehead rests against mine. "Did I ever tell you how sexy you look in a tee and those glasses?"

I shrug. "Not lately," I say with a wink as I place my arms around his neck.

"Well, you do."

He pulls me closer, his erection grazing my stomach, and my lips part on command. A small breath escapes me, and Paxton's mouth is instantly on mine. His tongue quickly slips into my mouth, playing twister with my mine, and suddenly, I need him more than ever. I stand on my tiptoes and kiss him harder. He groans then grabs two handfuls of my ass and effortlessly lifts me up off the ground. My legs immediately wrap around his waist as he carries me to my bedroom, never breaking our connection. I fist his hair, growing hungrier by the second, but the minute he lays me on my back, he pulls away. His eyes bore into mine while hovering over me.

"Talk to me," he pleads. *Moment over.*

I don't want to talk. All I want to do is push him off me and ask him to leave. At least that's what my head keeps telling me to do. My heart wants him to stay; to hold me until I fall asleep. And my body? It wants him on top of me, underneath me, inside of me. The question is, which one do I choose to follow? I close my eyes for a moment, releasing a long, drawn-out breath. When I open my eyes again, I slowly push him off until he's lying next to me, then I get out of my bed and head towards my door.

"Macy, where are you going?"

I turn to him. "Come on."

I walk out of my room and make my way to the kitchen. I grab two beers out of the fridge and hand one to Paxton, motioning him to the couch. He takes a seat against the arm, legs spread towards the other end, and I sit between them, my back to his chest.

Paxton places a kiss to the side of my head as I lean into him, and I take a swig of the beer in my hand. I feel his arms wrap around me and hug me a little too tight.

"I… can't… breathe," I manage to get out. A laugh falls from his mouth and he releases me, tipping his beer back. I tilt my head enough to place a soft kiss on his jaw. "Thank you for being here."

"Thank you for letting me be here. I wouldn't want to be anywhere else."

The aching in my chest is back. He's going to make it impossible to give him up at the end of this. All I want to do is lie here in his arms forever. I've only been his for two months, but I don't think any length of time will be enough. Not with him. Four months, that's all I have left, and then it's over for us. A tear escapes and slides down my cheek, so I quickly brush it away. But in true Paxton fashion, he notices.

"Hey, what's wrong?" He turns my face toward his, and suddenly I can't find the words to speak. "Please talk to me, Macy. I'm tired of doing this. I'm done with the runarounds. I want to be here for you, but you need to let me."

With every word, my heart shatters a little more. *I'm going to hurt you. I love you, but I can't be with you. I want you, for the rest of my days, but I don't know how to do this.* How do I tell him that? I can't, so I don't.

Instead, I only tell him the half-truth. "I just miss Lauren, that's all. I didn't realize how lonely I'd been until she came. And now, she's gone again." I bring the bottle to my lips again, drinking half the contents with one big gulp. Then I finish it off with one more large sip.

"Woah, woah. Slow down there, boozy." He jokes. I just roll my eyes and remove myself from the couch. I lean down until I'm eye level with him and close enough where he can feel my breath on his lips.

"I'm going to get another," I whisper. Then I slide my tongue across his bottom lip and hear him groan as I walk to the kitchen.

I bend over to pull another beer from the fridge, and when I shut the door, Paxton is standing in the doorway. I don't even get a chance to open my beer before he grabs me and lifts me onto the counter, causing me to shriek with laughter. His eyes are blazing with lust, and a prominent throbbing increases between my legs. His lips meet my neck, kissing and sucking each exposed piece of skin. My head falls back in pleasure as I wrap my hands in his hair.

Breathlessly, I ask, "I thought you wanted to talk?"

He pulls back from my neck for a brief moment and moves in closer. "Who's the tease now?" His teeth find my bottom lip, and he sucks on it, before releasing me. My breath hitches, and the friction between us is so hot that I might catch fire if I don't find a release soon.

I grip the bottom of my shirt and raise it over my head, tossing it to the side to expose my fully naked body from the waist up. His eyes go wide, sucking in a sharp breath, and I can't help but torture him a little more.

With my hand still in his hair, I pull him toward me until my lips reach his ear. "Still me," I whisper as I tug on his ear lobe with my mouth.

"Jesus Christ."

He slowly lowers my panties and drops them to the floor. His hands grip my waist, dragging me close to him until our bodies are flush, my legs on either side of him as he stands between them. Our lips connect in a hot and heavy embrace, and I peel Paxton's shirt off while he drops his sweatpants and steps out of them. He breaks our kiss momentarily to swipe a condom from his pocket then rolls it on. Once he positions himself back between my legs, his lips meet mine again. I scoot towards the edge of the counter where Paxton's hard length meets my entrance. In no time, he's inside of me, and I try to stifle the moans erupting from my mouth as he thrusts himself to the hilt.

I adjust myself so that I'm leaning back, resting on my palms. Paxton leans forward and snakes his right arm around my back. His left hand is massaging my breast as he kisses from my chest up to my shoulder and then my neck while still driving into me. My vision is starting to blur with the rise of my orgasm.

"Paxton," I pant. "I'm close." A deep moan escapes his lips, and I feel myself tipping over the edge. "Please, Paxton," I beg.

His movements become quicker and deeper, then I feel his fingers graze over my sensitive bud.

"Fuck, you're taking me so well, baby."

He grips my waist one last time and deepens inside me until we both hit our climax. I sit up and lean into him, my body going limp. Sweat is rolling down our bodies, and my hair is clinging to my neck and shoulders. Paxton tilts my chin up to meet his gaze and sweeps a feather-like kiss over my lips.

"Let's get you cleaned up." In one swift motion, he lifts me from the counter and carries me to the bathroom.

We fuck one more time in the shower for good measure and then drop to my bed, exhausted. Our naked bodies are tangled in the sheets, but sleep is on the horizon, so I snuggle up to Paxton and he falls fast asleep. Me, on the other hand? I lay there for another hour, coming to the realization that this man is my safe place, and these next four months are going to be hell on my heart.

Chapter 36
Paxton

Head over Heels

It's been nearly three weeks since my meeting with Jack. I haven't heard from him, and there hasn't been any new news regarding Jade and her impending plea. I'm hoping, whatever the verdict, the right person ends up behind bars. The justice system can be cruel and unfair at times, but we, as lawyers, do our very best to make sure our clients come out on top. I just hope Wyatt's lawyer knows what he's up against.

Finals are approaching this week, and my focus needs to be on passing, so I shake the details of the case off my mind. The next hearing isn't until the beginning of February anyway.

I'm ready to enjoy my winter break with Macy and my family. That is, if she agrees to join us. Occasionally, she's been hanging out with Payton in her spare time, so maybe that'll give me an edge when I ask her to be my plus one on the trip. But for now, I need to get my ass out of my car and head to class. I catch a glimpse of Macy's long, auburn hair towards the building. She's wearing a pair of navy dress pants with her long-sleeve white button-up top tucked in, and a skinny tan belt. She looks like heaven.

I open my door and hop out, running to catch up with her. I walk in stride next to her and place my arm around her shoulder, pulling her to my side and pressing a kiss to her temple.

"Hey, beautiful. I've missed you."

A curve appears on those perfect lips, showing off my favorite smile of all time.

She nudges me. "You just saw me two days ago, goof."

My hand immediately shoots over my heart as if she's wounded me. I earn an eye roll for that one, followed by a subtle laugh. Something about the sound of her laugh always sends a rush through my stomach. I'll never get tired of that sound for as long as I live.

"So, does that mean you didn't miss me, then?" I cock my eyebrow and shoot a mischievous look her way. Her hand playfully shoves the side of my head as she bites her bottom lip. Now all I can think about is kissing her. She catches me off guard by intertwining her fingers in mine as we walk.

"Someone's needy today," she teases with a half grin.

I shrug. "No shame in my game. I need you, always." Maybe that's a bit forward, but I'm done holding back how I feel about her. I'm so ready to tell her everything, but I need the timing to be just right.

We stop just short of the classroom. While everyone else is filing in, I lean my back against the wall and pull her close to me. When her eyes are on mine, I work up enough courage to ask her the question that's been burning a hole in my tongue. "What are you doing for Christmas?"

"Paxton, can we discuss this later? We have class." Her voice is just above a whisper.

"Come to Utah with me."

"What?" Her puzzled look is fucking adorable.

"Utah. It's our annual family vacation. Come with me," I repeat.

She checks the watch sitting on her left wrist, and her eyes dart to our classroom. She hates being late, but I'm not letting her go until she agrees. That beautiful hazel gaze meets mine once more.

"Okay."

Well, that took considerably less convincing than I expected. I had prepared myself for kicking and screaming and a hell of a lot of excuses, but much to my surprise, I don't need to bust out any of my rehearsed negotiations.

"Okay? Just like that?"

"Yes. Now can we get to class, please? You know I hate being the last one in there."

I nod and guide her through the door. Sure enough, we're the last two to be seated.

"Nice of you to join us, Ms. Callahan," Dr. Prelow announces. Macy's cheeks blush red, and she shoots me a warning glare with dagger eyes. "You too, Mr. Meyers."

I salute him, acknowledging that I heard him but couldn't care less about his attempt at embarrassing me. I'm too full of pride to care because my girl just agreed to spend an *entire week* with me—*without* a tantrum I might add.

"Since you're late, Ms. Callahan, do you mind telling me what the mens rea of murder is?"

"Gladly." Her tone is sarcastic, as usual. "The mens rea of murder is the intention to kill or intention to cause great bodily harm." She continues. "And if you're looking for examples, evidence of intention to kill is a premeditated attack that requires the use of a weapon, causing multiple wounds, whereas the intention to cause GBH is the act of injuring someone just to carry out a crime. This can be in the form of stabbing, breaking bones, or just fist-fighting."

Everyone starts clapping, and even Dr. Prelow can't help but join in. That was fucking impressive.

My dick is instantly hard. This girl has the ability to turn me on just by her *words*. That's a new one for me. She sneaks a look at me over her shoulder, a grin as wide as ever, and my chest tightens while my stomach is filled with a swirling sensation.

I'm in love with her. *Head over heels, completely and utterly in love with her.*

Monday, December 19 - 4:00pm

Taylor opens the door to her office, and I stride right on in with a smile plastered across my face. She follows and takes a seat in her usual spot across from me. I take it upon myself to spread out on the couch, my head on one end, my feet on the other, crossing them at my ankles. My hands are resting under my head as I just lay there in pure bliss.

"By all means, make yourself comfortable." She jokes. "But for real, what's going on with you?"

"I love her, Tay." I can't wipe the stupid, goofy grin off my face, and I don't want to. "I'm finally happy again."

I thought for sure Taylor would celebrate this win with me. She's seen me at my lowest, so she knows how badly I've been waiting to feel like this since I broke things off with Jade. But when I look over at her, apprehension is all I see.

"You okay over there?"

"Uh, yeah. I'm good," she lies. "That's great, P. There's nothing more I want for you than for you to be happy. Just promise me, you'll be careful."

Why does everyone keep telling me that? What does everyone know that I don't?

"Not long ago you were telling me to put myself out there, to tell her how I feel and exactly what I want, and now you're telling me to be careful?" The bitterness in my tone is apparent, but I'm slightly pissed off. "Is there something you're not telling me?"

Her face reveals an insulted expression. "No, there's nothing. Is it so wrong for me to want to protect my friend?" She releases a low breath. "You've been through so much, and I just don't want to see you get hurt again."

"And you think Macy is going to be the one to hurt me?" I know she's difficult. I know she has a past that I have yet to dive into, but who she is when she's with me is who I've fallen in love with. Where she came from, what she's gone through — none of it matters. She makes me better. I like the person I am when I'm with her, and *that's* what I care most about.

"That's not what I'm implying. All I'm saying is, it's still early in your relationship. Have you broken down her walls yet? Because if not, you still have so much to learn about her." Taylor fiddles with her pen between her fingers, something I learned she does when she's avoiding things. "Just promise me you'll consider what I'm saying before you rush into anything."

Rush into anything like what?

"I'm not going to up and propose to her if that's what you're indicating. But yeah, I'll take your advice into consideration." I sit up and run a hand through my hair. "Look, I have to go. See you after the holidays?"

"Yeah, sure," she agrees. "I'm leaving town Friday evening to go visit my parents. I'll be gone until the 5th. Can you come on Friday, the 6th at 3:30 instead?"

I stand and nod in agreement then she escorts me to the door, and I leave her office with a shallow wave. My body is buzzing with annoyance.

I had such a great day, and I came here, hoping to bask in that excitement with my friend, yet she was far from enthusiastic about my news. I'll deal with her later, though. All I want to do right now is go see my girl.

> You free for dinner tonight? I'm cooking.

MACY
> That depends. What are you making and are you doing it naked?

> The best damn beef tenderloin you've ever had. And no lmao, I was not planning on it. I'd like to keep my manhood in prime condition.

MACY
> Should I be worried?

> PTSD. That's a conversation for another time. I will remain fully clothed.

MACY
> What a shame. Lucky for you, I'm starving, so I'll make an exception.

> Wow, you're so good to me. Be there at six thirty.

I run to Mariano's to pick up the ingredients for dinner tonight, and then I head to my apartment to shower and change before heading to Macy's. I throw on my black sweats and an old, faded Chicago Bears tee.

After grabbing the grocery bags from my fridge, along with a bottle of wine, I slip on my shoes and make my way to my car. The engine roars to life, and "You're Still the One" by Shania Twain fills my speakers. I smile as the memory of Macy singing in my passenger seat resurfaces. That's the night I told her I had feelings for her. Every day since then has felt so right. It always does with her.

God, I can't wait to see her face.

Once I put my car in park, I grab the bags from the seat

next to me and head inside, taking the elevator to the second floor. I do my signature knock, and the door creaks open.

Macy is standing there, dressed in pink and white striped silk pajamas. Her hair is twisted into a loose braid that hangs over her right shoulder, and she's got her glasses on her makeup-free face showing off those freckles that I love so much. I cross the threshold, and she closes the door behind me.

"This is for you."

She takes the bottle of wine I'm holding out, and I give her a quick kiss on the lips before taking off towards the kitchen.

I preheat the oven and heat a cast iron skillet on the stove while I prepare the meat. First, I tie it up so that it's an even thickness Next, I season it with oregano, parsley, rosemary, salt and freshly cracked pepper, then coat the tenderloin in a garlic butter sauce that I made from scratch.

Macy walks in and pours us each a glass of red wine. She sits herself on the counter next to the stove, watching me do my thing. Even in long-sleeve pjs, she's still sexy as ever.

I take a sip of my wine then continue cooking. Once the pan is searing hot, I place the tenderloin in it, letting it cook for three minutes on each side. A savory aroma fills the air, and Macy's eyes flutter from the delicious smell. There's something I seriously enjoy about watching her watch me in the kitchen.

She finally breaks the silence after her first glass of wine is finished. "So, what did I do to deserve all of this?" Her hand gestures to the spread over the stove.

I decide to whip up some mashed potatoes and broccolini as well. She reaches for the bottle of wine and pours herself another glass, immediately taking a sip.

"Just existing," I say with a shrug and a playful smile. Her cheeks tint a shade darker than normal, and I can't tell if it's from my comment or the alcohol she's consumed. "Can't a boyfriend just do something nice for his girlfriend, just because?"

"He can." She nods. "But no guy has ever gone to the lengths for me like you do. I'm not used to it." Her head dips, losing eye contact with me.

After the beef is finished searing, I place it on a lined baking sheet and stick it in the oven, setting the timer for ten minutes. Then, I walk over to where she's sitting and settle between her legs. Lifting her face to meet mine, I search her eyes. She almost looks sad.

"Well, what are you used to?"

"Not much, honestly." She shrugs and takes two more sips from her glass. At this rate, she's going to be drunk before dinner is ready, but if she keeps spilling information like this, I might not have the decency to stop her. I know that's wrong of me, on more levels than one, but she's finally talking, and I want to know more. "I've never allowed any of my past boyfriends to get too close to me, so I've never put very high expectations on them. Not that I'm holding you to any standards, because I'm not. It's just that you're constantly showing me what I've been missing, and I don't really know what to make of it all."

The fact that she's never been treated like this makes me so damn angry at every guy who's ever been with her. Why wouldn't they want to spoil her and make her happy? I'd do just about anything in the world for her, whether she asks or not.

I lift my hand to her cheek, caressing it with my thumb then gently kiss those perfect lips of hers. "They're fucking stupid for not showing you how you deserve to be treated, Mace. Just know, you'll never have to wonder your worth when you're with me."

She kisses me this time, and we end up making out until the timer beeps on the oven, breaking our focus. I lower the temperature and set the time for another twenty-five minutes.

While we wait, Macy and I remain in the kitchen, consuming the tasty red blend. We're conversing and laughing. Her smile is a sharp white that contrasts against her deep, maroon-stained lips, and my mouth is drawn her to like a moth to a flame. I want so badly to kiss her, but she presses a finger to my lips to stop me.

"What would you like for dessert?" she asks. I'm about to answer 'her,' but she stops me from saying that too. "And before you say, me… don't." She chuckles. "I'll make whatever you want."

I think about it long and hard. I'm not really a sweets kind of guy, but if she's offering, I won't refuse.

"Uh, how about cookies?"

She digs through her pantry and fridge and pulls out everything we need.

"Hope you like chocolate chip."

With a mixing bowl in one hand and the bottle of wine in the other, she gulps down the rest and sets the bowl on the counter. Macy stumbles, and I catch her before she hits the floor. When I lift her back up, she's laughing so hard. She's *definitely* drunk. All I can do is laugh with her.

"Are you sure you're coherent enough to make cookies?" I ask playfully.

"Can I make them? Yes. Will they be edible? Who knows?" Another laugh escapes her mouth.

I stand behind her as she empties all the contents into the bowl and uses a mixing spoon to combine everything. There's flour all over the counter, chocolate chips doused across the floor, but she's enjoying herself too much for her to care.

I swipe some of the flour from the marble and wipe it across her cheek. Her head slowly cranes around until she's staring me dead in the face.

"You… did… not…"

"Oh, but I did."

The next thing I know, homemade cookie dough is flying

from her hand and plops me right in the forehead. *It is war.* Ten minutes later, her kitchen is a disaster. We're sitting on the floor, covered in a sticky mess, laughing so loudly that we were probably disturbing her neighbors. I use my index finger to remove some of the dough from her neck and she grabs my hand, placing my finger in her mouth and slowly sucking the remains off it, finishing the last bit with a 'pop.' I don't know that I've ever been so turned on in my life.

"Macy," I warn, and she bats her eyelashes at me knowingly.

Then the timer notifies us that dinner is finally ready. I sigh as I stand to remove the pan from the oven. All I know is, it's not the tenderloin I'm hungry for anymore.

Chapter 37
Paxton

I'm Not Going Anywhere. Ever

Though I insist we skip dinner and go straight for dessert, Macy suggests otherwise. She pleads starvation, so I give in and make us each a plate, and I cut her meat for her because honestly, I don't trust drunk Macy with a knife.

The kitchen is still a mess, but once she grabs two sparkling waters from the fridge, she plops back down on the floor and puts her back up against the cabinet. She opens both bottles, and I slide down to the ground, sitting across from her and hand her a plate and a fork.

Examining her food, she looks up at me with the most sincere eyes I've ever seen. "You cut up my food for me?"

She looks fucking precious right now, all wide-eyed and thankful. All I want to do is scoop her up and bring her straight to the bedroom, so I can rip all her clothes off and fuck her into tomorrow. But instead, I set my plate next to me and pull her by her thighs so that her legs hang on either side of mine then place a small kiss to her nose.

"Of course, I did. There's no way I'm allowing you to

handle cutlery at a time like this." I chuckle as I gesture to the empty bottle that was once full of wine.

That earns me a hard eye roll and a swat to the shoulder.

"And to think I almost called you a gentleman," she murmurs as she steals a piece of tenderloin off my plate and places it in her mouth. It elicits a moan from her and a shit-eating grin splits across my face. I take pride in a lot of things, but my cooking is one thing I'm always sure of. I try to steal a piece from her plate in return, but she fences me with her fork instead.

"Don't even think about it," she says with a daring glare. "And wipe that smug look off your face. It's not *that* good." The smile tugging at her lips says otherwise.

"Uh huh," I nod. "Keep telling yourself that babe." I take a swig of my water to wash down the contents of my bite.

Macy leans back against the cabinet behind her, picking at her food before taking a few sips of the bubbly liquid in her hand. Her head falls back, and a small chuckle leaves her lips.

I cock my head and lift an eyebrow, thoroughly curious. "What are you laughing at?"

She meets my gaze and studies me briefly before parting her lips, and I stare at the way her tongue sweeps across her bottom lip.

"This. Us. I don't know." She gives me a one shoulder shrug then knocks back the bottle, emptying it.

She absolutely does know, and for someone who doesn't have a filter, she surely loses her voice when it comes to vulnerability. The alcohol she consumed is making her bold, though, so I'm interested to see where this is going. I just sit there silently, waiting for her to continue.

"If I'm being honest, I don't know how to do this." She waves her hand, gesturing between the two of us. "I have zero clue what the fuck I'm doing."

Well, that's not where I thought this was going, and now I'm a little worried. And quite frankly, for the first time in God knows how long, I don't know how to respond. Because the truth is, I don't know what the hell I'm doing either. Nothing has been more than sex for me over the last four years—until now—so I'm still navigating this whole relationship thing.

Formulate a response, Paxton. Say something. Literally anything will do.

"I've never dated anyone for longer than six months," she adds.

I hold the track record for world's longest silence, because I'm an idiot. What do you say to a girl who just admitted she doesn't know what on Earth she's doing with you, then comes out and confesses she's never had a relationship last longer than half a year?

"Well, we're well on our way to surpassing that. Guess I'm the exception huh," is apparently what I decide to say when I open my big, stupid mouth. Now I'd like to crawl in a hole and die because that came out cocky as fuck, and that expression she's wearing does not confirm my assumption one bit.

She steals my drink from my hands and finishes it off before firing back. "It's only been two months, big guy. Don't count yourself out just yet."

Ouch. I feel that hypothetical punch right to my balls. Why only six months? Is that intentional? Or do things just never last that long? But the real question is, does she see this going beyond that? I use this as an opening to be a smart ass, because, why not?

"*Technically,* it's been seven months, if you count all of our non-dates since June." I try not to sound complacent, but I sort of do, just to prove a point. We've spent so much time together over the last few months, and she's still here, so that must mean something. Whether she wants to admit it or not.

"Those don't count," she retorts back. "We were friends. Nothing more."

Mother fucker. How many times is she going to theoretically assault me tonight?

I try my best to mentally ice the wounds.

"Right, right. Because I'm not your type." She nods in agreement, so I knock her down a peg or two just for agreeing with me. "If I recall correctly, you admitted that you classified them as dates in your head well before we started actually dating. So I think that means you like me, and now, you're sitting here on the floor getting drunk and eating dinner with me while still having cookie dough in your hair."

I flash her my best charming smile and she bites her cheek to keep from reciprocating. Then I lean forward and whisper, "Just admit that this right here"—I use my finger and motion between us— "is different, and we can wrap up this conversation so I can bring you to the bedroom and wreck your body."

"Never," she replies, and it comes out a whole lot breathier than I imagine she meant it to.

I place our plates on the floor then wrap one arm around her waist and grab her by the nape of her neck with my other hand until our chests are flush and she's straddling me. My lips are ghosting over hers as her breathing increases, and it's so quiet I'm almost positive I can hear her heart beating wildly against her ribcage.

"Paxton," she whispers faintly, and my cock springs to life at my name on her lips. The way this woman possesses my body is overwhelming but exciting all the same. With one damn word, she ignites every single cell in my body, causing me to lose my self-control. Macy tangles her hands in my hair, and with her forehead to mine, she says, "Kiss me."

And I do. God, do I. My lips cover hers so fast, hot and breathless as she opens her mouth to make room for my tongue. It quickly finds its way to hers, and we're slowly gliding, tangling them together.

She's grinding against my hips, heat unfurling in my belly, and it's taking so much restraint for me to behave;, to give us this moment of passion without stripping her bare.

"I've never wanted anyone the way I want you," I speak

against her mouth. "And I'm not going anywhere, Macy. Ever."

She breaks our contact, peering up at me with those hazel eyes. They hold so much pain and uncertainty that my heart aches for her. All I want to do is wrap her up and hold her for eternity; to let her know that whatever her past holds, I'm here for her, and I'll never let anything bad happen to her ever again. I want her to feel loved in all forms, and to show her how special she truly is because I can tell she doesn't believe it for a second that she's extraordinary.

A lone tear streaks down her cheek and I catch it with my thumb, wiping it away.

"I can't promise you forever, Paxton. I can only promise you right now. And I need that to be enough."

And with those words, my heart shatters.

Chapter 38
Macy

Ugh, Fuck Me

His eyes cloud, tears threatening to spill as he stares at me. My gut wrenches at the sight of him because I know I've destroyed every plan he has conjured up in his head for us. I don't know why I said it, but the words were out before I could take them back. He caught me off guard with his promises of a future where he'll never leave me, but it was never him I was worried about. Until now.

"Please say something."

He lifts me by my hips, lowering me to the floor then stands to his feet. I watch him as he fazes out of my kitchen, but before he makes his exit, he turns to me. "You don't see a future for us, do you?"

My chest constricts, and breathing becomes harder. I feel like the wind has been knocked out of me, like all the breath has been seized from my lungs, and I can't grasp for air. Because here it is, the moment I send every good thing in my life packing. Only this time, it's four months too soon.

I'm not ready to let him go. I don't think I ever will be, but right now, I don't know how to fix this. I don't know what words to say to make him stay. Lying to him about a future I can't guarantee won't do either of us any good.

Instead of an answer, more tears skate down my face, and Paxton looks unsure of his next move. He's hurt, that much I can tell, but he comes to me anyway, because that's the type of person he is. Someone willing to put his own pain aside to make someone else feel whole. And even though I'm broken in so many ways, I've never felt more whole than when I'm with him.

He kneels down next to me, hooking his finger under my chin, forcing my eyes to meet his. "So, what does this mean for us?" His voice is shaky as he speaks, and I can feel my heart ripping in two.

I stop crying long enough to formulate words, though I'm not sure they're all that coherent. "It means I can give you myself—right here and right now. I can promise you that I'm happy with you, and you're the only person I want and need in this very moment." The tears keep falling. "I've been honest with you tonight—more honest than I have been with anyone, but I need you to understand, I am scared. I'm not lying when I say I don't know what the hell I'm doing, because I don't. All I know is I like you, *really* like you, and I'd like to see where it'll go, but at our own pace, without a rushed destination."

He rests his forehead against mine while cupping my face and slowly nods. "Can you be honest with me one more time?" he asks as he holds my gaze.

"Yes." I barely manage.

"Why only six months?"

I inhale a jagged breath, unsure I want to go there. Paxton thumbs both of my cheeks, his eyes bouncing between mine, and I realize he deserves the truth, no matter how hard it is to admit.

"I don't let myself fall in love. If I feel myself getting there with someone, I end it."

The realization of what I have just confessed hits me hard, and I'm terrified he's about to walk away.

But true to his nature, Paxton answers me with another question. "And with us?"

My mind is racing with a million different answers I could give him, but I'm so tired of hiding from my feelings, so I tell him exactly what it is I feel. "I want to try. I'm done running."

His lips come crashing down on mine, and he picks me up off the kitchen floor, guiding my legs around his waist while I wrap my arms around his neck. He eats up the distance from the kitchen to my bedroom and sits me on the edge of the bed while slowly unbuttoning my silk pajama top. Our kisses become more aggressive, filled with desperation, and I lift Paxton's shirt above his head and toss it to the floor. Within seconds, we're completely undressed, and he fishes a condom out of my top drawer next to my bed. Soft kisses land on my lips.

"God, I want you so bad, Macy. So fucking bad." He rolls the condom over the length of him and rocks against my center, falling to his forearms as he hovers over me.

My need for him escalates. The unfulfilled sensation between my legs grows deeper, more heightened, and I grab I fistful of his hair, pulling his lips to mine.

"I want you too, Paxton." Then I repeat his words back to him. "More than I've ever wanted anyone else." Because it's true. Because no one I've ever been with has made me feel the way this man has, and though I can't promise him a future, I know I'm willing to work towards forever with him.

He lowers his lips back to mine, entering me at a slow, torturous pace while kissing me ever so gently. My eyes flutter shut, my back arching as he completely fills me. Paxton drags kisses down my neck, allowing his tongue to coax the length of my throat. I moan in pleasure while he barely slips out of me then back in with a little more force with each thrust.

He grabs both of my hands, reaching them above my

head and intertwining his with mine. His pelvis rocks into me as he pulses inside of me, and I cry out his name when he finally slams into me like he means it.

"Fuck," he whispers. "You feel so good, baby."

I whimper as he picks up his speed, our hips crashing into each other. My orgasm is climbing, and I'm on the brink of falling over the edge when he slows down.

Before I can protest, Paxton rolls me onto my side, tossing my left leg slightly forward. He settles in behind me, lining himself up at my entrance.

"Pax—" I try to protest but am immediately cut off by what happens next.

He enters me from behind, and I fist the sheets at the swift movement. My body is positioned in a way that he fills me up as deep as he can get, causing a delicious friction. He nuzzles his chin in the crook of my neck, feathering breaths down it, causing goosebumps to erupt and possessively drapes his arm over my middle, using me as an anchor to rail me from behind.

"*Oh my God. Yes, yes,*" I pant over and over. "*Please,* Paxton."

"Please, what, baby?" His voice is low, gravelly, the most luscious sound.

"Make me come, *please*," I practically beg.

A groan leaves his mouth, and he slides his hand from my stomach down between my legs until he's circling my clit.

"Tell me this pussy is mine and only mine," he demands.

I don't answer him right away, and he removes his hand. I cry out in protest at the loss, but immediately nod in response to his question.

"I want you say it." He takes my earlobe between his teeth, and I feel the tingling all the way down to my toes. "If you want to come, I suggest you give me what I want."

He pistons his hips one good time, hitting that spot that only he can, and I cave. "Yes." I scream. "It's yours."

Another thrust. "And?"

"And only yours," I admit. "Now *fuck* me."

He resumes pumping into me, and places his fingers back, repeatedly putting pressure on the bundle of nerves at my forefront. My orgasm fully explodes, leaving me crying out in pleasure. His movements slow as he lets me ride out the best sex of my life, and I suddenly feel guilty for not allowing him to come apart with me.

Once he pulls out, he rolls me to my back and settles in between my thighs, trailing kisses along my jaw.

"You're so fucking beautiful, Mace."

He swipes the hair from my forehead and places one kiss between my eyebrows. Then, he stands, disposes of the condom, and heads to the bathroom to grab me a wet washcloth. I follow him in there and turn on the shower instead. I pull the rough cloth from his hands and guide him into the steam-filled shower, pushing him up against the cold tile wall. His hands make their way from my waist, up my sides, coasting both arms, until he's cupping my face.

I close the distance between us, sucking his bottom lip between my teeth, biting him with enough force that he grips the hair at the nape of my neck. Pulling it taught, he tries kissing down my neck, but I quickly put that to rest, no matter how good it feels. I use both of my hands to slam him back into the wall and give him my best *fuck me* glare. He holds his hands up in surrender.

"Good boy," I tease while trailing my hand down his chest and over his rock-solid abs. His muscles tense under my touch and that sends a rush down my spine. His cock is hard as steel, and his eyes widen when I drop to my knees in front of him. Never breaking eye contact, I run my tongue from bottom to top, lapping over his tip. He fists my hair and drops his head back to the tile.

"Jesus fucking Christ," he pants.

Heat pools low in my belly, a spark igniting between my legs at his reaction. So much satisfaction floods me knowing

I'm the one who's making him feel like this. I cup him with one hand, massaging him, and wrap my other hand around his thick length before covering the rest of him with my mouth completely. He moans, and I suck harder and a little faster. His grip on my hair tightens, and a whimper escapes my lips. I flick my tongue on his underside while I continue to suck, my cheeks hollowing.

"*Fucking yes,* baby," he pants. "Right fucking there. Don't stop."

I speed up just a touch more, and he expels his orgasm into the back of my throat. His legs stiffen, and I swallow every last drop of him.

He swiftly lifts me to my feet. With a wicked grin, he lowers in front of me. "I want you to come on my tongue now."

I don't have time to argue. He pins me to the wall, drapes one of my legs over his shoulder and devours me like I'm his last meal, *twice.*

―――

I wake up to my alarm going off at 6:00 am with Paxton still spooning me. It's our last week of classes before Christmas break, and I'd be lying if I said I wasn't excited to spend eight days in a cabin with my boyfriend and his family. I've never enjoyed the holidays because there wasn't much to celebrate. Lauren and I were either alone or with a random babysitter my mom hired.

Though my mom worked an awful lot, presents were few and far in between, so I wasn't a kid who counted down the days until Santa came. I was the one counting down until the holidays were over—my birthday included. This year will be different though, which reminds me, I need to figure out what the hell I'm going to get this man as a gift.

Maneuvering as slowly as possible, I shift out of Paxton's grasp, but he lets out a growl and tries pulling me back to him.

"Come back to bed."

Truth be told, if we didn't have class, I would stay tangled in the sheets with him all day. He smells impossibly delicious, like aftershave and a hint of my charcoal body wash—all rugged and manly. It's intoxicating, and as much as I want to give in, we need to get up and get ready. I place a kiss to his lips and watch as a smile stretches across his face.

"Ugh, if you keep looking so damn adorable, I'm going to make us late," I tease.

"Please do," he dares, and I let out a small chuckle.

We're still completely naked, so I walk over to my dresser and pull on a matching white bra and panties set. Paxton's eyes rake over me as I slip into them, and my body suddenly feels all hot and tingly, my face flushing with a pink tint. Something about the way he watches me hungrily makes me incredibly shy. His gaze never wavers as I pull on my long-sleeved beige body suit and a pair of black business joggers, finishing off the look with an oversized belt, minimal jewelry, and nude heels.

He licks his lips like he's ready to pounce.

"Ugh, fuck *me*," he lets out, and I can't help but grin.

Picking up his boxers from the floor, I toss them at his head, and they hit him square in the face.

"Get up," I demand as I walk into the bathroom to do my hair and makeup. I opt for a smokey eye today to enhance the golden specks around my irises. I curl my hair and pin half of it up in a clip, leaving the bottom half to fall down my back. I swipe on a dark plum lipstick and smile at my reflection. I'm happy, and I look it.

Paxton appears behind me in just his underwear and wraps both arms around my waist, hugging me tightly. The warmth of his body makes me shiver, but in the most comforting way. I love the way he takes hold of me, claims me with his touch.

I'm his, and he's mine.

A broad grin breaks out across his face when he catches my eyes in the mirror, and my chest aches with how fucking beautiful this man is. He's my favorite part of every day, and I want him to know that. He deserves to.

A shy grin graces my lips, and I turn to him. He hooks my chin, tilting it up to meet his gaze, then places a series of small kisses on my lips to keep from messing up my lipstick. He's so perfect it physically hurts, and I just can't believe he chose *me*. I can't stop smiling, which he notices.

"What?" He asks.

I shrug, rising up on my tiptoes to kiss his cheek.

"Just trying to figure out how I hit the boyfriend jackpot."

His cocky little smirk lights up his face. "Consider yourself lucky," he teases back with a quick smack to my butt and a wink. "Now get your ass to the kitchen. I made you coffee."

His wink makes my lady bits run hot, and I'm seriously considering making us late. But like a good girl, I make my way down the hall, and sure enough, Paxton has coffee in two to-go cups waiting for us on the island. If I thought I couldn't possibly fall harder for this man, I was wrong.

"Have a great day, gorgeous" is written on my cup in sharpie.

He emerges from my bedroom in his clothes from last night then proceeds to put on his shoes. He drops a kiss to my forehead, and I hand him his cup.

"I'll see you in a bit," he says before he slips out the door. When it closes, I let a long sigh, coming to the realization that I might want Paxton more than I want the junior partner position. And that terrifies me.

Chapter 39
Macy

I'm Not in Control. Like, at All.

It's finally Friday, Christmas Eve, eve. Exams are finished. Bags are packed. And all I have left to do before we leave is head to my therapy session. Our flight isn't until five this evening, which will put us in Salt Lake City around 8:00 pm.

I'm running out of excuses as to why I can't meet Paxton earlier. *Do I really need to go today? I can just skip. I've been doing just fine, for the most part.* The internal battle between going and canceling has me struggling, but ultimately, I choose the latter. I pull up Dr. Reynold's number and hit call.

"Macy, hi," she says sweetly when she picks up. "All set for 2:30 today?"

"Actually, that's why I'm calling. I'm sorry to do this at the last minute, but I think I'm going to have to reschedule. I have a flight in a few hours, and I'm afraid I won't be able to make it on time if I come in." I let out a breath. "I apologize for the inconvenience."

There's some rustling in the background, but she seems sympathetic in her tone. "It's no big deal. I'm leaving for

Christmas break today too, so that gives me some extra time. I won't be back in town until after the New Year, so I'll see you on the sixth, okay?"

"Sure, thank you. Happy holidays, Dr. Reynolds."

"You too, Macy."

After we hang up the phone, I shoot Paxton a text.

> Change of plans. I'm ready when you are.

PAXTON
> Sweet. Any chance we'll join the mile high club?

> In your dreams, buddy.

PAXTON
> Good thing I sleep well on planes.

> Just come pick me up, idiot.

PAXTON
> Cumming in twenty 😉

I simultaneously roll my eyes while chuckling. In all honesty, sex in a 3ft x 3ft bathroom sounds quite intriguing. Spontaneity isn't my strong suit, but I've been trying to be better at branching out. Hence my agreement to go to Utah. It's not something I'd normally do—especially with a boyfriend and his family—but being in a cabin in the mountains beats spending Christmas alone. And at this point, I'd probably do anything Paxton asks of me. Except have a baby, because Lord knows I don't want to be a mom. Unless it's to his babies. Wait, no. Absolutely not. No babies. Right?

Jesus, what is happening to me?

My watch reads 2:18 pm, so Paxton should be pulling up within the next ten minutes. I head to my room to change into something comfortable for the flight. I settle on black joggers, a plain black tee with my bikini underneath since there's a hot tub, and my black LA hat. I finish off the look with a jean jacket and some white sneakers, then grab my winter coat to throw on as well. One swipe of my favorite nude lipstick, and there's a knock on my door.

I drag my suitcase down the hallway, opening the door to reveal Paxton grinning like a fool.

"What?" I ask, trying to hide my smile.

He wastes no time stepping over the threshold and wrapping his arms around me, lifting me up to meet his lips. I throw my arms around his neck and wrap my legs around his waist, lifting myself a little higher to reach his mouth better. His hands meet each one of my ass cheeks, giving them a squeeze, causing me to squeal.

I pull back and take a long look at him. His smile is still as wide as ever.

"I'm just excited to spend the next week with you, that's all," he answers in response to my question. "You look extremely sexy, by the way."

My cheeks flush pink, and I give him another kiss on the lips before sliding down his body. My feet hit the floor, so I step back, really taking him in. He's also wearing sweatpants—gray ones, *of* course—with a long-sleeve white tee and a backwards hat. All my insides heat at the sight of him.

Yep, the mile high club is sounding pretty good right about now.

His grin turns cocky as he catches me ogling him. "You're reconsidering, aren't you?"

His smug comment brings me back to reality.

"I am doing no such thing," I spit back. *Totally am.*

"Hmm, okay then." He steps in closer to me and bends down until his lips are brushing my ear. "That's too bad, though. I planned to suck your soul straight from your body on the bathroom counter."

I let out a shaky breath at that thought. Paxton slowly trails his hand up my thighs, stopping right over the spot where the bundle of nerves is lighting my whole body on fire.

235

My eyes fall closed, and chills run down my entire spine as he circles me over my pants. He's torturing me, and I'm putty in his hand, his very skilled hand that knows how to undo me.

"Let's get going before I take you right here, right now." He pulls away, still wearing that grin I love, yet hate so much.

I nearly whimper at the loss of contact, but there would be hell to pay. He's playing with fire, and I won't be the one to get burned.

Check-in is a nightmare. It's obvious everyone is leaving for the holidays, so what would normally only take us thirty minutes at most takes us almost two hours.

His family left for Utah yesterday, so they're already there. This will be the first time I'll be spending a consecutive amount of time with his family, and I'm starting to feel nervous. At least for Thanksgiving, I had Lauren to keep me at ease. She was there, being the buffer, as usual. She's always been the bubbly, likable one, and I've always been fairly reserved. I don't think I'm unlikable, I'm just not as extroverted as Lauren. She draws people in easily, whereas I keep people at arm's length. I knew Paxton's family would love her, but now I'm not so sure they will like me without her. Ugh, I miss my sister, and now I'm being a needy brat.

> I wish we were spending Christmas together. I miss you.

LAUREN
> Me too sis, but try to have fun, and don't die while attempting to ski. I need you alive for my wedding.

> Sure, I'll make sure I'm extra careful so you can reap the benefits. How selfless of you.

> **LAUREN**
> Just trying to assure that you'll live long enough for me to stand in your wedding. Have a safe flight! Love you.
>
> Now I'm going to throw myself off the ski lift. Love you!

My wedding. She said it so confidently that I almost let myself imagine it for a second. But the reality is, I've never made it past six months, and the thought of long-term commitment strikes a huge fear in me. I'm not sure it's scarier than being alone for the rest of my life, but it runs a close second. Because at least if I'm alone, no one can hurt me. No one can consume all of me, just to realize they no longer want me and then leave me broken. If I'm alone, I'm the one who's in control, and I need to be in control.

So don't ask me why I've agreed to a relationship and a family vacation with a man I think I'm in love with. That literally screams, *"I'm not in control."* Like, at all.

We didn't join the mile high club, but the flight was entertaining to say the least. The couple across the aisle from us had some fun of their own underneath the blanket they shared. I'm not sure if they didn't think people would notice, or if they truly didn't care, but they weren't very discreet. Despite what people say, watching other people get off is *not* a turn on. Not for me, anyway.

Luckily for us, baggage claim is much easier to get through than check-in, so we're out of the airport roughly twenty minutes after we land.

Preston and Payton are picking us up, and I'm excited to spend some time with them. Payton and I have become pretty close since Thanksgiving, which I'm grateful for since I don't have many girlfriends. We text regularly and try to hang out at least once a week if our busy schedules allow. The automatic double doors open as we walk outside to the designated pick-up area, and a rush of cold wind slaps me in the face. December in Utah is just as cold as Chicago. Even after two and a half years here, my southern ass is not used to these northern winters. I don't think I ever will be.

True to their word, Paxton's brother and sister are parked and sitting in their rental SUV. Preston hops out, engulfs me in a bear hug and takes my suitcase from me. He shoots a look at Paxton and shakes his head.

"Making your girl carry her own luggage, P? I thought mom taught you better than that?"

I stifle a laugh. "I insisted."

"Yeah," Paxton shoots back. "You heard her. She *insisted*, aka I didn't want to get my ass kicked for arguing with her."

Preston shakes his head again, grinning this time. "Smart man."

The guys throw our bags in the hatch while I slide into the back seat, instantly defrosting from the heat pouring through the vents. Payton is sitting in the passenger seat, scrolling mindlessly on her phone before turning around. Her smile is wide, showing off her perfectly straight teeth. Yet another pebble thrown into the ridiculously flawless gene pool that is the Meyers family.

"I hope you know I love you, and I would've jumped out to hug you, but it's cold as balls out there, and I love being warm more," she says with a laugh.

"I honestly don't blame you one bit. It's nice and toasty in here. Much more appealing than the artic weather out there," I say, gesturing out the window. "But it's the thought that counts." I wink at her, which warrants me another laugh.

The boys finally get in the vehicle, and we take off toward the cabin. Payton plays music, but I'm too awestruck to even hear what song is on. My eyes are glued to the snow-lined trees and long stretches of mountains as we drive. The scenery here is nothing like I've ever seen before. I absolutely hate the cold, but I'd bear the burden of it to live in a place like this.

Twenty minutes later, we arrive at the cabin, and my jaw becomes unhinged. When Paxton said cabin, my immediate thoughts were a small, log-style building. Maybe a small porch, and even a fire pit in the backyard with a couple of chairs.

This place is anything but that. The quote unquote *cabin* is a three-story, wood-panel lined mansion with a massive amount of large, bay windows and a tin roof. It does indeed have a porch, which looks to wrap around the entire house, as well as a balcony on the second floor that houses two rocking chairs and a small fire pit of its own. Off to the side of the house is a winding staircase that leads up to the second and third floors, which has me wondering where our room will be.

Preston and Paxton begin unloading the car, making me realize I'm still sitting in the backseat staring at my home for the next week. It's surreal, honestly. We never had money to afford the luxury of going on vacation when I was a kid, so I didn't get to experience life until I was old enough to afford to travel with my own money.

It's a miracle I even made it out of New Orleans for law school, given how expensive it is. But I keep telling myself that the debt will be worth the reward once I'm a kickass lawyer, making more money than I've ever dreamed of. That's the goal, anyway.

I step out of the car, taking in my surroundings. The air is crisp, wind whipping at my already chapped cheeks. The smell of pine trees fill the air, and I breathe it all in. After the car is unloaded, the four of us make our way up the few steps onto the front porch. Payton opens the door, and I allow Preston to walk in after her, then I follow behind with Paxton trailing me. Before I can take in the interior of the home, Lauren comes barreling down the stairs and wraps her arms around me.

"Surprise!"

I hug her back tightly, and glance over at Paxton, who's now standing next to me. With a smile on his face, he looks as proud as ever.

"Merry Christmas, baby."

My eyes are welling with tears because even though I didn't voice how much I had wanted my sister here, he knew it anyway. He made sure I get to spend the holidays with the only family I have, and at this moment, I know, without a doubt, that I will never let him go.

Chapter 40
Paxton

Two Can Play This Game

The look on Macy's face right now makes the money I spent to get Lauren and Dillon here worth every penny. I've never seen her look happier or more beautiful than she does right now. I'd do anything to continue being the reason she feels like this. We may only have been friends for six months—and only two months as an official couple—but I'm so gone for her. So desperately in love with her, and I'm going to tell her tonight.

When she and Lauren finally let go of each other, I place my arm around her shoulder and pull her into my side, kissing her temple. "I'm going to put our things in our room. I'll be back in a minute."

"Wait, I'll come with."

"You sure you don't want to catch up with your sister? I can get Dillon to help me with the bags."

"I have eight whole days to do that, thanks to you. She'll be fine for a few minutes." She gives me a knowing smirk, and there's no way I'm going to argue. I'm every bit willing to let her do whatever it is to me that she's plotting in that pretty head of hers.

Everyone else heads to the kitchen, and I lead us up the stairs to the third floor, bags in tow. There's only one bedroom up here, and it has its own private bathroom, equipped with a large, clawfoot tub and a steam shower with four heads, one of which is detachable. *Oh, we're going to have so much fun.*

As soon as we enter the room and I drop our bags, Macy slams me into the wall and mounts me like a starved kitten. Her mouth is on mine before I can do anything else, so I grip her waist and pull her to me until our chests are flush. Her fingers grip the small patch of hair on my neck peeking from underneath my hat, which elicits a groan from me. Who knew I was such a masochist? Macy's tongue dances along mine, and I have every urge to rip all her clothing from her body, so that's what I try to do, but she stops me.

Instead, she peppers kisses down my neck while she mumbles her thank yous against my skin and slowly grazes my erection with her hand. My eyes fall shut, only to instantly feel the loss of her lips and hand. When I open them, she's peering up at me from her knees, and all the breath leaves my lungs at the sight of her. God, she's so damn gorgeous, and mine—all mine. I close my eyes and let my head fall back against the wall as Macy tugs my sweatpants low enough to swipe her tongue across my waist. I shiver with pleasure. Her breath is hot, tongue searing my skin. I want more. I *need* more.

"*Baby*," I whisper almost breathlessly.

Suddenly, my skin is void of contact, feeling cold. I don't like it one bit. My eyes fly open, watching Macy smirk at me. Why is she smirking at me right now? I go to reach for her, but she puts even more distance between us, wagging her finger at me.

"Tsk tsk," she says with a devilish grin. "You don't get to tease me like you did earlier and get away with it, *Mr. Meyers.*"

Oh, so this is what we're doing then? I lunge for her, but she runs out the door and darts down the stairs shrieking before I can catch her.

My evil, evil girl. Two can play this game, and I always win. *Always.*

I put away our suitcases and head downstairs to join everyone, but when I enter the kitchen, only the guys are there. Preston clearly notices the way I unapologetically search for Macy because he informs me the girls went straight for the hot tub.

And because I'm so pussy-whipped, I make my way outside to the back porch. That's when I realized how fucked I am. My hot-as-fuck girlfriend is slipping her way into the steaming water, wearing the sexiest black bikini I've ever seen. Her hair is pulled up into a bun on top of her head, showing off her shoulders that I love kissing so much. The halter of the bikini is pulled tight, making her tits look extra perky, and those bottoms are cheeky, making her ass look even more fantastic than usual.

I look down, noticing my cock has tented my sweats, so I have to do some rearranging. Macy's gaze meets mine, and that incredibly infuriating look she's giving me right now only solidifies that I will not, in fact, be winning. *Zero chance. Throw in the towel. Give up now.*

Footsteps approach behind me and my brother's hand lands on my shoulder.

"What *the fuck* did you do to land a girl like *that?*" He laughs at my expense. "I'm way more handsome than you and entirely more successful. With a much bigger dick, might I add, and I'm still fucking single."

I shake my head, mostly because he's an arrogant asshole. He's picky as hell when it comes to women, and he knows it. *That's* why he's still single. He refuses to settle for less than perfect—which is highly unattainable—but I'll let him figure that one out on his own.

"One, you are *definitely* not better looking than me, asshole. Two, do you really want to pull out a ruler and measure right now? Because I will. And three"—I smack him in the back of the head— "if I wanted to be a fucking doctor, I would've. But I don't. Going the lawyer route *clearly* has paid off, hence the smokin' hot redhead you're drooling over. So obviously, I'm sexier *and* smarter, with a bigger dick."

"Bet I got a bigger dick than both of ya'll," Dillon snorts, interrupting.

Jesus. Looks like we're whipping out our swords later to compare. Preston and I both roll our eyes and huff.

"I heard the tail end of the conversation, but I am curious. Why don't you have a girl, Preston?"

My brother just shrugs. He's never been serious about many girls in his life. I can count on two fingers how many girlfriends of his I've met, and that was purely by accident. He doesn't bring girls home because my mom is relentless, and Payton can be a bit... let's say, judgmental. She's very protective of us, which is why I am relieved that she and Macy hit it off so well. Just another thing to love about her.

"My career's been my sole focus. I've dabbled in dating. Nothing too serious. It's hard finding someone who can deal with me *and* my schedule. Not to mention, being able to separate girls who like me for me and not just my surgeon status." Preston's gaze remains focused on the scenery, and I can tell from his tone that he really has given this a lot of thought. I've always known him to be a bachelor, but it's evident that he's finally ready for more and is having a hard time pinning down the right girl. "That, and I can't bring anyone around my family without them scaring them off." He pushes me, and I shove him back.

"Hey, don't look at me. Take that up with your mother and sister." I joke. "I can't help if they like me better."

"You both are nuts." Dillon chuckles. "I love my two little sisters, but I've always wanted a brother. I'm excited to be gaining two." His eyes travel to where the girls are sitting, talking in the hot tub, and he sighs. "That girl right there," he tips his chin toward Lauren and lets out another breath. "I can't wait to marry her."

My chest tightens as I watch Macy throw her head back in a laugh, completely unaware I'm transfixed on her. The way her smile takes my breath away. How her laugh is the only sound I want to hear on repeat like my favorite song, and all I can think of in this moment is: I can't wait for that too.

Chapter 41
Paxton

And You Say I'm Dramatic

"Are ya'll just gonna stand there and stare like a bunch of perverts or actually join us?"

Lauren and Payton full on belly laugh at Macy's comment. Imagine that; a smart-ass comment coming from the mouth of my sassy ass girlfriend. Even when she insults me and calls me a pervert, I still can't get enough of her sarcasm. It's one of my favorite things about her. She's so sure of herself and doesn't take shit from anyone, especially me, and it's such a sexy quality to have.

Many of my past conquests were beyond self-conscious, always fishing for compliments. Not that I mind complimenting a woman, because I don't. I love it, actually. It's something I make sure to do often, but I want to do it on my own accord. I don't like feeling uncomfortable or being forced to make up something just to satisfy a woman's ego. I like getting to know a person and letting them know what I like about them over time. It's more genuine that way, and it allows them the opportunity to trust me enough to fully open themselves up. And although the women I've been with over the past four years have only been in my bed, I still treat them with respect, even if I wasn't boyfriend material at the time.

"You coming, man?" Dillon's voice breaks me out of my trance.

Preston's already dipping in and taking a seat next to my girl. He throws an arm around Macy's shoulder and pulls her close to him, whispering something in her ear, making her laugh. If he wasn't my brother, I'd be seeing red right now, but I know how badly he likes to bust my balls, so I don't even feed into it. He can be a jackass, but I know he'd never do anything to hurt me. I'll let him have his fun, but when I get back, his hands will be off her.

"Uh, yeah. Let me go change real quick."

I step back into the house to find my mom walking through the front door with my dad. They're both dressed up, my mom in a floor length crimson dress with a fur shawl wrapped around her shoulders, hair done up in an elegant twist. My dad is wearing black slacks with a shirt to match my mother's dress and a black jacket over it. They clean up nice.

"Well, well, well. Look what the cat dragged in," I say in a teasing tone. I look at the clock on the mantle. It reads 10:41 pm. "Isn't it past your bedtime?"

My mother rolls her eyes, and my dad chuckles. They walk toward me, and my mom braces me in a hug. "Hi to you too, sweetie. How was your flight? Where's my girl at?"

I smile. My heart genuinely squeezes in my chest at her words. *My girl.* It makes me incredibly happy that my mother likes her so much, and I can't wait for my dad to meet her. I know he'll love her just as much. He gives me a half-pat on the back hug, then pulls back.

"It was good. Great, even. She's excited to be here with everyone for the next week. The girls went straight for the hot tub, so they're out back with the boys. I was just about to get changed and join them."

"Alright, honey. Well, we won't keep you. That charity event wore us out, so we're going to head to bed because you're right, it's way past our bedtime." She chuckles, and that makes me smile too.

My dad's already heading down the hall, so I give my mom a kiss on the cheek. "Sleep tight. Love you."

She reciprocates, and I head to my room to get changed. My phone dings. It's a text from Macy.

> **MACY**
> Would you mind grabbing my chapstick from my black duffle, please?
>
> Sure thing, babe. Don't want to be kissing any crusty lips.
>
> **MACY**
> You're the absolute worst.

I laugh to myself.

After I throw on my light blue swim shorts, I grab her bag from the closet and set it on the bed. I feel a slight pang as I stare at the bag, remembering it's the one I used to bring her things to the hospital the day she passed out on me. It's a memory I try not to think back on very much, but it's also the day she called me her boyfriend, so it wasn't all bad. I push past my thoughts, and rummage through it, searching for the small stick. This isn't working. I dump the bag out onto the bed to get a better look at the contents. *Found it!*

I start putting everything back into the bag when I grab ahold of a few pamphlets. *Eating Recovery Center, Avalon Heights – Eating Disorder Recovery, Sellars House – Anorexia and Bulimia Treatment.*

A wave of nausea rolls through me. *No.* She's not sick. She can't be. How the fuck did I miss this? I try thinking back on any signs I should've been picking up on. I can't think of a single thing. She's not afraid to eat in front of me. She puts away beer and wine like it's nobody's business. She works out and takes care of her body, so it doesn't make any sense. Another text alert from Macy pops up on my screen.

> **MACY**
> You get lost up there? I know it's a big house, but I didn't think you were that directionally challenged.

Despite feeling like I'll vomit at any minute, I manage a semi-smile. It doesn't reach my eyes, but it has the effect on me I need to get my ass in gear. I put the rest of her things back in her bag, throw it into the closet and make my way downstairs. We *will* talk about this. It's not up for debate this time, but it's a private matter I'd rather not discuss in front of an audience.

I step out onto the back patio, receiving slow claps from the assholes sitting in the hot tub. I flip them the bird then make my way over to Macy, handing her the tube of chapstick. She runs the balm over her lips as I slip into the hot water, putting myself between her and Preston. He offers me a half-hearted laugh, knowing exactly what I'm doing, and of course, my girlfriend has to open her big mouth.

"What if I wanted to sit next to him instead?" Her smug grin tells me all I need to know about the rise she wants to get out of me.

"Like hell you are. He had his fill, and now he's done. Don't make me knock my brother out, please."

She shrugs and giggles. I drag her into my lap and wrap my arms around her waist. With her back to my chest, she leans against me, placing a quick kiss to my cheek.

I'm trying to remain unfazed about the secret she's keeping from me, but it's eating at me. I don't want to make a scene in front of everyone, so I need to act like there's nothing wrong. It's a lot harder than I anticipate, because I don't even react when she kisses me, which is why she whispers in my ear.

"Everything okay?" Her voice is timid, and now I feel guilty. Her eating disorder doesn't make me love her any less.

If anything, I want to help her. I want her to let me be there for her. It's the secrecy that dangles over me like a dark cloud. I need her to trust me. I *want* her to trust me. I want her to *want* to tell me things. She needs to know she doesn't have to do things alone anymore. I'm here. I want to take care of her. But she needs to let me.

I swallow and clear my throat. "Yeah, all good." The lie feels dirty on my tongue, but I'll have time to be honest later. And I will because I'm not afraid to have hard conversations. I don't run from confrontation. I prefer to get everything out in the open, and that's what we'll do later. I don't know how convincing I'm being, given the wary look on Macy's face, but I'm rolling with it for now. I guess she is too because the shift in conversation changes.

"Me and Dillon are gonna go for a run in the morning then hit the gym before we start the day. You in?" Preston nudges my shoulder, waiting for an answer.

"Sounds good," I answer on autopilot.

"Sweet. Well, it's late, and I'm wiped. Bedtime for this senior citizen." The girls chuckle. Preston rises from the water and steps out of the hot tub. He wraps a towel around his waist then turns to face us. Pointing at me and Dillon, he says, "Six am wakeup call, fuckers." Then proceeds to disappear into the house.

"I'm pretty tired too," Payton says as she stands to her feet. "Girl's gotta get her beauty sleep." She yawns and grabs her things from the lounge chair. "See you in the morning."

The four of us collectively tell her good night before she walks inside. "Ya'll hungry?" Lauren breaks the silence. "I'm starving." I just got in, but truthfully, I couldn't care less about getting right out. My mood is sour, and honestly, I could go for something to eat. "I might actually die if I don't get food in me this instant."

"And you say I'm dramatic," Macy retorts with her signature eye roll. "We'll meet ya'll inside shortly."

With that, Lauren and Dillon leave us alone, and suddenly, I'm feeling uneasy. My stomach plummets at the thought of her harming her body. I run the palm of my hand up and down her torso, and she leans her back against me, dropping her head to my shoulder. Her muscles tighten under my touch, and thoughts are constantly swarming me, trying to figure out how her body is so perfect, yet so internally damaged.

She pulls me from my thoughts as she snakes her right arm around my neck and runs her fingers through the hair at the nape. Her left hand guides mine from her stomach down to her waistline. My dick immediately twitches in my swim trunks. I turn to look at her face. Her eyes are closed, and her breathing is becoming erratic as she pushes my hand into her bikini bottoms. She's distracting me because she knows my head is elsewhere. She can sense it, and instead of harboring me about it, she's giving me an out, which I'll gladly take right now.

I bring my lips to her neck, and she lolls her head in the opposite direction to give me full access. I press kiss after kiss down her throat until I come to the junction where it meets her shoulder, nibbling at first, then sucking the skin lightly. Macy's breath hitches, and guides my hand even lower, running my fingers through her slit. I groan. Even in the water, I can tell how wet she is. I'm full on hard to the point that it's painful, but I want to make her feel good, so I let her continue to direct me where she wants me.

"Paxton," she whispers. "Please. Do something. Anything."

I suck on her neck some more, and a low moan tumbles from her mouth. "Make me," I dare her.

She doesn't even hesitate. *There's that confidence I love so much.* Macy covers my hand with hers and pushes two of my fingers inside her, causing her pelvis to tilt off my lap. I grab her and press her back down with my right hand, while she works my left hand with hers. I've never had a girl take control like this before. Never have I done anything remotely like this, but I'm living for it. Having her forcefully use my hand to pump in and out of herself as I curl my fingers, reaching the spot I know she craves, is easily the sexiest thing I've ever experienced.

Before I know it, she's pushing a third finger in and bringing my right hand down over her clit.

Holy fucking shit.

One's pumping, the other's circling, and Macy's arching her back for release. I put her out of her misery by working her myself so she can focus on reaching her climax.

My lips reach her ear as I whisper, "Fuck, baby. You're so hot. Come for me."

And she does, with my name falling off her lips in a hushed voice. God, I'm going to explode if I don't empty myself soon. Macy's body is completely slack against mine, sated, floating on a euphoric high. The girl is a vision, and I'm so fucking happy she's mine.

When her head turns my way and her lips softly land on mine, my heart picks up, and I smile a genuine smile against her mouth. She deepens the kiss with a tug of my neck then pulls away, eyes hooded and tired.

"Let's go get a snack and head to bed. I'm exhausted."

Chapter 42
Macy

Tit Punched

The room is still dark when I open my eyes—due to the blackout curtains, I'm guessing. I don't remember falling asleep last night, but I do remember Paxton being slightly distant. He wasn't as clingy as he normally is, always needing to be touching me in some form. Which I didn't realize I missed until he retreated to his side of the bed before I had the chance to doze off.

I didn't push him to talk last night because I want us to have an enjoyable trip without any fights. I loathe confrontation, and it's easier to act like nothing is wrong than assessing the situation head on. Whatever is bothering him can wait until we get back to Chicago, unless he brings it up himself.

Is this the right way to handle things? No. And I'm well aware of that. Am I going to become a bigger person and learn to communicate my feelings all of a sudden? Also no. I'll figure it out one day, but today isn't that day.

I reach over to snuggle up to him, only to be graced with an empty bed. I snatch my phone off the bedside table to check the time. It's barely after seven, which means he's already gone for his morning run with the boys.

Not ready to get up just yet, I shoot a text to Lauren.

> Has Dillon said anything to you about Paxton?

I don't expect her to be up this early, so when my phone dings a minute later, I'm relieved.

LAUREN
> No? Should he have?

> I guess not. He's just been acting weird since last night, and he's not talking to me about it.

LAUREN
> If something's going on, I'm sure he'll talk when he's ready. If you're so worried, why don't you just ask him?

> Uh, because that would be the logical thing to do, and you know I'm anything but logical when it comes to relationships. Hence the reason I'm still single at nearly twenty-six while my sister is engaged.

LAUREN
> Are you saying you want to get married? Also, you're not single? Last I checked, you're here with your boyfriend?

Do I? Surely not. I don't know. Maybe one day, if the opportunity presents itself with the right guy. *Is Paxton that guy?* I guess he could be. If he checked all the boxes. Boxes which are still empty because I have zero idea what I'm even looking for in a partner. I have never even wanted long-term companionship before this. And even now, I'm still not sure that I do. Have I thought about maybe, possibly getting invested further with him? Like once or twice at best. Okay, maybe three times. Can't be sure. But marriage? Pfft. That's like eternal commitment. One I'm not sure I'll ever be ready for.

When I don't immediately respond to her, I get a follow up text.

> LAUREN
> Oh my god, YOU DO!

> Can't a girl take time to text back without you jumping to conclusions about her nonexistent thoughts of wedding bells? Maybe I was peeing. Or conjuring up a will. Never know when you'll need one of those.

> LAUREN
> Not when that girl is you. I think you like him, maybe even love him. I think you've thought about a future with him. And I think you might want to marry him one day. *squeals with joy* My little heart is so happy you've finally found someone to defrost that iceberg in your chest.

I roll my eyes. She really is the dramatic one here. Though she may be right, I won't give her that satisfaction. Not right now anyway. It's still too soon to tell if this is going anywhere, and I don't want to be put in a vulnerable position in case things don't work out. So, I deflect, per usual.

> And I think you're out of your damn mind. The empty black hole that used to harbor a beating organ is a little disappointed that you don't know me at all. It's cute of you to be hopeful, though.

> LAUREN
> Jesus, Macy. You're such a cynic. I truly don't understand how we share the same DNA sometimes.

> Mom's poor choice in men and lack of contraception is my guess. *shrugs*

> **LAUREN**
> For the love of all that is holy, get the fuck up, and let's go have breakfast. I'm done entertaining your sadistic notions.

    I just smile. She loves me and my aversion to all things romance, whether she wants to admit it or not. I hop out of bed and put on something more presentable than a silk pajama set. Once I settle on black leggings and an oversized sweatshirt, I brush my teeth, throw my hair into a messy bun and swipe my glasses on my face.

    Since it's still early, I sneak down to the second floor and push open Lauren's bedroom door. The bed is made, and she's nowhere to be found. I hear the faint sound of water running in the bathroom connected to their room. The door is wide open, and Lauren is standing at the sink, washing her face. I slink out of sight, just outside the door. When she comes walking out, I jump out and she punches me square in the tit as she screams. I double over, eyes welling with tears as I clutch my right breast. I'm heaving from laughter, trying to catch my breath.

    When I finally stand, she whisper-yells, "Mother, fucker! Was that freaking necessary Macy?!"

    "Excuse me? If you don't remember, *you* told *me* you wanted to go eat. Sorry I was being an honorable sister and coming to your beck-and-call." Massaging my boob, I say, "Plus I think you just gave me a hematoma. Looks like I'll be scheduling my first mammogram at the ripe age of twenty-six."

    She pinches the bridge of her nose, already annoyed with me before eight in the morning. I can't say I blame her, but really, it's her fault.

    "Remember how I told you to be careful while trying to ski so you can make it to my wedding?"

    "I do," I answer nodding.

"I will personally throw you down the damn mountain myself, if you keep this up."

"Perfect, you'll be doing me a favor," I say as I walk past her and out of the door. I turn for a moment to see if she's following. "You coming, Aileen Wuornos?"

Her mouth falls open, and I stifle a laugh. "You did *not* just compare me to the world's most notorious female serial killer."

"I did," I respond with a smirk. I pat her butt two times as she walks by. "Now, come on."

"You realize how insulting that is, right?"

"You insulted me first by threatening to murder me. Can we please go? I'm hungry."

She follows reluctantly, huffing while doing so. We descend the stairs quietly, making our way to the kitchen when the smell of cinnamon and coffee fills the air. My stomach grumbles embarrassingly loud, which warrants a look from Lauren. I haven't eaten much the past two days, so I just shrug. What she doesn't know won't hurt her.

Dr. Meyers is standing next to the oven, removing cinnamon buns when she notices us. She immediately sets the tray on the stovetop and barrels her way over to engulf me in a hug.

It's one of those things I'm still getting used to, but I awkwardly hug her back because I know she's an affectionate person. I'm almost positive that's where Paxton gets it from. All her kids, really. Both Preston and Payton are physical people from what I've gathered being around them.

She releases me then embraces Lauren, who squeezes her back and plasters on a huge smile. "It smells delicious in here, Mrs. Paige."

Mrs. Paige? *Mrs. Paige?* They're on a first name basis? Since when? I know she's my sister, and I love her, but this whole encounter has me feeling uncomfortable. *I* don't even call her Paige, and she's my damn boyfriend's mother. Insecurity swirls heavily in my gut. Just another thing to tip me over the edge of jealousy when it comes to my own family.

"Thank you, Lauren. I'm so glad to have you both here for the holidays."

I return from my thoughts to engage in conversation, realizing I've been standing here, silently reeling in my own misery. "We're happy to be here. Thank you for having us," I say, attempting to smile. "Do you need help with anything?"

"There's fruit in the fridge that needs to be cut. If you don't mind doing that while I ice the cinnamon buns, that would be great. Thank you."

I nod. "Of course."

Lauren pulls the fruit from the refrigerator while I grab the knife and cutting board. I notice Dr. Meyers has once again concocted an entire spread of food over the island, just as she did for Thanksgiving. Lots of carbs, pastries, jellies and syrups. My mouth is watering as I cut up the strawberries and arrange them into one of those clear bowls with dividers. I follow it up with bananas, cantaloupe, grapes, and blueberries.

Bare feet tap against the hardwood floors, and Payton comes into view in all her sleepy glory. Her blonde hair is pulled back into a braid with loose pieces falling out, and she's in red flannel pajama pants and a black long-sleeve tee. Her eyes are a bit groggy, like she wasn't ready to wake up just yet, but she perks up once she sees the food.

"Morning, sunshine," I greet her. "Get your beauty rest?"

Her playful scowl tells me all I need to know. Payton is *not* a morning person. Not until she's had coffee at least. But her FOMO wins out every time. She'd rather wake up early than miss out on anything.

Walking past the island, she pops a kiss on my cheek, then Lauren's, followed by her mom's. "The Keurig is ready to go, and there's cold brew in the fridge for anyone who wants that instead." Dr. Meyers finishes with the cinnamon buns and begins plating them. "I made Patrick buy six different creamers because I didn't know what everyone likes," she says with a smile. "I figured we'd make use of the dining table, so I'll start bringing everything over there, and we can eat when the boys get back."

And as if they were listening in, all four men walk through the back door from the patio—the fourth being Paxton's dad who I have yet to meet. Paxton walks in last, his eyes lingering on me before he gives me a half-assed smile and heads to greet his mom.

Okay, that was *different*. Usually, he greets me with a kiss hello, but instead, all I get is a fake attempt to appear like he isn't being distant. I don't and won't admit there's a small ache in my chest at his behavior. This is why I don't let myself fall. Because people tend to change or finally show their true colors.

Whatever, I'm not doing this with him. If this is how he wants to act, I'll enjoy my vacation with my sister and be done with it.

I shed my sweatshirt due to the temperature in the house. It has nothing to do with the increase in my blood pressure. Nope. That definitely isn't a thing, and I am perfectly fine. In just a t-shirt now, I notice the way Paxton's dad gives me a once over with a pinch between his brows. Nothing but disappointment written across his face. Well, isn't this fantastic. Can't imagine all the reasons why he would think I'm not fit for his son. Nose piercing? Full sleeve of tattoos and more? Maybe it's because I'm a redhead and he can tell I don't have a soul. Who knows? At the rate my relationship is going, I'm sure he won't have to worry about me much longer anyway. And I'm not a kiss-ass, so I'm not going to make some grand gesture for him to accept me. It is what it is.

"Honey." I hear Dr. Meyers say. "This is Macy, Paxton's girlfriend."

It's quite embarrassing that my own boyfriend can't even

introduce me to his father. He leaves his mother to do his dirty work. What a swell guy.

I stick out my hand and plaster on my best smile. "Nice to meet you, sir."

He nods. He freaking *nods*. "Mmmhm." That's all I get. *Kay*. This is fucking awkward because Paxton isn't even defending me. He's just standing there, watching it all unfold, like he could care less. Seriously, what the hell is his problem?

Dr. Meyers swats his shoulder. "Patrick, don't be a dick." All her kids snicker as he retreats to the dining room. She turns to me. "Sorry about him. He's a bit of a Scrooge around Christmas. He'll warm up." Great, can't wait.

I follow suit and give her a curt nod before walking over to the fridge and grabbing the cold brew and hazelnut creamer. Paxton opens the cabinet to the right of the stove and pulls out two mason jars with handles, filling them with ice. He hands one to me and pops a quick peck on my cheek then walks away. *What the actual fuck?*

Pouring my coffee into my mug, I add the creamer and some simple syrup, giving it a quick stir.

Lauren steps up next to me and leans in. "Well, that didn't go as expected." *Yeah, no shit.* "Was this your first encounter with him?"

"Yeah."

"So, there hasn't been any animosity?"

"No, Lauren. There hasn't been any interaction between us at all. He simply took one look at me and declared me unfit."

My shoulders slump because it just reminds me of the inadequacy I've felt when it comes to my physical appearance my entire life.

"Surely that's not the case. He seemed perfectly nice when I met him yesterday."

"Obviously. You're perfect. Golden blonde hair. Blue eyes.

Virgin skin. The exact representation of the girlfriend every parent wishes for their son."

Anger seethes through me. I shouldn't be taking this out on her. It's not her fault I'm damaged goods with a tainted exterior.

"That's not fair, and you know it." A hurt expression crosses her face, and I feel guilt tug at me. She's been nothing but supportive of me since we were kids. I don't get to blame my insecurities on her.

"You're right, I'm sorry," I apologize. "Do you want me to make you some coffee?"

"I'm actually going to have some water but thank you." She grazes my arm just as my stomach growls loudly. "Let's get you some food."

And with that, we join everyone at the table.

Chapter 43
Paxton

Plan B

I'm being a dick right now. I know I am. Preston even told me I am, regardless of the lack of information I fed him this morning. He knows something is up, but Macy's business isn't mine to tell, regardless of how badly I'd like my brother's advice. I could go to my mom, I guess, but even then, it still wouldn't feel right to have that conversation behind her back. If Macy wanted me to know, she'd tell me. And God, I wish she'd just fucking tell me.

The look on her face when I didn't kiss her good morning in the kitchen doesn't sit well with me. I'm not this guy, despite my lack of relationships the last few years. I'm a decent person, and a great boyfriend, but I just couldn't bring myself to pretend that I don't know what she's hiding.

And although I'm angry and hurt by her lack of trust in me, I am *seething* after watching my father degrade her with his stare, but I don't dare challenge him.

Macy might not be the type of girl I've ever dated before, but she's far superior in almost every way. She's beautiful, smart, driven, and kind. The girl uprooted her entire life for a chance to change her narrative. Not many people have the courage to do that, but she did, and she's managed to make her way to the top of our class.

I thought he'd at least give her the opportunity to prove herself to him. I honestly didn't think my dad would be the hard one to crack. But because he's old fashioned, he can't see past the inked skin or tiny hoop through her left nostril.

I wanted so badly to step in, to defend her when he so rudely brushed off her attempt to introduce herself, but I know better. I may not be afraid of confrontation, but the one person I refrain from riling up is my father. I learned growing up that it didn't bode well for me, and I refuse to make a fool of myself or Macy. So, I just stood there, inwardly cringing at the abruptness of their conversation, and try to shake it off as best as I can.

When Macy sits next to me at the dining table for breakfast, I can't help but watch her as she fills her plate. My eyes remain glued to everything she places on it. Scrambled egg whites, two triangles of wheat toast with butter, and a few pieces of fruit. That's it. I start doing the math in my head. She's consuming *maybe* one-hundred-and-fifty calories at most, and my need to fix people instinctively takes over. I place a large cinnamon bun on her plate.

"Babe, you *have* to try my mom's famous cinnamon buns. No Christmas Eve breakfast is complete without one."

I plaster on my best smile, trying to hide the fact that I'm testing her.

Her head whips in my direction, as if she's completely thrown off that I'm speaking to her, given my absence this morning and silence when I walked through the door.

She doesn't argue, so I begin eating, keeping an eye on her out the corner of my eye as chatter fills the room. To my surprise, my dad speaks up first.

"So, Macy. Are you from the Chicago area?"

I can't pinpoint if he's trying to conjure up conversation to actually get to know her, or if he's trying to badger her, but I make sure to listen attentively. The look on his face is flat, so I'm not sure the direction he's going. My mom gives him a wary look, but he just continues to wait in silence for an answer.

"No, sir," she says once she's finished chewing. "I'm from New Orleans, actually."

"I see…." He draws his response out. "And how did you end up in Chicago?"

Macy pushes her food around her plate before dabbing her mouth with a napkin. She sets it back in her lap before answering. "I've always known I wanted to be a lawyer." She pauses for a moment. "After graduating from college, I researched the top five law schools in the US, as well as the state with the highest crime rate and overall success in criminal law. U of C happened to fall into both categories, so I packed my bags, and here I am."

My dad washes down his bite with a sip of orange juice and sets it down, nodding. "Hmm. That seems incredibly far to be away from your family." Silence stretches across the table for what feels like forever, until he speaks again. "Once you finish in May, are you planning on going back home?"

Yep, this definitely feels like an interrogation. What the hell is he doing? *Is he trying to get her to leave me?* I'm feeling uneasy, but I'm not quite sure what to do about it. Inserting myself will only make it worse, so I let the conversation ride out. I just hope he doesn't scare her away after this. Not that Macy scares easily, but she's made it clear she's never put herself into this position before. Vacationing with a boyfriend, meeting his family. It's her first time and may very well be her last if this goes south.

I watch as the wheels turn in her head, wondering what her next words will be. She once told me she couldn't promise me a future. That she could only give me here and now. Is that why? Does she plan on leaving after graduation?

My stomach turns sour, feeling a bout of nausea roll in. I can't lose her. I love her, and I haven't even had the opportunity to tell her yet. If I could just get my head out of my ass, I'd have done it already. I promised myself I would, and I need to before she thinks better of it and high tails it back to where she came from.

"I don't know if I'll ever make it back south, but if I don't land the junior partner spot at the firm I'm currently interning at, I've considered New York. Maybe even California." She looks at Lauren with a smile on her face. One which Lauren returns.

Bile rises in my throat. I didn't once think about her leaving Chicago if she didn't get this spot, but now that it's a possibility, I'm scared shitless.

"Ah, the law firm Paxton is interning at as well?" My dad asks, even though he knows damn well it's the same one.

Macy nods. "That's the one."

"Have you started looking for jobs in either state yet?" He presses on, and I'm about to lose all fucking control. "I'm only asking because Paxton is a shoo-in for that position, so it's important to have a plan B."

"Dad!" I interject at the same time my mom yells, "Patrick!"

Not only is he being disrespectful, but he's going to end up leaking information that we haven't discussed, and I'm not ready for that conversation just yet. The last thing Macy needs right now is to hear about my previous relationship with Jack Sterling, or even worse—his daughter.

"With all due respect, sir, I'm at the top of my class alongside Paxton. He's a brilliant student, but I have just as good of a shot at getting junior partner as he does."

I know the last thing I should be doing is getting turned on, but having Macy stand up to my dad is fiercely sexy. And she's right. She *does* have the grades and the skills to take this position if the playing field was fair. The problem is, it's not, but she doesn't know that, and I don't plan on telling her. I want to protect her from Jack, and it's easier to do that if she doesn't have any knowledge of my history with him.

"Uh huh, and the tattoos?" He continues. "Were they just a delinquent phase or do you actually enjoy scarring your body?"

That's it. I've had enough, and apparently so has everyone else. Preston and Payton's faces have never been so devoid of color from embarrassment, and my mother is enraged. I'm too afraid to look at Lauren and Dillon at this point, so I scoot my chair back and extend my hand to Macy.

"That's enough!" Anger roars to life. "We're done here," I say, not even making eye contact with my father.

Macy grabs my hand and follows me out of the room, her head hanging low.

I really am ashamed of my dad's behavior. This time of year, he's always on edge. Christmas was Penny's favorite holiday. We all grieve the loss of her in our own ways, but he's taken it harder than the rest of us. She was his last child, his baby girl. One who he felt as though he failed because he couldn't help her medically. She contracted bacterial meningitis, but before anyone could figure out what the problem was, it was too late. There was severe brain damage that occurred, and for months, she rested in a vegetative state. After months of torture, my mom finally put her out of her misery, and that sent my dad spiraling. He's never been the same since.

I walk us up to the third floor and slam the door shut. Grabbing our bags from the closet, I toss them onto the bed and begin filling them with our things. I don't know that I've ever been as angry as I am in this moment, but I'm pretty sure steam is rolling off me because Macy comes to my side, stopping me from packing. The moment her hands grip mine, a calmness settles over me, and I can finally breathe.

"What are you doing?" Her voice is so faint, I can't even be sure I heard her question at all. But the look on her beautiful face wills me to answer her.

"We're leaving," I say with heaving breaths. "That was fucking brutal, and I'm sorry. I'm so damn sorry you were succumbed to that kind of disrespect." I bring my hands to cup her face, thumbing over her cheeks in attempt to soothe myself. "I won't defend him because I'll never allow anyone to treat you like that, but he isn't in his right mind. Not this time of year. With it reminding him of Penelope, he's just broken. But it's no excuse." I shake my head, trying to process that whole disaster. "We can get a hotel, or we can go home. Whatever you want."

For the first time all day, Macy embraces me. Her arms wrap around my middle, and I hug her in return, finding comfort in her arms. It's the most peace I've found since we arrived, and I feel like such an asshole for the role I've played over the last few hours.

With her face buried in my chest, I decide that I'll wait for the moment she's ready to tell me her struggles. I won't allow my own insecurities to steal what we have, because if I've learned anything from breakfast, it's that I refuse to lose her.

"No." It's a single word, and I'm not quite sure what it's an answer to.

Macy peers up to look at me through her glasses, and her piercing hazel gaze makes my chest ache. *God, she is so fucking perfect.* Pieces of her auburn hair frame her makeup-free face. Those light freckles dust the bridge of her nose and the apples of her cheeks. The dainty little nose ring that I love so much hoops perfectly through the edge of her nostril, and I can't help but place a kiss on the bow of her pouty pink lips. She looks at me with so much appreciation that my heart feels like it's going to burst. I want to tell her how I'll never let anyone hurt her. That I want to protect her with all that I am. I want her to know how much she means to me. *How much I love her.*

"I want to stay," she continues, bringing me back to reality.

"You do? Even after everything?"

She nods. "He brought a lot of perspective to the conversation. I might have a vision for what's next if I don't get the partnership, but I haven't exactly executed it. So he has a point. I do need to be prepared for a different outcome," she states matter-of-factly. "And he's your dad, he has a right to be concerned about who he lets into the lives of his children. I don't blame him for questioning me, and I don't take offense to his comments because I know I'm not the picture-perfect girlfriend on the outside." She continues, "I look like trouble to someone who doesn't know me."

Her grace in this moment has those three little words burning on the tip of my tongue. They're so close to erupting, and I don't know how much longer I'll be able to hold out before I'm spilling them to her. I wish I could just say them. I wish I wasn't afraid I'd scare her away. I wish I knew that she felt the same. But since I can't confirm or deny any of those things, I just stay silent.

Instead, I tilt her chin up with my knuckle, and gently kiss her, savoring the way she tastes on my lips. Macy rises on her toes, hands sliding up my neck and getting lost in my hair while she deepens the kiss. A groan escapes me as she teases me with her tongue, and I grip her hips, pulling her closer. My need for her is building, but just as I slip my hand under the hem of her shirt, there's a knock on the door.

We break from our kiss, Macy standing behind me, holding my hand. I slowly open the door. My mother stands on the other side of the threshold, scanning the room. Her eyes land on our bags, and a panic sets in.

"Please don't go," she begs. "Your father is being an idiot, I can admit that, but we want you both here." I cock a brow, and a deep sigh leaves her mouth. "I promise to keep him in line from here on out."

Macy chuckles.

My mother's expression softens, shoulders going lax. She peers around me, searching for my girlfriend. "Does that mean you'll stay?"

Hope beams in her eyes as Macy nods.

"Of course, we'll stay," she says, and my mom jumps up and down clapping like a little schoolgirl.

A smile touches my lips, and I don't take it lightly that this could have gone a completely different way. I'm one lucky sonofabitch to have such an amazing, understanding woman.

My mom throws herself into my arms, hugging me and reaching out for Macy to join us. When she does, she squeezes the life out of us, and we can't help but laugh.

"I'm making plans for the girls to go to the spa this morning. You boys can go do whatever it is that you do." She turns to leave, but before she exits, she adds, "Be ready in an hour, honey." Then she happily hums as she walks down the stairs.

I focus my attention back on Macy and grip her hips once again, pulling her until her chest is flush with mine. Painstakingly slow, she lifts her gaze until it meets my eyes, and a smile spreads across my face.

"Now, where were we?"

Chapter 44
Macy

Better Than Sex

The four of us are in a private suite, face down, laying side by side, each on our own massage table. There's faint music playing in the background and essential oils filling up the large space—lavender with a hint of some type of citrus if I had to guess. My masseuse, Sven—*yes, that's his actual name*—is working wonders on the kinks in my neck. If I didn't love sex so much, I'd say it's almost better than an orgasm. *Almost*. His big, strong hands are pushing and pressing my muscles in all the right places, melting away every ounce of tension the last few months of my life have caused me.

As I lie here, listening to the drawn-out exhales and miniscule grunts of pleasure coming from the other three, I wonder how the hell I got here. Not just physically in this spa—although yes, that's still a mystery how I got this damn lucky—but just life in general. I've never been one to believe in fate; I'm a cynic, after all. But in retrospect, I was the poor girl who grew up with next to nothing. I had a runaway father and an absent mother who cared more about her current boyfriend than her own kids. I struggled mentally with self-love and physically with an eating disorder that nearly ruined my life. So how did I end up here? In a new city, with a guy who I'm crazy about, and a welcoming family that I never got to experience first-hand growing up. You know, minus Paxton's dad.

People like me don't just get lucky like that. I didn't play the lottery and hit the mega-millions. I didn't draw straws and win the upper hand. I didn't find a four-leaf clover and immediately find my soulmate. And even though none of those things happened, it still feels as though they did. I've found a place I can call home for the first time in my life. In a few months, I'll have my dream job as a criminal lawyer, and I've finally convinced myself I'm deserving of love. No matter the time it took to get here, I gave in to my heart and opened it completely to someone I love whole-heartedly, and it's about time I told him. That's right. As soon as I see him next, I'm going to tell him. He deserves to know how I feel, and I don't want to wait a second longer.

"How does sushi sound for lunch, ladies?" Dr. Meyers—well Mrs. Paige, as she told me to refer to her, minus the Mrs., but I'm a polite southern gentlelady—asks as she lifts her head from her table. She starts spouting off some of the best sushi joints in the area, as well as the most popular rolls from each one of them. I inwardly groan because I'm just not feeling it, but beggars can't be choosers, now can they? I was hoping for something with more substance, like a good pasta or a juicy burger.

"Mom, please no," Payton speaks up. *Thank God.* "I threw up volcano rolls for six hours last weekend when the girls and I went out to celebrate the end of the semester. Literally anything else will do. *Please.*"

Have I mentioned how much I love my future sister-in-law? Well, I'm hopeful she will be one day. That's how serious I've become about my and Paxton's relationship. Payton has become one of my best friends. Not that I have many. I didn't go out of my way to mingle when I got here, mostly because I've been intently focused on getting my degree and landing this partnership. The girls in my class haven't exactly been Elle Woods, either. They've been more of a Vivian Kensington, if I'm being honest, and I don't know if I'd chalk that up to my attention from Paxton or being the recipient of the internship.

Probably both.

Either way, I keep to myself.

"You know what sounds good?" I hold my breath, waiting for Payton's suggestion. "Stanza's. I could *really* go for their carbonara and an arugula salad right about now."

Payton, I love you. I really, really love you.

"Oh, yes!" Mrs. Paige yells in excitement. She turns to me. "They have the *best* gnocchi and their tomato basil soup is to die for." A dabble of drool falls from her bottom lip onto her chin. She swipes at it unknowingly. "Is that drool?" We all burst into a fit of laughter. "Shit, I'm drooling." A laugh bubbles from her lips. "I told you it's good!"

Another wave of laughter rolls through us, and suddenly, all I can think about is food as my stomach rumbles. I haven't been eating much lately, which I'm sure isn't surprising, given my history. Plus, that disastrous breakfast cut my meal short, so now I'm starving.

I tried to take every interrogating comment and question in stride—even the offensive ones. I don't know what it's like to have a dad, much less a parent that cares about you or anything pertaining to your life, so I don't fault the man. Did he come off like an asshole? Sure, but I know his intentions are to protect his kids, and I don't rattle easily. I might not be confident when it comes to my physical body, but I like who I am as a person, and I won't let him scare me off with his concerns. I love his son, and I plan to be around as long as Paxton will have me. *Preferably forever.*

We finish our morning with a facial and a pedicure, foot massage included. It couldn't have been a more relaxing visit, which was severely overdue on my end. Now, we're on our way to the Italian restaurant for lunch. Mrs. Paige and Payton are sitting up front with me and Lauren in the back seat. I pull my phone out of my purse and turn it back on. The spa specifically makes all their customers turn off their phones and put them away in a locker to ensure they're getting the most out of their stay.

Once powered up, my phone vibrates, and my screen is lit up with texts from Paxton. I can't help but smile.

> **PAXTON**
>
> I miss you already, gorgeous.
>
> I hope you're enjoying yourself. You deserve it.
>
> We spent the morning at the Rec Center. Tell Lauren I'm grateful her fiancé is a beast at basketball because I suck and am dragging him down, just like last time. I did apologize to him profusely but tell her I'm sorry too. Anyway, I can't wait to see you later. 😚

The last one has me giggling, which warrants a shoulder check from Lauren, so I show her the text. Her head falls to the headrest in a laugh, and it just makes me laugh harder.

My poor guy. He might have one of the sexiest bodies I've ever seen, can bench press twice my weight in the gym, even run six miles without breaking a sweat, but he cannot play basketball to save his life. I don't know why he continues to put himself through that kind of torture.

Payton whips her head around. "What's so funny?" Her tone is playful, interest piqued.

"Your brother is getting his ass handed to him in basketball, again," I say reluctantly. "Does he like embarrassing himself? Why does he keep playing?" I shake my head, unable to comprehend.

"Easy," she responds, not even questioning which brother

I'm referring to. "Preston is great at it. Which means he will suggest playing against Paxton any chance he gets , since he knows he will win." She adds, "And Paxton is too proud to turn down a challenge, even if he knows he'll lose."

"Hmm," Lauren chimes in. "Must be the first-born syndrome." She continues, "Macy used to threaten to not play with me when we were kids unless it was what she wanted to do." She folds her arms over her chest, clearly reminiscing and pouting like the brat she is. "I could never have my favorite Barbies, drive *my* Barbie jeep, or play my favorite characters when we played pretend because they were conveniently also *her* favorite."

Payton snorts, and I give Lauren a heavy eyeroll.

Rolling my shoulders back and puffing my chest with pride I say, "And look at me now. A successful lawyer-to-be, all because I take charge."

"Damn right, baby!" Mrs. Paige yells. "You tell 'em!"

I swear her personality is infectious. She's so bubbly, but also a badass who seems like she doesn't take shit. Exhibit A: her husband. And the fact that she's an ER doctor only proves that even further and showcases the fact that she knows about determination and hard work. Plus, she's raising three highly intelligent and successful children. I know it takes a strong woman to do that.

What I would have given to be raised by someone who made me want to strive to follow in their footsteps versus the alternative. I saw how my mom lived her life, and I knew that I wanted no part in that lifestyle. I knew that as soon as I was able, I was going to leave and make something of myself. So I did just that. I applied for as many scholarships as I could, took out loans to cover the rest and studied my ass off to make sure I had the grades to get into law school. Once I graduated, I packed up and moved to Chicago.

Haven't looked back since.

We pull up to a restaurant labeled *Stanza, Italian Bistro &*

Wine Bar. It's a two-toned brown brick building with floor to ceiling glass windows and a wrap-around outdoor patio on the second floor. The railings are also made of glass, giving it a completely elegant and upscale vibe.

Payton leads the way, guiding us to the main entrance. The aroma of Italian dishes hits my nose as soon as we walk through the door, and my mouth begins to water. I can't wait to eat my weight in pasta.

Once we reach the hostess stand, Mrs. Paige requests a table on the balcony for the four of us, so the hostess guides us upstairs then directs us through a set of double doors and onto the spacious patio. The roof is covered in wall-to-wall exposed beams and softly lit with warm glowing light fixtures. It's breathtaking.

We're then seated at a round table covered in a white tablecloth, surrounded by wooden chairs that are lightly stained to match the wood panels above us. The cushions are a hideous shade of pea green, closely resembling baby food. *Ew.* Of all the colors they could've chosen, that's what they went with?

I'll bet any money that Lauren is concealing an aneurysm due to these seats. She is an interior designer, after all. If I had to guess, she'd probably suggest using taupe or dark gray to match the flooring.

My phone pings, and I try to stifle a laugh when I read the message on my screen.

> LAUREN
> Pistachio green? Really? They couldn't have gone with graphite instead? It's hideous, Mace. I think I threw up in my mouth a little.

Do I know my sister, or do I know my sister? I just shake my head with a small smirk as we take our seats. I open my menu and begin looking it over whenever my phone goes off again. I assume it'll be Lauren, judging the names of the dishes, or telling me what she's planning to order, but instead, it's another text from Paxton.

PAXTON
Babe. I lost. Bad. Like, really bad. So bad that Dillon left me, and we played three-on-one. So, if you haven't already apologized to Lauren for me, forget it. Tell her that her fiancé is a traitor.

> Brutal. I'll pass along the message. How's your ego holding up?

PAXTON
Not great, honestly. My dick might need some stroking. It took a beating.

Whoops, that was supposed to say ego*, not dick. Stupid autocorrect.

> You're insatiable, you know that right?

PAXTON
You mean charming?

> No, in fact, I do not.

PAXTON
Ah, sorry. The phone is breaking up. I can't hear you.

> BYE.

"Macy, what would you like to drink?" Payton pulls me from my phone.

I take a quick glance at the menu. "Uh, I'll take a water and the Cagliari Sunset, please."

"Great choice. It's a house favorite," our waiter says to me with a wink. He's handsome. Tall, tousled brown hair with eyes to match. And when he flashes me his award-winning smile, I feel my cheeks heat. I just hope that no one else notices.

It's not that I'm looking for attention elsewhere, but I'm just not used to it. Growing up, boys never glanced my way. Not until I was older and lost all my baby-weight. It makes me slightly uncomfortable when I notice a guy hitting on me, hence the blushing.

I hold my menu up in front of my face while skimming it. Everything sounds so fancy, and the prices reflect just how fancy they must be. *Tagliatelle, Mollusco, Diavolo.* Why the hell does everything have peas in it? Must be where the cushion color inspiration came from.

When our waiter returns with our drinks, he serves them one by one, saving mine for last. He steps next to my chair, placing it down in front of me and brushes my shoulder on the way back up. If the wink wasn't intentional enough, this *definitely* was. Luckily, everyone is buried in their own menus to witness his display of affection. With his close proximity, I notice the name on his nametag: Ryan. Hmm, never would've pegged him as a Ryan. He looks more like a Connor.

Connor, I mean Ryan, takes everyone's orders. Again, saving me for last. Although I was craving pasta, none of them sound even remotely appetizing, so I end up ordering a cup of tomato basil soup and The Piedmontese sandwich, no mushrooms, because *gross*. Beef, mozzarella, roasted red peppers and caramelized onions?

Yes. Please.

After ordering, I excuse myself to find the restroom. Walking through the double doors, I search the large dining area for a sign signaling the women's room. This place is huge, so I begin wandering around, only to bump into, you guessed it.

Connor. I mean, Ryan.

"Excuse me, I'm sorry," he says before realizing it's me. "Oh. It's you."

It's me? What does that even mean? How do I respond to that? Uh, yes, it's me? Hey, it's you, too? No. Because that would imply I was looking for him, which clearly, I am not. Nope. Just looking for the good ole loo. Do they still call it that? Either way, I'm still standing here, trying to search my brain for a damn response, but coming up short. He probably thinks I'm an idiot, unable to speak. So I just smile.

That's it.

That's my brilliant response.

He sticks out his hand toward me. "I'm Ryan, by the way."

My silence has not deterred him, obviously. Again, I give him a quick smile, but this time I reach for his hand and give it a shake because I'm a nice gal.

"Gathered that by name tag." I point to it, and he looks down with a sheepish expression. "Macy."

"Nice to meet you." He returns the handshake with that perfect grin of his. I'm sure that smile gets him in a lot of trouble. *And panties.* Good thing I'm immune. "Is there something I can help you with, or were you just looking for me?"

Oh dear God.

Abort! Abort!

Maybe if I'm a little less lady-like, he'll be turned off and leave me alone. "Nope. Just looking for a place to empty my bladder. That's all."

Annnd there's a laugh. *Come on, dude.* I'm not even that funny. Ask anyone.

"Right this way." He gestures for me to follow him, which I do. You know, so I don't pee my pants in this very restaurant. Although maybe *that* would get him to finally give up. But then I think better of it because I don't have a change of clothes, and I really don't want to sit through lunch smelling like urine. "I don't assume you're from around here since I've never seen you before."

So it continues.

"I'm not, but Salt Lake City is a pretty big area. I could be from here, and there's still a large possibility that we'd never cross paths." Why the hell do I need to elaborate? I could've just said no. Leave it to me to go the extra mile.

He cocks his brow, a smile playing on his lips. "Well, that was a little hostile." He chuckles, leading me down a narrow hall. "But I guess it's also valid."

"Sorry," I apologize. "I blame the lawyer in me. She always needs to defend her answer."

"Lawyer, huh?" Ryan makes a sharp right and points down the short hallway. "That's pretty hot."

Once again, my face feels like an inferno. This feels wrong on so many levels, and I'm not even doing anything. It's not like I'm flirting back or allowing him to make any moves. So why the hell do I feel so guilty?

He thumbs behind him. "Second door on your left. Good luck with your urinary endeavors." And without another word, he shuffles back in the direction we came and leaves me to my business.

After what feels like an eternity—but in reality was only eleven minutes— I return to the table. The girls are engaged in conversation, sipping their drinks. I take a long pull of mine, and try to immerse myself in their chatter, but my mind goes straight to Paxton, guilt settling in. The gut-wrenching feeling in my stomach has yet to subside, so I try to run through the events of lunch thus far.

Did I unknowingly make a move? *No. I literally sat down and ordered like everyone else.*

Was there any flirting on my end? *Not that I recall.*

I backtrack over every word, every movement, all my body language. Nothing screamed, *come on to me.*

After wracking my brain for a solid five minutes, I realize that his actions aren't my fault. What he chooses to do is not a reflection of me. I didn't invite his flirting, and I didn't reciprocate it either, so I need to stop blaming myself.

"So we were just discussing a makeover for my apartment," Payton announces. "Lauren has some really cute ideas."

"Yeah, we were thinking boho chic meets minimalist." Lauren pulls out her phone and shows me the Pinterest board her and Payton created while I was in the bathroom. "Totally her style, right?"

She shows me pictures of cream-colored living rooms with bright art on the walls, a sleek and stylish bedroom with a white comforter and colorful throw pillows, and a very sleek kitchen with accent cabinets.

I nod in agreement, doing my best to take part in their excitement. "The pops of color will look amazing, P." I turn to Lauren. "You're the best in the business, Lo. I know if anyone can make it come to life, it's you."

That answer satisfies them both, and they get back to pinning their ideas. Not long after, our food arrives. Ryan sets a large tray on the table next to ours and begins unloading our plates. I'm not sure why he chooses to serve me last, but at this point, I expect it. He sets down my soup and sandwich, then politely asks if we need anything else. We all shake our heads, and Mrs. Paige thanks him.

Once he heads back inside, all of us tear into our meals. And holy crap, this soup is heaven. Hearty, creamy, and the perfect consistency. I tear off a piece of my sandwich and dip it into the tomatoey goodness. *Orgasmic.*

By the time we're all finished eating, Ryan collects our plates and drops off the check. Of course, Mrs. Paige snatches it up without a second thought.

We all thank her as we rise from our chairs and head inside toward the exit. Before we make it fully out of the door, an arm catches my elbow. I spin around to find Ryan, a receipt in his hand.

Lauren, Payton and her mom are standing behind me, and I can only imagine the looks on their faces right now.

He hands me the piece of paper with his full name—Ryan Adams, in case you're wondering—and a phone number scribbled on the back.

"I know you're not local, and I'm not sure how long you're here for, but if you ever find yourself back in Utah, I'd love to take you on a date." He flashes me that charming grin of his one last time. "I'm in my last year of engineering, by the way. I won't be waiting tables for a living."

As if that'll change the fact that I have a Paxton.

I return the paper to him. "I appreciate the gesture, but I have a boyfriend." His shoulders deflate, and his smile falls flat. "Thank you for lunch."

He nods.

Mortified, I turn around, and we all walk out the door and toward the car. I train my eyes on the ground, keeping them from going anywhere near those three grinning women.

Chapter 45
Macy

Good. Fucking. Girl.

As soon as the engine comes to life and we're in route back to the cabin, Payton spins around in the front seat, Lauren turns to face me, and Mrs. Paige eyes me from the rearview mirror. Each of their faces are plastered with narrowed, humorous gazes.

"Not. A. Word." I pin them all with a death glare as their warning, but do they listen to me? Of course not. Why would they ever be nice to me?

Payton shrugs. "I mean, I think you should've taken him up on his offer." She then receives a flick to the temple from her mother. "Ow! What was that for?!"

"Oh, I don't know," Mrs. Paige responds sarcastically. "Paxton Andrew Meyers. Ring any bells?"

Pretending to mull over her answer while Lauren buries her laugh behind her hand, Payton finally answers. "Not any good ones." She pauses then adds. "Besides, he was delicious. I think you should go for it."

This time, it's a smack to the arm resulting in a girly

shriek, and I can't help but grin a little. I may not have had this type of relationship with my mom, but I'm glad I get to partake in it now, with a bonus sister added to the mix.

I snap my fingers as though I just came up with a brilliant idea, *because I did.*

"Here's a thought. How about, drum roll please..." Lauren initiates my pretend drums on her thighs because she has a love for the dramatics. When she stops, I announce, "*You* date him then."

Her face twists in disgust. "Okay, one, I don't have time for a boyfriend. You know, med student and all that jazz. And two, even if I did, I wouldn't be chasing someone who is so clearly interested in someone who is *not* me." She rolls her eyes so hard I'm surprised they don't get stuck back there.

Payton does have a point though. I wouldn't pine over someone who didn't want me either. Let me rephrase that. I wouldn't pine over someone who didn't want me *again*. Because let's be real, no one wanted me before the age of seventeen. Crushing on guys I had no business even looking at was something I did all throughout middle school and high school. But now, I know my worth. I've used that to my advantage over the years.

Was it right? No, probably not.

Did it feel good to finally have the upper hand for once? Hell yeah, it did.

Knowing I don't have to worry about feeling unwanted anymore gives me a sense of peace I've never had before. And that's all thanks to Paxton. He's been nothing but loving and attentive. He shows me he's attracted to me and wants me. Not only does he prove it to me physically by the way he can never keep his hands off me, but he throws out words of affirmation, always telling me how beautiful I am. Some might think that's superficial or shallow, but when you're someone who's struggled with their self-image her entire life, it means more than all the annoyingly sweet things most women expect from their significant other.

So, who needs Connor Ryan Adams when I have Paxton Andrew Meyers?

I shoot off a text to my boyfriend, so he knows I'm thinking about him.

> I need to talk to you about something.

Almost immediately, those three bubbles appear.

PAXTON
> Okay, talk.

> When I get back.

PAXTON
> You're not serious.

> I am.

PAXTON
> You don't get to text me "we need to talk" and then not talk about said thing.

When I don't respond, he calls. When I don't answer, he calls again, and then a third time. At this point, I'm grinning so hard my cheeks hurt. I don't normally condone this behavior. *Who am I kidding, yes, I do.* But since it's news he won't be expecting, I'm being childish about it. Can't a girl be excited about telling her boyfriend she loves him for the first time??

PAXTON
> Just know, you are a cruel, cruel woman.

> Also, if die from a heart attack due to your lack of response, just know it's all your fault.

Wow. He's so dramatic. And cute. Incredibly cute. But still dramatic.

And what do you know? As soon as the cabin comes into view, there stands Paxton, pacing the front porch—waiting for me, I assume.

"What the hell is he doing?" I hear Payton ask.

I bite the inside of my cheek to stop my laughter. "I may or may not have told him we need to talk."

All three heads whip in my direction. "Oh, so he's finally having that mental breakdown about him being alone forever then," she says nonchalantly. "I've been waiting for it for four years now."

Well shit.

Now I'm afraid to get out of the car. He looks distraught. Maybe this was a bad idea. But it's too late now. The minute Mrs. Paige puts the car in park, Paxton flings my door open, gesturing for me to evacuate the back seat.

With a sheepish grin, I slowly remove myself, avoiding his eye contact.

"Upstairs, now," he commands, pointing to the house.

Three chuckles fill the air behind me, which warrants them the most vicious glare I've ever seen Paxton wear. They all drop their laughter and hold their hands up in surrender as we step through the door.

Immediately, he drags me up the stairs by my wrist. Like, literally drags me, and I think at this point I may have taken it too far.

Paxton pushes the door open and releases my arm. He points to the bed.

"Sit. Talk. Right now." His tone is edgy, and I might be a bit terrified to admit what I'm about to say. I thought about it on the way over, and I'm not a very romantic person. I didn't want to plan anything special or make a big deal out of it because even though I've never said these words out loud to a guy before, I don't want it to be cheesy. All I care about is that he knows I mean them, no special occasion necessary.

"Okay…" I drag out, sitting at the edge of the bed. When I sink down, my shoulders fall with the long breath I release.

Come on. You can do this. Just tell him.

My heart is beating so fast in my chest that I fear it might escape my body. Nerves swarm my stomach. What if he doesn't feel the same way? Surely, he does. Doesn't he? He pursued me first. He was the first to admit his feelings for me. He's been nothing but all in this entire time, right?

Paxton must notice the doubt swirling around in my head because he kneels on the floor between my legs and takes my face with both of his hands. "Hey, what's going on?" His voice is now filled with concern, and my heart constricts.

Of course, he loves me. Look at the way he tends to me in a time of need. No guy behaves like this just for the hell of it.

Quit stalling.

Quit overthinking.

I cover his wrists and lower his hands from my face, holding them instead. I look into his beautiful blue-green eyes, getting lost in the overflowing love and appreciation I have for this man. He's everything I never knew I wanted. He's the reason I finally see a future with someone. The ring, the house, maybe even the kids; I want all of it—with him.

"Babe, you're scaring me," Paxton says softly, directing my attention back to him.

Just say it.

"I love you." The words are foreign, but they don't feel wrong. In fact, they've never felt more right. Like I was meant to save them just for him. But when his head falls to my lap and a sigh leaves his lips, I start to regret opening my mouth.

No. You love him. Regardless of reciprocation, you love him.

I can hear my heart beating wildly in my ears, and I think I might throw up from embarrassment. What was I thinking?

"Jesus. *Thank fuck*," Paxton curses.

I'm sorry, what was that?

He lifts his head, meeting my gaze again, a crease forming between his brows. I'm expressionless because I really don't understand what's going on at this point. My heart is still hammering, waiting for an alternate response.

But instead of words, he braces my face with both hands and presses a demanding kiss to my lips then releases me, dropping his forehead to mine.

"I love you too, Macy." He sighs again.

He does? Fireworks erupt and butterflies take flight in my belly. The beating of my heart is scarily increasing to the proximity of a-fib, and everything in my world is right. *He loves me.*

"Could you maybe, like... say that again?"

"I love you," he whispers, kissing me again. I smile against his lips then pull back.

"One more time. I don't think I heard you correctly."

"Macy Brooke Callahan, I love you. I have for a while, but if you ever think of pulling some shit like that again, there *will* be consequences," he threatens. "I was worried fucking sick."

"I'm sorry. But uh, what kind of consequences are we talking?" I ask playfully. "I like spankings, in case you need ideas."

His eyes grow dark, lustful. And before I know it, my back hits the mattress and Paxton is hovering above me, arms on either side of my head. This man is so fucking sexy. I can't even begin to comprehend how he's mine. How he chose me, out of everyone. I'm more than willing to accept it though.

He lowers himself down, his lips connecting with mine. It's soft and sweet, but perfect in every way. I snake my hands over his shoulders, sliding them up his neck and into his hair. As I fist it tighter, Paxton groans and deepens the kiss, so I open my mouth slightly to give him access. Our tongues become a tangled web, sending a jolt of pleasure right between my legs.

My roaming hands find their way down to the band of his sweatpants. I slide them down over that perfectly chiseled ass of his, and he swiftly tears my leggings off, taking my underwear with them.

"Condom," I mutter while sitting up to pull his shirt over his head, him taking mine off in return.

Butt naked as the day he was born, Paxton heads to the closet to grab his bag. Rifling through it, he begins getting frustrated. "Did you pack any condoms? I guess I forgot."

All hope of getting railed so hard I feel him for the next week, diminishes. How the hell could we forget to bring protection? I figured he would remember, so I know I didn't grab any. I shake my head in return to his question.

"It'll be fine just one more time, right?" He waggles his brows and stalks towards me; within seconds, he's on top of me again.

I place a hand to his chest. "Abso-fucking-lutely not." I stop him. "No condom, no sticking your dick in my tight, wet..."

Paxton pins me down, and my breath hitches, not finishing that sentence. "Don't fucking tease me like that," he says, nipping at my bottom lip. "Six more days of not fucking you? I don't fucking think so."

He grinds his pelvis into mine, and I can feel his entire length up against my center. It's both heaven and hell because I want him. No, I *need* him, desperately. And I am on birth control, so it's not like we're one-hundred percent unprotected.

Fuck it.

I'm about to agree, when I decide to push him just a little bit further. Maybe he'll give me that spanking I so rightfully deserve.

So I continue. "Welp, sorry bud. You're not getting a ride on my magic carpet without proper attire." It's killing me not to laugh in his face right now, but I somehow manage to keep my shit together.

His expression reads defeat, but he doesn't push me any

further. Instead, he pecks my lips ever so gently and says, "okay."

Then slowly, he starts to rise off me, planting himself at the foot of the bed. I adjust myself so that I'm leaning back on my elbows, staring at him. Honestly, his self-restraint is impressive, but this is *not* how we're ending things.

"Okay?" I question. "That's it? Just 'okay?'"

I'm still completely undressed, nipples hardening from the lack of contact they just had.

"Well yeah," he replies. "You said we're not having sex. Ergo, I stopped."

Rising to my knees, I make my way toward him. I run my hand down his cheek and over the slight stubble he's accumulated since we've been here.

"I appreciate your gentleman-like ways, but I was just busting your balls." With my mouth now brushing his ear, I whisper, "I'm on birth control, so if you don't find your way inside me within the next five seconds, I'll be forced to please myself."

His throat bobs, taking a long swallow.

"And no, you will not be allowed to watch."

With that, I'm immediately spun around and pushed down so that my forearms are resting on the bed. Ass in the air, Paxton grabs my hips and lines himself up to my center. Without warning, he simultaneously places a stinging slap to my right cheek while thrusting into me.

"*Oh, God,*" I cry out from both pain and pleasure.

"I told you next time you gave me shit, there would be consequences." His voice is gravely, like it's taking all his restraint to speak. When he twists my hair in his fist and pulls it taut, I moan loudly. I blame all the romance novels for turning me into a masochist. Who knew pain could pull so much euphoria from your body? "Are you going to be a good girl from now on?"

Those books also confirmed the fact that I, indeed, have a

praise kink. Please, tell me I'm good— the best, actually. I want to know that I'm the reason behind every moan, every breathless pant, every grip to the sheets. I gain so much satisfaction by hearing those words.

But because I want him to spank me again, I disagree. His body stills.

Smack.

Oof. That one stung. Maybe it'll leave a handprint. I'd love for him to mark me.

I push back against him, circling my hips trying to gain some friction.

Smack.

"We finish when I say we finish." *Jesus Christ, I love a commanding man.* "Now, would you like to revisit that last answer?"

When I nod, he says, "good fucking girl," and plows so deep into me, I can feel him in my throat. It's the fullest I've ever felt, and it's fucking delicious.

Paxton slams into me again, harder this time, and I see spots. White hot pleasure ripples through me, and I know my climax is approaching.

I reach between my legs, running my fingers over my clit as he continuously takes me from behind.

"That's it. Play with that pretty pussy while I fuck you like this."

His words send me into a spiral and his name falls off my lips, over and over. "Fuck baby, I'm coming," is the last thing I hear before my orgasm explodes and I collapse onto the sheets, Paxton falling on top of me.

Holy shit.

I don't know if it's the aftermath of saying I love you, or the fact that there was no barrier between us, but that was the best sex of my entire life, and I can't wait to do it again.

Chapter 46
Paxton

Birthday Girl

I'm sated. Completely and utterly spent as I collapse behind Macy and roll onto my back next to her. I stare at the ceiling, taking shallow breaths, trying to come down from my high. If that's even possible. And even though the sex was mind-blowingly out of this world, the grin on my face is for an entirely different reason.

She loves me.

She fucking loves me.

Part of me feels like this is all just a figment of my imagination, like something I conjured up in my head to finally coax me through my feelings for her. I know I love her. I have for longer than I care to admit to either of us, but Dillon's words have been on a constant loop in my head for weeks, causing all sorts of fear to take hold of me.

She's dealt with a lot, and Lauren says it's clouded her perception of love. Just be careful.

I know she doesn't love easily. She doesn't take relationships lightly. She told me so herself. That any time she would get close to falling for someone, she would end her relationship. So for her to love me is a big damn deal, and I'll make sure to never do anything to mess that up. This is a forever kind of thing. For me, at least.

Macy rolls onto her side, clinging to me as her hand absently runs up and down my chest and torso. Goosebumps break out over my skin at her touch. She inches her face closer, resting her head on my shoulder. I can feel her looking up at me, but I don't allow myself to reciprocate.

"I can hear you thinking," she says quietly. "Talk to me."

Rather than making eye contact with her, I maintain my focus on the ceiling, watching the fan spin in circles. Sort of like my emotions right now. They're all over the place. I'm starting to fall from cloud nine as my thoughts take on a mind of their own. She might love me now, sure; but what if she decides later that she doesn't? That this is a mistake. That *we're* a mistake. I can't go through another heartbreak or failed relationship.

"Paxton." My name is a whisper on her lips. Cupping my cheek, she turns my gaze to meet hers. Beautiful hazel eyes stare up at me, questioning every moment that just unfolded between us. "I—"

I cut her off with a kiss because I'm too afraid to hear what she might say, and equally as afraid that I might say something I don't mean out of fear. I don't regret telling her I love her. I've been wanting to, but fear is a funny thing. It makes you second guess every decision you've ever made, every word you've ever spoken or will speak. And I don't want this to be one of those times. So I won't let it be.

My fingers tangle in her hair, pulling her in closer. I lose myself in this kiss, pretending that everything will be okay from this moment forward. Because it will be. It has to be. She loves me and I love her. Nothing can take that away.

Christmas flies by in the blink of an eye. Macy somehow scored us tickets to the last Bears game of the season; *did I mention I love her?* And I got her a brown leather briefcase with her name engraved into the gold handle for her future endeavors, which may or may not have made her tear up. In case you're wondering, it did.

But my favorite gift of all? The look on her face after giving her a spare key to my apartment. It's a big step, I know, and it's not like I'm asking her to move in or anything. But I want her to feel comfortable enough to come and go as she pleases. And if she happens to be waiting in my bed in lingerie when I get home one day? Well, win-win.

We've been busy all week, and now it's already New Year's Eve. We're spending the day on the slopes—the bunny ones, I might add. Macy got tired of busting her ass, so we've resorted to snow tubing. Would I rather be snowboarding? Sure, but whatever makes my girl happy is what we're going to do. And from the constant smile on her face and overflowing laughter, I'd say she's pretty damn happy.

I'm standing at the bottom of the slope with Preston while all three girls pile onto one inner tube. Dillon stands behind them, ready to send them on their way. He gets a slow running start and pushes off the tube, sending them sailing down the slope. Macy throws her head back, my favorite sound exiting her mouth, and my heart squeezes in my chest. The rate at which I fell for this girl may have been incredibly fast, but she's everything I want and more. Which is why I've planned a surprise party for her tonight at one of the local ski lodges in town for her birthday.

Will she be mad? Probably.

Do I care? Yes and no.

Yes, because I love her and truly don't want to see her upset; but no, because she deserves to be celebrated, and I want to be the one to make that happen. She's spent her entire life taking care of someone else. It's time someone takes care of her.

I know she hates to be the center of attention, and under any other circumstance, I wouldn't put her through that. This is the only exception though. Earlier this year, she made me promise not to get her a present in exchange for telling me when her birthday is. And because I don't go back on my word, this is my compromise.

Since she won't let me spoil her directly, I put Lauren and Payton on shopping duty this afternoon. I gave them my card and told them to let her pick out whatever outfit she wanted today, on me. Sneaky, right?

"You ready for tonight?" Preston's voice cuts through my thoughts as he nudges my shoulder.

The girls are going for another round down the slopes with Dillon trailing behind them, so Preston and I are left alone once again.

I nod, sticking my freezing hands in my snowsuit pockets.

"And you're sure she has no idea?"

"I'm still alive, aren't I?" I answer. "She knows we're going to a New Year's Eve party tonight; she just doesn't know it's for her."

My brother crosses his arms over his chest and gives me a pointed look. "You're really going all out for this girl. You in love or something?" He arches a brow, waiting for my answer, though I think he already knows.

I remove my right hand from my pocket to scrub it over my face. Preston and I have always been close. We're not afraid to talk about relationships, though he's a lot more private than I am, and we've always been open and honest with each other about everything. All of us have. It's just the way we were raised.

Our parents established open communication at a young age because they've always wanted us to know it was okay to come to them about anything. None of that "boys don't cry or talk about their feelings bullshit," which I was thankful for. I leaned on my parents a lot growing up, especially my mom. And on days when she didn't know the right thing to say, I had Preston doing his best to work through those hard times with me.

"Yeah, actually. I am." I pause. "And before you tell me it's too soon—"

"I wasn't," he cuts me off. "I think she's good for you. I like her a lot. She's laid back, quick as a whip with sarcasm and just fits in with us." A breath leaves him, clouding the air in front of us with cold, white smoke, before he continues. "I know I'm not the first to say Jade wasn't exactly my favorite person, but I will be the first to say that Macy is everything Jade wasn't. And I think that's my favorite thing about her. You deserve to be happy, P, and I can see that girl makes you insanely happy."

Preston isn't typically a sap. That title is normally reserved for me, but I think he might have me beat right now. Which is weird. To see him so... emotional is new for me. Like I said, we're open with each other, but he always keeps his personal life more guarded. Usually, unless I pry, he's pretty quiet. Part of me wonders if the loneliness is creeping in on him.

"Well I appreciate that. She does make me very happy." Finally making eye contact with him, I admit, "She's the one. She's it for me."

A chuckle leaves his lips, as if to say, "*I already figured as much.*" He's always known me best, besides Penelope, so I'm sure my confession didn't come as a surprise to him.

"Just try to keep this one, okay?" His laugh fills the air around us, but there's a dull ache, reminding me that my first engagement failed miserably. I know he didn't mean anything by it, but it still stings. And although I wasn't the cause of our undoing, I still wonder if there was something more I could've done to save us.

No.

Stop.

That type of thinking is what landed me in therapy in the first place. She was sick—mentally and emotionally. There was nothing I could do to fix that. *She's* the one who went off the deep end. *She's* the one who destroyed our relationship with her control issues and incessant need to fight all the time.

I rarely play the victim card, but I know I'm not the one to blame. I was on the receiving end of her constant wrath, and eventually, I had to get out.

I need to stop justifying the situation and see it for what it is.

My past.

A lesson learned.

The end.

The realization of our screwed-up relationship may have left me damaged for the last four years, but it brought me right where I'm supposed to be. Here with Macy.

I can feel my brows furrow as I'm deep in thought, which only means Preston must notice too.

"Hey man," he says in a low tone. "Get out of your head. I was just poking fun."

When I nod but don't respond, he fires back, "Seriously, I wasn't thinking when I said that." Then he pulls me into his side with his arm wrapped around my shoulder. "It wasn't your fault, so quit thinking it."

Before I can form a sentence, both Preston and I are taken to the ground. I'm flat on my back, staring up at the crystal blue sky while laughter fills my ears. To the right of me, all three girls are piled on top of each other, laughing in hysterics. The inner tube is somewhere off in the distance, and Dillon stands above us with a shit-eating grin.

"Oops," he says nonchalantly, like he didn't just try to dislocate both of my knees with brunt force.

He helps the girls up first then lends a hand to me and helps me to my feet.

Out of the corner of my eye, I see Macy charging toward me. The minute I turn, she's hopping into my arms, legs winding around my waist. Instinctively, I grip her ass with both hands, hoisting her up my body. When she's good and settled, her arms find my neck as she pulls me in for a kiss. It's quick, but it doesn't stop from sending a bolt of pleasure straight down to my dick.

And now I'm turned on. Perfect.

"Thank you for being a good sport today. I had a lot of fun." She pecks my lips again, and I smile against hers.

"Anything for you, babe," I whisper.

Macy is abruptly pulled from me, and she shrieks. My body instantly shivers from the loss of warmth of her body wrapped around me. Payton and Lauren are hauling her away while both giving me a wink.

"We're going shopping! See you idiots later," Payton shouts behind her.

Then they disappear down the slope until they're no longer in view.

I turn to Preston and Dillon. "Time to get to work, boys."

They both huff because they're assholes, but they follow me to the car, and we head to The Snowpine Lodge to set up for tonight.

Once the ballroom is draped in gold, silver and black décor, we head back to our cabin to pregame. The girls are still out doing their thing but should be back shortly, according to Payton. Apparently, they decided to treat themselves to lunch—on me, *secretly*—which is what's taking them so long. She also mentioned that they will be getting ready together, so I shouldn't wait. It's coming up on eight o'clock, so I take a quick shower and begin getting myself ready.

I stand in front of the mirror, observing myself after I'm fully dressed. I decided on black dress pants, a black blazer and a white button up with the top two buttons undone.

Freshly groomed face?

Check.
Hair perfectly styled?
Check.
Macy's favorite dimple? I grin at myself.
Check.

I look dapper as fuck, if I do say so myself. If Macy doesn't want to sneak me off to a closet tonight after seeing me, I might need to get her head evaluated. Am I being a bit cocky? Sure, but seriously, I look like I just walked out of a GQ magazine. All so I can impress my girl.

I make my way down to the kitchen where my parents are talking quietly in the corner, each drinking a glass of wine. Dillon and Preston are lining up shots of some sort. The small glasses are filled with a light-yellow liquid, lemon wedges sitting next to each one. Which only means one thing: *lemon drops*. My mouth waters. It's been a while since I've drank, and I'm anticipating a good night ahead of us, so I join the guys at the island as we wait for the girls to arrive.

The sound of heels hit the hardwood steps and in walk two long-haired blondes dressed to the nines. Lauren, in white pants that flare at the ankles and a white sequin top with a fluff of feathers attached at the wrists. Payton is also wearing white pants, high-waisted, with a white blazer, half buttoned and a silver sequin crop top underneath. Both look gorgeous, but when my girlfriend walks through the threshold of the kitchen, all the breath in my lungs ceases to exist.

Jesus fuck.

She looks phenomenal in all black. Her black pants sit just above her belly button, and she's wearing a one-shoulder, long-sleeve black sequin top. The exposed arm shows off her entire sleeve of tattoos, as well as the one across her collarbone. And damn if I don't want to kiss that spot right now.

Macy's makeup is dark and smoky, bringing out those golden flecks in her eyes. Her long, auburn hair is pulled back into a slicked-back ponytail, but it's still long enough that it hangs between her shoulder blades.

I'm going to request that she keep it up later, so I can wrap it around my fist and pull her head taught while I fuck her from behind.

I can feel my dick thickening behind my zipper. He's going to have to cool it for now. We still have roughly three hours before midnight. But once that clock strikes twelve, I'm going to give Macy the best birthday sex she's ever had. I'll make sure of it.

Payton's hand lifts my jaw off the floor and closes my apparently open mouth. That's when I snap out of my trance.

"Now that you're done openly ogling your smokin' hot girlfriend, can we get this party started?" She grabs the sugar shaker from the cabinet and douses each piece of lemon with some.

Macy smirks my way then walks toward me and places a kiss on my cheek. She leans in a little closer and whispers, "I can't wait to get you out of that suit later."

And with that, my dick comes to a full salute that I need to adjust before everyone catches a glimpse of how badly I want to nail this sexy redhead in front of me.

I think we're about four shots in when Preston announces our Uber driver is waiting outside to take us to the lodge. We each down one more shot for good measure and head out the door. We ordered an extra-large vehicle so we could all fit comfortably. Everyone piles into the Tahoe one by one, excluding my parents. They said they wanted to drive so they could leave whenever they were ready.

The drive to The Snowpine Lodge is only ten minutes, but because of the snowfall, it's taking a bit longer. Utah in the winter is gorgeous, but the nights are exceptionally cold. I feel Macy shiver next to me, so I wrap her in my arms and rub my hands up and down hers to warm her up. It does the trick because she instantly relaxes.

A few short minutes later, we pull up and the driver lets us out. We file out individually, but I stay back to hand him a tip. "Thanks for the ride, man. Drive safe."

Everyone hurries inside to escape the cold. When we walk through the doors, Lauren and Macy crane their necks to take in the place. The high ceilings, the modern art and sleek furniture. It's a complete one-eighty to the cabin vibe you'd expect a lodge to possess.

I guide us down the hallway that leads to the ballroom while checking the time on my watch. It's almost eleven, which means everyone should be in place. Preston checks his phone for an update then gives me the signal to walk in. With Macy's hand in mine, I push open the double doors and let her lead.

The moment she enters, the entire room erupts with confetti and cheers of "Happy birthday!"

Immediately, she stops in her tracks and turns to me.

If looks could kill, I'd be a dead man.

Chapter 48
Macy

Leave the Pony

I'm going to kill him.

I'm. Going. To. Kill. Him.

I manage to put on a brave face and redirect my attention to the room full of complete strangers. They're all staring at me with gaping smiles, confetti poppers in hand, waiting for a *thank you.*

It's the least I can do, I guess. Even though I have no idea who any of them are.

Paxton slides in behind me, resting his arm around my waist, and instantly I feel at ease. I'm still mad at him for this, make no mistake, but at least he's bringing me the comfort I'm desperately seeking. So I do what any good girlfriend would do, and I smile at the nameless guests, then follow it up with a collective "thank you" to close out my appreciation.

"Can I speak with you for a second?" I ask as I gesture toward the private area curtained off at the back of the ballroom.

Once again, I lead and Paxton follows. Only this time, I'm not being ambushed.

As soon as we're alone, I fist his perfectly ironed shirt at the collar and yank him into me. A little too hard because I lose my balance and shift backward. Luckily, Paxton has proven time and time again to have ninja-like reflexes because he catches me from the back and rights us before we topple over.

His stupidly charming grin breaks out over his face, and I already know to expect a smart-ass comment in three… two… one…

"If you want me that badly, baby, all you have to do is ask. No need to cause a scene."

And there it is.

I casually roll my eyes as I often do before sending attitude his way. "What I *want* is for you to tell me what the hell this is. And who the hell are all those people?"

I motion to my right, as if he doesn't already know there's an entire room full of randoms on the other side of this curtain. Of course, he does. He orchestrated this whole damn thing!

"You said no presents. I obliged. You never said anything about a party."

A long sigh escapes me. He really is impossible, I swear.

"You're the most stubborn man I have ever met. You know that, right?"

A nod and a feather-light kiss to my lips is all it takes to break my resolve. "I know. But I didn't break my promise. That's all that matters." He brushes his thumb across my cheek. "Now can we get back out there, please? You look too good not to show off."

A smile plays on my lips, but I'm still going to make him work for it. No matter how charming he can be. And honestly, how can I be angry when did all of this for me? Am I full on embarrassed? Mortified would be a better term. But I'm also grateful for him and his thoughtfulness. Birthdays were celebrated few and far in between when I was a kid, if at all. So I am a *tiny* bit excited. He doesn't need to know that, though.

"Damn right, I do," I quip back before flipping my perfectly sleek ponytail and strutting away while he watches.

Now that I've had time to mingle—uncomfortably I might add—I do notice a few people we've met over the last week while doing touristy things. Two couples to be exact. Brynna and Miles are around our age, both twenty-seven. They're from South Carolina and are vacationing with their families for the holidays as well.

Jensen and Noelle are closer to Preston's age. She's twenty-eight and he's thirty. According to Noelle, they're on their babymoon. With their first due in February, they needed a getaway to spend some much-needed quality time together before his arrival. She wears pregnancy extraordinarily well, too; dressed in a midnight blue jumpsuit that hugs her bump just right.

I've never wanted to be a mom. I still don't know if I do. Not much has changed in that department, except for the tall, dark, and handsome man following me around tonight. But if I ever do consider it, in the distant future, I hope I look half as good as Noelle.

"Happy birthday!" She wraps me in a hug. "You look incredible."

I stifle a laugh. This woman is eight months pregnant and effortlessly wearing three-inch heels.

"Me?" I point to her. "You literally look like you belong on a runway. How you're managing to walk around on those things while harboring a baby the size of a watermelon is beyond me."

We both chuckle and take a sip of our champagne flutes—hers filled with cider, of course.

Paxton wraps his arms around me from behind, his hand ghosting over my stomach. He leans in close, his lips brushing against my ear. "You're going to be the sexiest MILF in the entire damn world," he says in a hushed tone.

The words catch me off guard because we've never once talked about a future with a family. A future that I'm not sure I can give him. But now, the thought of him coming inside me bare sends my body temperature skyrocketing.

I down my drink to hide the flush on my face, and Noelle and I pick back up in conversation. We talk for a considerable amount of time before I realize that we're alone.

At some point during our conversation, the men wandered off to the bar. I pull my phone from my wristlet to check the time. Six minutes till midnight, so we make our way over to our guys. Lauren and Dillon are standing at the far end taking shots, with Preston across from us, talking to some gorgeous brunette in a silver dress. She's laughing, which is a good sign. No ring, I also noticed. Maybe they're hitting it off and he'll finally find his person.

Wouldn't that be wild, I think to myself.

I scan the room to look for Payton. White sequins catch my eye, and low and behold, she's grinding on some guy in the middle of the dance floor. Her back is to his chest, arms around his neck. His hands are splayed across her waist while he matches her rhythm. I inwardly smile. It's safe to say everyone has their New Year's kiss.

The countdown begins.

Ten…

Nine…

Eight…

At midnight, Paxton snakes one hand around my neck and the other around my lower back. In one quick swoop, he crashes our bodies together while his lips descend on mine.

Confetti and balloons fall from the ceiling. Paper horns are blown in celebration. Loud cheers erupt, signifying the new year. But all I can focus on is the fireworks between the two of us. The feeling of this kiss. His body against mine. My racing heart.

Tonight, something shifted. I don't know what it is yet, but I can feel it deep within. Something's different between us. *I'm* different. But in the best way. Things can only get better from here.

When we finally come up for air, Paxton grabs my face with both hands and rests his forehead against mine. "Happy birthday, gorgeous. I love you."

I reach up for another kiss. Lightly pressing my lips to his, I smile. "I love you too, Paxton."

It's after two am when we all stumble back into the cabin. We're a mess of tangled bodies, clacking heels that are quickly discarded onto the floor, and hushed whispers that are a little too loud.

"Shhhhh," Preston whisper-yells. "Mom and dad are sleeping!"

Fumbling down the hallway, Payton runs straight into the wall and falls to the floor. Numerous laughs expel from multiple mouths. I don't think we've ever been this drunk before, and it's showing.

The door at the end of the hall creaks open, followed by a head poking around the doorframe. Payton looks up from her place on the floor, and the grin on Mrs. Paige's face reveals that she's just as amused by our intoxication as we are.

"Well, I'm glad to see you all made it home okay." She chuckles. "Now go get some sleep."

"Yes ma'am," we all somehow manage to say in unison.

Then she wanders back into her room and shuts the door.

Dillon helps Payton up and guides her and Lauren upstairs to their respective rooms. Preston nods to me and Paxton and takes off towards his bedroom. Before he makes it too far, Paxton stops him.

"Hey Pres?"

"Yeah?" He turns around to look at us.

"Who was the brunette you were locking lips with tonight?"

Preston's teeth run over his bottom lip before answering. "I don't know, man. She wouldn't even tell me her name. She's here on vacation. Said it was better this way."

"Damnit. I thought she was your *it* girl." Paxton presses in a teasing tone.

"Nope," he says, popping the P. "Just a random New Year's kiss that I'll never see again." He shuffles, looking like he's ready to crash. "Now if you'll excuse me, the bed is calling my name."

And with those final words, he continues towards his bedroom, leaving the two of us to climb to the third floor. Which turns out, is really freaking hard when you feel dead to the world.

By the grace of God, we make it to our room and barrel our way inside.

First order of business: taking my hair out of this godawful ponytail. I attempt to release my hair, but Paxton catches my arm instead. He sidles up behind me, pulling my back flush with his front. He lowers my hand and peppers kisses down my neck. My head lolls to the side, giving him full access to the slope of my exposed collarbone and shoulder, where he latches his mouth.

A moan escapes me as he trails his way back up to my ear. "Leave the pony," he says, then nips my earlobe causing my head to fall to his shoulder. "I'll need something to grab onto while I'm thrusting inside you in two minutes."

His mouth. Those words. The alcohol. They're all a deadly combination for creating the intense heat burning low in my core.

My body is on fire as his hands roam every inch of me. First, they land at the hem of my crop top, lifting it above my head. Next, he unhooks my bra, tossing it to the side. Working his way down, he slips his fingers in the band of my pants and pushes them down until they're a pool at my feet. I step out of them, and Paxton leads me to the edge of the bed.

Instead of putting me on top, he stands me at the foot and places my hands on the mattress. Still standing behind me, he fists my ponytail and pulls my head taut, just like he promised. He kisses my lips, my cheek, my ear, my neck and down my spine, where he finally lets go of my hair.

My underwear is next to go. While on his knees, he helps release them from my ankles. I'm fully naked and exposed to him, yet all I can concentrate on is the lust pulsing between my legs.

I shiver as his fingertips graze the back of my thighs and whimper when he squeezes my ass with both hands. But it's not until he spreads me and swipes his tongue from back to front that I full on gasp. The sound spurs him on, pushing me further onto the mattress until I'm face down, ass up.

"This fucking ass," he groans. "Do you trust me?"

I nod.

Another long, languid lick and I'm almost a goner. The mattress muffles my cries as he slides two fingers inside me, pumping in and out while his tongue circles my clit from behind. His thumb is inching its way between my ass cheeks, heading straight for the puckered hole we have yet to experiment with. And that's when he starts massaging it. I don't know what prompts him to slowly start pressing in, but the sensation is overwhelming. The pressure is almost too much to bear, even if I am loving every second of it. His fingers work both holes rapidly. My legs start shaking, and my vision goes blurry.

He removes his fingers and holds tight to my thighs, licking and swirling and finally sucking until intense pleasure slices through me, and my body goes limp.

"That was the hottest fucking thing I've ever done," he admits.

Paxton makes his way back up to me, trailing kisses in his wake. "I'm not done with you. Don't move," he demands.

Not like I could, even if I wanted to.

I look over my shoulder as he undresses himself. He orders me to move to the head of the bed.

With what little strength I have left, I crawl to the spot he directs me to. Paxton climbs on behind me, lifting my hips until I'm back on my knees. His index finger swipes my center, where he finds me dripping wet for him. The groan that escapes him turns me feral.

I immediately turn around and push him onto his back. There's protest in his eyes, but I choose to ignore it. Instead, I straddle him. Lust takes over, and he grips my hips, guiding me down onto his hard length. His eyes roll behind his head as he bottoms out, and I lift before slamming down again.

"*Baby,*" he moans. "I need this. I need *you.*"

Those last words are my undoing.

I place one hand on his shoulder and tightly grip the headboard with the other. His hands help guide me up and down, repeatedly until we're nothing but a panting mess. At some point, both of my hands end up in his hair, and I'm pulling it so hard I might yank it out.

"Fuck, Mace," he pants. "That's it. Ride me. Just like that."

His fingers find my clit as I ride him faster. "Come for me, baby."

My lips find his; his tongue finds mine. And we finish with him calling out my name, just the way I like it.

I slowly lift myself off and lie beside him. He pulls the sheet over me and climbs out of bed. With a swift kiss to my temple, he lets me know he's going to clean up. I nod and lean over to check the time. I tap Paxton's phone, but instead of focusing on the clock, I focus on the text sitting on the screen.

TAYLOR (12:01 AM)
Happy New Years, P. I hope you're enjoying your trip. We still on for next Friday?

My stomach rolls, and I think I'm going to be sick. Actually, I *know* I'm going to be sick. I reach for the small trashcan beside the bedside table and empty everything I drank tonight. When I come up for air, I'm shaking... *and sober.*

One text. That's all it takes for everything good to crumble.

Who the fuck is Taylor?

Chapter 48
Paxton

Not Today, Satan

I walk back into the bedroom after a quick shower to find Macy hurling into a trashcan. I rush to her side as she empties her stomach, tears falling down her cheeks. Pulling her hair back, I rub my free hand up and down her back. The last time she got sick like this was after the football game, where we drowned our sorrows in shots and beer.

I know we drank a lot tonight, but I didn't think it was *this* much. Maybe our sexcapades ruffled her stomach. Either way, I'm going to take care of her.

After another three heaves, she finally stops.

"Hey," I say as I brush the fallen strands of hair away from her face. "Are you okay? Do you need me to get you anything?"

She doesn't look at me, just nods. Rising from the bed, she escapes to the bathroom without a word, the white bed sheet trailing behind her like a train from a wedding gown.

I sit on that thought for a minute. Macy in a wedding

dress. Only she's walking toward me, instead of away. Something in my stomach flutters at the image I've painted so clearly. I'm so in love with this girl, and I want to make her mine, forever. But God if I don't need to slow my ass down. She'd probably be scared indefinitely if I voiced the thoughts in my head.

While I wait for her to return, I sit against the headboard and pick up my phone to busy myself. There's a message from Taylor from midnight.

> TAYLOR (12:01AM)
> Happy New Years, P. I hope you're enjoying your trip. We still on for next Friday?

Not thinking twice about it, I respond.

> Happy New Years, Tay. Thanks for reminding me. I'll see you on Friday at 3:30.

I hear the bathroom door open, and Macy emerges, still wrapped in the sheet. I click my phone off and set it back on the end table next to my side of the bed to give her my attention. Her gaze tracks my movement, but she still doesn't say a word. Instead, she makes her way to the closet and pulls out her suitcase. Rummaging through her clothes, Macy snags a pair of underwear, sweatpants, and an oversized t-shirt, then disappears back into the bathroom without even so much as a glance my way.

What the hell is going on?

When she appears for a second time, she's fully dressed and her hair is tied up in a messy bun. With her face clear of distraction, I notice the splotches on her cheeks. It's evident she's been crying, but why? I'd chalk it up to having thrown up the contents of her stomach, but surely that wouldn't be the reason for the silent treatment she's obviously giving me.

I start backtracking over anything I could've done or said but come up short. She was perfectly fine five minutes ago when I was fucking her senseless. My skin starts to prickle with irritation at the lack of communication. If there's something going on, I wish she'd be an adult about it and just talk to me. But when she climbs into bed after brushing her teeth and faces away from me, I realize that isn't going to happen. I want to comfort her, but I can't do that when she doesn't let me in.

It won't do me any good to dwell on the shortcomings of tonight, so I choose to be passive instead. I scoot behind her, tucking her body into mine. She stills for just a moment as I wrap my arm around her waist, tugging her closer. When I rest my chin in the crook of her neck, she melts into my touch, finally giving up the fight of whatever internal battle she's having with herself. I feel her breathing even out, and I can't help but match her rhythm as we lay in silence.

I'm struggling to keep my negative thoughts at bay. *Does she really love me? Will she leave eventually? Is it me? Am I enough for her?* The darkness only magnifies the voices in my head, willing me to spiral out of control. I try to remember the tactics Taylor taught me during our early sessions, when my nightmares would keep me awake for days. So I shut my eyes and focus on the steady breathing of the woman beside me.

I don't know how long I lay there, but eventually, sleep pulls me under and everything fades to black.

Morning comes quickly. I can tell by the faint sunlight barely peeking in that it's an ungodly hour. When I check my phone, my suspicions are confirmed. It's quarter after six, which means I've gotten roughly three hours of sleep, if that. We don't have to be at the airport until eleven, so I do my best to snuggle back up to Macy, in hopes that she's somehow in a better place when she wakes up.

Just as my mind starts slipping into limbo between being awake and asleep, my phone vibrates. This time, when I look at it, the message is from someone I have no interest in speaking to right now.

Jack.

It's not even seven am. Why the hell is he texting me so early? I pick up my phone to read the text.

JACK
We need to talk.

I haven't heard from him in a few weeks, so an uneasy feeling settles deep in the pit of my stomach. I begin typing out a response, but then I think better of it. Instead, I put my phone down to try and get some more sleep. Surely, whatever it is can wait.

The next time I wake up, it's barely after nine. I'm still not well-rested, but it'll do for now. Macy is still asleep next to me. She looks so peaceful that I hate to wake her, but I know she needs to get packed. We both do. So I trail small kisses from her neck up to her ear, slowly breathing around the shell.

She groans, and I'm graced with a boner after that sound.

"We gotta get going, babe," I remind her. "It's time to get up."

Macy tries to swat me away, but I quickly pop a kiss on her cheek and roll off the bed. When she doesn't follow suit, I yank the covers off her. Still not stirring, I grab the mouthwash cup from the sink and fill it halfway with water. Now I know what you're thinking, *this is a bad idea.* I'm aware. Apparently, I just like to test the limits of life. I slowly walk over to the bed and douse her like the Wicked Witch of the West, which warrants me a high-pitched scream.

"Paxton!" Her eyes are like daggers, ready to pierce me at any given moment.

Aw, she looks so cute when she wants to kill me.

As soon as her feet hit the ground, she lunges for me. I shriek like a middle school girl and make a beeline for the bathroom, shutting the door and locking it.

Not today, Satan.

"Open the damn door, you coward!" Her banging is becoming a little incessant, and I'm quite literally scared for my life.

"Are you going to hurt me?"

"No…" she responds slowly.

Well, that's a lie if I've ever heard one.

"I don't believe you!" I don't know why I'm yelling, but I figure it makes for good theatrics. I can't hide in here forever though, and eventually I'm going to have to come out. I just don't know how safe it is at this moment.

"Paxton, honey," Macy says sweetly. "Open the door. We're going to be late."

Mother fucker. She's right. I can do this. She's just a tiny redheaded girl, how dangerous can she be?

Whew.

Okay.

I start counting in my head. Three… two… one. Letting out a ragged breath, I unlock the door and take my time opening it. On the other side stands my five-foot four firecracker of a girlfriend ready to pounce. Before I have the chance to react, she throws an uppercut to my stomach, and I fall to my knees.

Wasn't prepared for that one.

A little "hmph" of victory escapes her as she saunters off back towards the bedroom. I shamelessly watch her ass sway to the closet to grab her things, then remember I'm still doubled over on the floor.

Picking up what pride I have left, I stand up and gather my things, packing alongside her. Since her minor assault, she hasn't as so much looked in my direction. The peacemaker in me wants nothing more than to fix this, talk it out, do the responsible thing and ask her what's wrong. Then there's the stubborn part of me that wants her to come to me, talk to me, lean on me. But because I'm such a pusher, the softer side of me wins out.

"You good?" It's not exactly an exploratory question, but it'll at least break the ice. Allow her to be vulnerable on her own terms, but also let her know I'm here and willing to talk if that's something she wants to do.

"Hmm?" Her head shifts up as she absentmindedly shifts her gaze to meet mine.

"Is everything okay? You've been pretty quiet since last night."

"Oh," she says somberly. "Yeah, all good."

I'm about to respond when she grabs her things and heads for the door.

"I'm going to say goodbye to Lauren and Dillon. Meet you downstairs?"

I don't bother disagreeing. I just nod and finish packing. In a perfect world, Macy wouldn't have been burned. She wouldn't have lived through trauma, and she'd be well equipped with communication skills. Whatever it is that she's dealt with has made her so closed off that she fights willingness at all costs. And as hard as it is for me to deal with, I know I need to be patient and let her go at her own pace. Pushing her will only cause her to run, and we've already established that's not something I'm willing to let her do.

Once we're all at the airport, we go our separate ways. Lauren and Dillon head to their terminals and the four of us head to ours. My parents are staying an extra day. Said they wanted quality time.

Luckily, we were able to book the flight back to Chicago with Preston and Payton. I'm thanking my lucky stars for that right about now, considering all things. I've tried to give her space all morning, but I'm more than ready to talk. Only, as soon as we board, she asks Preston to switch seats with her so she can sit with Payton.

When she puts her duffle in the overhead compartment, Macy looks over her shoulder at me. She looks sad, defeated even. My heart squeezes in my chest because I want nothing more than to put that smile back on her gorgeous face. I hate seeing her like this, and quite frankly, I just want her to be happy.

Preston sits in Macy's seat next to the window, and I walk toward Payton's row, taking her by the arm and lifting her from her seat. I plop down in hers and nod for her to go sit with our brother instead.

When I turn to Macy, I'm greeted by another death glare, followed by a huff.

What's new?

Crossing her arms over her chest, she faces toward the window and leans against it, closing her eyes. Now, I'm just pissed. I won't cause a scene in front of a plane full of strangers, but I make no promises once we land. The excuses I'm constantly making for her? I'm done.

She ignores me for the duration of the flight and the Uber ride to her apartment where I left my car.

I have four unanswered texts. One from Payton. One from Preston. Both inquiring about the same thing. Which makes three of us because I have no idea what the fuck is going on. And two messages from Jack, wanting me to call him immediately. I don't answer any of them. I'm too distracted to have a civil conversation with anyone right now, including the woman powerwalking to her apartment building.

"So, you're just not gonna talk to me?" I'm chasing after her, coming to a stop in front of her.

"There's nothing to talk about. I just wanna go in and go to bed." She's avoiding my gaze, and I'm about to lose my shit.

"Right. Because that's what you do," I spit back. "Hide from everything instead of saying what you really feel."

When she finally looks me in the eyes, her face is molten, ready to combust.

"Excuse me?"

"What? That's what you're doing, right? Same shit as always." My voice is louder now, and I'm no longer in control of my emotions. "Pushing me away. When the going gets tough, you get going."

"Oh, fuck you."

"There's a start. Tell me how you really feel, huh." I push. "Then maybe we can get past this high school bullshit and talk like civilized adults."

The blaze in her eyes tells me I've gone too far.

"You wanna talk?" She shoves my chest and causes me to stumble. "Let's talk then, Paxton. And we can start with Taylor."

I wince at the sound of her name.

"Who is she?"

My mind whirls for a second, wondering how the hell she even knows about Taylor. Then I start to panic. I can't even form a response without unloading it all, so I stand there in silence.

"Yeah," she quips. "That's what I thought. Just go! Leave!"

"You haven't even given me a chance to explain myself and you're already shoving me out the door the first chance you get." I'm still yelling, and now pacing. "That's not fucking fair, and you know it."

"Then explain." Her voice is cold and unlike her. "I'm standing here. Waiting."

"I promise I will if you just give me some time. It's complicated."

"No." She laughs. "What's complicated is this. You. Me. This whole relationship. I won't stand by and be kept in the dark. Not like this."

Now it's my turn to laugh. "That's real rich coming from you."

"And what's that supposed to mean?" she questions.

"Oh, I don't know, Macy. How about the fact that you've

been hiding a fucking eating disorder from me this entire time?"

The moment the words leave my lips, I know I've fucked up. Her face is now completely devoid of fight. I can see it plain as day. The slap in the face I just served her. But she quickly schools her features and begins walking away.

I go after her, trying to grip her arm, but she manages to escape my touch. I run my fingers through my hair and grip it at the root. Any harder, I'd be pulling handfuls from my scalp.

"Fine!" My near confession brings her to a hault. "You wanna know who she is?" I pause before continuing, "She's my therapist, okay?!" I'm damn near panting, wishing I could just be done with this conversation. "Are you happy now? Knowing your boyfriend is fucked up in the head? That I'm not this well put-together machine that you always seem to think I am?" I stop pacing and let my hands fall to my side. "Well, there you have it. I hope you're happy with your answer."

"Paxton," she whispers as she walks forward to embrace me.

I step back and hold up my hand to stop her, letting my gaze linger on her for a moment. And then I see it. See the new way she looks at me. Eyes full of pity. I don't want it, and I sure as shit don't need it.

She tries to step toward me once more.

"No." I stop her. "Don't." I back up towards my car. "You're right, I should go."

I get in my car and take one last look at her, standing in the parking lot of her apartment complex, then I drive away, leaving her in my rear-view mirror.

By the time I reach my own apartment, I'm fully drained. Emotionally. Mentally. Physically. All I can think about is collapsing in my bed and sleeping through the rest of the weekend.

I grab my bag from my trunk and haul it over my shoulder. I pass by the reception desk and give a brief nod to Dani, then make my way to the elevators. I hit the second-floor button and lean against the wall, letting my head fall back.

This isn't how it was supposed to be. Where the fuck did it all go wrong? My eyes are closed, and my mind is racing a mile a minute.

When the elevator dings, I step out and head to my door. Slipping the key in, I turn it, only to find it already unlocked. I could've sworn I locked the door prior to leaving. I know I did. I always do. Double, even triple checking is a habit of mine after the fire incident. And there's no way Macy could've made her way here before me, even if she was speaking to me. So who the hell got into my apartment?

I take small, slow steps inside and close the door behind me. dropping my bag, I examine the perimeters. Nothing seems to be out of place. No forced entry, that much is obvious. All my belongings are as I left them, so I scope out the rest of the place.

I check the guest bedroom first.

Empty.

No one in the guest bathroom either.

A faint smell of something sweet catches my nose. It's coming from down the hall. I creep open the door to my bedroom, and every ounce of blood leaves my body at the sight of *her*.

Sitting on my bed.

Candles are lit across my dresser and nightstand.

I don't even register her talking at first. Her lips are moving, but I don't hear a thing. Then, I finally snap out of it.

"Hey baby," she purrs—or tries to at least. "Long time no see."

The words are like nails on a chalkboard to my ears. I'm not her baby. Not anymore. I'm frozen in time. My feet are rooted to this very spot, unable to move. What? How?

And then I remember the texts. This must be what Jack wanted to speak to me about. She's out.

A sinking feeling worries me to my bones, and suddenly, I feel like I've just walked into a trap.

"Jade," I manage to croak, her name tasting like ash on my tongue. "What the fuck are you doing here?"

Chapter 49
Paxton

It Was You

"What?" she questions. "Not happy to see me?"

I stand there, staring at her in disbelief. One—because how is she out right now—and two—because seriously, *what the fuck* is she doing here? How did she even get in here is the better question?

Which is the next thing that comes out of my mouth.

"What gives you the impression that I'd ever be happy to see you here, in my damn apartment?" The silence is thick, but she plasters on that grin I used to love so much. One that I now loathe. I continue speaking. "And how on earth did you fucking get in here?"

Jade stands to her feet. I hadn't noticed until now, but she's wearing nothing but one of my t-shirts. It stops mid-thigh on her petite frame. Her dark hair flows over the front of her shoulders, and her blue eyes bore into me, like she's trying to decipher my next move. Seeing her in my clothes makes my skin crawl. It doesn't have the effect on me that it used to. No one will ever be wearing my shirts again—except the crazy-ass redhead who I need to apologize to immediately.

She closes the distance between us, and I take a small step back, not wanting to be near her presence.

"Oh, don't be like that," she whines. "Can we please just talk?"

"I don't want to talk, Jade," I voice. "I want to know how the hell you got into my place."

"Well, if you'd let me talk, *baby*, I'd get to that."

Once again, she steps towards me. This time, she runs her hand up my arm, and reflexively, I pull back. I don't want her touching me. It feels foreign. Like she was never my girlfriend for years, or my fiancée for months. No, the girl standing in front of me is a stranger. Someone I don't recognize anymore.

"I miss you, P," she finally says. "Can you honestly say you don't miss me at all? Miss us?"

I rear back like I've just been slapped. Is she serious right now? After all she put us through, she thinks I'm going to miss her? Miss *that*? That's gonna be a hard no. I'll never miss her narcissistic tendencies or her controlling behavior. I'll never want back the days where she played head games with me and used reverse psychology to make me the bad guy. I'll never miss any of it.

"Yes, Jade. I CAN say it," I answer honestly. "I don't miss you. I don't miss us. I don't miss our relationship or our engagement." I huff out a breath. "Now that we've gotten that out the way—tell me how you got into my apartment. I'm done playing games."

She laughs. The bitch is *laughing*. And I am fed up. I back away from her, leaning against my tall dresser across from my bed, folding my arms over my chest. My patience is wearing thin.

"You never really were good at hiding your keys, P." She's laughing, again. This one sounds a lot more sadistic than the first. "You really thought leaving your spare key in the light fixture was a smart idea?"

She runs her fingers along the candles on my dresser, and my heartrate picks up. When she turns back to face me, I see it written all over her face. The admission. And the next words out of her mouth solidify it.

"Same hiding spot as our house," she confesses. "It wasn't hard to find then, and it surely wasn't hard to find this time either. You're predictable."

There's a lump in my throat that feels like I've swallowed a handful of cotton balls. I've known it all along, but somehow her admitting it out loud has my stomach in knots.

"The fire," I say breathlessly. "It was you."

She gives me a shrug, as if she didn't just set my whole world up in flames. Not once, but twice. My fight or flight response is on high alert, and my initial reaction is to get the hell out of here. I'm clearly in over my head with this psychopath.

But instead of fleeing, I press for more information, wondering if she'll give me the answers I've been pleading from her for months.

"And Josie?" I question. "Was that you too?"

There's no emotion on her face. Nothing but the look of a broken, soulless girl as she stares at me. The light that she had once upon a time is no longer present. Her eyes are tired, rimmed in blue, and her face is sunken below her cheekbones. That girl that I loved so many years ago has now been replaced by a shell of a human. Possibly even a murder. But she gives nothing away.

"I'm not here for your interrogation, Paxton." Her tone sends a chill down my spine. "I want you back. I want us to fix things."

Before I can mouth off an answer, another voice interrupts us. One very familiar—and one I'm not expecting to hear.

"He's not fixing anything with you," Macy says as she

charges in the room. "You lost your shot a long time ago. And as long as he's with me, you'll never get him back."

I rush over to her, unable to comprehend the fact that she's here right now. I block Jade's view of Macy and hold her face with both of my hands. My breathing is uneven due to the unsafe situation she's walked in on. *Why* is she here? *How* is she here?

"Baby, what are you doing here?" I manage to choke out. "It isn't safe. You need to leave."

"I'm not leaving you here with her," she whispers. "Come with me, please."

"I have so many questions, but my first is—how are you not freaking the fuck out right now?" My mouth carries out the next question before she can answer. "And about Jade, how did you know?"

"I told you, I'm not one to scare easily. As for her, it wasn't that hard to put together after I started thinking about all the little signs," she admits. "Her death glares in the court room. Her tendency to only talk to you and her father. Jack constantly calling you at odd hours of the day and night."

I rest my forehead on hers, completely forgetting Jade in the moment, but quickly realizing we need to leave. I let go of Macy and turn myself around to stand in front of her with my back to her chest.

Jade is standing there, staring at us like she's ready to erupt at any moment. But the thing about psychopaths? They remain calm and collected. They have a presence about them that gives outsiders the illusion that they're harmless. I've seen it countless times before in these types of cases, and Jade is no exception.

A small chuckle leaves her mouth. "You think you can just replace me with my dad's slut of an intern?"

Jade makes her way to each candle, blowing them out one by one. The aftermath of the smell lingers around the room, causing nausea to roll in the pit of my stomach.

She steps around me to glance at Macy. I guard her protectively, unsure of what Jade's next move might be. Then she looks at me, her glare chilling me down to my core.

"Did you really think daddy was going to let me stay in there?" She continues. "That he wouldn't find a way to get me out so we could be together again?"

"It's over, Jade. It's been over, for years," I remind her. "I'm not coming back. What will it take to get you to understand that? I'm finally happy again. Let it be."

She scoffs. "Happy? With *her*?" Jade cocks her head to the side, and it's her telltale sign she's about to lose her shit. "Does she know, P? About your past?"

"Stop it; right the fuck now," I demand. "Just shut up."

"Ah ha." She laughs. "Of course, she doesn't know. She wouldn't be with you if she did."

Macy then whispers, "What is she talking about, Paxton?"

"You don't think he was assigned to this case because he wanted to be, do you?" she questions. "No, sweetheart. He's being blackmailed by my father for saving his ass years ago. Go on, Paxton. Tell her."

I'm sure I'm going to throw up. This isn't how this conversation is supposed to go. I'm supposed to have more time. I'm supposed to be able to do things the right way. But instead, I'm being forced against my will by the devil herself. Everything I've tried to keep hidden is coming crashing down around me, and there's nothing I can do to stop it.

"Tell. Her," she reiterates. "You do it, or I will."

I turn to Macy and grab both of her hands in my trembling ones. "Promise me we will get through this," I demand. "Please, whatever I say next, just promise me that you'll walk out onto the other side with me."

"You're scaring me," she admits, and I feel my chest tighten with those words. "What did you do, Paxton?"

"Oh, Jesus Christ." I hear Jade lose it. "You're fucking weak, P. You know that? Maybe if you cared half as much about losing our relationship you wouldn't be in this position right now." She's fuming and continues to lash out. "Your perfect, precious boyfriend was involved in an accident five years ago. Hit a young girl because he was too busy texting."

"Please, just stop!" I yell. Then I turn back to Macy. "It was just that—an accident. A moment of stupidity, and I've never felt worse about anything in my life."

I try to steady my breathing before I go any further. "That scar you asked about? The collision sent her car into flames. And by the time I was able to pull her out of the car, my shirt had caught fire, which is what caused it before I could tear it off. The girl was burned pretty badly, and I didn't know what to do, so I called the only person I knew who could get me out of trouble. I was young and scared. When Jack arrived, he told me to run. He took care of everything, and no one except him and my parents know about it. And my therapist, Taylor." I'm gasping for air, praying that whatever love Macy holds for me outweighs the secrets pouring from my mouth. "I check on her—the girl. Not that she or her family knows. But she did survive, and every month I send her parents an anonymous check to help cover any underlying medical bills."

Macy lets out a breath and runs her hand down the side of my face. "It's okay," she says, so sure of herself. "Let's go." She intertwines our fingers as she leads us out the bedroom and down the hall.

Jade is hot on our heels, and I can feel the steam radiating from her body. She wanted a reaction out of Macy that she isn't going to get, and now all hell is about to break loose.

"That's it?!" she screams. "It's okay?! He deserves what he has coming to him."

Jade rushes into my kitchen and begins opening every cabinet, and throwing all my dishes onto the floor. Clash after clash, Macy and I both flinch. We watch as she tears my place apart, dish by dish. The sympathy I would have had for her at one point in time is now replaced by anger and resentment.

But we can't leave her like this. There's no telling what she'll do.

I ask Macy to head home but of course, she refuses. In the blink of an eye, Jade comes charging towards me, a kitchen knife in her hand, and nothing prepares me for what comes next.

My hands are covered in blood, but I don't feel any pain. And that's when I realize it's not mine. It's Macy's. The faint screaming I hear is drowned out by my own blood pumping through my ear drums because I know this isn't happening. My girlfriend is lying limp on the floor, bleeding out onto my hardwood while my murderous ex-fiancée is standing there with no remorse.

I'm yelling for help and suddenly hear banging on my apartment door. I can't feel anything. I can't move. I'm numb, holding onto Macy like I'll die if I let her go. So, I just sit there, shaking her and begging her to wake up.

Chapter 50
Macy

Worth the Hurt

My eyes are heavy, but I'm able to open them enough to see the flashing lights. Red and blue, just like before. Only this time, it's daylight. And instead of my mother being on the other side of those two closing doors, it's Paxton. His shirt is stained red as he stands there yelling something at the paramedics. But I can't hear him, and then I can no longer see him. That's when my vision goes hazy once more, and I slip into a familiar black hole.

The next thing I know, I'm being hauled through the emergency room doors, and the squeaking of the gurney has me wincing. It feels like déjà vu all over again.

The trauma bay.

The nurses surrounding my bed.

The blur of voices floating around the room.

It's all too familiar.

Is this it? The part I've always been so afraid to admit I wish would have come true? Is this the end for me? The day I flatline for real and never wake up again?

I keep waiting for the code to be called, but it never comes. Instead, I hear someone yell that they're rushing me up to the OR and sometime later, I'm waking up in a hospital room with a sleeping Paxton by my side.

He's still in his clothes from earlier—blood stained and all—and his head is resting on my bed as he sits slumped over in what I assume must be the most uncomfortable chair known to mankind. His right hand rests firmly on my right thigh, and I do my best to adjust my position without waking him. I'm sore, I know that much, but I can't recall exactly what happened.

I shift slightly, pulling myself into a sitting position when Paxton's sleepy grin greets me. As if he's just now realizing I'm awake, he jumps to his feet and assesses me before scooting into bed next to me. There are no words between us as he holds me like his life depends on it. He places several kisses to the top of my head then my temple while he squeezes me against his chest.

I flinch in pain and only then does he loosen his grip.

Turning onto his side to face me, his breathing is heavy as he lets out a few shaky breaths. He pushes away a piece of loose hair that has fallen onto my face and cradles my cheek with his hand.

That's when I realize the tears staining his cheeks, and I can't help but let a few tears run down my face as well.

I wipe his with my free hand and ask, "Baby, why are you crying?"

His eyes close briefly, like he's gathering his thoughts before speaking.

"I thought I lost you." The confession is strained. "I don't know what the fuck I would have done if you hadn't made it out of there alive."

The memories start flooding back, and I wince in pain.

"I'm okay," I reassure him. "I'm right here. With you."

Pausing for a moment, I ask, "What happened? Where is she?"

"They have her in custody," he explains. "I've never been more thankful for nosy neighbors in my life. But they heard screaming and plates crashing, so they called the cops. That's who broke down the door after she went off the rails. She couldn't even escape."

He doesn't give me any time to absorb the information before he continues. "There's something else I need to tell you."

I swallow thickly, trying to hide the nerves. "Okay," I manage to get out.

"A few years back, there was a fire at my house. The fire department said it was caused from a single lit candle." Tears start to form at the brim of my eyes again. "I don't burn candles, and the fire so conveniently started while I was in the shower. But luckily for me, I designed the home. I knew the ins and outs, and I was able to escape before it came collapsing down." He continues. "There was no evidence that she did it, but today confirmed my suspicions. She didn't deny it, and she got into my apartment by finding my spare key the same way she did the night of the fire. So, she was wrong. The only person who got what was coming to them today—was her."

"Oh, Paxton," I cry as the tears rain down. My heart squeezes in my chest at the thought of someone so cold and calculated trying to harm him. How anyone could ever want to cause him pain is beyond me. I sit there, stroking his face, not wanting to stop touching him.

He grabs my hand from his cheek and kisses my palm. Then he wraps his hand around the back of my neck and pulls me in for a kiss. It's delicate at first, but quickly turns frantic, like he's scared this is the last time he'll ever kiss me.

When his lips part from mine, he exhales long and hard. Paxton peers up at me through dark brown lashes, and the next words out of his mouth are words I never expect to hear.

"Move in with me." It's a plea, the way he says it so desperately. "Or I can move in with you if being at my place is too hard. Or we can find a whole new place together. Something brand new and not tainted. I don't even care at this point. All I know is that I don't want to be apart from you another night—ever again. Please say yes."

It takes almost no time to think about it before my lips are moving, giving him the answer he so badly wants. "Yes," I whisper. It may be quiet, but I mean it more than anything. I know I want this man forever. I've known it for a while. And making a home with him is the first step to letting myself finally have the happiness I know I deserve.

"Thank fuck." He kisses me again, softer this time. "I love you so much, Macy. Thank you for standing by my side when I needed you most. For loving me through the darkness of my past. But we will be having a discussion about your unwillingness to get your ass out of that apartment, you stubborn, stubborn girl."

I smile, knowing that our *discussion* will be more of a punishment. The good kind. The one I love so much because it earns me a handprint across my ass cheek. Sometimes, being a bad girl has its payoffs.

"I'm sorry, you know," I say sincerely. "I'm sorry for not trusting you with my truths. For not giving you the chance to explore my demons with me. For not allowing you to pull me from my own darkness. I was afraid of what you'd think of me if you knew my struggles with my body. That you'd somehow see how damaged I really am and change your mind about me. I've been fighting this battle for as long as I can remember, and I just didn't want you to find something to hate. But through all of this, I'm so sorry that you felt like you had to hide your struggles, too."

He pierces me with this look that breaks my soul into a million tiny pieces, but when he smiles, it puts me back together. This man owns every single part of me, and I am more than okay with never getting those pieces back.

"I've lived with my secrets long enough that they became a burden. I didn't want anyone else to have to carry that weight with me, so I never allowed them to. But now that you know, if you're ready to walk with me, we can face the light together. You don't have to do this alone anymore. I'm here now. Forever."

Forever. The word echoes in my head. It spins on repeat, like a broken record player. Yet, I've never loved a sound more than I do right now.

I slip my hand into his, ready to take on the world as long as he's by my side. Because in this very moment, I realize something.

Paxton Meyers is worth the hurt I endured to get me here, and I wouldn't change a thing.

Epilogue
Paxton

Six Months Later

I hear a car door slam which signals that Macy is home. Home. *Our* home. A few weeks after the incident, we started searching for places. It only felt right that we start fresh in a new house. Leaving everything else behind was a lot easier than we both anticipated, even if we're both still a little damaged.

We decided to settle down in a small, gated community not too far from the city. She wanted an all-white exterior with rustic beam poles and black accents, so that's what my girl got. It's a cozy little two-story house with a manicured lawn and a two-car garage. Perfect for just the two of us. For now, anyways.

We've talked about starting a family in the future, but Macy isn't in any rush. Though, if it were up to me, I'd make her my wife and baby mama all in one night.

Between earlier this year and now, Macy and I both graduated from U of C and started therapy as a couple to work through some of the trauma. During our sessions with Taylor,

I learned more about Macy's eating disorder and why my birthday is such a trigger for her. I also learned more in depth about her habitual habits to sabotage herself where relationships are concerned. And though being vulnerable with each other has presented some struggles, I know we're so much stronger for it now.

Prior to graduation, we gave up our intern spots at Jack's firm and both declined the junior partner position. After word got out that he made some calls to get Jade out, his business hasn't been trusted anywhere in the state of Illinois. In fact, I believe he lost his license to practice. It worked out for the best, though, because I plan to start my own firm with my soon-to-be fiancée. If she says yes, that is.

Payton proposed Macy for a girls' day on my behalf so that I could get her out of the house. I want tonight to be special, but I also don't want her suspecting a thing.

Because I know Macy isn't a fan of attention, I'm making this night about us and only us.

No crowd.

No photographer.

Not even our families, though they're well aware that I'm proposing.

We're having our monthly movie night on the couch, so I gather all her favorite comfy blankets, as well as her newfound favorite snacks. Eating in moderation has been a work in progress, but she's managing. Which is why I make sure she has a little bit of everything. From Sour Patch Kids to Ring Pops. Chocolate covered pretzels to spicy sweet chili Doritos.

The sound of the deadbolt clicks as I finish plating our Pad Thai, and Macy walks through the door and into the foyer with a huge smile on her face.

She's smiling. *Why is she smiling?*

She abruptly turns my way, giving me a grin so wide that I'm sure her cheeks are hurting.

I swear to God I will have my sister's ass if she somehow

spoiled this surprise. The nerves I'm feeling are tenfold in comparison now that she's here, but I have to keep my shit together.

I place the bowls on the counter next to the two glasses of wine and walk in her direction. When I reach her, I wind my arms around her waist and kiss the top of her head.

Looking up at me, she's still wearing that beautiful smile I can't get enough of.

"Hi," she says, never losing her glow.

I kiss her lips quickly then pull back and look down at her.

"Hi," is all I manage to say. I've clearly lost my ability to form sentences in her presence.

"Well," she starts. "Aren't you going to ask me why I'm so happy?"

Now I'm the one smiling like a fool. Her happiness is contagious. I never knew I could be this happy with another person before, but being with her has proven otherwise. I push the fallen strand of hair out of her face before inquiring.

"So, baby." I pause for a moment. "Why are you so happy?"

Nerves begin swirling in my stomach, silently pleading that it isn't because of my plans for tonight. But what she says next catches me off guard.

"Lauren and Dillon are moving to Chicago." Her smile is beaming brighter, if that's even possible, and my pulse begins to slow down in relief. I grab a fist full of her ass and hoist her up, winding her legs around my waist. She throws her arms around my neck and buries her face in my shirt.

"That's the best news I've heard all day, Mace," I tell her truthfully. "I know how much having her close means to you, and I couldn't be happier for you."

"Thank you, babe. I love you," she says before pulling back and examining the setup in our living room. "What's all this for?"

Before I can answer it dawns on her.

"Oh, right. Movie night."

I nod, giving her another peck on the lips. "Correct."

She slides down my body, grazing my dick in the process.

And now I'm hard. Great.

"I'll be just a few minutes. I'm gonna go throw on something comfortable." She heads toward the hallway. "Be right back!"

I take this time to bring our food to the coffee table in the living room. I set everything down, making sure it's all perfect. Then I make my way to the guest bedroom to grab the ring from the closet. After fishing it out of a buried shoebox, I slip the small velvet box in my pocket.

Somehow, I manage to make it back before Macy and drop down on the couch, propping my feet up on the coffee table. Tonight is my turn to pick the movie, so naturally I'm choosing something I know she loves. As I'm pulling up *Pearl Harbor* on Netflix, Macy flops down next to me, grabbing her bowl of Pad Thai and placing it in her lap.

"Smells delicious." She inhales and takes a bite, a small moan escaping her mouth. "So good."

I grin. "Anything to keep you making those sounds." I joke.

She playfully nudges me. "Shut up."

I laugh then take a sip of my wine and shovel a forkful of noodles into my mouth to stop myself from asking her to marry me this very second.

We eat in comfortable silence while we watch the movie, and once we're nice and full, Macy grabs a handful of snacks and cuddles up beside me. She feeds me a Sour Patch Kid while she sucks on her Ring Pop, and my dick is twitching thinking about her sucking on my cock instead. The mental image of her on her knees for me when we christened this couch is now playing in my head, and I'm hard as a rock.

Focus for two fucking seconds, dude.

"So, what did you do today?" she asks, breaking my thoughts.

Okay, now is the time.

Just tell her.

"I looked at a few properties for sale. Made some calls. Toured a small office in the city."

"Oh? What for?"

The part of the movie where Evelyn finds out she's pregnant is playing, and it stops me in my tracks.

This woman sitting beside me is everything I've ever wanted. There is no future for me if it's not with her. So, I tell her just that.

"Well, I was hoping we could start our own firm," I admit.

She looks at me in adoration, and my heart speeds up in my chest. "Together?"

I nod. "Together. You and me."

A huge smile graces her face, which puts a smile on mine in return. "I'd love that. What would we call it, though?"

"I was thinking Meyers and Meyers, LLC."

Something crosses her face, and I'm not sure what. Whether she's thinking, or putting the pieces together, I can't tell. But I think I might throw up if she doesn't say something soon.

"Meyers and Meyers," she repeats. "But—"

I cut her off before she can say anything further. I pull the box out of my pocket and get on my knees between her legs. She's sitting on the couch and I'm kneeling between them.

Tears fill her eyes, and I do my best to choke out my next words.

"Macy Brooke Callahan. I've told you before, and I'll tell you a million more times if you let me. I am so fucking in love with you. When you came into my life, I was not expecting you. I wasn't even looking for you, but somehow you came to me when I needed you most. I tried my hardest to resist you, not wanting it to begin. Because I knew that by giving in, I was giving someone another chance to break my heart again. But the moment I looked into your eyes, *really* looked into them, I felt myself give way. I knew my heart would be safe with you, and that's where it would stay forever. You are the best thing that has ever happened to me, baby. And I don't want there to be a day in this life when you're not by my side. So please, marry me. Continue to make me the happiest man in the world, and I will spend every second of the rest of my life proving to you why I was worth the wait."

I open the box to a solitaire pear-shaped diamond sitting on a gold band. Macy covers her mouth, and nothing prepares me for the full-on tears falling down her face. I can only hope it's a good sign.

"Babe," I say to break the silence. "An answer. Please."

She wipers her cheeks while nodding her head over and over. "Yes. Yes. A million times yes."

I release the breath I'm holding. "*Thank fuck.*"

I slip the Ring Pop off her finger and replace it with the one she's going to wear forever.

Macy lunges forward off the couch and launches herself at me until I'm flat on my back and she's laying on top of me. She peppers kisses all over my face while crying what I'm assuming is to be happy tears.

"I'm so fucking in love with you too," she whispers as we get lost in the best kiss of my entire life.

Acknowledgments

As an author, it's easy to get carried away with words. I could write a novella alone thanking the people who got me to this point. The fact that I have a book published is surreal in itself. But I wouldn't be here without the help of everyone who's been in my corner since day one.

To my mom, thank you. Thank you for never doubting my writing abilities and always reminding me that I'm capable. Ever since I was a kid, you said I'd either become a lawyer because I was good at arguing or an author because of my talent for telling stories. I may not be in the court room, but the characters of my BOOK are. How fucking cool is that?

To my husband and kiddos. Not being present is hard, but on the particularly rough days when I was tucked away, writing nonstop, ya'll took it like champs. Thank you for understanding that an author's job is never done and loving me through the tough moments anyway.

To my girl, Holly. Thank you for your consistent and never-ending support since my very first chapter. You were the one who always pushed me to write the next and pulled me out of my writer's block when I was deep in the trenches. You never let me give up and rooted for me until the very last word.

To my beta readers. I'm not sure there are enough words in the dictionary to describe the love I have for you. There would be no book without you. I wouldn't even consider writing another word if it weren't for the kind words you showered me with daily. Or the immense amount of love and support you guys have shown me every single day. Or the overwhelming excitement that filled our group chat every time I proposed a new idea, showed a teaser, or dropped a design. Your friendships mean more to me than any words on the pages I write, and I am so thankful to be on this hot-mess-express train with each of you.

To my loves, Kim and Maddy, aka the best PR duo a girl could ask for. This release would be nothing without your undeniable talent. The work both of you have put in to make all my dreams come true has been nothing short of amazing. I am truly grateful for the time and effort given to every project I've conjured up. You both have knocked every expectation of mine out of the park. I love you endlessly.

To my cover designers. Brey, thank you for jumping head first into this project without me ever asking. I am eternally grateful for your friendship, and I love what we created for this entire series. And Melissa, thank you for your amazing talent that brought my special edition vision to life. The way you so effortlessly created a cover on the very first try blew me away. It's everything I could've hoped for and more.

To my editor. Lord knows she deserves all the praise after me threatening to throw in the towel on a daily basis. Caroline, thank you for never giving up on me, even when I wanted to give up on myself. When I would text you crying that the book wasn't good enough, you assured me it was. I'm so lucky to have you in my corner, and I can't wait to see your red marks on all my future pages.

To my formatter. Cathryn, thank you for all the time you

spent making things perfect for this book. Thank you for dealing with the whiplash my mind tends to create. For never complaining about the never-ending changes that I could never settle on. You're a rockstar.

To all of the wonderful author friends I've made over the last few months. Thank every single one of you for being so kind and welcoming. Thank you for answering my obscene amount of questions and always pointing me in the right direction. I could not have done this without your help.

To my release event team. The Author Agency, thank you for taking on the brunt of my workload so I could focus on writing. I'm so grateful to have had your help with this release!

And to my readers, who in turn, became friends. I'll never be able to thank the book community enough for the friendships I've made. You guys are some of my very best friends. The people I can count on day in and day out to make me laugh and smile. Had I not found this community, I don't know that I'd be sitting here writing this. Because of the connections I've made, I now get to share my passion with all of you. It's surreal, to say the least. I appreciate each and every one of you. Thank you for everything you do. This world is a better place with you in it.

About The Author

Ashley Dranguet is a new and upcoming debut author, who has a love for all things romance. She has a flare for the dramatics but will always give you a happy ending!

An Alumna of University of New Orleans and Northwestern State University, Ashley has two degrees. One in biology and another in Radiologic Science. She's currently finishing up her third and final degree in Radiation Oncology but hopes to eventually pursue writing full time.

Her love of writing began early on in life, where she started winning contests and awards for her participation in essay contests in school. In addition to writing, she's also an avid reader and has been since a young age. Reading has always been an escape for her. Knowing she could do that for other people instantly sparked her dream of becoming an author.

When Ashley isn't reading or writing, you can find her spending time with her husband and two children, playing piano, baking/cooking, or having carpool karaoke.

Connect With Ashley:
Instagram: @author.ashleydranguet